PRAISE FOR ISLAND 731

"Robinson (Secondworld) puts his distinctive mark on Michael Crichton territory with this terrifying present-day riff on The Island of Dr. Moreau. Action and scientific explanation are appropriately proportioned, making this one of the best Jurassic Park successors."

— Publisher's Weekly - Starred Review

"Take a traditional haunted-house tale and throw in a little Island of Dr. Moreau and a touch of Clash of the Titans, and you wind up with this scary and grotesque novel. Robinson, a skilled blender of the thriller and horror genres, has another winner on his hands."

— Booklist

"[Island 731's] premise is reminiscent of H.G. Wells' The Island of Dr. Moreau, but the author adds a World War II back story...vivisection, genetic engineering, Black Ops, animal husbandry and mayhem. This is the stuff that comic books, video games and successful genre franchises are made of."

— Kirkus Reviews

"A book full of adventure and suspense that shows 'science' in a whole new horrific light. This is one creepy tale that will keep you up all night! And it is so well written you will think twice before taking a vacation to any so-called 'Island Paradise!'"

— Suspense Magazine

PRAISE FOR SECONDWORLD

"A brisk thriller with neatly timed action sequences, snappy dialogue and the ultimate sympathetic figure in a badly burned little girl with a fighting spirit... The Nazis are determined to have the last gruesome laugh in this efficient doomsday thriller."

— Kirkus Reviews

"Relentless pacing and numerous plot twists drive this compelling stand-alone from Robinson... Thriller fans and apocalyptic fiction aficionados alike will find this audaciously plotted novel enormously satisfying."

— Publisher's Weekly

"A harrowing, edge of your seat thriller told by a master storyteller, Jeremy Robinson's Secondworld is an amazing, globetrotting tale that will truly leave you breathless."

— Richard Doestch, bestselling author of THE THIEVES OF LEGEND

"Robinson blends myth, science and terminal velocity action like no one else."

— Scott Sigler, NY Times Bestselling author of PANDEMIC

"Just when you think that 21st-century authors have come up with every possible way of destroying the world, along comes Jeremy Robinson."

— New Hampshire Magazine

PRAISE FOR THE JACK SIGLER THRILLERS

THRESHOLD

"Threshold elevates Robinson to the highest tier of over-the-top action authors and it delivers beyond the expectations even of his fans. The next Chess Team adventure cannot come fast enough."

— Booklist - Starred Review

"Jeremy Robinson's Threshold is one hell of a thriller, wildly imaginative and diabolical, which combines ancient legends and modern science into a non-stop action ride that will keep you turning the pages until the wee hours."

— Douglas Preston, NY Times bestselling author of THE KRAKEN PROJECT

"With Threshold Jeremy Robinson goes pedal to the metal into very dark territory. Fast-paced, action-packed and wonderfully creepy! Highly recommended!"

— Jonathan Maberry, NY Times bestselling author of CODE ZERO

"With his new entry in the Jack Sigler series, Jeremy Robinson plants his feet firmly on territory blazed by David Morrell and James Rollins. The perfect blend of mysticism and monsters, both human and otherwise, make Threshold as groundbreaking as it is riveting."

— Jon Land, NY Times bestselling author of THE TENTH CIRCLE

"Jeremy Robinson is the next James Rollins."

— Chris Kuzneski, NY Times bestselling author of THE FORBIDDEN TOMB

"Jeremy Robinson's Threshold sets a blistering pace from the very first page and never lets up. For readers seeking a fun rip-roaring adventure, look no further."

— Boyd Morrison, bestselling author of THE LOCH NESS LEGACY

INSTINCT

"If you like thrillers original, unpredictable and chock-full of action, you are going to love Jeremy Robinson's Chess Team. INSTINCT riveted me to my chair."
— Stephen Coonts, NY Times bestselling author of PIRATE ALLEY

"Robinson's slam-bang second Chess Team thriller [is a] a wildly inventive yarn that reads as well on the page as it would play on a computer screen."
— Publisher's Weekly

"Intense and full of riveting plot twists, it is Robinson's best book yet, and it should secure a place for the Chess Team on the A-list of thriller fans who like the over-the-top style of James Rollins and Matthew Reilly."
— Booklist

"Jeremy Robinson is a fresh new face in adventure writing and will make a mark in suspense for years to come."
— David Lynn Golemon, NY Times bestselling author of OVERLORD

PULSE

"Rocket-boosted action, brilliant speculation, and the recreation of a horror out of the mythologic past, all seamlessly blend into a rollercoaster ride of suspense and adventure."
— James Rollins, NY Times bestselling author of THE SIXTH EXTINCTION

"Jeremy Robinson has one wild imagination, slicing and stitching his tale together with the deft hand of a surgeon. Robinson's impressive talent is on full display in this one."
— Steve Berry, NY Times bestselling author of THE LINCOLN MYTH

"There's nothing timid about Robinson as he drops his readers off the cliff without a parachute and somehow manages to catch us an inch or two from doom."
—Jeff Long, New York Times bestselling author of DEEPER

"An elite task force must stop a genetic force of nature in the form of the legendary Hydra in this latest Jeremy Robinson thriller. Yet another page-turner!"
— Steve Alten, NY Times bestselling author of THE OMEGA PROJECT

ALSO BY JEREMY ROBINSON

ALSO BY SEAN ELLIS

Jack Sigler/Chess Team
Callsign: King
Callsign: King – Underworld
Callsign: King – Blackout
Prime
Savage
Cannibal

Cerberus Group Novels
Herculean (2015)

Mira Raiden Novels
Ascendant
Descendent

The Nick Kismet Adventures
The Shroud of Heaven
Into the Black
The Devil You Know
Fortune Favors

The Adventures of Dodge Dalton
In the Shadow of Falcon's Wings
At the Outpost of Fate
On the High Road to Oblivion

Novels
Magic Mirror
Wargod (with Steven Savile)
Hell Ship (with David Wood)
Oracle (with David Wood)
Flood Rising
(with Jeremy Robinson)

Secret Agent X
The Sea Wraiths
The Scar
Masterpiece of Vengeance

CANNIBAL

A Jack Sigler Thriller

JEREMY ROBINSON
WITH SEAN ELLIS

BREAKNECK MEDIA

Visit Jeremy Robinson on the World Wide Web at:
www.jeremyrobinsononline.com

Visit Sean Ellis on the World Wide Web at:
seanellisthrillers.webs.com

Sean would like to dedicate this book to:

"Bonnie Osborne, the first person to believe I could do this. Thank you, wherever you are."

Special thanks also to Ian Kharitonov for Russian language translation.

CANNIBAL

"And having well considered of this, we passed toward the place where they were left in sundry houses, but we found the houses taken down, and the place very strongly enclosed with a high pallisade of great trees...and one of the chief trees or posts at the right side of the entrance had the bark taken off, and five feet from the ground in fair capital letters was graven CROATOAN."
~John White,
Governor of the Roanoke Colony,
August, 1590

"When a man is denied the right to live the life he believes in, he has no choice but to become an outlaw."
~Nelson Mandela, 1995

And ye shall eat the flesh of your sons, and the flesh of your daughters shall ye eat.
~Leviticus 26:29

PROLOGUE: JUDGMENT

PROLOGUE

Virginia Colony, 1588

"Run!"

The exhortation still rang in Eleanor Dare's ears, but instead of offering the possibility of hope, it sent her reeling to the edge of the abyss.

Run? From that? *Impossible.*

Over the sound of her frantic breathing, the rustle of grass and the snap of twigs underfoot, the hungry snarls of her pursuers closed in.

So close.

A shriek erupted from the darkness somewhere off to her left, but it was almost immediately cut off, replaced by an unholy gurgling noise and the wet tearing of limbs being ripped apart.

She wondered who it had been, and she wanted to say a silent prayer for the soul of the fallen man. Instead, she found herself begging God that the man's sacrifice might buy them just a few more seconds, and salvation for her, her husband Ananias and for little Virginia.

Ananias gripped her arm and dragged her forward faster than her legs could move, repeating that desperate word. "Run!"

She clutched her infant daughter closer to her bosom and focused on the bobbing flame of the torch. Eleanor knew little about the man holding it. John was the name he had given them, but whether it was his true name, who could say? He was an Englishman, a privateer, or so he claimed, who had washed up in their midst a few weeks earlier, warning them not to expect relief supplies anytime soon. England, he had said, was at war with Spain, and no ships would be spared. Ananias and several of the surviving elders had believed him, trusted him, so she had as well. It was he who had urged them to flee the trap that had been waiting for them at the Secotan village—though in truth, not much urging had been required. He had also advised against accepting the natives' invitation in the first place. If only they had heeded his earlier admonition, there would have been no need for the latter.

He told us to go to Croatoan. We should have listened to him.

Virginia had been asleep just a few minutes ago when their flight began. Now she was wailing in protest at having been disturbed from her slumber, completely heedless of the horror that stalked them. Against all her motherly instincts to offer comfort, Eleanor ignored her daughter's cries. The flame was the only thing that mattered.

The flame was life. Behind them, in the darkness, death waited.

"If you cannot silence the whelp," James Hynde said, panting, from a few steps ahead, "I'll dash its brains out and leave the both of you to them."

John wheeled around, his blade glinting in the orange light and aimed at Hynde's throat. The latter barely skidded to a stop before impaling himself on the point.

"No one will be left behind," the privateer said, "except you, if you speak again."

As soon as the threat was uttered, John turned back and resumed running. As Eleanor passed him, she saw Hynde swallow nervously, and then he, too, was running again.

Behind them, the crunching of bones diminished with the distance, then it fell silent altogether. Did the sudden quiet mean the brief reprieve was already at an end?

John stopped abruptly and began waving the torch over his head.

Hynde uttered a harsh blasphemy, while beside Eleanor, Ananias shouted, "Where are the boats?"

Eleanor realized that they had left the woods behind and were now standing upon the sandy shore, where they had made their arrival only a few short hours before. The Secotan village was here, on the mainland, but the fort, the home of Eleanor and the other members of the colony—those few who survived—lay on the eastward edge of the island the natives called Roanoke. Between the two lay a narrow marsh with a tangle of braided channels too shallow for a ship to pass through. The Secotan warriors had brought them to the village in their birch longboats, drawing the fragile looking craft up above the tide line when the journey was finished. Now, all that remained to mark the spot where they had landed were long grooves in the damp earth.

"They took the boats," Hynde raged. "This was their plan from the beginning. Their bloody vengeance!"

Eleanor did not doubt that. It had been naïve to think that the natives would simply forget the violence that had been done to them. Yet, in her heart, she knew that was not the real reason for what had befallen them on this night.

God has cursed us for the evil that was done in our midst.

She hugged Virginia tighter, rocking her, murmuring soothing words that felt like a lie.

"Into the water," John shouted.

Hynde and several others did not hesitate, but splashed out into the marshy shallows. Ananias however remained with Eleanor. "Not all of us can swim. And what of the child?"

A scowl crossed the privateer's face. "Would you rather face—"

He broke off suddenly, dropping his torch and raising his musket. Eleanor gasped and turned involuntarily, following his gaze in the direction from which they had come. Her eyes could not penetrate the darkness, but her ears could. Something was crashing through the trees, something so large that she could feel the vibrations of its footsteps.

This cannot be, she thought. *Unless...*

The rest of the thought was too terrible to contemplate.

There was a faint huffing sound as the privateer blew on the length of match cord attached to the gun, coaxing the ember to a cherry red. A click as he pulled the trigger brought it in contact with the powder charge in the firing pan. Even though she knew what was coming next, the report startled her. Through the sudden ringing in her ears, she could hear Virginia, no longer merely crying, but screaming as if scalded.

The privateer threw down the now useless musket and drew his sword. It seemed a paltry weapon against what pursued them, and Eleanor knew the man was almost certainly going to his death. He shouted something as he ran toward the shadows, perhaps urging them to keep going, or maybe it was just a battle cry. Ananias must have heard the former, for he scooped up the fallen torch, grabbed hold of his wife's arm and dragged her into the shallows, following after the other colonists.

God save him, she prayed. *If you will not save us, then at least spare him, for he is not a sharer in our sins.*

The man did not seem the sort to simply throw his life away. Perhaps he was more skilled with a blade than she imagined, or maybe he had scored a hit with his ball, wounding or even killing one of their pursuers.

Even so, she did not think she would see him again.

Ananias drew her toward the water, but his steps were tentative and Eleanor knew why. Her husband, a London bricklayer who had never even crossed the Thames until the day he had boarded the ship her father had hired to carry them to the New World, did not know how to swim.

He would have to learn very quickly.

Something seized hold of her shoulder, and she cried out in alarm, trying in vain to pull away for a moment. Then, through ears that were still deafened from the noise of the musket, she heard a man's voice.

John's voice.

He was still alive, and shouting something into her face.

She gaped at him, wondering if he was...truly alive. That by itself was no source of comfort. He was barely recognizable. His clothes were torn and he was drenched in gore, but if any of the blood was his own, he was in the grip of some powerful demonic rage that made him immune to the pain.

Just like the others, Eleanor thought, frightened.

"Give me the child," the man shouted again, and this time she heard. "I will carry her."

Eleanor shied away, but even as she did, she realized that John posed no danger to her. If he had, he would have simply taken Virginia by force, probably from her dead arms. *But to give him my daughter?*

If I do not, I won't be able to swim. I must trust this stranger. Mayhap God has sent him to deliver us from this curse.

She thrust the child into John's hands, and she was surprised to see him cuddle the little girl close to his breast. It was an astonishing sight: her little child, not even a year old yet, being comforted by this tall, rough man who wore the blood of a vanquished foe like the war paint the savage natives sometimes used. Virginia was evidently not bothered by his appearance; her screams faded even as Eleanor's hearing returned in full.

Ananias stared at him, incredulous, but he quickly overcame his disbelief and turned his eyes to the darkness behind them. "Are they—?"

"Dead. I killed two, but there might be more." He plucked the torch from Ananias's hand and somehow maintained his balance while holding the child in his left arm and keeping both the torch and his musket high and dry. Eleanor gathered her sodden skirts in one hand and continued forward, the water already waist-high.

After just a few steps, John shouted, "Here. Help me with this."

Braving the uncertain marsh, Ananias plodded forward to join him, and a moment later, the two men managed to drag and push a fallen tree trunk out into the water. It sank with a splash, but then bobbed back up. It was tricky work with John's arms full, but they succeeded.

John carefully laid his musket atop the floating log and proceeded to jam the end of his torch into the wood. The brand easily pierced the bark and went deep into the rotted wood. "It won't bear our weight, but if you hold fast to it, you won't drown."

Working together, the three maneuvered the tree trunk out into the channel. As the water rose higher, almost to Eleanor's throat, she threw an arm over the log and began to kick with her legs. She was not a strong swimmer and the treacherous conditions filled her with apprehension, but even death by drowning seemed a kinder fate than what would have happened if they had remained on the shore. Nevertheless, the wood was buoyant and although the water was cool, she found that the simple act of moving her legs, paddling like a dog, kept her mind off both the physical discomfort and the horror that they had just left behind.

Perhaps God has not entirely abandoned us after all.

It was easy enough for her to believe that he had. From the day they had set foot upon the shores of the New World, the colony had been plagued by one sort of misfortune or another. The worst irony was that they had never intended to establish the colony on Roanoke Island. It had been her father's intention to settle further north, on Chesapeake Bay, stopping at Roanoke only long enough to take aboard the men of an earlier expedition who had garrisoned at a fort on the island. To their dismay, they found no one alive, but only a single unidentifiable skeleton. Yet, that had not been the worst of it.

The commander of their fleet, a Portuguese navigator named Fernandes, refused to allow them back aboard the ships, insisting that they establish their colony on Roanoke. Her father, John White, the colony governor, suspected that Fernandes secretly wanted a base from which to conduct privateering raids, but this was of little consolation to the one hundred and seventeen souls—

including young Virginia, who had been born shortly after their arrival, the first child of English parents born in the New World— who were compelled to build a new life for themselves on the inhospitable outer bank island. It was already too late in the year to plant crops, and as the colonists soon learned, relations with nearby natives were badly strained. Their predecessors had massacred a native village after the alleged theft of a silver cup, and it could only be assumed that angry natives had wiped out the men of the garrison. The passage of time and an appeal to civility had not eased the tension, and soon thereafter one of the colonists had been murdered by the natives while gathering crabs on the north shore of the island.

Without enough supplies to last through the winter and with no reliable help from the native population, Eleanor's father had made the difficult decision to leave friends and family behind, making the dangerous, late-season voyage back to England to gather relief supplies.

No one had been under any illusions about the tough days that laid ahead. Food stores had been rationed. The colonists had gathered what little they could and prepared for the coming of the snows.

Then the situation had truly become dire.

"Something is wrong." John's voice snapped Eleanor out of her musings. She looked up and realized that they were now within sight of the shore. The shadowy woods certainly looked ominous, but she did not immediately see the reason for John's wariness. As soon as they reached the shallows and were able to stand, the privateer handed the now quiescent Virginia back to Eleanor, then quickly loaded and primed his musket.

"What do you see?" Ananias asked.

John shook his head as if to dismiss the question and raised a finger, warning them to silence, as he retrieved the nearly burned out stub of the torch.

The guttering brand held in John's fist made Eleanor realize what was wrong about the situation—what the privateer had noticed right away. The fort was dark. There were no torches or lamps, no watch fires, not even the smell of wood smoke. Where were the forty souls who had remained? The able-bodied men who had been instructed to set watch fires to guide them home?

Figures began emerging from the shadows, drawn to the light of the torch, but these were the people that had escaped the village with them, those who had made the water crossing. Some of them, at least. Eleanor hoped the others had simply come ashore somewhere else.

John directed the men to gather behind him and the women behind them, then proceeded toward the gate, which stood open but unguarded. The privateer paused there, studying something on the ground, and then raised his musket as if sensing danger, before he proceeded inside. Eleanor reached the gates a moment later and saw what had arrested his attention. It was a basket, the kind used by the Secotan women for storing and transporting food. They had all eaten from similar containers back in the village, right before the nightmare had begun. This basket lay discarded near the gate, half its contents—pieces of cooked fish—spilled out upon the ground. Eleanor saw the wasted food and immediately felt a pang. Even now, on the cusp of summer, food remained scarce, too precious to be indifferently cast aside. But something about the basket frightened her, and a moment later, that clue also fell into place. The natives had brought food to the colonists who had stayed behind.

Eleanor's heartbeat quickened as the full significance of this dawned, but it was already too late.

She heard one of the men gasp, and then John's voice boomed, "Out. Everyone."

Eleanor raised her eyes involuntarily. *Oh, God. No.*

The settlement had become a slaughterhouse. Everywhere she turned her gaze, she saw torn pieces of people she had once known, limbs, entrails and chunks of meat that were recognizable only because she knew they could be nothing else.

Ananias gripped her arm, dragged her back toward the gate. John's musket thundered again, the sulfur smell of powder a sharp contrast to the foul stench of death that hung like a fog over the fortress. In the flash, she caught a glimpse of something moving, emerging from one of the houses. The shape was thrown back by the ball, but then just as quickly, it reappeared or was replaced by another.

Another shape moved in the shadows further down the square.

And another.

And another.

At her breast, Virginia began to wail again, but Eleanor did not hear her daughter's voice. Her ears were filled with the sound of her own screams.

C   N

                                    CAPTURE

ONE

Quintana Roo, Mexico

Raul Campos held the walkie-talkie out at arm's length, shook it, then keyed the 'talk' button again. "South gate, come in."

This time the response was immediate. "South gate. All clear."

Campos recognized the voice of Antonio Garcia, but the delay in the man's response, albeit a delay of only a few seconds, troubled him. He hit the transmit button again. "Tony, where is Rico? Is everything okay out there?"

"It's good. Rico is on the west entrance."

Some of Campos's apprehension faded, but not all of it. He ran a tight ship and believed that there was no such thing as a minor lapse.

"Carry on," Campos replied, clipping the radio to his belt. He turned his attention to the bank of flat-screen TVs that displayed closed-circuit camera feeds from thirty different locations in and around the compound, studying each one in turn for any sign that something was amiss.

"Do you think there's a problem?" Chuy Rivera asked from his assigned station at the desk in front of the monitors.

Campos didn't answer right away, not until he had studied every single feed for at least five seconds, a process which took almost three minutes. There was nothing on any of the displays to warrant his anxiety, but he was still not satisfied. When he finally spoke, it was not to answer the question. "Come with me. We're going to check out the south gate."

Rivera grabbed his weapon off the desktop—an Uzi 9mm submachine gun—and rose to his feet. He knew better than to second-guess Campos, but he did ask one question. "Should we tell Mano?"

Campos, who believed in following his own rules to the point of obsession, balked. There was probably a very simple explanation for Garcia's slow reply; maybe he had been taking an unauthorized smoke break and left his radio in the gate shack. While that was the kind of thing that Campos might rightly get worked up over, it certainly didn't justify bothering the boss while he was working. "No. It's probably nothing."

They exited the office, stepping out into the humid night air. Campos slipped behind the wheel of a small electric cart, and with Rivera seated beside him, they drove away from the security office toward the south gate.

The compound was dark, kept so intentionally to hide it from reconnaissance aircraft. Not that the compound's existence or its whereabouts was a closely guarded secret. The local *campesinos* knew exactly where it was, and they had no doubt passed the information along to the *federales*. Everything was kept dark so outsiders would not know what truly went on inside. There were rumors, of course. Part of Campos's job as head of security was to monitor the flow of those rumors and to ensure if accurate information did get out, it would be quickly dismissed as superstitious gossip.

The darkness posed no hardship to Campos. He could have navigated the compound blindfolded. It took only a couple of minutes to reach the south entrance to the compound, but as soon as he stopped the cart, his senses went on high alert. Rivera started to get out, but Campos stopped him. "Wait."

He put the cart in reverse and backed up twenty yards, coming to a stop behind a tree. The cart's electric motor, which wasn't very loud to begin with, fell silent as soon as Campos let go of the controls. He cocked his head sideways, listening for any unusual sounds or the silence that might indicate a lurking intruder.

The night seemed perfectly ordinary, filled with the chirp of crickets.

Still, he was not satisfied. He unclipped the radio again and brought it to his lips. "South gate, come in." He spoke in a low voice, barely louder than a whisper.

The reply was immediate this time. "South gate, here."

Definitely Garcia's voice. So why does something feel wrong? "Be advised, Chuy is headed your way for a spot inspection."

There was a slight pause. "Is something the matter?"

"That's not your concern," Campos snapped. Garcia should have known better than to question him. "Just be ready for Chuy when he gets there."

"Understood."

Campos lowered the radio and turned to Rivera, hefting his own Uzi as he spoke. "Go check it. I'll cover you from here. Be careful. Something doesn't feel right."

Rivera slid out of his seat and strode up the path. Campos got out as well, ducking down behind the tree and training the barrel of his weapon on the door to the gate house. He held his breath, listening to the soft noise of Rivera's footsteps. His eyes were adjusting to the darkness, and in the starlight, he had no trouble distinguishing the moving silhouette. Rivera reached the gate house, paused just a moment, then opened the door and entered.

Campos waited. Five seconds passed. Ten seconds.

Rivera should have come out by now. Something is definitely wrong. I have to warn Mano.

He laid the walkie-talkie on the ground and took a mobile phone from his pocket. When he touched the button to turn it on, the screen was so bright that he winced and looked away quickly, just in time to see something flash out of the darkness toward him.

He jerked away, feeling the air move as the object—*a blade, it's a knife blade!*—sliced through the air above his head. His reflexes, honed from hours spent training and dozens of cage battles, not only saved his life but gave him the edge he needed to immediately strike back at his attacker. He lashed out with a foot, striking something so solid that, for a fleeting instant, he wondered if he had kicked the tree. But then the man toppled forward onto him, and he knew that he had scored a hit.

The man—he was sure it was a man—was huge, at least six feet tall and solidly muscled. But Campos had fought bigger and stronger. As the man threw his arms wide to regain his balance, Campos caught hold of the knife hand, trapping wrist and elbow in an arm-bar hold. He fell back, pulling the already unbalanced man down, and brought his legs up to immobilize and dominate his opponent.

For a moment, he held the man fast, their two bodies entangled like some kind of blacksmith's puzzle. He could feel the man straining, trying to break the hold. Campos felt a thrill of excitement at the sound of the other man's labored breathing—the almost bestial growl of exertion.

He will exhaust himself in a futile effort to break free, and when he is too tired to go on, I will—

Campos howled involuntarily as pain shot through his right arm. He tried to fight through the agony and maintain his hold, but even the act of trying to close his fingers unleashed a fresh wave of torment.

He broke my arm! That's not supposed to—

Campos screamed again.

There was another stunning eruption of pain, this time from his left arm. He could hear the radius and ulna bones in his forearm snap like twigs. He felt the jagged ends piercing through muscle and skin. Through the red mist of agony, he saw his assailant towering above him, silhouetted in starlight. Campos tried to throw up his hands to ward off the imminent attack, but his appendages dangled limply, like dead things. The pain took him to the edge of unconsciousness.

"No," he whimpered. "You're not supposed to beat me."

Then something slammed into the side of his head, and the darkness took him.

TWO

Stan Tremblay, callsign: Rook, stared down at the motionless form for several seconds until he was satisfied that the man wasn't going to be a problem for him—or anyone else—ever again. "What was that he said?"

"Dunno," was the casual reply from the small woman standing behind him. "*No hablo Español.*"

"I know for a fact that you *habla*," Rook grumbled, but let it go. *Probably some kind of macho death curse. 'I spit at you with my final breath.' Whatever.*

He placed a booted foot on the dead man's forehead and wrenched his knife loose from where it had pierced the man's temple.

The woman was Zelda Baker, and in addition to being Rook's teammate, she was also his girlfriend. When she was on the clock, as she was now, she went by the callsign: Queen. Her pert features and blonde hair were obscured from view by an adaptive camouflage head covering, but Rook knew underneath she was grinning. She shook her head in amused disbelief. "Why'd you go Conan the Barbarian with the blade? Why didn't you just shoot him?"

In the perfect clarity of hindsight, Rook had to ask himself the same thing. The truth of the matter was that he had been waiting for Knight—Shin Dae-jung, the team's designated marksman—to reach out and touch the guy with a round from his silenced

CheyTac Intervention M200 rifle. Knight probably had a good reason to hold back, but when it had become apparent that the target was about to make a phone call that would alert the whole compound to their presence, Rook had taken action.

"If I had shot him, he might have survived long enough to get off a few shots with that pea shooter. Then we'd have a gaggle of hombres to deal with."

"Right," Queen said, making no attempt to hide her sarcasm. "So instead you just went all Chewbacca on his ass, ripped his arms off and beat him to death with them."

"First I'm Conan, then I'm a Wookie? I'm sorry, when did you change your callsign to Nerd Princess?"

She laughed, then continued more soberly. "You had me worried there for a couple seconds. Thought you might need to tag me in."

"Naw. The guy was a Nancy. I eat his kind for breakfast."

"Yuck."

"What is this about blades and arms ripping off?" another voice chimed in, also a woman's but colored with a harsh Slavic accent. "Rook, why did you not just shoot him? That's what I did to his partner."

Rook turned to face the pair of figures that were moving toward them from the direction of the gatehouse. Like himself and Queen, the two were covered head-to-toe in gray chameleon camouflage that masked their faces and jet black hair, but he had no trouble identifying his teammate, Asya Machtcenko, callsign: Bishop, or the team's leader, Jack Sigler, callsign: King.

Despite the facts that they were brother and sister, and they shared nearly identical orange-brown eyes, the two were completely unalike in build and mannerisms. King was over six feet tall with a muscular physique—a narrower version of Rook, while Asya—*Bishop*, Rook corrected himself, *She's Bishop now*—was petite, though no less capable or deadly than her big brother. Yet, even absent these identifying factors, Rook could have distinguished them from a thousand yards away thanks to the blue icons—each a two-dimensional likeness of the chess piece that corresponded to their respective callsigns—that hovered above their heads. A similar icon hung over Queen, and in the distance, not quite four hundred yards away, another marked Knight's location on a hillside looking down into the compound.

The icons were not literally floating above their heads. They were instead integrated into a cutting-edge virtual environment that was projected onto the retinas of each team member. The display was courtesy of the very latest in virtual reality and quantum computer technology, all neatly packaged in a pair of nearly indestructible, black, sport-frame sunglasses. The chameleon suits utilized the same quantum computer in tandem with electro-magnetic sensors and a fiber-optic mesh fabric made of advanced meta-materials that could change color in response to the surrounding environment. Their weapons were also synced with the VR network to allow pinpoint, precision aiming. The five of them were, if not the deadliest special-operations warriors on the planet, at least the best equipped. Which was probably why Rook still felt a little foolish for having gone after the target with his comparatively low tech SOG Ops M40TK-CP combat knife.

King studied the motionless body of Rook's fallen opponent. According to facial recognition software, another feature of the VR glasses, the man—Raul Campos—was a career criminal with ties to other cartels and a long string of unprosecuted crimes. There was no record of his ties to the emerging *El Sol* drug cartel, but based on the radio transmissions they had intercepted and appropriated, thanks to some audio-wizardry courtesy of the team's resident tech expert, Lewis Aleman, they had learned Campos had earned his way to a position of responsibility in the El Sol organization.

Job opening, Rook thought with a morbid smile.

King nodded in Rook's direction. "Not your best work, but there's something to be said for doing things the old fashioned way."

Rook turned to Queen. "Was that a joke? I can never tell with him."

King ignored the comment, and when he spoke again it was for the benefit of the one team member who had not yet joined their little pow-wow. "Knight. Pick up and come to us."

"On the move." The reply was unusually terse, reminding Rook that if Knight had just done his job, the whole ugly wrestling match with Campos could have been avoided. He wanted to give his friend and teammate the benefit of the doubt—maybe he just didn't have a clear shot—but he couldn't help but wonder if...

He shook his head. Now wasn't the time to start doubting his teammates or second-guessing King's decisions. *Besides, even in his current condition, Knight is still worth a dozen of these* narcotraficante *shitheads.*

Mexican drug cartels were not the team's usual fare, but Rook thought the chance to use his deadly skills against an *ordinary* human threat was a welcome change of pace. When they had originally been brought together from various United States military special operations units to form a new elite team—the Chess Team—it had been with the understanding that they would go up against threats that were of an extraordinary nature. The last nine years had opened Rook's mind to a whole new definition of the word 'extraordinary.' As vicious as these drug cartels were, they were monsters only in a figurative sense. Chess Team usually fought actual goddamned monsters.

There were, of course, some aspects of the current assignment that were maybe not extraordinary but certainly atypical. First, there were the political considerations. The Mexican Drug War, which had been going on for nearly ten years, was largely an internal conflict—a turf war between rival drug cartels. The Mexican authorities and armed vigilante groups were trying to mitigate the collateral damage, but the cartels preferred terrorist tactics to open combat, resorting to assassination, kidnapping and outright brutality. The violence had more than once spilled over onto American soil, adding fuel to the already volatile issue of illegal immigration. The U.S. government had a legitimate interest in supporting Mexico's efforts to bring down the cartels. That support ranged from providing funds to sharing intelligence and even sending military and law enforcement officials to 'consult' with their counterparts in the Mexican government. Sometimes circumstances called for a more direct intervention, and that was something that had to be done very discreetly.

Chess Team was the very soul of discretion.

Although they had originally been organized as part of the US Army Special Forces 'Delta' teams, four years ago they had severed their ties—officially at least—from the military. Now they operated as a completely independent, and strictly speaking illegal, paramilitary force, ready to go into action on the orders of the president—or if circumstances warranted, of their own volition. While they still received occasional operational support from the military and other government agencies, their handler and the man chiefly responsible for creating the team in the first place, Tom Duncan, was an old hand at covering their tracks. Duncan went by the callsign: Deep Blue, a reference to a famous chess-playing computer from the late 20th century. For the first five years of their existence, Duncan had successfully managed the Chess Team as a second job, which was no mean feat, considering that unbeknownst even to the team at the time, his first job was President of the United States. Although he had ultimately resigned that office, his knowledge of the political landscape and his well-established network of connections had made it possible for Chess Team to continue doing what it did best: saving the world.

Aside from the politics of the current situation however, there was something about the El Sol organization that put it in a different class than rival cartels, which were typically more of a testosterone fueled hybrid of street gang and business enterprise. El Sol was into some very weird shit. So weird in fact that no one could quite agree on what exactly, but the most plausible accounts made El Sol sound more like an ancient bloodthirsty religious cult than a crime syndicate. It wasn't the first time that religion and superstitious beliefs had been co-opted by criminals to enhance their power, but El Sol had done it with exceptional speed and efficiency, crushing the other cartels in the Yucatan region, and scaring the hell out of the locals.

The less believable rumors mentioned demons and monsters lurking inside this gated compound. Rook, who had seen more than his share of both, was adopting a wait-and-see attitude.

The blue horse-head chess piece moved toward them with a preternatural smoothness, like a drop of quicksilver sliding across a sheet of glass. Without the VR marker, Knight would have been able to sneak up on them all.

Well that's one skill he hasn't lost, Rook thought. *But sneaky is only the first part of the job. You've got to actually pull the trigger once in a while.*

He felt guilty for doubting Knight. They were blood brothers, a bond that meant as much to him as the oath he had taken to defend America, and yet he couldn't simply set aside his reservations about Knight's operational fitness. The guy had been through hell. During their last field assignment in the Congo, a piece of shrapnel had taken Knight's left eye. The subsequent infection had nearly taken his life. He had survived the fever, but the damage to his optic nerve had been irreversible. For anyone else, the loss of an eye would have meant the end of his shooting days and a medical retirement, but Deep Blue had promised Knight that, if he so desired, they would find a way to get him back in the fight.

Knight had accepted without hesitation, and Aleman had gone to work designing an ocular implant that would give Knight back his eyesight, or at least something approximating it. Rook wasn't privy to the design specifications, and probably wouldn't have been able to make heads or tails of them in any case, but he did know that it had taken Knight several weeks to learn how to 'see' with the implant, and while his shooting accuracy was now as good as it had ever been, Knight seemed...off. Rook couldn't put his finger on exactly what it was that was different about his friend.

Maybe it had to do with what else had been lost in Africa.

When Knight was still fifty yards away, King spoke again. "Rook, take point. Queen, you're behind him. Head on a swivel."

Rook knelt to retrieve an M240B medium machine gun, which rested on bipod legs nearby. The thing weighed damn near thirty pounds loaded, and it was pretty much useless for the kind of surgical strike they were hoping to pull off tonight, but machine guns were like motorcycle helmets—better to have them and never use them, than need one and not have it. The 240B was his primary, but not his only weapon. Like the rest of the team, he also carried a compact H&K MP5 SD machine pistol, equipped with sound suppressor. Rounding out his personal arsenal were 'the Girls'—a pair of IMI Desert Eagle Mark XIX Magnum .50 caliber semi-automatic pistols, one on each hip. He slung the machine gun across his back, out of the way, and led with the MP5. In the event that they made contact, the whisper-quiet machine pistol might be able to neutralize a threat without waking up everyone for twenty miles. If the shit really hit the fan, the need for subtlety would have already gone out the window, and then he could make as much noise and fling as much lead downrange as he liked.

He started forward, covering the right side of the path while Queen watched the left. The glasses had low light capabilities that were far superior to even the best 4G night vision devices currently available to elite military units. The glasses also acted like a miniature heads-up display, showing a top down GPS map of the compound. Unfortunately, the one thing the glasses could not do was tell them where to find their objective, a senior member of El Sol known only as Mano—literally, the Hand. Their mission was to retrieve Mano, preferably alive, but if alive meant taking an unnecessary risk, then in a body bag was an acceptable alternative. Mano's true identity was unknown, but reliable intel placed him inside the gates of this remote property. If he was the important leader everyone believed him to be, then odds were good that they would find him in the largest building, which in the satellite photos, appeared to be a colonial-style hacienda at the center of the compound.

During their approach, they had reconnoitered the guard posts and tagged each of the El Sol gunmen in the virtual environment. Their locations appeared as red dots on the map, all distributed around the perimeter. There were no guards or patrols inside the compound but Rook remained vigilant as he made his way up the path to the cluster of dark buildings at the center of the perimeter.

"Stack on the front door," King said, his low whisper perfectly audible through the bone-induction speakers that transmitted sound vibrations from the glasses' earpieces and into the skulls of the team members. "Two to a room. Slow and quiet. Rook, Queen, you're up first."

Rook crept onto the porch and waited for the others to line up behind him. At a signal from King, Knight moved up and with a light touch, tried the door knob. It turned without resistance. He nodded to Rook, initiating a silent three-count, and then pushed the door open.

Rook moved inside and turned to the right, getting clear of the doorway and scanning for a target. Queen was directly behind him, moving left. Room clearing was something they rehearsed almost obsessively under a variety of conditions and threat configurations. As soon as he and Queen cleared the first room, Knight and Bishop would leapfrog through and clear the next room, repeating this procedure until the house was completely secure. King would watch their six o'clock, making sure that no one wandered in from outside. Staying focused, prioritizing threats and remembering which way to turn could be a matter of life and death, so it took a second for Rook to realize that what lay beyond the doorway was nothing like what he had expected.

"What the hell?"

THREE

"**Rook, talk to** me," King said. "What's happening? Is the room clear?"

"Uh, I'm not really sure." He straightened out of his slightly hunched over stance and took in the panoramic view that lay before him.

The hacienda exterior was a façade, an empty shell. Instead of a house of rooms, the interior was a vast open space at least two hundred feet across, the floor about ten feet below the balcony where they now stood.

"What is this place?" Queen asked. "A warehouse?"

Rook caught a whiff of the air and wrinkled his nose. "More like a barn."

"You would know, farmboy."

Rook ignored the jibe. Even if he hadn't grown up on a New England farm, the smells of livestock—musk and manure—would have been unmistakable. "I don't think we're going to find our guy in here."

"You're probably right," King said. "But do a quick walkthrough. Look for hidden storerooms, tunnels, secret passages. There's already more going on here than meets the eye."

"Copy that, Optimus." Rook's gaze was drawn to the center of the open space, where someone had partitioned a twenty-foot square with eight-foot high sections of chain-link fence, topped with a coil of razor wire. The structure looked like an animal pen or a dog run, but its conspicuous central location suggested another purpose.

"I think they've been using this place for cage matches."

No one asked him to elaborate. Of all the brutal and inhuman crimes attributed to the Mexican drug lords, one of the most heinous was forcing kidnap victims and captured enemies to participate in brutal gladiatorial fights. Here it seemed was proof that the El Sol cartel was doing just that.

Rook tore his gaze away from the cage and headed down a flight of wooden stairs to the floor of the open room. From there, he and Queen moved out to search the perimeter of the room. About halfway around, he found another section of chain-link fence that appeared to be a gate blocking access to a recessed alcove about twenty feet deep. The floor was strewn with what looked like hay bale-sized lumps of fur. Rook zoomed in on the nearest of them. "What the hell are those—"

The lump he was inspecting erupted into motion, crossing the intervening distance and slamming into the chain link right in front of him. Startled, he stumbled back with a yelp. The movement had been so sudden that it took him a moment to process what had just happened, and in that brief instant, the rest of the furry shapes were roused.

Rook got his MP5 up and thrust it in the direction of the snarling, snorting mass that seemed about to burst through the bulging chain link gate. His first thought was that this was a pack of dogs, but one look at the hideous snouts that lashed back and forth against the diamond-patterned barrier, raking the links with gleaming tusks, told him that these were a different animal entirely.

"Goddamned pigs," he said, his voice still a little shaky from the adrenaline spike.

"Wild boars, to be precise." The voice sounded like it was coming from right beside him, but the person speaking was actually two thousand miles away in the team's headquarters in New Hampshire.

"There are thousands of them roaming Mexico and the Southwest," Deep Blue went on, "Wild boars and feral hogs. Distant cousins to Porky and Wilbur."

Rook grunted a vague acknowledgement. 'Distant' was putting it mildly. About the only thing these creatures had in common with the pigs Rook had grown up with, was a distinctive flat nose. Aside from that, the boars were just plain ugly, with bulbous rat-like bodies about five feet long from snout to stubby tail, covered in coarse brown bristles, and supported on short, spindly legs that evidently were a lot faster than they looked. Razor-sharp canine teeth—nearly three-inches long—protruded from the pig-faces, and Rook had no doubt that those tusks could rip a person wide open with a single slash.

The fence continued to bulge and buckle under the combined assault of the boars. Rook guessed that each of them was probably in the neighborhood of two hundred pounds, and it seemed prudent not to test whether the so-called 'cyclone' fence material could stand up to the relentless battering, so he backed away slowly, keeping his MP5 trained on the creatures.

"Well, that explains the smell," he muttered. "Hey, Knight. You got any good family barbecue recipes?"

"Oh, I get it." Knight replied in a dour voice. "It's funny because I'm Korean. Really, Rook?"

Rook grinned. It wasn't much of a reaction, but it was a hopeful sign that there was a little bit of the old Knight still trying to break through.

"Something tells me they aren't raising these things for the bacon," Deep Blue went on. "They're a lot bigger than the boars found in the wild, and judging by their aggressive reaction, I'd say they're probably feeding them a cocktail of anabolic steroids and growth hormones, along with a lot of fresh meat."

"Why grow 'em big if not to slaughter them?"

Queen, who had come over to join Rook, jerked a thumb in the direction of the cage in the center of the open room.

"What? They're fighting them?"

"No," she said. "I think they're making their hostages fight them. Man against beast. And pigs are omnivores, so no clean-up required afterward."

Rook winced. There was only so much that light banter and dark humor could do to cushion the impact of such inhuman brutality. "These bastards need to go down."

"I'm glad you feel that way," King interjected. "So if you kids could hurry up and finish checking out the petting zoo, we've got work to do."

Rook continued backing away from the boars until their weird barking grunts were no longer audible, and then he turned and resumed searching the perimeter of the enclosure. Further along the wall, they found another gated alcove, which Rook gave only the most cursory inspection. At the far end of the room, they found a wide doorway blocked by a metal roll-up door.

Rook frowned. This was something they had not anticipated. "What's the call, boss?"

There was a long pause and Rook knew King was working through all the possible outcomes. That was King's gift; he was a highly analytical strategic thinker. It was no coincidence that they had chosen the appellation 'Chess Team.' King could manage the battlefield like a grandmaster moving pieces on a game board.

"We've got to know what's on the other side of that door," he said finally. "Stand by. We'll come to you."

Rook felt a strange sense of relief at King's decision, and he was about to say as much when, with a harsh metallic rasp, the door was thrown open.

The glasses instantly adjusted to the sudden brightness of incandescent light bulbs, saving Rook's eyes from flash blindness. Nevertheless, the suddenness with which the door had opened left him momentarily stunned. Fortunately, the man standing just beyond, a mere arm's length away, was even less prepared for the encounter. His eyebrows creased together in surprise and consternation, but not alarm.

He can't see us, Rook thought. *He sees something, but doesn't know what it is. His eyes haven't adjusted to the darkness, and with the chameleon suits, we blend in.*

Rook knew the illusion wouldn't last, but before he could bring the MP5 up, lines of text began scrolling across his heads-up display. A familiar name—Juan Beltran, one of the prime suspects believed to be the mysterious Mano—and a long list of criminal offenses.

This is the guy.

Rook shifted his weapon ever so slightly, and a red targeting dot appeared on Beltran's chest. The drug lord did not appear to be armed, and they had instructions to take him alive if possible.

Was it possible?

Beltran's eyes suddenly went wide.

He sees me.

In the instant it took for Rook to make his decision, Beltran overcame his panic and darted to the side. Rook pounced after him, swinging the machine pistol like a club, and he felt the resounding crunch of metal against bone, but as Beltran slumped to the floor, Rook saw the man's hand fall away from a bright red button mounted on the wall.

"What was that?" Queen asked, stepping forward to inspect the button. "An alarm?"

"Whatever it was, I don't think he got to it," Rook said, bending over to check Beltran's pulse. *Still alive.*

Great, now I have to carry him, too.

Queen placed a hand on the button, as if testing it, then she hooked her fingers around it and pulled. The button popped out with an audible click. She faced Rook with a grim expression. "I hate to rain on your parade, but I think he did get to it."

"A silent alarm?" Rook tilted his head, listening for the claxons of a security system, but he heard something else instead, a clicking noise, like teeth biting together, and with it, a sound that was somewhere between a dog's bark and a pig's snort.

He glanced back through the doorway. The gates to the alcoves on both sides of the big room stood wide open, and charging across the floor, like bristly guided missiles, were two dozen amped-up slavering boars.

FOUR

King was just starting down the stairs when a flash of artificial light at the far end of the room warned him that something was wrong.

"Bishop, watch the door. Knight, you're with me." He didn't ask Rook or Queen for an explanation. The fact that they had not immediately updated him could mean only trouble. Yet, despite the premonition of danger, the metallic rasp of the gated pens sliding open sent a chill down his spine.

The floor was alive with movement. Furry shapes, each about two feet high, spilled out of the alcoves. These were the boars Deep Blue had identified, and yet their appearance still came as a shock. The wild pigs looked like enormous bloated ticks, and they moved like lightning. Most of them charged toward the distant light, but four of the porcine heads turned in the opposite direction and shot toward the stairs.

King trained his MP5 on the nearest one but it was moving so fast he couldn't keep the aiming dot centered. To make matters worse, the virtual display wasn't marking the boars as targets; the software could easily distinguish human features and tag them accordingly, but it wasn't configured to do the same with animals.

Low tech it is, then. He squeezed the trigger. The machine pistol made a mechanical clicking sound as it started hurling 9mm rounds in the direction of the advancing boars, but the suppressed report was so soft that he could hear the creatures grunting and squealing as some of the bullets found flesh. Blood and fur erupted into the air all around the creatures, but none of them fell. They didn't even slow down.

Shit. It's like throwing pebbles at them.

The pigs were so close now that he did not need to bother with the aiming dot. He pointed the barrel at the closest beast and held the trigger. Bullets raked into the thing's head, gouging long bloody furrows, but the boar's skull was like an armor plate.

There was a whoosh of air from beside him, and then the boar popped like an over-inflated balloon. The thick hide and dense bone was evidently no match for a .408 round from Knight's sniper rifle.

King took a step back, switching to another target. The MP5 chattered a few more times then went silent. "Reloading!"

There was another hiss of displaced air, and a second boar went down just twenty feet away. Its momentum carried it forward, a tumbling fountain of gore that came to rest at King's feet. He slotted a full magazine into the machine-pistol and dropped down behind the carcass, aiming his weapon lower, at the spindly legs of the remaining boars. Then he let lead fly.

The bullets skipped off the concrete floor, filling the open space with a noise like a jackhammer, but the new tactic bore immediate fruit. One of the beasts stumbled, veering directly into the path of the other, and the two lumbering shapes collided in a flurry of limbs and slashing tusks that ended when they slammed into the dead animal King hid behind. They hit with such force that the carcass slid back and knocked King down.

He scrambled up, ready to engage again, but the entangled boars were already in their death throes, felled by two more close-range shots from Knight's rifle.

King let out the breath he had been holding and gave Knight a grateful nod. He knew that the team's sniper was dealing with a lot of self-doubt stemming from his injury, but there was no question in King's mind that Knight was one hundred percent ready-for-action.

Two more of the boars broke off from the main stampede and were lumbering toward them, but King looked past them to the square of incandescent light and the overlapping blue icons that marked the location of the rest of his team.

Rook's voice suddenly filled his head. "Get out of the fucking way!"

King immediately grasped Rook's intent and sprang into motion, running for the right side of the room. He had taken only a few steps when the chainsaw report of Rook's 240B thundered in his ears.

"There's too many of them," Queen yelled, barely audible over the din of the machine gun. "Fall back!"

There was another burst from the big gun, and then with the abruptness of a guillotine blade, the noise ceased and the distant light blinked out.

FIVE

When she realized that her MP5 was going to be about as effective at stopping the boars as a BB gun, Queen started looking for a better alternative than making a desperate last stand.

She had been a few steps behind Rook when Beltran had thrown open the roll-up door, and in the pregnant pause that had followed, she had gotten a good look at what lay beyond it. The door opened into a long tunnel, big enough to drive a truck through it. If there was any doubt about that, the idling Ford F-150 right behind Beltran erased it.

When Rook had taken Beltran down, Queen's attention had turned to the matter of the red button on the wall, and then to the stampede of boars charging toward them. Her machine-pistol was next to useless, and she didn't think she would fare much better with her back-up—a SIG Sauer P226 chambered for .357 ammo— which meant it was up to Rook to hold back the charge with his machine gun.

After shouting a warning for King and Knight to get out of his field of fire, Rook had swept the front line of the advance with a storm of lead, knocking the wild pigs down like bowling pins. But unlike human combatants who know better than to run headlong into the muzzle flash of a machine gun, the boars just kept coming. Rook began concentrating his fire on specific targets, felling one after another with short bursts, but it was plainly evident that some of them were going to make it through.

"There're too many of them. Fall back."

Rook nodded and kept firing while she went for the door post. The bottom of the door was out of reach, but she managed to leap high enough to snare the cord that hung down from it, and as her feet touched down, she pulled with all her might. Rook jumped back out of the way as the metal door slid down.

There was a squeal as the metal barrier crunched down into the skull of the fastest boar, slamming it to the floor. The creature's crushed skull prevented the door from closing completely, leaving a gap that was at least six-inches wide. Queen stepped onto the metal lip at the bottom of the door, trying to force it lower, but the barrier shuddered as more of the beasts arrived, bulldozing mindlessly into the obstacle. Then black snouts and gleaming tusks started appearing in the gap, and Queen felt the door lurch up as their combined efforts began wedging the door open again.

Rook darted forward and delivered a field-goal kick that knocked the dead boar back, then added his weight to the door, forcing it down. There were more tortured shrieks as the enraged animals pulled back, leaving bloody smears on the concrete, and then the door met the floor with a loud bang.

Rook leaned against the door, which continued to shudder with repeated impacts, as he panted to catch his breath. "Who...in the *fuck*...has a 'turn the hell-pigs loose' button?"

"That guy." Queen nodded in the direction of the motionless figure of Beltran. She took a few quick breaths of her own, then said, "King, we stopped those things."

"Yeah, I see that." King sounded uncharacteristically irritated. "They're headed our way now."

Rook winced. "Oopsie."

"We're in some kind of tunnel," Queen said, ignoring the remark. "I'm pretty sure it leads back to the surface. And we got Mano. If you can get clear, we can meet you at the extraction point."

"Do it," was the terse reply. "We're bugging—"

Bishop's voice cut in. "I have problem here."

Queen did not have to wait for an explanation. In the head's up display of her glasses, she saw several red dots moving toward the front door of the hacienda, where Bishop stood guard. The red button might not have been an alarm, but the battle with the boars had alerted everyone in the compound to their presence.

"Well, shit." King was silent for a millisecond, then continued. "Get Beltran to the extraction point. He's our priority."

"Screw that," Rook said. "I'll clear a path through the hell pigs with the 240 and we can all leave together."

"Negative. You wouldn't be able to shoot them without shooting us. We're going out the front door."

Queen counted the red dots, eight of them in all. She didn't doubt that her teammates could handle those odds, but those were just the bad guys they knew about. There was no telling how many cartel gunmen were waking up and grabbing their Uzis.

She glanced around quickly, searching for inspiration or a better answer...and she found it. "King, stay where you are. I've got an idea."

SIX

Bishop.

I am Bishop.

Rook wasn't the only one having trouble getting used to that change. Although she had been using the designation exclusively for months now, training for hours on end to truly integrate with the team, now that she was in the field, now that the bullets were real, Asya felt a gnawing inadequacy.

I am not Bishop.

She watched the red dots moving through the compound, drawing relentlessly closer. Her weapon was trained on the nearest man, the aiming dot in the virtual environment showing the cone of probability where the bullet would strike. In a moment, she would have to pull the trigger, take a human life.

She wasn't squeamish about killing, especially not men such as these. She had been a soldier for much of her adult life and had killed before. She knew what it felt like. That wasn't the problem. Except in a backwards sort of way, it was. She was a soldier, she had been part of the Russian Army, but there was a world of difference between being a rifleman in a front-line unit, and being part of the most elite special operations group on the planet. She had learned that the hard way several months earlier when, as Pawn—the designation reserved for personnel working with the team on a temporary basis—she had taken a bullet and nearly bled out in the subsequent firefight and escape from rebel forces in the Congo. Instead of giving her a nice safe job guarding the outer perimeter of Endgame headquarters, her brother and Thomas—*Deep Blue*, she thought, *I must remember to think of him as Deep Blue*—had promoted her to fill the vacancy left when the former Bishop, Erik Somers, had been killed in action.

'You are Bishop now.'

Once she had gotten over the emotional shock, she had quickly demurred. "I cannot do this," she had told them. "I cannot replace Bishop."

"No," King had told her. "You can't. No one can replace him, and we don't expect you to try, so get that idea out of your head."

Months of intensive training had almost convinced her that she could do exactly that, but now, once more facing a life or death situation, she felt like a pretender. It was as if the ghost of the real Bishop was watching her, judging her, waiting for her to fail, just as she had failed in Africa.

I am not Bishop. I am just Asya.

Bishop—Erik Somers, the *real* Bishop—had been a fierce giant, a force of nature. He had been the team's heavy weapons specialist, carrying machine guns around like they were feather-light and battling fearsome monsters, with his bare hands if necessary. In the end, he had given his life to save millions. How was she supposed to live up to expectations like that?

The answer was easy. She couldn't.

Asya tightened her finger on the trigger—*At least I can do this*—and squeezed.

The approaching gunman went rigid and then dropped, as three sound-suppressed rounds from her MP5 punched into his chest. She swiveled the gun to the next target, only a few feet away from the first and evidently unaware of the fate that had befallen his comrade.

A yellow dot appeared at the edge of her field of view. Her glasses, which saw the entire landscape in front of her even where she was not looking, had just marked the presence of another person emerging from one of the smaller buildings in the compound. A moment later, the yellow dot turned red as the facial recognition software put a name to the face—a minor street criminal with known cartel affiliations.

Another yellow dot popped up right behind him. Then another showed up on the other side of the compound. In the space of five seconds, the number of targets doubled.

Reinforcements were arriving.

"*Chyort vozmi*," she muttered in her native Russian, then switched to English for the benefit of the rest of the team. "Now I have a real problem."

Behind her, the animal noises—squeals and the weird chattering sound of tusks rubbing together—had reached a fever pitch, but King's voice cut through the din. "Hold them off a few more seconds. And prep the door. We're leaving by a different route."

A different route?

With a twinge of guilt, she realized that she had not been paying attention to the exchange between King and Queen. They had come up with a plan but she didn't know what it was.

No matter. She had her orders.

Instead of trying to pick off the isolated targets, she directed her fire wherever there were two or three gunmen clustered together. The effect was immediate and exactly what she had hoped for. Shouts went up all across the compound, as men dove for cover.

With their advance slowed almost to a crawl, she set the gun down and took a fragmentation grenade from her gear pouch. This, at least, was something she could do well.

"Thom—I mean Deep Blue, you will let me know if any of those guys get too close."

There was a trace of amusement in the reply. "Affirmative, Bishop. I'll be the eyes in the back of your head."

Asya shook her head over the strange American idiom for a moment as she quickly taped the grenade to the doorpost and then ran a length of fine wire across the threshold at ankle level. She tied one end to the ring on the grenade's safety pin, carefully working the pin out of its hole until only a fraction of an inch of metal kept the device from arming.

"Bishop, heads up."

She grimaced at the timing. One slip and her trap would blow up in her face. She slipped the pin back in place and grabbed the MP5, firing blindly through the doorway. The burst ripped into a man who was just ten feet away, but as he staggered back, he loosed a barrage of unsuppressed gunfire that scorched the air above her head. Red and yellow dots scattered again, but only for a moment. If there had been any doubt about the nature of the disturbance and where it was focused, the unintentional discharge had removed it completely. Wary of sniper fire, the gunmen were heading for the corners of the big empty house, clearly intent on flanking her position.

There was a sudden eruption of noise behind her as Rook opened up with the machine gun. She glanced back quickly and saw a bright spot moving across the vast open floor. As the glasses adjusted to the changing light level, the image resolved into a pickup truck tearing across the concrete floor with Queen at the wheel and Rook standing in the bed, blasting the swarm of boars that were now converging on the vehicle.

"Bishop," King yelled. "Move it. Our ride's here."

Ah, so that's the plan.

Asya turned back and finished preparing the grenade, then emptied her machine-pistol in the direction of a nearby group of gunmen. Without waiting to assess the results, she headed for the steps, slotting in a fresh magazine as she ran.

The situation below was almost surreal. There were still a dozen boars moving about. Many of them were wounded, leaving a trail of bloody hoofprints as they zigzagged in an effort to home in on the moving truck, but either their ferocity had inured them to pain or their tough hides were stopping the bullets with only superficial damage. The pigs seemed unimpressed by the moving vehicle, and as she watched, she saw one of them crash into the rear wheel.

There was a noise as loud as a gunshot, but when the boar tumbled away to lie in a bloody misshapen lump, she realized that the sound had been something else. The animal had ripped into the tire with its tusk, and although the resulting blowout had nearly taken its head off, the tire was now coming apart in an eruption of rubber chunks. Before the truck could go another twenty yards, the naked rim hit the concrete floor in a spray of sparks and with a shriek so piercingly loud that Asya had to fight the impulse to clap her hands over her ears.

Queen just revved the engine higher and kept going.

At the bottom of the steps, Asya found King and Knight, walking side by side, blasting every boar that stood between them and the truck. The relentless barrage of 9mm rounds from King's MP5 was taking its toll, but every time Knight pulled the trigger, letting a .408 caliber round fly, a pig came apart like an overripe melon.

The truck skidded around a hundred and eighty degrees, so that the bed was pointed toward the three, and Rook began waving frantically for them to climb aboard. King and Knight did so without hesitation, but Asya faltered as a squealing boar emerged from a blind spot at the front end of the pickup. The beast slashed its head back and forth, flinging gobs of bloody drool from the ends of its tusks. She had a vision of the razor-sharp teeth slicing her legs to the bone and almost started back for the stairs, but then the boar's head came apart to the sound of a burst from Rook's machine gun.

"Move it, Bish!" he shouted, sweeping the area for another target.

Asya sprinted for the bed of the truck and reached for King's outstretched hand.

"And watch your step," Rook added.

Asya thought the warning unnecessary, but as she vaulted into the open cargo tray, she almost faltered a second time. The entire bed of the truck was covered with corpses.

Naked human bodies.

A thunderous eruption filled the air, and a wave of pure force pummeled Asya's gut. She ducked reflexively, as did everyone else, as a spray of molten metal fragments flew through the air overhead.

"Looks like someone won the door prize," Rook shouted.

Door prize? Her English was good, but sometimes she had trouble making sense of what her teammates were saying, especially Rook. This time, however, the meaning was clear enough: someone had tripped the grenade booby trap she had set. The blast would probably make the rest of the gunmen take a healthy pause, but they would eventually brave the door again. This time, there would be nothing to slow them down.

The mystery of the truck's grisly payload would have to wait. Living bodies were her concern now.

Queen floored the gas pedal, and the pickup lurched ahead with another torturous wail of metal. Despite the fact that she was redlining the engine, the truck dragged itself forward. Asya felt King's hand grip her arm to keep her from spilling out the back, and for a fleeting moment, she felt gratitude toward her older brother. Then she realized what the gesture meant. *He does not think I can do this. And why should he? I do not believe it myself.*

Despite the blown out tire, the truck finally reached the far end of the room with the tunnel that had been initially blocked by the roll-up door, but there were still half a dozen boars pursuing them, easily keeping pace with the damaged pickup. Queen tried to thread the truck into the narrow gap, but the missing wheel played havoc with the steering. The rear end fishtailed at the last instant, scraping against the doorposts and knocking everyone in the bed off balance. The truck ground to a halt for a moment, and even with King's restraining grip, Asya was thrown backward into the pile of bodies.

A grunting boar leaped onto the back of the truck, its grotesque tusked head whipping back and forth like the blade of a scythe. Asya fumbled for her weapon as the creature got its forelegs over the tailgate, but before she could fire, King lashed out with a foot and connected solidly with its snout and sent it tumbling backward. At almost the same instant, the truck broke free of the snag and entered the claustrophobic confines of the passage.

Asya righted herself and crawled to the rear, thrusting the MP5 over the tailgate and firing into the rest of the pack. She felt King and Knight on either side of her, doing the same.

"Eyes front," Queen called out. "We're not the only ones that know about this tunnel."

Even before she had finished saying it, the air was filled with staccato reports. Asya whipped her head around and saw a veritable forest of red and yellow dots directly in front of the truck, standing between them and whatever lay at the end of the passage. Queen kept steady pressure on the accelerator, but the truck was barely moving at a running pace, not nearly fast enough to blow through the enemy lines.

The back window of the cab fractured as a round passed through, and Asya felt something slice across her upper arm. Rook, braving the incoming fire, heaved his machine gun onto the roof and swept it across their path, but the weapon fell silent almost immediately. Without looking back, he heaved the empty gun off the roof, letting it drop unceremoniously into the pile of bodies. Then he drew his Desert Eagles. The pistols boomed like cannons, first one then the other, in a perfectly synchronized rhythm of death.

Asya saw King and Knight both rise up to either side of Rook, adding their firepower to the desperate charge through the gauntlet. The three men were like a solid wall in front her, blocking her field of fire. She felt completely useless. The others had known exactly what to do, working together seamlessly to meet the threat, while she just sat there trying to keep up.

Her gaze fell on the discarded machine gun. Maybe there was something she could do, after all. She grabbed a spare drum magazine from her gear pouch—they each carried one to offset some of Rook's burden—and deftly loaded the linked rounds into the feed tray. Then, she hefted the barrel onto the side of the truck and started looking for something to shoot.

The tunnel abruptly sloped upward and then they were out in the open, emerging into the compound through a garage door in one of the buildings near the east wall. As the pickup slipped through the doors, Asya alone was in a position to see the gunmen lined up on either side of the building, and as they started to fire at the exposed rear end of the truck, she slid the machine gun around and pulled the trigger.

Hot brass and spent links started piling up under the weapon as a torrent of 7.62-mm rounds raked the building and the open tunnel mouth. Only a few of her shots found their mark, but the barrage broke the ambush before it could happen. She let off the trigger just long enough to start discriminating targets, and then she resumed firing short but lethal bursts.

The next thirty seconds were absolute mayhem, with the machine gun and Rook's pistols thundering in the night, interspersed with short bursts from the cartel gunmen, but then the attack seemed to fizzle out. By the time Queen crashed through the south gate, through which they had initially made their covert entry into the compound, the targeting dots behind them started blinking as the gunmen were lost from direct line of sight.

The break did not last long. When they had gone only a hundred yards or so down the dirt road leading away from the compound, two sets of headlights appeared on the road behind them.

"We're going to need an extraction," King said. "Now, if not sooner. Our wheels are about to fall off."

"Understood," Deep Blue said. "There's a clearing about two clicks ahead. Your ride will be waiting."

King stuck his head through the gap where the rear window had been and addressed Queen. "Can we make that?"

"It won't be pretty, but I'll do what I can."

"That's all I can ask." He turned back to the others. "Let's do something about the tailgaters."

Asya put the aiming dot squarely between the headlights and loosed a burst that tore the engine of the chasing car apart. There was a small explosion as spilled fuel ignited, and then the car veered off the road and crashed into a tree. As she switched to the other car however, multiple tongues of flame erupted all around it.

"Down!" King said.

Asya didn't need King's warning. She threw herself flat, pressing low behind the tailgate even as rounds began creasing the air where she had been only a moment before, or hammering against the tailgate. None of the bullets penetrated, but she could feel pulses of heat and kinetic energy radiating off the metal with each impact. She knew that trying to aim and fire the 240 in the face of the onslaught would be suicidal, but the machine gun wasn't the only weapon in her arsenal. She dug another grenade from her pouch, pulled the safety pin and let the spring-loaded trigger spoon fly free.

One matryoshka... two matryoshka... three! "Frag out!" She lobbed it out the back in a low arc that she hoped would send it skittering under the approaching car. She kept counting until, just a second and a half later, there was another enormous blast.

Asya's stomach lurched as the pressure wave lifted the rear of the pickup a few inches off the ground then let it fall back down. When the truck stopped bouncing and settled back onto its three good tires, she popped her head up just long enough to survey the damage. The grenade had detonated in front of the car, which wasn't what she had been hoping for, but it was better than nothing. One headlight was still shining through the cloud of dust and smoke, but the car wasn't moving.

Her measured triumph fell flat when she saw more muzzle flashes.

"*Crescent*'s here!" Queen shouted.

Asya didn't have to look to know that their ticket out of trouble had arrived. *Crescent II*, a super-sonic stealth transport plane with vertical take-off and landing capabilities, had just passed directly above them.

The plane was now a one-of-a-kind prototype, its twin having been destroyed. Thanks to some bureaucratic sleight-of-hand on the part of Domenick Boucher, the former head of the CIA, the plane had been set aside exclusively for their use, along with a permanent flight crew that left the United States Army 160th Special Operations Aviation Regiment, more commonly known as 'the Night Stalkers,' to join the Endgame organization. Now equipped with a slightly less sophisticated version of the chameleon adaptive camouflage system, the aircraft was nearly invisible against the night sky, but there was no mistaking its presence. The downdraft from its turbofans hit them like a gale-force wind.

Crescent settled to the ground right in front of them, its loading ramp already deployed, and Queen steered onto it. When the wheel rim hit the metal deck plate, there was another ungodly shriek and a shower of friction sparks, which lasted until Queen slammed on the brakes twenty feet into the plane's cargo hold. To Asya, it was like fireworks and music to her ears. They had made it.

"We're on," King yelled. "Good to go."

The turbo fans revved louder, and Asya felt the world tilt ever so slightly. The ramp closed behind them, shutting off the noise. For a few seconds, the five of them just sat quietly, looking at each other in disbelief. Then one by one, they pulled off the camouflage mesh that obscured their faces. In the normal light conditions, the photosensitive lenses in their glasses were clear, making them look like shooting glasses.

King ran a hand through his unruly black hair and cleared his throat. "I guess a LACE report is in order."

LACE, Asya had learned, stood for 'liquid, ammunition, casualties and equipment,' and it was the standard operating procedure for American military units after an engagement. The team used the term a little less formally; King was basically asking if everyone was okay.

Rook answered first. "No hits, runs or errors here, but I've pretty much used up all my bullets. Oh, and I seem to have misplaced my 240."

"And I seem to have found it," Asya said quickly, a smile coming unbidden to her lips. The simple fact of their survival had done wonders to lighten her mood.

"Maybe we should have let you take the big gun after all," King remarked. He gave her arm a squeeze. "Good job, up there." Asya was acutely aware of the fact that everyone could hear him. "I think you've got the high score for the day."

The praise only made her feel her rookie status more acutely.

"Any injuries?"

She shook her head, but then remembered that something had struck her arm in the tunnel. There was a gash in her camouflage suit, and when she probed the spot, her fingers came away sticky with blood, but there was no pain and no apparent swelling. *Probably just a small cut from a piece of flying glass*, she decided.

"I wish I could say the same," King said. "One of those pig-things got a piece of my ankle. Which is why I'm glad we didn't have to walk out of there."

"Sara's not going to like that," Rook said.

"She knows what I do," King replied, a little defensively. Sara Fogg was King's fiancée, and she knew all too well the risks inherent in his life. They had met during a crisis several years earlier, when the Chess Team had been called on to protect her, while she had investigated a deadly disease outbreak in the jungles of Vietnam. As a star epidemiologist with the Centers for Disease Control and Prevention, Sara lived with her own brand of danger; disease investigators were at the highest risk for contracting the contagions they tried to stamp out.

"That's not what I meant," Rook countered. "You're supposed to be *walking* her down the aisle in a couple days."

"Ah," King sighed. "That. Well, I'm a quick healer." He leaned his head through the window. "Queen?"

Queen's blonde hair was plastered to her face by sweat, but she was grinning triumphantly. "Fully mission capable. No injuries. You know, I don't think I actually fired my weapon. But I could definitely use a drink."

Rook cocked his head sideways. "What's that? Blue is buying?"

Disembodied laughter rang in Asya's ears. "I've got a cooler full of Sam Adams chilling on the back deck, but please tell me that you actually managed to accomplish the mission objective."

Rook thrust a hand into the pile of corpses and pulled up one that was still dressed and looked fresher than the others—so fresh in fact that he was still breathing. "Meet Mano, a.k.a. Juan Beltran."

"Excellent work."

Asya's curiosity finally got the better of her. "Please, what are all these dead people?"

Rook shrugged. "Came with the truck. As you can smell, they're all a little ripe. Been dead a few days. Here's something that will give you nightmares." He pointed to the torso of one of the male victims.

A ragged slit had been cut across the man's diaphragm, right under the rib cage. "I think someone cut his heart out."

Asya felt her gorge start to rise. "What are they doing in this truck?"

"Pig chow."

She shuddered. "That's terrible."

Rook stroked his long blond goatee like a mystic warrior in a kung fu movie. "That's why they call them the bad guys."

King deftly changed the subject. "Knight? You good?"

Asya glanced involuntarily at her teammate. Even though she had worked side by side with him for several weeks, his appearance still filled her with sadness. She still remembered the man he had been when they had first met; his broad, genial face, and eyes that were full of laughter. Now he just had one eye, and there was not a trace of humor in it. Where his other eye had been, there was a black and silver orb that bulged against his eyelids, as if it was trying to pop out of his head. As if conscious of her scrutiny, Knight reached up and removed his glasses, sliding a black eye-patch down to cover the artificial orb. Then, in a voice that felt like rain on a picnic, he said, "I'm fine."

SEVEN

Knight had not been injured in the battle, but he was not fine. Not by a long shot.

The eye patch automatically initiated a sleep cycle for his ocular implant, and that brought some relief, shrinking the railroad spike of pain that rammed through his skull down to something a little more tolerable, something more like a mere ten-penny nail.

It was hard to share the upbeat mood of the rest of the team when he felt like clawing his face open to end the constant throbbing. Harder still because he didn't dare tell anyone.

No amount of technical wizardry or medical science could restore the sight to his ruined eye. That had been the first hard truth he had been forced to accept. The loss of an eye meant losing stereoscopic vision and depth perception. Both were important but not absolutely critical to his performance as the team's sniper; he did most of his work with just one eye anyway, peering through a high-powered scope at targets that were too far away to see unaided. But there were other aspects of his job where it mattered a lot more. The simple task of being able to sneak through almost any environment undetected relied completely on his ability to judge the distance and placement of objects in the environment.

Lewis Aleman, who was to Chess Team what Major Boothroyd of Q section was to James Bond, was uniquely sympathetic to Knight's plight. He too had seen his career as a Special Forces sniper cut short by an injury, and he knew how devastating it felt to be declared unfit for duty. Aleman at least had been as passionate about working with computers and electronics as he was about killing bad guys from a distance, which had made his transition to the rear echelon a little easier to bear. Knight had no such fallback position. Everything he loved, his work and his extreme sports obsession—the more extreme, the better—would suffer without binocular vision. And that did not begin to touch the disfiguring nature of his injury. The metal fragment that had taken his eye had also left a ragged scar on the surrounding tissue. Even with a perfect artificial replica, even if he could master the tricky muscle control techniques required to make a glass eye behave like what it had replaced, that scar would mark him.

In his younger days, he had earned a reputation as a ladies' man. His platoon mates had half-jokingly, half-jealously dubbed him 'the Korean Casanova,' perhaps none too subtly trying to diminish his romantic successes with the reminder of his ethnic heritage. He had settled down in recent years, and was currently in a committed relationship with Anna Beck, the head of security at Endgame, but even if that relationship failed—and since his injury, he had grown increasingly worried that it might—he didn't want to go back to the night life. Yet, if he had been so inclined, he would have had to do so with a ruined face. Even going out in public was hard. He could not endure the looks of revulsion that made him feel like a carnival freak, and the pitying looks were even worse.

For a few weeks after the return from the Congo, he stood on the razor's edge. Anna had been nothing but supportive, as had the rest of the team, but Aleman had been the one person capable of understanding what he was going through, and he had had the means to do something about it.

"I can't give you back your eye," Aleman had explained, repeating that hard truth, "but there is something I can do that will compensate for it, and maybe even give you an edge you didn't have before."

The loss of depth perception, Knight's occupational therapist had informed him, was easily enough overcome simply by learning to see a different way. For routine tasks, it was easy enough to find workaround solutions. For example, when driving, you could gauge stopping distance by looking for fixed cues in the environment—lane markers, mileposts, rocks on the side of the road. For other situations, he could employ the technique of shifting the focus of his good eye back and forth, to get two side-by-side perspectives on an object, creating the illusion of binocular vision.

"We can use that technique," Aleman went on, "in conjunction with the glasses and the quantum computer net, to show you the world in three-dimensions."

Aleman had started by designing an artificial eye that was loaded with hardware he had been unable to fit into the glasses the team wore. Thermal sensors that could see through thin walls, an electromagnetic spectrum detector that could actually 'see' electrical fields, an optical scanner that could read anything from barcodes to Sanskrit and instantly translate it into readable text. "I could probably make this thing shoot a laser beam if you want," Aleman offered.

Knight had politely refused.

"The implant will see things just like an ordinary eye would, but the tricky part is turning that into something you can use. Maybe in a few years we'll be able to figure out how to turn digital code into something the brain can process, but for now what we're going to have to do is put the feed from the implant into the VR net and then project it into your good eye."

Knight's reaction had been skeptical. "So I'll be seeing two different things at the same time?"

"Yes and no. You know the old magician's saying: 'the hand is quicker than the eye?' Well, it's the literal truth. It takes the human brain about a tenth of a second to process visual inputs. That's how a movie projector can turn thousands of still frames into a motion picture. What I'll do is configure the VR network to show you those feeds, alternating between them so fast that you won't consciously recognize the change."

"That will work?"

"Your brain will have to learn to process what it's seeing, but yes, I think it will."

"I'm getting a headache just thinking about it."

Knight's comment had been eerily prophetic.

It had indeed taken him nearly two weeks to learn how to process the inputs from the implant, during which time, Knight had had to confront a second hard truth.

King and Deep Blue had avoided bringing up the subject of Knight's ability to continue field operations, but as he struggled to master the implant, they paid him a visit and broached the subject directly. Knight knew what was coming, but like pulling off a Band-Aid, it had to be done.

"You know what's at stake when we go out," King said. "We put our lives in each other's hands every time. You know that better than anyone. If you aren't one hundred percent confident in your ability to keep doing the job, then you need to step aside."

Knight wasn't bothered by King's forthright manner, but rather by the fact that the burden had been placed on him. *You know whether or not you can do it,* King had basically told him. *We're not going to make the decision for you.*

It would have been easier if they had just fired him.

"I will be," he promised. "Better than one hundred percent."

Now he had to live up that promise, and that meant he couldn't tell them the truth about the implant.

Aleman had warned him of discomfort as he got used to it, but the reality was a migraine that left Knight virtually paralyzed. Anna had been on the verge of taking him to the emergency room. The painful sensation did abate somewhat as the days turned into weeks. By the time his brain learned how to process the inputs, showing him a world that was in most respects similar to what he had lost, the migraine was no longer a constant companion. Instead, it only reared its ugly head when the implant was active.

He didn't dare tell Aleman or the others just how bad it was.

A further complication had arisen when he had begun showing signs of hypersensitivity to the implant, similar to the body rejecting an organ transplant. A regimen of immunosuppressant drugs had alleviated the symptoms, but at the cost of a somewhat compromised immune system. That risk was manageable, but he would always be at risk for infections, and in the dangerous environments in which the team often found themselves, what might be a nuisance to the others could prove fatal to him. Like the headaches, it was a price he believed himself willing to pay.

He had not expected it to be a recurring fee however.

Months later, that second hard truth was knocking him upside the head. *'If you aren't one hundred percent confident...'*

I'm not. I don't know if I can keep doing this.

The mission to take Mano's compound had taken about three hours, which included the time spent traveling from the drop zone to the target. The migraine had begun almost as soon as he had activated the implant, and by the time he had arrived at his overwatch position, the pain had been intense enough to make him feel nausea. As he sat on the hill, peering through the scope, trying to decide whether or not to take a shot at Raul Campos, the voice of doubt had wormed its way to the surface.

What if this mission lasts longer than a few hours? What if it goes on for several days?

The fact that he was asking those questions told him that he couldn't meet King's confidence test. He was lying to himself and putting the others in danger.

When we get back, I'm going to tell Blue that I can't do this anymore. I'm going to pull this goddamned fake eye out with my bare hands, and then I'm going to take Anna and...

And do what?

Doesn't matter. Anything is better than this.

We'll go to Disney World. Visit Grandma Knight. His grandmother, his last living relative, was in the late stages of Alzheimer's disease, and the doctors at the St. Augustine nursing home where she was a patient had warned him to prepare for the inevitable. He had been paying for her care for several years now, and even though she was no longer responsive, it seemed only right that he should be there for her final days. *I guess she won't be 'Grandma Knight' once I quit. I'll have to go back to calling her* Halmi *like I did when I was a boy.*

The decision brought him a little comfort as he laid on a cot in the cargo bay of *Crescent*, but not as much as putting the implant to sleep. After a while, the pain subsided enough that he was able to doze off.

He awoke to a sensation of heaviness, and he realized that *Crescent* was lifting off. He had evidently slept through their first stop. When he sat up, he saw that both Mano and the pickup were gone, along with the truck's grisly cargo. The thought of who those people had been burrowed into his consciousness like a sliver of glass. Were they rival cartel soldiers? Policemen? Judges? Or perhaps just randomly selected civilians, torn from their homes and fields, and executed to enhance El Sol's reputation for cruelty?

I won't miss that.

When he looked around for his teammates, he was reminded that even a simple task like that was now twice as hard as it had once been, but he resisted the temptation to activate the implant. The headache had finally let go, and he was in no hurry to bring it back.

He spied Rook, fast asleep on another cot. Queen had somehow managed to squeeze onto it as well, sitting in the hollow of Rook's fetal curl, doing a Sudoku puzzle. Asya and King sat together on the deck, cleaning their weapons and conversing quietly.

"Where's Bish?"

Even as he said it, he realized his mistake. Asya and King glanced up, and he knew they had heard him, but he waved a dismissive hand. "I mean, what's up? Where are we?"

"Just left a little airstrip outside Mexico City," King said. "We dropped off our passenger. And the bodies. It's Mexico's ball now."

"For all the good that will do." Mano's arrest probably wouldn't make much difference in the ongoing conflict. The cartels had almost as much power as the government, and their money had a lot of influence inside it. Knight however wasn't as interested in the politics of the drug war as he was in hitting the 'delete' key on his comment about Bishop.

It had been a stupid slip-up. This was their first field assignment since the Congo, and even though he had come to terms with Erik Somers's death, being in the familiar environment of *Crescent*'s cargo bay had transported him back in time, if only for a moment.

It was the nature of their business that people died. *'There are old soldiers and there are bold soldiers,'* so the saying went, *'but there are no old, bold soldiers.'*

They didn't come any bolder than Erik Somers. He had proved that with his final sacrifice.

And while Knight had initially refused to accept that his teammate was actually dead—his body had not been recovered—it was only because Erik had always seemed invincible. That belief, which he had held onto for several weeks, long after they buried an empty coffin in a cemetery outside the town where Erik had grown up, was not just Knight stuck in the denial stage of the grief process.

King regarded him for a moment. "I think this time might be different. What we saw tonight... That fighting cage, the bodies, those... What did Rook call them? 'Hell pigs?' That's the kind of evil that wakes people up."

"I hope you're right."

"Me, too. You sure you're okay?"

"Of course." Knight said, and then wondered why he had lied.

CURSE

EIGHT

Manns Harbor, North Carolina

Jason Harris swerved into the outside lane and then whipped the Ford Escape into a parking lot. Ellen Dare, in the passenger seat, looked up from the papers on her lap. "Careful, Jason. These hick town cops can turn a traffic ticket into the Midnight Express."

Jason looked at her sideways even as he slowed the Ford to a crawl. "Hick town? That's no way to talk about your peeps."

"Peeps?" Ellen arched an eyebrow, then shook her head in disgust. "Just because my ancestors once lived here, does not make the people my 'peeps.' And nobody talks like that anymore. You're a graduate student now, Jason. Grow up."

The frizzy blonde head and self-described 'pleasantly plump' upper body of Haley Stephens leaned through the gap between the two seats. "What's Midnight Express?"

My graduate student thinks he's in a nineties boy band, and my videographer knows nothing about film history. We're off to a great start.

"Never mind," Ellen turned her gaze forward just as Jason steered into the drive-thru lane of a fast food restaurant. "Mr. Pig? Really, Jason? It's only nine-thirty. Find a Starbuck's, for God's sake."

"These guys have the most incredible chorizo breakfast burrito."

"Chorizo?" Haley made no effort to hide her disgust. "Do you know what goes into that stuff?"

"As a matter of fact, I do. Which is more than anyone can say for Chicken McNuggets."

Ellen tuned out the conversation. The fare at the fast food chain wasn't her idea of a balanced breakfast, but there would be coffee and probably some kind of variation on hash browns, and that would be enough to get her day started. Today, at least. If they were going to spend the next two weeks on Roanoke Island, she would have to come up with a better plan.

The one thing she was sure of was that she wouldn't have time to prepare meals. She had just ten days to find the evidence that would support her theory about the fate of the so-called Lost Colony. It wouldn't have to be much. A button from a coat, a tool, a bone... *What*, wasn't as important as *where*. Context was everything.

The mystery of the Lost Colony was largely a fiction, romantic folklore designed to add an aura of drama to the historical record. Mystery was what brought the tourists around. The reality, which had been amply demonstrated by forensic science and extensive historic research, was far duller. The Roanoke Colony, after enduring a series of compounding misfortunes, had left the island and been assimilated by one or more Native American groups in the region. Much of what people believed about the Lost Colony was simply wrong, the result of embellishments made for dramatic effect or confusion with completely fictitious ghost stories.

It was popularly believed for example, that when John White returned to the colony three years after leaving it, he found houses put in order, tools stored and tables set with plates of uneaten food, as if the entire colony had been teleported away in an instant while sitting down to dinner. In truth, there were no houses, no tables, no tools. The houses had been disassembled and completely removed. Archaeologists had found no evidence to support the idea that the houses had been burned or attacked by hostile natives, which meant that the colonists themselves had torn down the settlement and carried everything to a new location.

Yet, when the fanciful elements were peeled away, there remained a compelling mystery and an untold story—a true story— that Ellen wanted the world to know, the story of her ancestor: Eleanor Dare.

Although she had refuted Jason's suggestion otherwise, Ellen felt a strong connection to the Outer Banks. She had been to the site of the Lost Colony three times previously, and while she—a die-hard urbanite—got along with the residents of the remote island towns about as well as oil got along with water, whenever she visited the old site, she felt like it was a homecoming.

Although more than four centuries had passed, Roanoke Island still remembered the colonists, and in particular, Virginia Dare, the first child born of European parents in what would one day become the United States. The county was named for her. The five-mile four-lane span that now bore them across the Croatan Sound was called the Virginia Dare Memorial Bridge. Yet, aside from that bit of historical trivia, nothing else was known about Virginia Dare, or the fate that had befallen her and her parents. Nothing that could be conclusively proved, at least. That was something Ellen hoped to change.

She had always loved history, particularly that moment in time where the cultures of the Old and New Worlds collided, for she was a product of that collision. Although there was no formal evidence of her mixed heritage, her red-blonde hair and fair skin, as well as family and tribal tradition, were testimony enough to the fact that, at some point in the history of the Native American people who now called themselves the Saponi Nation, there had been an introduction of European DNA. Many believed the source of that infusion was the missing colonists of Roanoke. Ellen had taken that hypothesis one step further.

She took a sip from her coffee, then set it in the cup holder and shuffled through the sheaf of papers until she found the photographs. The images were burned into her memory, but looking at them was like a form of meditation. The pictures were of a quartz block that had been discovered in 1937 in the woods near Edenton, North Carolina, sixty miles northwest of Roanoke. Her fingers touched the letters and numbers, as if feeling their texture, and she murmured the message displayed there:

Ananias Dare & Virginia went hence vnto heaven 1591.
Anye Englishman Shew John White Govr Via.

"Ananias Dare and Virginia Dare went hence into heaven, 1591. Any Englishman, show John White, Governor of Virginia."

She slid the photograph aside to reveal the second, which showed the reverse side of the stone:

Father soone After yov goe for Englande we cam hither
onlie misarie & warretow yeare
Above halfe DeaDe ere tow yeere moore
from sickenes beine fovre & twentie
salvage with mesage of shipp vnto vs
smal space of time they affrite of revenge rann al awaye
wee bleeve yt nott you/ soone after ye salvages faine spirts angrie
suddiane mvrther al save seaven
mine childe ananias to slaine wth mvch misarie
bvrie al neere fovre myles easte this river vppon smal hil
names writ al ther on rocke
pvtt this ther alsoe
salvage shew this vnto yov & hither wee promise yov
to give greate plentie presents E W D

She had read the message so many times that she no longer struggled with the unusual language and spelling.

EWD stood for Eleanor White Dare, the daughter of John White, the governor of Virginia Colony, who had returned to England in a futile effort to resupply the Roanoke colonists. The quartz block became known as the Dare Stone, and over the course of the next few years, several more stones were found. Forty-eight in all, each purporting to be a record of the events that followed the abandonment of the Roanoke colony. Soon, the inconsistencies in the language and the narrative provided by the stones led to an investigation. It exposed the Dare Stones as a hoax, perpetrated by one or more stone-cutters with a penchant for dealing in forged Native American artifacts. But a few scholars maintained that the first stone was authentic. Ellen's own research supported this position, and if the record contained on that stone was true, if those truly were the words of Eleanor Dare, then the solution to one of America's oldest murder mysteries was within her reach.

According to Eleanor Dare, only twenty-four of the colonists had survived the first year at Roanoke, a survival rate of just twenty percent. Exactly what had happened thereafter was not clear, but the fact of the Dare Stone's existence and the location where it had been discovered suggested that the survivors had attempted to find refuge among the natives where they lived, evidently without incident for another three years. Then, a misunderstanding with their native hosts led to the massacre of all but seven. Eleanor Dare survived, but her husband and daughter did not.

The Dare Stone—the first, authentic Dare Stone—was the foundation upon which Ellen had built both her professional career and her sense of who she was. As she developed and refined her hypothesis about the fate of the colonists, she began to see how the story of Eleanor Dare was the beginning of her own story.

"Here we are," Jason announced, as he pulled into the parking lot of the Fort Raleigh National Historic Site.

"Nobody move," Haley trilled, hastening to disentangle herself from the back seat. A moment later, she was standing in front of the Escape, video-camera in hand, motioning for them to get out.

Ellen gathered her papers and ordered her thoughts before opening her door. Once outside, she spoke to the camera. "We're here at the Fort Raleigh National Historic Site, the location of the Lost Colony. Archaeologists have been looking for evidence of what happened to the colonists for decades and come up empty-handed. That's good news for us, because it means we know where *not* to look." She paused, staring into the camera for a moment, then said, "How was that?"

"Good enough for now," Haley said, not lowering the camera. "We can reshoot if we come up with a better hook."

Ellen nodded. "Jason, get the equipment."

With Haley filming every moment, they made their way out of the parking lot and into the woods to the west. Ellen held up the GPS receiver for the camera. "Many people have wondered how the Lost Colony could have vanished so completely. This has led some scholars to conclude that the colonists packed up and took everything when they left, presumably to live with the Croatan Indians on Hatteras Island. But if the message in the Dare Stone is authentic, then nearly one hundred of the colonists perished in that first year, *before* the survivors left. Their remains are here." She made a sweeping gesture. "Somewhere. Somewhere nobody has thought to look.

"It has always been accepted that the area where we are now standing is the site of the Lost Colony, but from the time that it was abandoned until the nineteenth century, the island was mostly uninhabited. After John White's return in 1591, the next time the Lost Colony appears in the historic record is in 1709, when explorer John Lawson visited what he believed to be the ruins of the colony. The location has been fixed ever since. But what if the fort Lawson visited was not the site of the Lost Colony?

"According to John White, the original fort first occupied by Richard Grenville's expedition and later by the Roanoke Colony was situated on the north shore of the island. But the shoreline of the Outer Banks islands changes dramatically every year. A comparison of the coastline between 1851 and 1970 showed that over nine hundred feet of coastline were lost to erosion. That means there's a very good chance that the original site of the colony could have washed away long before Lawson's visit. Unless, of course, Lawson was looking in the wrong place."

A gesture from Haley stopped her before she could go on. "We're gonna do all this background stuff in post, remember?"

Ellen gave a guilty nod. "I'm a history teacher. Lecturing is what I do."

"Well, today you're digging. That's what we want to get on camera."

The GPS chirped, announcing that they had arrived at their destination. Ellen glanced at it, then showed it to the camera. "We've arrived. If I'm right, this is the graveyard of the Roanoke Colony, where all but twenty-four of the settlers were laid to rest. We've been given permission to make several exploratory excavations. If we can find anything to support my theory, we'll return next year..."

She broke off when she spied Haley making a 'get on with it' gesture.

Jason dropped the bundle he was carrying, a collection of small folding shovels and garden trowels, which they would be using like surgeons' scalpels to slowly peel back the layers of soil, which, Ellen hoped, concealed the last resting place of the Roanoke colonists. "Is it just me," he mumbled, "or does having that camera watching your every move make this feel like the start of *The Blair Witch Project?*"

"Don't you forget it, sweetheart," Haley replied playfully. "The camera sees all, every time you scratch your ass or pick your nose."

Ellen ignored their banter and started placing survey markers at specific intervals to mark the area where they would be digging.

Her hypothesis turned on the idea that the colonists would have buried their dead far from the settlement, and well away from the constantly moving shoreline. Given their limited resources, it was unlikely that the survivors would have made any kind of permanent grave markers, and wooden crosses would have long since decayed away to nothing. She had settled on this location as the most likely site of the cemetery, but there were more than a dozen other possible locations they would be checking out over the next two weeks. None of them had been excavated by archaeologists working for the US Forest Service. Ellen did not dare hope that they would get lucky on the first try. There was every chance that nothing remained to be found at all. The bones might have dissolved in the soil, or she might have been wrong in her assumption that the cemetery had been located away from the eroding shoreline. But if they did find something, some piece of evidence to confirm that at least some of the colonists had died and been buried here, it would be the first step toward proving that the Dare Stone was a real and accurate record of Eleanor Dare's life. And if it was, then she would be one step closer to proving that she herself was the woman's direct descendant.

There was no doubt in Ellen's mind that she had some of the blood of the Lost Colony in her, but making the case for Dare ancestry hinged on the numbers. According to the stone, Eleanor Dare was one of only seven colonists to survive the massacre in 1591. That meant there was a roughly one-in-seven chance that Ellen's family line traced back to Eleanor Dare herself.

It was impossible to resist the urge to fantasize about what might have happened. Had Eleanor conceived a second child with her husband in the intervening years? Had a native warrior taken her for his own wife after the death of Ananias?

One thing at a time, she told herself. *First, I have to prove the Dare Stone authentic. Then I can begin looking for the graves of Ananias and Virginia.* Once she located the remains of Virginia Dare, DNA testing would provide solid evidence that 'Dare' was not merely an appellation she had chosen and changed legally eight years earlier, but her true family name. The Dare Stone provided ample clues to narrow the search, but she would need a lot more in the way of resources to begin that quest in earnest. That was why it was so important to hit a home run with this expedition.

The shovels made a harsh rasping noise as she and Jason began digging. At first, she jumped excitedly every time the metal blade hit something harder than the sandy island soil, but after uncovering numerous roots and rocks, she tempered her enthusiasm and fell into an automatic routine. She dug until she reached bedrock, and then she climbed out of the hole, filled it in, and moved to the next marker. After a few hours, she was so unplugged from herself that it took a moment for her to register Jason's excited shouts. When she finally did, all of her earlier enthusiasm returned in a rush.

She found Haley standing over the waist-deep pit, training the camera on the object Jason held up. "What have you got?"

Jason turned slightly to reveal his prize, and even from a distance Ellen could see that it was a bone—a femur, judging by the round protuberance at one end. She reached out and took it from him, but her excitement began to ebb when she realized that the bone could not possibly be human. The ball joint at the top was much too large, and even though the rest of the bone had broken off at some point, it was far too long to belong to a human.

After she explained this to the camera, she added, "This could be a hopeful sign, though. If we find other animal remains nearby, it could mean that we've found a trash midden, and that could shed a lot of new light on the lives of the colonists." *Or*, she didn't add, *this could just be where a deer dropped dead five hundred years ago.*

"Should we bag it?" Jason asked.

Ellen considered the question for a moment. "Not yet. If we find anything else, then we'll break out the baggies."

Jason laid the bone on the edge of the excavation and resumed digging, and Ellen went back to her own hole and dropped back in. She had just picked up her own shovel when Haley cried out in alarm.

For a fleeting instant, Ellen hoped the cry meant that they had found something real, a human skull, perhaps. That would certainly elicit the kind of horrified shriek Haley had just uttered. However, the moment that she reached the edge of Jason's pit, she knew that the scream had nothing to do with a discovery.

Jason was bent over, on hands and knees, shivering and retching. For several seconds, she could only stand there dumbfounded, her brain reeling off messages of denial. *He'll be okay. He just needs to take a break.* But when the fit seemed to get worse, she broke free of her paralysis and slid down into the hole with him.

She gripped his arm, intending to offer comfort and reassurance, but immediately drew back her hand in astonishment. "He's burning up." She looked up and found Haley, still recording every moment. "Put that damn thing away, and call 911. Hurry!"

As if to underscore the urgency of the plea, Jason threw back his head and let out a feral howl of agony.

The camera dropped from Haley's hands, completely forgotten, as her eyes fixed on the horror of his face. Ellen saw it a moment later, and clapped her hands over her ears to shut out the screams—Jason's, Haley's and her own.

NINE
Washington, D.C.

Senator Lance Marrs sighed as he listened to his chief of staff, Rob Sorrel, run down the items on the day's schedule. Between his duties as a US legislator and the much more arduous job of launching his campaign for the highest office in the land, there was simply too much information for Marrs to track. It was the chief of staff's job to keep him organized, to make sure he got where he needed to be and said what he needed to say. The details didn't matter that much, so instead he listened for specific words and phrases that he knew might require him to actually pay attention.

"There's a procedural vote scheduled for the Jobs Bill at two-thirty."

'Vote' was one of the keywords. Marrs straightened in his chair. "Where do we stand on that?"

"Against."

Marrs frowned. A jobs bill sounded like a good thing for the American people, and voting against it would be just the kind of thing a political opponent might use against him. On the other hand, if the bill was signed into law and the president could claim an economic victory, it would weigh against him in the general election. "Continue."

"You are speaking at a Chamber meeting this evening."

Speaking engagements didn't interest him that much. He would show up, read the talking points and press the flesh. The Chamber of Commerce could be counted on for decent food and a well-stocked bar, at least. "Is that it then? Sounds like a light day. Let's try to work in nine holes."

"Yes, sir."

As Sorrel took out his cell phone and called the country club to arrange a tee time, Marrs turned his chair around and gazed out the window like a despot surveying his realm. He had a good view of the Capitol dome and several other Washington landmarks, but the thing he desired most, despite being only a few blocks away, was hidden from his eyes.

Soon, he told himself. *Soon it will be mine.*

Based on current polling, it was not merely wishful thinking. Although there was a crowded field of primary contenders, many of whom were striking a much more populist note, playing up their 'political outsider' credentials—a back-handed way of accusing Marrs of being an establishment candidate—most would run out of money long before the primaries were in full swing. He would need only a few early victories to guarantee his anointment as the party's choice, and from there, it would be a steamroller ride to the Oval Office. His role in bringing down the Duncan administration would be his strength, and his opponent's weakness. The opposition party would be toxic for years to come because of the disgraced former president; Marrs would make sure of that, both with sanctioned advertisements and a coordinated 'dark money' campaign that would pile on the innuendo, until anyone who had ever shaken Tom Duncan's hand was buried up to their neck in it.

"Sir, I just got an e-mail from a donor who wants to discuss...um, some concerns. May I suggest inviting him to join you on the course?"

"Donor?" That was another word that commanded his attention. "Who?"

"A Mr. Bell, from Mid-Atlantic Diversified Holdings, LLC. He's maxed on personal donations, and has contributed a million to your SuperPAC."

The name meant nothing to Marrs, but the amount was all he needed to get his blood pumping. He rose from his chair and grabbed his coat. "A million? Hell, yeah. Tell him I'll meet him at the club. I may even let him win."

Sorrel tapped in the message, and then just thirty seconds later reported. "They're sending a limo to pick you up."

"Even better. You say that vote is at two-thirty? What's the spread?"

"Unlikely to move forward."

"So no one will miss me if I decide to spend the rest of the day with my new best friend."

Sorrel grinned. "No, sir."

Marrs grabbed his jacket and headed out the door, contemplating how to wheedle another million from the beneficent Mr. Bell. Mid-Atlantic Diversified sounded like the kind of company that had lots of money to burn.

The promised limousine was waiting for him. It was at the far end of a gauntlet of journalists who turned his way like a school of fish when he exited the main lobby of the Russell Senate Office Building. He made eye contact with the few that he could count on to give him good press and tossed out a few quick sound bites— mostly barbs directed at the president. Then he strode quickly to the car, sliding into the darkened interior. The chauffeur closed the door, silencing the more pointed questions of the less friendly muckrakers. Marrs settled into the plush seat with a sigh of relief.

Seated across from him was a stern-looking man in a better suit than the one Marrs was wearing. "You must be Mr. Bell," Marrs said, extending a hand.

The man ignored the offer of a handshake. "No. Mr. Bell is not in the country."

"But then...?"

The man opened a portable computer and placed it on his lap so the screen faced Marrs. The display showed a live web-cam feed of a middle-aged man with strong features, black hair and an olive-complexion. He wore a white dress shirt that was open at the throat, revealing a thick gold chain and a hint of hidden tattoos.

Marrs bit back a complaint and put on his best smile. "Mr. Bell. A pity that you are only able to join us by telepresence. I had so looked forward to shaking the hand of my biggest supporter." It was not strictly true, since Marrs received considerably more support from the petroleum industry, but diversification was just good business practice, as was some harmless ass-kissing.

The man on the screen returned a predatory smile. "That's right, Senator. I am your biggest supporter. You need to remember that."

Hispanic, Marrs thought, noting the strong accent. *Well, as long as his money is green, I don't care if his skin is brown, black, yellow or purple. And if he's not American, I don't want to know.*

"Rest assured, Mr. Bell, when I get into the White House, I will personally lead the fight to solidify the United States' position as a bastion of free-enterprise."

"Save it," the man snapped. "Whether you become the president or not will depend on what you can do for me right now."

"Well, of course, I will continue to use my authority as a United States—"

"You really don't know who I am, do you?"

Marrs swallowed nervously. In fact, he didn't know who Bell was, but he was starting to get an idea. "What I know is that we share a vision—"

"Last night, some *pendejos* attacked one of my facilities in Mexico. They took my brother. Killed several of my loyal associates."

Marrs let his breath out with a sigh. *Shit. The guy is some Mexican mob boss.*

He had let visions of dollar signs blind him, and he hadn't taken the time to ask the right questions. *Dammit, Sorrel is supposed to make sure things like this don't happen. I guess I can kiss that million good-bye.*

"I think there's been a misunderstanding," Marrs said, speaking to the man holding the laptop. "If you'd just let me out."

"Oh, there's been a big misunderstanding," the man on the computer continued. "And you're going to take care of it for me. You're going to make people understand."

"I'm afraid I have very little influence with the Mexican authorities. Now, if you'll just let me out—"

"You think I care about *federales*? The men who did this were American soldiers."

Marrs was about to repeat his request a third time, but the declaration stopped him. "American soldiers? You can prove that?"

"Prove it? They came in an invisible plane. You think the *federales* have that? You think anyone has that but your Army?"

"An invisible plane?" Marrs could almost hear the jackpot bells ringing. This was better than a million dollars. "Some kind of stealth aircraft?"

"That's what I said," the man snapped.

"Mr. Bell, or whatever your name is, what exactly is it that you want me to do? I don't have the influence to free your brother."

The man on the screen made a savage cutting gesture. "I will take care of my brother."

"Then what do you want from me?"

"These *pendejos* who attacked me. I want them. I want to tear their hearts out and eat them while they watch. You hear me?"

Marrs had a sick feeling that the other man was not speaking figuratively, but in his own way—his own much less literal way—he wanted the same thing. If someone in the administration had authorized an incursion into Mexico, particularly without the permission of the Mexican government, then Marrs had just struck a political mother lode. He had already taken down one president; if he could prove that Tom Duncan's successor was fighting an illegal drug war in a sovereign nation, without the approval of congress, Marrs's ascension to the presidency would be assured.

Hell, they'd probably skip the election and just swear me in.

"Mr. Bell, I need you to stop talking for a moment and listen to me. I am going to help you, but first I need you to do something for me." He could see a building volcanic eruption of ire in the man's eyes. "If you want this... If you really want this, then we're going to do this my way."

"And you will give me these *pendejos*?"

Marrs smiled conspiratorially. "I'll serve them to you on a platter."

TEN
Endgame, New Hampshire

Knight peered through the Schmidt and Bender PM II/LP 3-12x50mm scope and watched for the target to appear. The high powered optics shrank the intervening eight hundred yards, bringing the objective into sharp relief, making it appear close enough to reach out and touch. But there was a trade-off; he could see only a few feet to either side of the crosshairs, which made acquiring the target in the first place, tracking it and leading it, to compensate for the bullet's travel time, a real challenge.

That challenge was exactly what he was looking for.

Contrary to the myth of the lone wolf, snipers usually worked in teams of two or three—a shooter and at least one spotter. The exceptional technology of the VR glasses and quantum computing had eliminated the need for a spotter, and for that matter, had rendered the scope itself obsolete. Once a target was tagged, the glasses could track it and the computer could perform all the necessary calculations to ensure that the round would unerringly hit exactly where he wanted it to.

Therein lay the problem.

Knight was no Luddite, nor was he inclined to sacrifice results in the interest of professional pride or slavish devotion to tradition. In the field, where those results could mean the difference between the success and failure of the mission, and more importantly, life or death for his teammates, he willingly embraced anything that gave him an edge. But reliance on technology, like the extreme magnification of the scope, came with a trade-off. Technology had given him back his eye, after a fashion, but the trade-off was simply one that he couldn't endure any longer.

The target appeared at the edge of the scope, moving at a walking pace, which, magnified by the lenses, seemed astonishingly fast. He pivoted the rifle on its bipod, keeping the crosshairs just ahead of the target. Then he took a breath, let it out and squeezed the trigger. The suppressor muffled the report, but the rifle buck-ed just enough to remove the target from view momentarily. He brought it back quickly to where it had been, just in time to see the automated target drop.

"Good shooting."

Knight started at the sound of the voice, which had come from his blind side. He rolled away from the gun and scrambled to his feet as if meeting a threat. In the brief moment it took for his body to do that, his brain processed what he had heard. The voice, the thick Slavic accent—it was Asya...Bishop.

He took a calming breath to steady his nerves. "Congratulations. Not very many people can sneak up on me."

"I am stealthy, no?" she replied with a mischievous smile. "But you were very focused, so it was not that hard to do, I think."

"Maybe." *Or maybe it's just a lot easier to sneak up on a one-eyed man*, he thought. *As if I needed one more reason to quit.* He turned back to his rifle and started breaking it down. "I'm done here if you want to use the range."

"Actually, I thought you might want an extra set of eyes." She stopped suddenly, embarrassment reddening her cheeks as she realized what she had said, then she waved the binoculars in her right hand. "I mean as a spotter."

He tried to hide his own dismay. "It's okay."

She gestured out across the range. "I guess you do not need a spotter. That was an ace shot."

"Automated targets are predictable. I've shot this range so many times, I could probably do it without the other eye."

"You are not using the glasses." It was phrased as a statement, but Knight heard the implicit question.

"No. I like to keep my shooting skills sharp. Doing things the old-fashioned way is more of a challenge." It was partly true, but there were a lot of reasons why he had decided to keep his implant covered up. Aside from the pain, which he could tolerate for short intervals, another of the trade-offs that came with the implant was its constant connection to the virtual network.

"Old-fashioned is good," Bishop said. "In the Great Patriotic War, Vasily Grigoryevich Zaytsev killed four hundred Germans using a standard-issue *Vintovka Mosina* rifle."

"I didn't realize you were such a history buff."

"It's a Russian thing."

"Ah. That must be where King gets it."

She laughed. "I think my brother's interest in history is... different."

Knight felt some of his initial irritation letting go, replaced by curiosity. He settled back down behind his gun and then craned his head around to watch her get into position. He was mildly disappointed to see her take her glasses from a pocket. "I thought you wanted to go old school."

She regarded the glasses for a moment then put them away. "Good point."

He put his eye to the scope and began scanning down range. The next target would be a thousand yards out, and he trained the rifle on the point where he knew he would have the best chance of scoring a hit. "So why are you really out here?"

There was a conspicuous pause. "I...thought you might..."

Her dissembling served only to confirm what he already suspected. "You're worried about fitting in, right? Wondering if you can really cut it?"

Another pause. "Target is up. One thousand yards."

He saw it, right where he expected it to be. "How do you think you did?"

As soon as the question was out, he pulled the trigger.

"Target down," she said, matter-of-factly. Then with far less certainty, she added, "I...I'm not Bishop. I'm not him."

"That's not what I asked." When she did not respond, he went on. "Look, I know I'm not the first to tell you this, but no one expects you to be what Erik was. You have your own unique skill set. Blue and King both see your potential, and that's what they expect you to bring to the team. Focus on doing that, not on trying to be someone else."

"I know what you are saying is true," she said finally. "It is just... You have all worked together for so long, and I am like a child with short legs trying to keep up."

"You're going to do just fine," he said, but the platitude rang hollow in his own ears. Asya could no more stop competing with the ghost of Erik Somers, than he could with the man he had been. The only difference was that he knew it.

As he shifted the gun to the twelve hundred yard target, he felt a buzzing in his pocket. Leaving his glasses behind was one thing, but every member of the team had to be on-call at all times. With a sigh of exasperation, he dug out his quantum smartphone and tapped the screen to accept the incoming call.

"Dae?" He was surprised to hear Anna Beck's voice. She never made personal calls while on duty. Her role as head of Endgame security kept her too busy for idle conversation, and besides, she knew as well as anyone that the Q-phones were not to be used for anything but team business. When she continued, there was no mistaking the note of concern in her voice. "You need to come back right now."

Knight felt a chill pass through him. "What's wrong?"

"Dr. Friedmann just called. Grandma Knight... I'm so sorry."

ELEVEN
Washington, D.C.

Colin Parrish gazed up at the uniformed doorman for several seconds, appraising him with a cool stare. At just slightly over five feet tall, Parrish often looked up at people, but he was never intimidated. "I'm supposed to meet someone."

"I'm sorry, sir." The doorman did not sound the least bit apologetic, and he spoke the last word with palpable contempt. "The club has a strict dress code. At the very least you need to be wearing a jacket and tie."

Parrish ran a thumb along the lapel of his weathered brown leather bomber jacket.

"Not that kind of jacket," the doorman clarified.

Parrish looked past him, first at the dark glass pane in the elegant wood and brass door, and then into the lens of the inconspicuously mounted security camera. Finally, he returned his stare to the doorman and shrugged. "Oh, well."

He was halfway down the block when he heard the sound of rapid footsteps. "Sir, wait."

The doorman jogged past him and turned, blocking his path but with hands outstretched, palms up, as if beseeching Parrish for a benediction. The change in the man's demeanor was like night and day. "Sir, forgive me. I didn't... If you'll just follow me, I'll show you inside."

Parrish suppressed a smile, maintaining his indifferent expression. "Thank you."

He was led through the main entrance into a richly appointed foyer, where a maître d' was waiting to usher him into the lounge. Parrish ignored the shocked looks of the handful of patrons. Their disdain meant exactly nothing to him, though he found their sense of superiority amusing. A few seconds later, he found himself in a small private room, decorated in the same elegant style, all red velvet and hardwoods. There was a single table in the room, and seated at it was the man who had asked to meet with him. Parrish strode to the table and took a seat opposite him.

The man, who was nursing an amber-colored beverage in a tumbler, gave him the same haughty look as the people in the lounge. "Are you..." He paused and wrinkled his nose distastefully. "Bulldog?"

Parrish leaned forward, smiling like a used-car salesman, and offered his hand. "Senator Marrs. A pleasure to make your acquaintance."

Marrs stared at the proffered hand, clearly signaling that he had no intention of taking it, but Parrish did not draw back. Instead, he maintained his pose, statue still, until Marrs admitted defeat and gave him a quick limp clasp. "Let's get on with it. I'm told that you're someone who can, how shall I say it, take care of unpleasant business?"

Parrish glanced around the room. "Where'd the waiter go? I'd like a drink."

"You're not here for a drink," Marrs snapped.

Parrish brought his gaze back to Marrs. "I've read a lot about you, Senator. You're a very powerful man, accustomed to getting your way. You know exactly what you want, and you don't let anything stand in your way."

"That's right." Marrs's arrogant expression remained unchanged, but he seemed pleased at the characterization.

"And you're smart, too," Parrish went on, "Which is why I'm sure that you'll have figured out by now that the only way to get what you want from me, is to stop acting like an asshole."

The senator's face went beet red. "I will not stand for—"

Parrish calmly pushed his chair back and started to rise.

"Wait." With a visible effort, Marrs brought his ire under control. "You're a tough customer. I'll give you that."

Parrish settled back into the chair and folded his hands on the table, but said nothing until a waiter appeared and asked for his drink preference. "A glass of water, please. No ice."

"Water?" Marrs said, but then quickly shook his head. "Get the man some water, for Christ's sake."

Parrish waited until the waiter was gone then said, "Tsk, tsk, Senator. What would your constituents say?"

"Fuck them. And fuck you, too. Are we going to talk business or not?"

Parrish placed his hands on the table, palms down, as if he was about to push himself away. "I know that it's important for you to be the alpha dog here, Senator, but your posturing is wasted on me. This little bit of theater has not brought you any closer to getting what you want, so why do you persist in it?"

"Fine. Let's talk about what I want."

"Let's."

Marrs grabbed his tumbler and drained the contents in a single gulp before lowering his voice to a conspiratorial whisper. "I need you to find somebody for me. Several somebodies, actually. And I need you to—"

"Senator, let's save some time and dispense with the cloak and dagger routine. Just say what you mean."

Marrs brought the glass down with a bang like a judge's gavel. "All right. Here it is. There's a guy in Mexico. A cartel guy. And I owe him a favor."

Parrish made a rolling gesture. "Better."

"His operation was attacked by a rogue outfit. I'm not sure who they are, but I think someone in the government is backing them. I want you to find out who they are, and then I want you to..." He glanced around the room as if only now fearful of being overheard, then lowered his voice. "I want you to deliver them to him. Is that something you can do?"

The waiter returned with a glass of water and another drink for Marrs. When he was gone again, Parrish gave his answer. "In very broad terms, yes, that is something I can do. But understand that to fulfill a request like this expediently, I will need your full cooperation."

"I can pay you whatever you want."

"I'm not talking about money. Money is overrated. What I will need, money can't buy." He chuckled. "Well, I suppose that's not strictly true, is it? It bought you, didn't it?"

Marrs reddened again. "What *do* you want?"

"Access."

"To what?"

"Anything and everything. If, as you say, this rogue element has backing from someone in a position of authority, the only way I'm going to be able to root them out is with full access to classified information."

Marrs's forehead creased in a frown.

"I'm guessing that what you really want is deniability," Parrish went on. "You could find these people yourself, but the rest? How did you put it? Delivering them? That's what you really need me for."

Marrs relented, nodding. "Fine. Whatever you need. Just be discreet."

"That goes without saying." Parrish picked up his water glass and took a sip. "So, let's get started, shall we? Tell me everything you know about this rogue operation."

TWELVE
Endgame, New Hampshire

King stared at the mirror, looking for some trace of himself in the reflection. Over the course of his very long life, he had fought countless battles and worn a dizzying array of uniforms and every type of battle armor imaginable. He had even fought stark naked once or twice. Never, in all that time, had he felt quite so exposed, so vulnerable, so unlike himself, as he did now.

"You look fantastic," Sara Fogg remarked, standing beside him. "It's perfect."

King met her eyes in the reflection and gave a half-hearted smile. "I look like a butler."

From the doorway, his adopted daughter Fiona gave a low whistle. "You look like Prince Charming, Dad. Gonna take the car and make a run to the Snack Shack, 'kay?" She disappeared without waiting for an answer.

"Prince Charming." King rolled his eyes. "At last, all my dreams have come true, and now I can die."

Sara gave him a sideways hug. "Don't worry. You can survive this."

"It's really not fair that you get to see me all dressed up like this, but I don't get to preview you."

"You know the rule. You don't get to see me in my dress until the wedding day."

"I'm more interested in seeing you out of it."

She slugged him playfully. "That's exactly why it's best to leave the planning to the woman. Men only have one thing on their minds." She made a circuit around him, smoothing wrinkles in the tuxedo jacket and straightening his bow tie. "Okay. Let's get this thing off you."

He gave his best lascivious grin. "Thought you'd never ask."

Her wink was very encouraging. "How's the leg?"

"It was just a scratch. Almost healed already." In truth, the three-inch-long gash he'd received from one of the crazed boars had cut deeply, requiring twenty stitches and a heavy duty antibiotic injection. The treatment had been administered during their homeward journey aboard *Crescent II*, by Queen, who had seemed to enjoy poking needles in him just a little too much. The leg was still sore, and he favored it when he moved to avoid reopening the wound, but he was a quick healer—a family trait. He knew in another day or so, he would be able to remove the stitches and walk normally.

"Well, take it easy anyway. Especially tonight." She loosened his bow tie. "Any idea what Rook has planned for you?"

"Knowing Rook, it will probably involve beer, barbecue and various displays of manliness. We're not leaving the grounds, though. Pinckney isn't exactly brimming with nightlife."

"You're telling me. Still, I'm glad we're having the wedding here. It's a beautiful place."

King studied her face, looking for any indication of insincerity, but saw none. The Pinckney Bible Conference Grounds was a remote private park, which unbeknownst to the evangelical organization that owned and operated the rustic campground, concealed the entrance to the sprawling underground complex that had once been Manifold Alpha. The vast laboratory had been built by insane geneticist Richard Ridley, and was now Endgame's headquarters. It had been Sara's idea to have the ceremony outside in the campground, but he was worried that the suggestion might have been made solely for his benefit. The extreme secrecy that surrounded Chess Team's operations and personnel, to say nothing of the fact that Deep Blue—or rather, former President Tom Duncan—could not exactly move about freely in public, meant that a very private ceremony was best for King.

But was it what Sara really wanted? Had she dreamed of a fairy tale wedding in a big church, surrounded by friends? The fact that he didn't know troubled him, but theirs had not been a typical romance and courtship. As an infectious disease investigator for the CDC, she was gone as often as he was. Their life, such as it was, amounted to stolen weekends together, either at Sara's seldom-used apartment in Atlanta, at King's house in Richmond or in a hotel room wherever their paths crossed. Marriage would likely not change that. They would be joined, their commitment to each other formalized, but getting to truly know one another might take the rest of their lives.

"Actually," she went on, "it's those displays of manliness that have me worried. A game of horseshoes is one thing, but you've got to promise me, no Indian wrestling."

"Scout's honor. I will be a spectator only."

"Will Knight be there?"

King didn't know the answer to that question. He had only just heard the news about Knight's grandmother. Her passing had come as a surprise to no one, least of all to Knight, but it was one more blow in what had been a very rough year. "I hope so. He could use a distraction."

She slid the jacket from his shoulders. "It's not always that easy, you know."

King did know. He had endured his own share of losses. Even after uncounted years, he still felt a measure of grief for his sister, Julie, who had inspired him both with her life and her death in a fighter jet training accident. He was reminded of her every time he saw his childhood friend George Pierce, who had been engaged to marry Julie. "That reminds me," he said, not explaining the apparent non sequitur. "I've got to pick George up at the airport."

"You should take Fi. I'm sure she can't wait to show Uncle George her brand new driver's license."

"Not much chance of getting the keys away from her," he said with a nod and a grin. It was still a mystery to him how little Fiona had grown up so quickly. How old had she been when she had come into his life? Twelve? Now she was seventeen, an energetic, intelligent, attractive—maybe too attractive—young woman, eager to assert her independence and take on the world. "But she's gone now. I figure we've got...twenty minutes?" He glanced at the stainless-steel Omega Speedmaster Professional chronometer on his left wrist. "So if you'll help me get the rest of this monkey suit off—"

He was interrupted by the familiar but ominous notes of the Jaws movie score. The ringtone on Sara's phone. She uttered a low growl but then answered in her most professional voice. "Sara Fogg, here."

As she listened, the look of irritation gave way to disappointment and then morphed into real concern. "Understood. Send a plane." She glanced over to King. "George is coming into Logan, right?"

He nodded.

"Send the plane to Logan. I'll be there in two hours."

King waited until she ended the call to speak. He had been worried about the mission in Mexico spilling over into several days and encroaching on their big day, to say nothing of the possibility of sustaining a real injury. The last thing he had expected was for Sara's work to get in the way. "What's up?"

"Maybe nothing. A weird case in North Carolina. Might not be an outbreak, but the local docs are spooked." She tried for a wan smile. "Should just be an overnight thing. Show up, advise routine precautions and head home."

"And you're the only one who can do that? Doesn't the CDC have other disease detectives?"

"None with my experience." King waited for her to elaborate, but instead she said, "Don't worry. The wedding isn't for three more days. There's plenty of time."

"Did I ever tell you about a little thing we have in the military called Murphy's Law?"

"Too many times. Call Fi. Tell her to get back here ASAP. I have to pack."

THIRTEEN
Washington, D.C.

Despite his short stature, broad powerful build and pugnacious manner, Colin Parrish's nickname—which he had adopted as both *nom de guerre* and job description—had nothing at all to do with his physical appearance. In another life, when he had served in the United States Army Criminal Investigations Division, a superior officer had called him 'Bulldog' for the way he would seize onto a lead and drag it to the ground. It was a trait that had served him well, first as a law enforcement officer and subsequently as a private contractor.

Bulldog seemed an appropriate name for what he did. He was more than just a private investigator, more than just a mercenary and a fixer. He was whatever the situation demanded. The only limit to what he could do was his level of interest. The more challenging a situation was, the more interested he became. When he sank his teeth into the mystery of Senator Marrs's rogue operators, he immediately sensed a diversion worthy of his time, but to run this lead down, he would need to be more bloodhound than bulldog.

Identifying 'the cartel guy' had been fairly easy, even without Marrs's description. The capture of Juan Beltran—the notorious Mano— had already hit the cable news outlets. His older brother, Hector, was almost certainly the mysterious Mr. Bell, the true leader of the El Sol cartel. That information would prove useful for the delivery phase.

The one clue that Marrs had given him—the stealth plane—had been more than enough to get the ball rolling. Half an hour of Internet searching turned up a series of UFO sightings going back several months. One from Belgium was particularly interesting, but to pursue it fully, he would require the kind of access that only Marrs could provide. Using a disposable cell phone, he called the senator.

Marrs answered quickly, speaking in a low voice. "Dammit, not now," he said, and then hung up immediately.

Parrish calmly hit 'redial.'

Marrs picked up even quicker. "I told—"

"That was your only freebie, Senator. If you hang up, our arrangement will be concluded."

Marrs whispered a string of profanity, then Parrish heard him speaking to someone else, asking to be excused. When he spoke into the phone again, he was breathless and hurried. "This better be good. You can't just interrupt me any time you like."

"I can and will, if necessary," Parrish replied. "That was our deal, as you'll recall."

"What do you want?"

"About six months ago, NATO air defenses in Europe reported an anomalous supersonic contact. There was no accompanying radar signature, so fighter jets were scrambled to intercept and investigate, but just a few minutes later, the planes were recalled. All forces were instructed to stand down. That would suggest that a senior NATO member nation was conducting a clandestine operation using a stealth aircraft and did not want it to be compromised."

"A stealth plane," Marrs murmured. "All right, you have my attention. Is it the plane we're looking for?"

"At the same time that was happening," Parrish continued, "there was a very curious incident near Brussels. Police responded to a break-in at the Royal Museum for Central Africa, where they found dead security guards and a lot of property damage. Eyewitness reports from the area also mention an unidentified aircraft in the sky above the museum. The official reports don't mention the aircraft, but European UFO enthusiasts were all over it."

"That's got to be the plane we're looking for."

"There are also similar reports out of the Democratic Republic of Congo for the same period, though as you might imagine, those are harder to track down and verify. The people of equatorial Africa are too busy trying to survive to worry about flying saucers and updating their Twitter feeds."

Marrs was speechless for several seconds. "Congo. God damn. I was there. I met the bastards. CIA black ops, two of 'em. A man and a woman. It's gotta be the same people."

"The plane is their vulnerability. You can subpoena the Director of National Intelligence and demand a full accounting of their stealth assets." He recalled that the directorship was currently vacant, filled by an interim successor since the retirement of long-time CIA head Domenick Boucher. Boucher would have to be subpoenaed as well. The incident in Belgium would have occurred on his watch, which meant he was almost certainly involved in the creation of the rogue unit. "That will open the window and let in the sunlight."

"That kind of thing will take time, and that's something I don't have right now. That gangster in Mexico wants his pound of flesh, and I don't think he's the patient sort."

"Here's some free advice, Senator. You need to cut all ties with Hector Beltran. You don't need anything he has to offer."

"Free advice is worth exactly what it costs," Marrs snapped. "Besides, this isn't about him or what he wants. It's about bringing these bastards down in a very public way. Big and loud. That's what the Mexican will do for me. But it has to happen now. That's why I brought you in. I was told that you were the man for the job, but maybe I was told wrong."

Parrish considered his reply carefully. His gut was telling him to walk away. Marrs was mercurial and dangerous. It was a wonder his ambition had not already destroyed him. On the other hand, the senator was also almost certainly going to be the next President of the United States, and having the leader of the free world owing you a favor was not something to be taken lightly. He closed his eyes for a moment, already sure of his answer, and now wondering how he would make it happen.

"Are you still there?" Marrs growled, when the silence stretched out for more than a minute.

"I am. Very well, Senator. You want big and loud, and you want fast. Are you truly prepared to do whatever it takes to make this happen? Because once I set things in motion, there won't be any backing out. Do you understand that?"

"Yes," Marrs answered, too quickly to have actually considered all the angles. "What's the plan?"

Parrish told him.

FOURTEEN

Logan International Airport, Boston, Massachusetts

Over the years, King had endured many long hours traveling from one part of the world to another, but the longest transcontinental flight was nothing compared to the two-hour drive from rural Pinckney to Boston's Logan International Airport. As they cruised down Interstate 93, with Sara in the back seat, busily sending texts and e-mails from her phone, and Fiona behind the wheel, singing at the top of her lungs to the strangest pop music King had ever heard, there was little for him to do but sit, stare out the window and wince at the occasional missed high note.

There was a brief respite from the aural assault when they arrived at the airport. He said his good-byes to a clearly pre-occupied Sara, and then headed to the international terminal to wait for George Pierce's flight to arrive.

He was looking forward to seeing Pierce again. Theirs was an odd but enduring friendship, punctuated by moments of gut-wrenching grief and suffering. The death of King's sister—George's fiancée—had pushed them apart for a while. Pierce had gone on to pursue a career in archaeology, teaching in Europe, while King had enlisted in the Army and ultimately joined the Special Forces, but their paths had crossed unexpectedly when Pierce had discovered the remains of an ancient creature out of legend, only to be abducted by Richard Ridley and subjected to inhuman experiments. King and the Chess Team had rescued him from Ridley's clutches, and in so doing, initiated Pierce into their very secretive world. Pierce's unique knowledge had proved invaluable on several occasions thereafter, making him one of the few people outside the cocoon-like environs of Endgame in whom King could confide. Indeed, he had trusted Pierce with a secret to which no one else on Earth—not Sara, not even Deep Blue—was privy.

Nevertheless, the old wounds could never completely heal. King's wedding would no doubt be a painful reminder of Julie's death. Pierce had never married; as far as King knew, he had never even been in a serious relationship after Julie.

When George finally emerged from the plane and entered the terminal, the initial reunion was brief, and dominated by Fiona, who had a special attachment to 'Uncle George.'

"My goodness," he told her, as he disentangled from her crushing embrace. "Look at you. You're... What happened to little Fi?"

"I got my license," she said, as if that somehow explained everything.

"Uh, oh." Pierce glanced at King. "Does that mean she's driving us?"

"We've survived worse," King said.

"Ain't that the truth."

King turned to Fiona. "Go get the car. Meet us out front."

Fiona, clearly pleased with the chance to fly solo, hastened away, leaving Pierce and King to catch up. Pierce shook his head as he watched her go. "It doesn't seem like it's been that long. What are you feeding her?"

"She eats everything. It's hell managing her sugar." Despite her apparent good health and abundant energy, Fiona Lane, the sole survivor of a devastating attack on the town of Siletz, Oregon, was an insulin-dependent diabetic. As a side project, Lewis Aleman, who had also earned the title, 'Uncle,' had designed a very high-tech 'bionic pancreas' to augment her insulin pump, but even with the hardware, it was a constant struggle to keep the teenager from indulging in the veritable all-you-can-eat buffet of junk food that was twenty-first century America.

"Speaking of that," Pierce said, followed by a somber pause. "What are her plans? School? Career?"

"Ah, I don't even like thinking about that." Fatherhood had been unexpected for King. After plucking Fiona from the ruins of her hometown, he had adopted her and raised her as his own daughter, but the process had been a little like walking in on a movie at the half-way point. He had not watched her grow up from infancy, hadn't encouraged and cultivated her innate interests from early childhood and he certainly had never thought about the fact that she was moving inexorably toward adulthood and independence. "She talks a lot about getting into a linguistics program. We're going to try to get her into the Defense Language Institute in Monterey. She can't enlist because of her diabetes, but I know people who can pull a few strings to get her in as a civilian." The strangeness of Pierce's question finally sank in. "Why?"

"Have you considered letting her study abroad?"

King stopped in his tracks. "You mean...with you?"

"You know how special she is, Jack. We've only scratched the surface of what she can do."

King felt a strange chill come over him. Pierce was right, about everything, and yet the course that his friend was suggesting carried a great deal of risk, and not just for Fiona's health and happiness.

Pierce seemed to sense that he had touched a nerve. "We've found something unusual, and I think she might be the key to unlocking it. She would be perfectly safe."

"We both know there's no such thing."

Pierce inclined his head to cede the point. "As safe as she is with you."

"You're not talking about waiting until after she finishes high school, are you?"

Pierce shook his head ruefully. "Want to hear about it?"

"No. When I said I trusted you with this, I meant it." King sighed. "Well, on the plus side, it might be good for her to get away.

See a little more of the world. I think some of the local boys have started to notice her."

"We can't have that."

"I suppose it's not really up to me, is it? We can talk to her after the wedding, but I'm pretty sure I already know what she'll say."

Pierce nodded then clapped King on the shoulder. "It's good to see you again, Jack. Now, isn't there a party waiting for us?"

"First we have to make it back to Endgame alive."

"Is her driving that bad?"

"Her driving is the least of it. Have you heard what passes for music these days?"

FIFTEEN
Pinckney, New Hampshire

Beltran had accepted his part in the plan without question. Parrish thought that he had actually appeared a little too eager during their Skype video-conference, which had left Parrish feeling unsettled, and that was a rare thing for him. He had dealt with all manner of criminals, and he knew that, aside from possessing some areas of moral ambiguity, most were not that much different from ordinary 'righteous folk.' But there were those rare exceptions—people who possessed no sense of morality whatsoever. Sociopaths and predators, who made him believe that there really was such a thing as evil in the world. Beltran was definitely in that category. The man was also obviously very intelligent, and not just in the canny 'street smart' way that many criminals were. The cartel lord was a force to be reckoned with. Parrish was not looking forward to actually meeting the man, but it was necessary to the plan.

The plan—Parrish's plan—was already gathering momentum, a freight train about to crest the hill. If Beltran had kept the schedule, then the first part of it was already done, and it would be hitting the news at any moment. Provoking the desired response would be a little trickier, but Parrish's research into the Congo incident—hushed rumors of a small but elite group of American operators who had stopped a civil war and restored order to the DR Congo—had left him confident of success. They would take the bait. They would be unable to resist.

Tracking down former CIA director Domenick Boucher had been an unexpected challenge. Unlike most men of his ilk, Boucher had not left public service for a much more lucrative job as a defense industry lobbyist or a foreign policy pundit. Instead, he had, at least to all appearances, literally retired to a cabin in the woods. Parrish had contacts in the Company who might be able to shed some light on what had become of the former director, but he didn't dare approach them with direct inquiries. Boucher could not be allowed to know that someone was looking for him. In the end, Parrish had found what he needed by posing as a literary agent interested in brokering a deal for Boucher to write a memoir of his service. Boucher's former friends had been only too happy to point him in the direction of the retired CIA director's new home, on the edge of the White Mountain National Forest in New Hampshire, in a sleepy little hamlet called Pinckney.

Pinckney, it turned out, was a very unusual town. Parrish had run a search on several UFO forums hoping to find a reported sighting of the stealth plane, but instead he had found numerous references to some mysterious event in 2009. It read like something from a Stephen King novel, with weird science experiments, tales of monsters and a lot of explosions. Several people claimed to have been eyewitnesses to the incident, yet local news reports attributed the entire incident to a toxic chemical leak. Parrish smelled a cover up, and after just a few casual inquiries, he had learned about the secret history of Pinckney, New Hampshire.

It was a strong circumstantial case, but what he did have was an explicit connection to Boucher.

It was just after dusk when he arrived in the small town just off Route 27. Parrish consulted his GPS unit and saw that his destination—the address he had been given for Boucher—lay just ahead. It was not a house, as he had anticipated, but a large, privately operated campground, something called the Pinckney Bible Conference Grounds, if the painted wooden sign was to be believed.

"Guess he got religion," Parrish murmured, as he pulled his car into the gravel parking lot beside the front office. A chalkboard on the wall under the eaves by the door listed upcoming events and their locations. There was a private party already in progress, a wedding scheduled for the upcoming Saturday and some kind of convention celebrating the work of a popular thriller novelist. Parrish recognized the author's name; the guy wrote books about giant monsters and weird shit like that. Evidently, the people who operated the resort weren't too picky about who they allowed to use the facilities.

As he skirted the office and walked along an unpaved road called 'Hallelujah Lane,' Parrish felt a rising sense of apprehension. The area was densely wooded, but through the trees he could see rustic cabins, most of which appeared to be shuttered tightly, awaiting the arrival of the tourist season. There were too many possibilities, and there was no way of narrowing them down. A search like this might take several days of painstaking surveillance, casually plying the locals with indirect questions. He now felt the momentum of his plan bearing down on him. If he didn't find Boucher soon, the window of opportunity would slam shut.

At the intersection of Hallelujah Lane and Praise Street, he could hear music playing in the distance, no doubt from the private party mentioned on the event calendar. Crashing the party would be risky, but maybe one of the revelers would let something slip after a few beers. He wandered down Praise Street toward the sound, but as he got close enough to make out the silhouettes moving against the orange glow of a well-fueled fire-pit, a bright light flashed in his face.

He threw up a hand to shade his eyes, resisting a reflexive urge to dive for cover in the woods. "What the—? Get that thing out of my face."

The light lowered, but the damage to his night vision was already done. He could still see the flashlight, but the person holding it was virtually invisible in the near total blackness. "Can I help you find something, sir?" inquired a voice that, to Parrish's practiced ear, sounded disingenuously cheerful.

"I'm on my way to the party," Parrish snapped.

"It's a private party, sir," The man's tone was abruptly as hard and cold as steel. "And you aren't on the guest list."

Parrish felt a rush of adrenaline in his veins. He had made a big mistake in trying to bluff his way into the party, but his instincts told him that he was close to finding what he was looking for.

"Not on the list?" He affected umbrage. "Listen, I paid my registration fee six months ago. My name better be on the damned list."

"Registration?" There was doubt in the voice now.

"Yes. For the convention. I came all the way from Phoenix."

"Sir, this party has nothing to do with any convention. You must have the wrong event."

Parrish did his best to look crestfallen. "You're kidding. I paid my registration. I've been looking forward to this all year."

"You can inquire at the office. I'm sure they'll be able to help you."

"The office." Parrish nodded gratefully. "I'll do that. Thank you."

His eagerness to end the encounter was not an act. The man that had accosted him was evidently some kind of security guard, which in itself was not that strange, but the way in which he had intercepted Parrish was very telling. The man wasn't just some local rent-a-cop.

Parrish retraced his steps to Hallelujah Lane without glancing back, but when he was half-way back to the front office, he ducked into the woods behind a bookstore that looked like a small church. He waited there, expecting the guard, or possibly an entire security team, to descend on him, but nothing of the sort happened.

Nevertheless, with painstaking caution, he began moving through the woods, following a course that was roughly parallel to Praise Street. His trek brought him to an unoccupied cabin, and he scrambled up onto its rickety roof. Using a small but powerful monocular, he managed to catch a glimpse of the private party where he was now certain he would find Domenick Boucher.

He peered through the lens for several minutes before finally spotting one of the attendees—a big man with short blond hair and a long goatee. Parrish thought the guy looked like he belonged in a biker gang. For a moment he wondered if he had misinterpreted the significance of the encounter with the flashlight-wielding guard. But then he saw more figures moving through his very limited field of view, and one of them was definitely the former CIA director.

Parrish's breath caught in his throat as he recognized the man with whom Boucher was speaking. Without waiting for further confirmation, he dug out his phone and called Marrs.

When the senator picked up, there was no trace of his earlier surliness. Instead, he seemed to be eagerly champing at the bit. "Well?"

"I found him."

"Then it's time?"

"Yes. But listen, Boucher is here with someone else." He allowed a dramatic pause. "President Duncan."

Marrs was speechless for several seconds. "That can't be. Boucher is the one who helped me take Duncan down."

"Well, they appear to be thick as thieves now. Is it possible that they might have played you, Senator? The whole affair with Duncan's resignation might have been a diversion to hide what they were really up to."

"That's absurd. Duncan was the President of the United States. You don't just give that up."

You might not, Parrish thought, but didn't say. Duncan was a former soldier, and a strategic thinker. He wouldn't have given up the Oval Office unless it was for something he thought was even more important. "Whatever they're up to, we're about to pull back the curtain on it. Make the call now."

SIXTEEN
Manteo, North Carolina

The drive from Pitt-Greenville Airport, where the chartered Lear Jet dropped her off, to the Dare County Hospital took nearly as long as the flight itself, but there were no closer airports that could accommodate the small jet aircraft. Sara did not mind the drive itself. She actually preferred being in a car, even a rental, to air travel, where all too often there was an overabundance of strange smells and sounds. What bothered her was the simple fact that the patients were still at the rural hospital where they had first been diagnosed. There was no valid reason, at least none she could think of, for critically ill patients to remain in a facility that was not equipped to provide the kind of treatment they might need. She intended to make resolving that issue the first order of business when she met with the hospital administrator.

When she pulled into the parking lot shortly after sunset and got a look at the facility, her first impulse was to double-check the address. It was a one-story structure that looked more like a strip-mall urgent care clinic than a hospital, but then with a total population in the county of less than thirty-five thousand, there was little need for more. Serious cases could be transported by helicopter or ambulance to any number of first-class medical providers in the region. Still shaking her head in disbelief, she got out and retrieved the duffel bag that contained everything she would need to set up a field-expedient bio-lab. She could work with less—and often had, but never on American soil.

The emergency room was strangely subdued. There were no patients waiting to be seen and just a handful of staff, along with two men wearing the khaki and black uniforms of Dare County Sheriff's deputies. As she stepped inside, something—she had no idea what—triggered a twinge in the back of her throat that made her eyes water. The sensation was like biting on aluminum foil. She had to swallow several times to keep from breaking into a coughing fit. After a few seconds, the feeling began to abate, but she made a mental note of the episode nonetheless. There was something here, something unusual, a smell perhaps, that was unlike anything she had ever experienced before.

"Are you the CDC?"

She turned in the direction of the voice and spotted a slim, middle-aged man with hair gone prematurely gray and a salt-and-pepper beard, wearing a long white lab coat.

"That's right." She held up her credentials, hoping that the gesture would keep the man from offering to shake her hand. "Are you Dr. Foster?"

He gave a relieved sigh. "Thank goodness, you're here. What do you need? We're a pretty bare bones operation here, but—"

"About that. Dr. Foster, why weren't the patients airlifted out of here?"

Foster's eyebrows drew together in a frown. "Given the unusual nature of their symptoms, I made that call. The patients appear to be in...stable condition. I thought moving them might pose an unnecessary risk of exposure to others."

"You don't sound too sure, Dr. Foster."

"I'll be honest, Doctor...?"

"Fogg. Sara Fogg."

"I'm in way over my head, Dr. Fogg. I'm the first to admit it. That's why I called you."

Sara looked around the ER, aware that their conversation was being observed with great interest by everyone present. A doctor with the humility to admit his own inadequacy was a rare thing in her experience, and Foster was being very public about the admission. "Tell me what you know. Start at the beginning."

He motioned for her to follow, but he walked immediately toward the Sheriff's deputies. "Early this morning...about ten, right, Jim?"

One of the deputies nodded.

"About ten," Foster continued, "we got a 911 call from a researcher working out at Fort Raleigh. She said one of her associates had collapsed. By the time the paramedics arrived, there was a second victim."

"Tell me about the symptoms."

"Fever, sweating, convulsions, profuse salivation."

"Salivation? They're drooling?"

Foster nodded. "That was how they presented initially. By the time they got here, there were other... Well, you'll have to see that for yourself. When one of the first responders began showing the same symptoms, I knew we were dealing with something contagious."

That was news to Sara. "How long after exposure?"

Foster glanced at the deputy. "Five minutes?"

The man shrugged. "More like two."

Sara's mind raced to keep up. Viral or bacterial contagions took days, sometimes weeks, to incubate. That meant they were looking at something else, a toxin perhaps. But what was the vector? "Anyone else?"

"No. But everyone who has had any direct contact with the patients is here. Under quarantine. That includes all of us."

Her respect for the doctor went up another notch. For someone who felt out of his depth, he had already started making good decisions. Without further discussion, he led her to the hospital's laboratory. It was only slightly better equipped than a high school science classroom. She quickly set up her own gear and then donned a biohazard safety level-four environment suit. She felt a little self-conscious in the suit. It was unlikely that the hospital had BSL4 suits, so Foster and the rest of the staff had probably been treating the patients using standard isolation precautions: disposable paper scrubs, surgical masks and gloves. However, it was the nature of infectious disease that caregivers were often at the greatest risk, so taking precautions, even those that seemed extreme, wasn't simply a matter of self-preservation. If all the doctors died, then there would be no one left to fight the outbreak.

The Tyvek over-garment was similar to the suits used by her colleagues at the CDC research laboratory in Atlanta, but it was meant for one use only. Once she sealed herself in, she would have about a half an hour until her self-contained air supply was exhausted. After that, the suit would be useless, but one assessment visit would be enough to determine whether the hospital's isolation protocols were sufficient. If they were not, she would have to declare a hot zone, and that would initiate a much more comprehensive response from the government.

When she finished putting on the suit, she asked Foster to take her to the patients. As the two of them, accompanied by a pair of nurses, made their way to the isolation ward, he filled her in on their identities. "First patient is Jason Harris. Twenty-three year old male, grad student at NC State. I'm afraid I haven't been able to get his medical history yet. An eyewitness on the scene says that he was fine one minute, and then fully symptomatic the next."

"Eyewitness?"

"Dr. Ellen Dare, his thesis advisor. She's the one that called 911. She's here, if you want to talk to her."

"She's not symptomatic?"

"Not in the slightest. She and the second patient started first aid while they waited for EMS. The other girl—Haley Stephens, twenty year old female, undergrad, also at State—was already fully symptomatic when EMS arrived. Miss Stephens was shooting video at the time, but I don't think there's anything useful on it."

"I'll want to take a look at it anyway."

They had reached the end of a corridor, but between them and the heavy metal doors that led into the next ward, someone had erected a barrier of thick transparent plastic, held in place with silver duct tape. "Best we could do, I'm afraid."

"It's fine," she assured him.

"There's a decontamination area on the other side of the doors, where you can remove the suit. Disinfectant shower, biohazard disposal bags. We're still following our isolation protocols, though I'm not sure how much good it's doing at this point."

"Tell me about the third patient."

"Doug Stovall. Thirty-four year old male. Lives in Manns Harbor, across the sound. Volunteer fire-fighter and paramedic. He was working to stabilize the patients and get them loaded into the ambulance when he went down, too. He was wearing gloves, but given the circumstances, they wouldn't have made much difference."

"What do you mean by that?"

"The convulsions are quite severe. The patients were thrashing and biting, so he was certainly exposed to their bodily fluids. But so were the other paramedics, and most of us here, and we aren't showing any—"

"I'm sorry, did you just say 'biting?'"

He gave an almost embarrassed nod. "All of them are doing it. We had to use restraints, and even then we don't dare get too close."

"You've tried sedatives? Tranquilizers?"

"Tried. Failed. They won't let us get close enough to put in a line."

Sara didn't like what she was hearing, but she sensed that the only way to learn more was to actually get a look at the patients. She waited for Foster and the nurses to pull on isolation garments, and then proceeded through the door.

Beyond the designated decontamination area lay the main hospital floor. Foster guided Sara past the abandoned nurse's station and into the first room. As soon as the door opened, she could hear low guttural noises, like grunts or snarls of fear. Despite that warning and Foster's earlier description of the symptoms, she was unprepared for what she saw next.

"Which—?" She couldn't get the rest of the question out, but Foster seemed to understand.

"That's Jason Harris. Patient Zero."

Sara was having trouble reconciling what she now saw with what she had been told about Harris. The gaunt figure strapped to the bed did not look like a young graduate student.

It didn't even look human.

Harris appeared emaciated, as if starved to the point where his body had devoured every ounce of muscle tissue, leaving little more than a skeleton covered with hairless skin. The skin itself was almost transparent, and underneath it, Sara could see cords of gray muscle and sinew, and a spidery map of blood vessels and nerves. It was as if he was fading out of existence. Yet, despite the evident wasting of his body, Harris was thrashing in his restraints, shaking so violently that the heavy hospital bed was now askew and creeping across the room.

Even stranger was the skeletal deformity.

Jason Harris's bones—all of them—were unnaturally long, as if they had been softened and stretched like taffy. His arms, fixed to leather straps attached to the bed rails, were almost twice as long as they should have been. Through the papery skin, she could see that the bones were spindle-thin.

"The skeletal deformity." Sara wasn't sure what else to call it. "Tell me that's a pre-existing condition. Acute Marfan Syndrome or something like that?"

"I'm afraid not. All three of them look like this. It's definitely a symptom of whatever they've got."

"That just isn't possible. Bones don't change like that. Not in twelve hours' time."

Foster spread his hands helplessly.

Sara realized she was breathing fast, her exhalations fogging the face-plate of her environment suit. Impossible was not an option. She was a scientist, obligated to deal with the facts of the situation, no matter how unbelievable they seemed.

Focus, Sara. Do your job.

She took a deep breath and started forward into the room.

Harris's head swiveled toward her. His skull was grotesquely long, stretched and distorted like a melting wax effigy. The skin was pulled taut, the lips drawn back from teeth grown so large that even on the abnormally large jaw, they were jammed together crookedly. Some protruding like tusks.

But the eyes...

Although drawn back and nearly covered over by bone growth around the occipital cavity, his eyes looked normal. Bloodshot but otherwise unchanged. In their blue depths, she thought she could see an echo of the human he had once been. As their stares met, she felt the urge to offer whatever comfort and reassurance she could.

Suddenly, with a convulsion so violent that it lifted the bed several inches off the floor, he thrust his head toward her, biting at the air. His teeth gnashed together so forcefully that, even through the barrier of the suit, Sara could hear the enamel chipping away.

Sara had watched a lot of people die over the years. That was the nature of her profession. But she had never seen anything like this. Even if, by some miracle, this young man recovered—and it was her scientific opinion that nothing short of divine intervention could effect that outcome—the changes to his body, and probably to his psyche as well, would be permanent.

She struggled to order her thoughts.

"I'll need a blood sample," she told Foster.

The doctor exchanged an unhappy glance with the nurses, but they all knew that it had to be done. As they ventured closer, the patient seemed to grow even more agitated, like a mad dog straining to break free of a chain. Sara felt a rising trepidation. Without a blood sample, there would be no way to even begin looking for a cause, but getting it meant risking exposure, and not just for herself.

Sara was willing to take that risk, but she wasn't so sure about asking the others to do so, especially since there was no way of knowing whether the potential benefit outweighed the danger.

Before she could voice these reservations however, Foster and the nurses moved in quickly and braced Harris's upper body. The nurses each grasped an arm while the doctor managed to wrap his arms around the patient's misshapen forehead.

"Go!" Foster yelled, snapping Sara out of her uncertainty. She moved forward quickly, dismayed to see that, even with three people holding him down, Harris was thrashing so violently a clean stick would be almost impossible. Still, this might be her only chance.

She struggled to fix the rubber band tourniquet in place, just above the elbow, then placed her left forearm atop the patient's and leaned onto him, adding her weight to that of the nurse. She could still feel him trying to move. Using just her right hand, she worked the plastic sheathe off the syringe needle and brought it close to his arm. She had no trouble finding a vein through the almost transparent skin, but trying to hit it while Harris was struggling against them was a challenge. She held her breath, trying to anticipate his next spasm, and then stabbed the needle into the vein.

The vial started filling up with viscous blood that was so dark it seemed almost black. Harris jerked again, and she had to press down hard on his arm to keep him from shaking the needle out. She needed at least three vials, but it was immediately clear that she would be lucky to get even this one filled. Holding the syringe with her right hand, she cautiously lifted her left and loosened the tourniquet.

What happened next was a blur.

There was a flurry of movement beside her, and then something slammed into her, knocking her backward. There was a sharp inexplicable pain in her hand, but she was more concerned with trying to arrest her fall. She stumbled backward, flailing in vain. She caught a glimpse of something red against the austere white ceiling tiles. Then hands were grasping her, pulling her along the floor, away from the trembling hospital bed. She fought them for a moment, caught in the grip of a reflexive urge to assert some control in the midst of the chaos.

As the panic began to ebb, she started to piece together what had happened. Harris was still restrained, but somehow he had slipped out of Foster's grip, and that had been enough to send the three medical professionals scrambling. One of them had knocked her down, and then together, they had dragged her away, out of danger.

Sara recalled the pain she had felt, and for a moment she feared she had been pierced by the syringe. The vial lay on the floor, a few feet from the bed, leaking crimson droplets onto the floor but still mostly full.

But did it stick me?

She looked down at her hand and immediately saw that the answer to her question was irrelevant.

A section of the suit, from her fingertips all the way up to her left elbow, had been torn away, exposing her to whatever pathogens were circulating in the air of Jason Harris's hospital room, but even that was now unimportant. She watched in disbelief as fat drops of blood—her blood—spattered the floor, flowing freely from the semi-circular wound on the side of her hand.

Harris had bitten her.

SEVENTEEN
Pinckney, New Hampshire

King sat on the picnic table, gazing into the radiant flames dancing above the fire pit and idly rolling a bottle of Sam Adams Boston Lager between his palms.

"My bachelor party," he murmured.

It sounded strange in his ears, but no stranger than some other words and phrases that had found their way into daily conversation, like 'my wedding' and 'my fiancée.' Still, those were things he had willfully embraced with his commitment to Sara. The notion of a bachelor party had not even entered into his mind.

Rook, of course, had been all over it. Yet, much to King's surprise, the festivities were subdued. Instead of a post-adolescent stag party, this was a quiet, almost introspective gathering of men who had sacrificed—or at the very least postponed—marriage and family life to make the world a little bit safer for everyone else. Even the normally extroverted and irreverent Rook seemed to get this, though this apparent shift toward maturity probably had more to do with Queen's influence in his life.

Those two are definitely good for each other, King thought with a grin. *I should probably start thinking about* his *bachelor party.*

He glanced up as Knight stepped out of the shadows to join the group. The team's sniper looked conspicuous in his black designer slacks and white Egyptian cotton shirt, dressed more for a night on the town than a few hours of hanging out around a bonfire. King jumped down from his perch, wincing at the stab of pain in his leg, and crossed over to greet him.

"Dae-jung, I was very sorry to hear about your grandmother." The offer of sympathies, like everything else about the night, felt strange to him, but Knight returned a grateful smile.

"Thank you, Jack." Knight seemed oddly serene, which was both encouraging and a little disconcerting. "I'll probably need some personal time, but it can wait until after the wedding."

"You don't even need to ask," King assured him, and he meant it.

Before he could say more, the rest of the group gathered around to offer their condolences as well, and King faded away, returning to the table to continue nursing his beer. With Knight's arrival, the roster of King's friends was nearly complete: Deep Blue, Rook, Knight, Lewis Aleman, George Pierce and Domenick Boucher. There were a couple of other familiar faces—men from

Endgame security who were present in a semi-official capacity—but it was, as Rook had planned and as King wanted, an intimate evening with close friends. The only man not present was his father, Peter Sigler—sometimes known as Peter Machtcenko, depending on which identity he was using. King's feelings toward his father were conflicted enough that he was unsure of whether to count the man as a friend.

Of them all, Boucher was someone King did not actually know very well, even though the man had been an integral part of the creation of Chess Team. In fact, he had been present at what King now thought of as the first assembly of the team, though only he, Rook and Erik Somers had been present at the time. Boucher, the longest serving director of the CIA in the Agency's history, had worked with Deep Blue from the beginning to make Chess Team possible, providing black budget funding, logistical support and most importantly, mission-critical intelligence. But his interactions with the team had usually been indirect, filtered through Deep Blue. In the last few months, however, ever since his retirement from public service, Boucher had begun working more closely with the team, stepping back into the role that had begun his career: intelligence analyst. It was now his job to review all the information coming into Endgame and determine where intervention might be required. Thanks to the many active and passive channels he had established during his tenure with the Agency, there was a deluge of intel for him to filter. Boucher also acted as an intermediary with the current president, an arrangement that had been forged several months earlier during the Congo crisis. President Chambers knew only that Boucher could field an elite paramilitary team to deal with extraordinary situations while maintaining a buffer of absolute deniability. The capture of Mano—Juan Beltran—had been carried out at the president's behest.

As if sensing that he was the subject of King's contemplation, Boucher, accompanied by Deep Blue, wandered over to join him at the table. "You boys sure know how to party," he remarked with a wink.

"It's a bit slow now," King replied, "but wait until the entertainment shows up."

"A stripper in a cake?"

"Even better. Rook hired Garrison Keillor and the whole gang from A Prairie Home Companion to do a live show."

Boucher grinned. "I must be getting old because that actually sounds like—" He broke off with a frown, and dipped a hand into his pocket to retrieve a cell phone. He glanced at the display and raised an eyebrow. "Uh, oh. It's the Chief. No rest for the wicked." He turned away before accepting the call, leaving King with Deep Blue.

"The President does realize that we're unavailable for the next few weeks, right?" King said.

"When you sit behind the Resolute Desk, the whole idea of time off becomes a little fuzzy. Even when you're on vacation, you're working, and you assume it's that way for everyone else, too." Despite his off-hand manner, the former president appeared apprehensive about the phone call. "I'm sure he wouldn't call unless it was something very important, and if it is..."

Deep Blue didn't finish, and King didn't need him to. The job they had all willingly signed up for wasn't the sort of thing that allowed for time-outs.

But still, it would be nice if the world could take a break, just until I get back from my honeymoon.

When Boucher turned back around, King could tell by the look on his face that the world had other ideas.

EIGHTEEN

Manteo, North Carolina

Sara stared at the crescent-shaped wound in mute disbelief. *I'm supposed to do something*, she thought, *but for the life of me, I can't remember what.*

There was a sharp twinge in the back of her throat, almost like an electric shock. It was the same sensation she had experienced upon entering the hospital, but much, much stronger. *It's something in the air,* she realized. *Something that got in when the suit ripped.*

She was only faintly aware of Foster and the nurses, hustling around her, tearing back the damaged suit and irrigating the wound with saline solution. All the while they watched her for some sign that she was about to become what Jason Harris and the others like him had become. Her heart was pounding, and the strange sensation only added to the feeling of lightheadedness. Was it the first stage of infection, or was she just panicking?

'Five minutes?' She recalled Foster asking the deputy.

'More like two.'

Either she was infected or she wasn't. If she was, there was nothing she could do about it. So there was no sense in worrying about it. What was important was to provide documentation, so the next disease investigator to arrive on scene would have some place to start. Meanwhile, she still had a job to do.

"I'm okay," she lied. It was an effort just to get the words out.

"I'll be the judge of that," Foster said, continuing to rinse the bite.

"Can we at least get out of here?" she said, her voice and nerve a little steadier. "Maybe he'll calm down if we're not in the room."

Foster was receptive to this idea, and after pressing a large gauze pad to the wound, he helped her to her feet. Before exiting, she ducked in to retrieve the syringe. When they were back in the hall, she turned to Foster again. "I think I'm okay, but I'll let you know if I feel even the slightest bit symptomatic," she said, her professional calm now fully restored. "If I give the word, you'll need to strap me down and call my superiors."

Foster gave a wide-eyed nod.

Has it been two minutes?

Her hand was starting to throb in time with her pulse, but aside from the strange sensation in the back of her throat—and even that was diminishing—she felt perfectly fine. "I'll start analyzing the sample right away." Even as she said it, she knew that finding anything in the specimen of Jason Harris's blood would be a long shot. "We might not be dealing with a contagion here."

"Then what?"

"Something environmental, maybe. A toxin." She shook her head. "No, the blood sample can wait. I need to talk to the survivor."

She rinsed in the disinfectant shower and stripped off the ruined bio-hazard suit, now well past the five minute mark. Although a hopeful sign, it didn't completely allay her concerns. Most viral and bacterial infections took anywhere from several hours to several days to incubate in the body. The rapid onset described by the first responders was almost certainly some kind of statistical outlier. Maybe the two college students and the paramedic had all been exposed at some earlier time. She would not be able to declare herself free of infection until she could isolate the exact cause and check her own blood for the presence of the contagion.

After placing a fresh sterile dressing on her hand, Foster led her to another private room, where she found a woman with auburn hair who appeared to be in her mid-thirties. Although she was seated on a hospital bed, the woman was fully clothed, as if expecting to be released at any moment.

Dr. Foster made the introductions. "Dr. Dare, this is Dr. Fogg, from the CDC. Dr. Fogg, Dr. Dare."

"Call me Sara."

"Ellen." It was evident from the woman's demeanor that she had long since passed the point of fear, and was now chafing at the restrictiveness of the quarantine. "What's happened to Jason and Haley? No one will tell me anything."

Sara glanced at Foster. "Well, it's a violation of federal law to share medical information," she explained. "But I can tell you that they're receiving treatment and being watched very carefully, the same as you."

"I don't need treatment," Ellen said, an edge of desperation creeping into her tone. "I saw what happened to them. What they...turned into. There's no treatment for that."

Sara ignored the comment. "I need to know everything that happened. Can you talk me through it?"

Ellen gave a frustrated shrug. "There's nothing to tell. One minute Jason was digging, and then next he was..." She struggled to find the right words for a few seconds, then threw her hands up.

"Digging?"

"Yes. We're conducting an archaeological survey of the Lost Colony."

"Lost Colony?" The reference was vaguely familiar, but Sara was mostly just trying to get Ellen to loosen up a little.

"The very first British colony in the Americas was located here on Roanoke Island, just a few miles from here. Back in 1587."

"I think I remember that. They disappeared, right?"

Ellen nodded.

"What were you digging for?"

"According to one historical source, most of the colonists died in the first year, but a few survivors managed to integrate with the local native population, including my ancestor, Eleanor Dare. If that source is accurate, then the remains of nearly a hundred settlers are buried somewhere on the island, but so far no trace has been found."

"And did you find anything?"

Ellen shook her head. "Jason found an old animal bone, but nothing of significance."

"Where is the bone?"

"Probably still at the excavation. It wasn't important."

Sara made a mental note to visit the site and collect the insignificant bone anyway. "Did you uncover anything else unusual? It wouldn't have to be manmade. Did you notice any unusual odors?"

Ellen shook her head again.

"What about insects? Did Jason or Haley mention being bitten?"

Ellen threw up her hands. "Do you seriously believe a mosquito bite could cause that? They turned into monsters, for God's sake."

In her most patient but authoritative voice, Sara replied, "I'm trying to isolate exactly what it was that did cause it."

"I already know what caused it."

"Oh?"

Ellen faced her, and with all the gravitas of her academic expertise, said simply, "The curse."

NINETEEN
Endgame, New Hampshire

They reconvened twenty minutes later around a table in the command center, minus George Pierce, but with the addition of Queen and Bishop. Boucher had spent the interval working with Deep Blue and Aleman to organize what little intel they had into something approximating a mission briefing. When everyone was present, he nodded to Aleman, and a moment later, a grainy surveillance photograph of a dark-haired man appeared on the wall-mounted plasma screen.

"The man in this photo is believed to be Hector Beltran, the older brother of the man you captured last night in Mexico. I say 'believed to be' because he's notoriously camera shy. In fact, he's a mystery to just about everyone. We know very little about him, and what we do know is probably wrong."

Rook yawned loudly.

Boucher ignored him. "Beltran and his brother came up in the Los Zetas cartel, but evidently Los Zetas was too tame for them, so they struck out on their own to form El Sol, which seems to be more of a religious cult than a drug cartel. Certain aspects of their practices borrow heavily from ancient Aztec religion."

"Like ripping out people's hearts?" Rook asked, suddenly taking more of an interest.

"There was a lot more to Meso-American religion than just human sacrifice," King said, his voice low but nonetheless authoritative.

"That may be true," Boucher said, "but judging by the rumors, and of course what you found during your last excursion, that's the part of the old religion that Beltran is most interested in. El Sol—the Sun—is what the locals call it, but the name they use among themselves is..." He consulted his notes and spoke the next word very slowly. "*Tepilhuan Huitzilopochtli*. Think I got that right. Loosely translated, it means Children of Huitzilopochtli."

Aleman tapped a few keys and Beltran's likeness was replaced by a picture of what looked like a native warrior wearing feathers and holding a snake.

"Huitzilopochtli was a very important god in the Aztec pantheon, and the one most often associated with warfare and the underworld, as well as ritual human sacrifice and cannibalism. He was also a sun god, which is presumably where El Sol takes its name. The Aztecs believed that only the shedding of blood could keep the sun god moving through the sky, so the worship of Huitzilopochtli was particularly brutal."

King leaned forward. "This is all very interesting, Dom, but we all got an up close and personal look at El Sol's brutality last night. Can we cut to the chase?"

"No offense, Jack, but what you saw last night was nothing. Just little brother disposing of some bodies. However, in the interest of moving this along... Two hours ago, a charter bus full of American tourists—forty-six altogether—disappeared in Mexico City. Even before the bus was reported missing, someone claiming to be the leader of El Sol called the Mexican authorities and told them that if Juan Beltran was not released by sunrise tomorrow, they would start sending the hostages' heads home to their families by express mail."

Rook, for once, had no comment.

"The Mexican government has made it clear that they are not going to release their prisoner. Their position, much like that of our own government, is that they do not negotiate with terrorists."

"He'll butcher them," King said. "If he hasn't already."

Boucher nodded gravely, then Deep Blue cut in. "I know some of you might be thinking this is your fault. It's not, so get that idea out of your head."

"Never mind whose fault it is," Queen snapped. "How do we save them?"

Boucher looked around the room, studying each person in turn. King did the same. He saw mirrored in their faces the same anger and resolve that he now felt.

Except for one.

Knight's face was an unreadable mask.

King knew that Knight was a consummate professional, but even the best shooter wasn't immune to personal tragedy. Knight had been through the wringer. On top of everything else, he had just lost his last living relative, and he was now being asked to put all that aside and jump back into the deep end.

Not just him. Maybe we need to slow things down a little.

King cleared this throat. "Dom, with all due respect, why us? This is exactly the kind of thing Delta was created for. Shouldn't they be handling it?"

He felt their eyes on him, not just Boucher, but Queen and Bishop and Rook. Even Knight seemed surprised by the unexpected show of reticence. Then Deep Blue spoke up. "I'm afraid I have to agree with King. We're here for extraordinary threats, and I'm not sure that this qualifies. I had serious reservations about the mission to capture Mano in the first place."

Queen brought her fist down on the table hard enough that everyone jumped just a little. "I don't believe this. I never thought I would hear 'not my job' from anyone in this room."

Deep Blue fixed her with an intense stare. "What is it you think we're doing here?"

Queen glared at him, but after a few tense seconds, she unclenched her fist and sat back in her chair.

Deep Blue was not finished. "We came together because sometimes there are situations that no one else can handle. Situations that require immediate action and can't wait for the politicians to pull their heads out of their asses and work together for the greater good. But here's something that maybe you haven't thought about. We're breaking the law, and so is the President, every time he calls us up. Now, I just happen to believe that sometimes you have to bend the rules to get the job done, but when it gets to be a habit... Well, then we have a problem. We may be off the books and outside the chain of command, but we are *not* the President's private army, and the day that we become that is the day that I hit the lights and walk away for good."

Rook tilted his head back and stared at the ceiling. "The people on that bus should find that comforting."

King stood up. "All right. The point has been made, but the question stands. Dom, why did the President call you for this?"

Boucher looked a little uncomfortable with the question. "Honestly, I think Tom may have hit the nail on the head. President Chambers knows we can get the job done, fast and without a trail that leads back to him. But yeah, maybe he's starting to take this arrangement for granted."

"Just so we're clear on that," King said, cracking a smile. "Saving forty-six innocent Americans is a good enough reason for me to make an exception, but if any of you want to sit this one out, for any reason whatsoever, that's your prerogative." He made a determined effort to avoid looking in Knight's direction, and then quickly added. "Hell, I'm tempted. It seems like there was something I was supposed to be doing this weekend."

His comment produced the desired chuckle. Without waiting to see if Knight would excuse himself, King turned back to Boucher. "We got a little taste of what El Sol is up to. Can we expect more of that?"

"I wish I could give you an answer, but the truth is that we don't actually know where Beltran is keeping the hostages. El Sol controls more of Mexico than any other cartel—the entire eastern coast, from the Texas border to the Yucatan—but their real strength is their secrecy. We don't know where or even if they have a base of operations. Until you rounded up Mano, we didn't know anything about their central leadership. So far, he's not saying much, and I don't think we're likely to learn anything useful from him anyway. The hostages could be anywhere in El Sol territory."

"So we just got all spun up for nothing," Rook said, tilting his head back again. "I say we head back to the party. Who's with me?"

"We'll find them," Aleman said, with easy confidence. "I'll have the exact location before you cross into Mexican airspace."

King regarded the tech expert for a moment, then turned his gaze on Deep Blue, as if to say: *It's your call.*

"I guess I'd have to agree with King," he said after a long pause. "Forty-six innocent Americans is a pretty compelling reason to bend the rules, regardless of whether we have an official sanction. But if anyone wants to sit this one out..." He nodded toward King. "Just say the word."

Nobody spoke.

King sneaked a look in Knight's direction and saw him looking exactly as he had before, stone-faced and inscrutable.

"All right, then. Get prepped. Wheels up in two hours."

TWENTY

Manteo, North Carolina

"**Curse.**" **Sara did** her best to maintain a neutral affect and tone. It was not unusual to hear talk of curses and God's wrath when investigating an outbreak in a remote community on a far-flung continent, but she would not have expected it from a university professor in the United States.

Ellen showed no embarrassment whatsoever. "There was a curse on the colony. I didn't want to believe it, but now? It's just like the Dare Stone says."

"The Dare Stone? Tell me about that." Sara's request was not merely an act of patronization. Whether it was in a river village in central Africa, or the hollows of rural Appalachia, there was often relevant information to be found just under the surface of traditional wisdom and folklore.

"My ancestor, Eleanor Dare, left a record of what happened." The woman abruptly reached out for a folder on the chair beside the bed. She opened it and removed a black and white photograph of a rock covered in cryptic writing. She pointed to what looked like a random spot and began reading. "'About half are dead for two years or more from sickness, we are four and twenty. Savage with a message of a ship was brought to us. In a small space of time they became afraid of revenge and all ran away.'"

"What does that mean?"

"The 'savages,' the Native American people that lived here before, knew that the English would blame them for the sickness, so they abandoned the remaining colonists when they heard there was a ship in the area."

Sara parsed this and immediately grasped the significance. "The sickness that killed the colonists, that was the 'curse?'"

Ellen nodded. "It's right here: 'Soon after the savages, fearing angry spirits, suddenly murdered all, save seven.' Angry spirits. The natives believed the colonists had offended their spirit gods. We know that earlier expeditions encountered hostile tribes, but those were isolated events. The tribes were often at war with each other, so fighting with one tribe wouldn't anger them all. In fact, it often presented an opportunity for an alliance. Like the old saying, 'the enemy of my enemy is my friend.'"

Sara was not as interested in the reason for the curse as she was in determining how it functioned. "Are we talking a toxin of some kind? An herbal concoction? A viral agent to which the settlers might not have an immunity?" The latter was a long shot. Although even primitive cultures had a grasp of how to use infectious pathogens in a crude form of bio-warfare, she doubted very much that the Native Americans of the period would have grasped immunology.

"A curse," Ellen repeated, as if that answered everything. "The colonists had committed a sin so grave that they were universally reviled." She sounded miserable, defeated. "I grew up with the stories, but I didn't want to believe it. I have their blood in me."

"I'm sure that had nothing to do with it," Sara said, trying to steer the woman out of the downward spiral of survivor's guilt. "After all, you're still healthy."

The other woman brightened at this. "Of course. They let Eleanor Dare live. She was innocent. She probably didn't even know what was going on."

"Ellen, I need you to focus on the curse itself. Tell me what you know about it. How did it make the colonists sick?"

Ellen shook her head. "Aside from the Dare Stone, all I really know is what's been handed down in oral histories."

"Okay, tell me about those. Do they describe symptoms like what happened today?"

The woman looked up suddenly, her eyes haunted by some terrible revelation, and then she nodded slowly. "Among the native peoples that inhabited this region, and all across North America really, there are legends of creatures called 'wendigos.' Hideously deformed humans, with gray rotting skin stretched over their bones, eyes sunken into the skull, and a ravenous appetite for human flesh."

Sara had almost stopped listening at the word 'creature,' but Ellen's description of the wendigo was too similar to the physical deformities that Jason Harris was exhibiting to be dismissed. She didn't believe in evil spirits or curses, but if the ancient natives had witnessed someone undergoing the same transformation, they would naturally have ascribed a supernatural explanation to it.

It has to be something environmental, she decided, *something they uncovered at the dig. Fungal spores, perhaps.* But why had it affected the paramedic, yet spared Ellen Dare, who had been in direct contact with the other victims? *I've missed something.*

"This Eleanor Dare, your ancestor... She was immune? I mean, the curse didn't affect her, right?" There had to be a genetic component to it, something passed down through the generations.

"She was spared," Ellen said. "She was not a sharer in their sins."

"Spared? Are you saying that the natives were able to selectively target their victims?"

Ellen's face twisted with uncertainty and for the first time, Sara sensed the woman's inner conflict. She was an intellectual, an erudite scholar, who like Sara, believed there was a rational explanation for everything, and yet she was also the child of a culture with deep-seated traditional beliefs that included things like spirits and people who transformed into monsters, and right now, what she was experiencing seemed to more closely resemble the latter.

"No," she said, in a small voice. "They didn't need to. The curse would only affect those who had..." She faltered. "Only the guilty."

Sara shook her head. "I don't understand."

"The curse of the wendigo comes upon those who have eaten human flesh. Before they disappeared, the Lost Colony had become cannibals."

TWENTY-ONE
New Hampshire

Crescent II **was** waiting for them in a clearing on the edge of the White Mountains National Forest. It was a twenty minute ride, along a rutted dirt road that was actually in much better shape than it appeared at first glance. Anna Beck drove them, as she often did, taking full advantage of her position within Endgame to see her boyfriend off.

As he watched them talking, then embracing and kissing, at the foot of the loading ramp, King had to fight the urge to tell Knight to sit this one out. Knight was too much of a professional to ever voluntarily step back, but if anyone had earned some time off, it was he. But the truth of the matter was that Knight, as their designated marksman, was arguably the most important member of the team. Like the chess piece for which he had been named, he was not limited by the physical shape of the battlefield. He was their eyes—which was bitterly ironic—and their protector, ready to strike down threats that they couldn't even see. He was not irreplaceable by any means; in a pinch, any one of the team could have taken his place, but King was glad that such a last minute shuffle had been unnecessary. It didn't ease his conscience any, but it certainly made him feel better about the mission.

Before boarding the plane, King took out his personal cell phone and tried calling Sara again. He had said his good-byes to Fiona and George in person, though he fully expected to be back at Endgame about the time they were waking up. Sara hadn't answered his earlier attempt, just before he left Endgame, and while that probably meant nothing, he was nonetheless worried. He always was, when she was called out to a hot zone. This time, she answered on the first ring. "Hey, how's the party?"

She sounded distracted, but then that was typical Sara. "It kind of fizzled," he said, wondering how to let her know that the team was being deployed again.

"Sorry to hear it. Listen, Jack. This thing is turning out to be a little worse than I originally thought."

King felt a chill pass through him. "Are you all right?"

"Of course," she said, just a little too quickly.

"What's wrong?"

"Nothing. It's just a really weird case. What I'm trying to say is that..." She drew in a breath. "This might run a little longer than... We might need to postpone the wedding. Just a few days."

King felt some of the panic ebb away. "Postpone the wedding? That's all?" He had to stifle a chuckle.

"I'm so sorry."

"Don't be. This is who we are. We both know that. And everyone will understand. Trust me."

"You're not mad?"

"Of course not. To tell you the truth, I—"

"I gotta run, Jack. I'll call when I can, but don't wait by the phone. Give Fi a hug for me. Love you."

Before he could reply in kind, an electronic tone signaled that the call had ended. The abrupt end to the conversation brought back his nagging concerns about the nature of the crisis with which Sara was dealing. He handed the phone over to Anna for safe-keeping, and then lowered his glasses into place.

"Blue, are you live?"

Deep Blue's voice filled his head. "I'm here, King."

"I need a favor. Can you access the list of current CDC operations?" He searched his memory. "Anything in North Carolina?"

After a short pause, Deep Blue said, "It looks like there was a request sent by the Dare County Hospital in Manteo. That's in the Outer Banks, not too far from Kitty Hawk, where the Wright Brothers flew their airplane."

"I know where it is," King said, more impatiently than he intended. "What's the crisis? What kind of disease?"

"It says non-specific, agnogenic illness with morphological and behavioral abnormalities."

King felt his heart pounding faster. *Could it be? No. It's impossible.* "Agnogenic? What does that mean?"

"It's a fancy word that means they don't know the cause."

"I need..." He stopped himself. He couldn't back out of the mission, not now, not for what might amount to nothing more than a case of the jitters. "Can you send someone down there to back Sara up?"

Deep Blue answered without hesitation. "Absolutely. I'll send Anna." There was a pause, and then he asked the question King was dreading. "Why? Do you know something about this?"

King knew what Deep Blue meant. "I know a lot of things. It's probably nothing. But just in case."

"I understand. I'll send Anna as soon as you're in the air. Whatever it is, she can hold the fort until you're done in Mexico. We'll drop you off on the way back."

King breathed a little easier. "Thanks, Blue. I owe you one."

"No you don't, but I'll remember you said that."

TWENTY-TWO

Mexico

The black Range Rover was waiting for Parrish in the hangar where the chartered Gulfstream IV parked, after it taxied off the runway at Benito Juarez International Airport. The surly muscular men who got out of the SUV moved with a melodramatic swagger that would have been almost comical, but for the small fact that it was no act. Although Islamic terror groups like Al Qaeda and ISIL dominated the headlines, they did not hold a candle to the cruelty of the Mexican drug cartels. Parrish took a deep breath, steeling himself for what would happen next, and descended the stairs from the jet.

He did not expect to be greeted hospitably, and was only a little relieved at the complete indifference of the group. One of the men made a beckoning gesture.

"I have some luggage," Parrish said, in English. He was fluent in Spanish, but thought it best not to reveal that detail to the men. They might speak more freely among themselves if they believed that he wouldn't understand them, and that was the kind of advantage he would need to survive what was probably coming. He jerked a thumb over his shoulder, in the direction of the open hatch. "It's in there."

The cartel men exchanged a glance, then one of them—a young man with a permanent sneer and a chest that was pushed so far out, he appeared to have a spinal disorder—said something to the others, presumably translating, though whatever he said was not in Spanish or any other language with which Parrish was familiar.

So much for my advantage.

Another of the men answered in kind, and then two of them started forward, brushing past Parrish to enter the plane. They emerged a moment later, carrying between them a large olive-drab container that looked almost like a coffin. The man in the lead shouted something in the strange language, and even though he couldn't understand, Parrish had a pretty good idea what had been said.

'Get the other one.'

It took about ten minutes for the men to secure the two containers to the roof of the Range Rover, after which the sneering man brusquely pushed a heavy cloth bag into Parrish's hands. "Put it on."

Parrish slipped the bag over his head, all too painfully aware of the fact that he was now totally at their mercy. Still, the men had to know that without him, the contents of the two containers would have little value, and their boss would not get his revenge.

The men said very little, or at least, very little that he could hear over the painfully loud music that blasted from the sound system. Parrish, whose tastes ran to New Orleans jazz, could not identify the style, but there were a lot of horns and guitars. The beat of the songs let him tick off the minutes, which helped him estimate that the ride had lasted about an hour. For the last twenty minutes, the going was slow, the Range Rover bouncing along a deeply rutted, probably unpaved surface. Finally, it came to a stop, and the music went silent. Parrish was hustled from the car, and one of the men yanked the bag off his head.

Although the only source of light was a row of what looked like tiki torches, Parrish nevertheless winced and shaded his eyes against the sudden brightness. There was bare dirt underfoot and a featureless black sky overhead, which meant they were outside, but other than that, he could discern nothing about where he was. He elicited a roar of laughter, at least a dozen different men taking pleasure in his discomfort. He blinked tears away and tried to bring his eyes into focus.

His initial estimate wasn't even close. There were more than twenty men, most wearing woodland camouflage fatigues, all holding assaults rifles—AR-15s along with a few well-used Kalashnikovs. They stood in a circle around him, with more men right behind him.

This just keeps getting better.

He drew in a breath and then in the loudest voice he could muster, he said, "They're already on their way, so if you really want to do this, I suggest you stop screwing around."

There was an ominous silence, then from the midst of the gathering, someone started laughing. The crowd parted and Hector Beltran stepped into view.

Parrish knew the man's face well from their earlier Skype conversations, but even without prior knowledge, he would have had no trouble identifying the man as the leader of the group by virtue of his attire—or more precisely, by his lack thereof. Beltran was almost completely naked, adorned in a cape of brightly color-ed feathers and a strange headdress. His bare chest and arms were marked with an elaborate intaglio of tattoos that resembled scales or feathers of green and red, so that it was hard to tell where the cape ended and the man began.

Beltran was only a few inches taller than Parrish, but the headdress made him look much bigger. He was broader and bulkier than Parrish, too, with swollen biceps and pectoral muscles, as well as puffy cheeks—all classic signs of steroid abuse.

Come to think of it, a lot of these guys look like juicers.

Beltran came forward and clapped him on the arm. *"El Buldog!"* He turned to look at his men. "You heard him. Quit screwing around."

Parrish endured the attention stoically. "I wasn't kidding. The people that hit your facility are already on their way here. If they have a supersonic stealth aircraft, they've probably been cruising around looking for you for the last couple of hours."

"Good. I want them to find me."

"No," Parrish countered, shaking his head. "You want them to find you on *your own terms*. These people are the best of the best. If they find you before we're ready, you can kiss your ass good-bye."

Beltran laughed again and thumped his tattooed chest with a fist. "Maybe we should find out, eh?" He shouted something in the unfamiliar language, and the assembled men thrust their rifles skyward and shouted in unison.

Beltran caught Parrish's look of confusion. "We speak the language of our ancestors, the Nahua people. You would call us Aztecs."

Parrish shrugged. "You can speak in pig-Latin for all I care. I'm just here to do a job."

It was the wrong thing to say. Beltran's eyes flashed with anger and he took a step forward. "Be very careful, *Buldog*," he said, speaking in a soft tone that was even more threatening than his chest-thumping aggression. The roar of crowd noise fell silent, as even those among the group who did not understand English realized that something was happening between their leader and the gringo visitor.

Parrish was faced with a dilemma. If he backed down, appeared contrite, he might smooth the ruffled feathers, but any hope of getting control of the situation would be gone. But if he stood his ground, asserted that he was, at the very least, Beltran's equal, he could very well end up dead.

No guts, no glory.

"I don't need this shit." He turned back toward the Range Rover, fully aware of how futile the display of bravado was.

In the total silence, he had no trouble hearing Beltran's laughter. "I like you, *Buldog*. You got some big brass balls on you."

Parrish stopped, turned slowly. "I meant what I said. I just flew two thousand miles to set this up. We've got a very small window of opportunity, after which our chances of success—of *survival*—begin to fall off dramatically. So let's stop dicking around and get ready."

Beltran advanced again. There was a dangerous gleam in his eyes, and Parrish knew that despite what the man had said, Beltran had not forgiven the perceived insult to his heritage. "Yes," he said in the same low voice. "We must get ready. Come with me." He shouted another command to his men, and a moment later, the gathering began to move.

As the men began to shift out of the way, Parrish got his first good look at his surroundings. As he had surmised, they were indeed outdoors, but he was unprepared for the sight that greeted his eyes.

Instead of an open field, he found himself standing in what appeared to be a courtyard or plaza, surrounded by walls of well-weathered stone. At one end of the plaza, a steep stone stairway rose up, and after a moment's scrutiny, Parrish realized he was looking at a step pyramid. The plaza, pyramid and everything else around him were the ruins of a pre-Columbian civilization—probably Aztec if Beltran's earlier comment was to be believed. In the torchlight, Parrish could see that the flank of the pyramid facing the courtyard was stained with large splotches that glistened wetly in the torchlight.

The men did not ascend the stairs, but instead gathered at the base of the structure, collecting around large clay pots. The smell of cooking food wafted over the plaza, something spicy and sweet—pork in a mole sauce, Parrish decided—and under any other circumstances, he probably would have found it appetizing, but at that exact moment, it just made him feel nausea.

What the hell? These guys are having a midnight snack?

It was all Parrish could do to keep silent as he watched Beltran reach into the pot nearest the staircase. With his bare hands, he plucked out a dripping morsel the size of a golf ball, put it in his mouth with a dramatic flourish and began chewing with almost obscene vigor. "*Buldog*, you should have some."

"I ate on the plane. Look, I really don't mean to offend you and your ancient traditions, but shouldn't you save the victory celebration until after you win?"

"Believe me, we will feast. But this meal is not a celebration. This is a communion with Huitzilopochtli. We share a meal with our god so that he will be in us when we fight our enemies."

Parrish held his tongue. He had known from the outset that Beltran was not somebody who could be reasoned with, but whatever was happening here went beyond mere machismo and obstinacy. The men, all of them, were deep into what could only be described as a religious trance. They attacked the repast with a strange mixture of gusto and reverence, and as they savored their portions, they seemed almost to transform, like something from a superhero movie. Their muscles swelled, some of them actually seemed to grow taller before his eyes. Parrish could almost feel the aggression boiling off their bodies. If he interfered now, there was not a doubt in his mind that the outcome would be fatal.

He shook his head, convinced that there had to be some kind of hallucinogen in the food, or maybe in the smoke from the torches or the cooking fires. Something that he was inhaling for a contact buzz. If Beltran wanted to get his guys all cranked up before the fight, that was none of Parrish's business. His part in this was nearly done.

Beltran shouted something in the Nahuatl tongue, and a moment later the sound of drums filled the courtyard, beating out a fast rhythm. The men continued to eat, but Beltran was evidently finished, for he took hold of one of the torches and motioned for Parrish to join him as he began ascending the steps. Parrish had to jog to catch up to him, and as he stepped across the dark stains on the stairs, he could smell the metallic tang of fresh blood.

They must have slaughtered the pigs up here, Parrish thought, and he was very glad that he hadn't eaten.

The pyramid was not very tall, only about sixty feet high, but Parrish was winded by the time he reached the platform at the top. Beltran was waiting at the entrance to a squat structure. The man led the way into the dark interior with his torch. The room was empty but for a single stone slab—possibly a sacrificial altar, judging by the veritable sea of blood that drenched it. Sitting atop it, looking completely out of place, was a small microwave oven.

"We collected all their phones," Beltran said. "And put them in here, just as you instructed."

Parrish nodded. "The oven is designed to contain electromagnetic radiation, so it's blocking the cellular signals. When your men are in position, we'll open the door and allow the phones to start looking for a network. They'll immediately become visible to anyone looking for them, and anyone with a computer will be able to pinpoint the GPS coordinates."

"Won't they suspect a trap?"

"They might, but it won't matter. They have to go where the signal leads them. Which means you need to decide where you want them to go."

Beltran extended his arms over the altar, palms down. "Right here. They will be offered to Huitzilopochtli."

Parrish tried not to think about what that might mean. "I'll show your men how to use the TOW system I brought. But first, we need to talk about the hostages."

Beltran made a dismissive gesture. "I've taken care of them."

"You were supposed to turn them over to me. That was our deal."

"I don't make deals," Beltran said with a sneer. In the torchlight, with his ritual garments and tattooed body, he looked more like a beast than a man. "You should have figured that out by now, *Buldog.*"

"Where are they? What did you do with—" The chill returned suddenly. His gaze was drawn magnetically to the blood on the altar. It seemed to be moving. The whole room was moving. "What have you done?"

"I told you. I took care of them." And then, with a maniacal grin, Beltran reached for the microwave oven and opened it.

TWENTY-THREE

The Chess Team flew through the sky on their own wings. Unseen and virtually invisible to both the naked eye and radar, they soared like raptors, four miles above the night-dark landscape.

On their previous visit, just twenty-four hours ago, they had HAHO jumped—high-altitude, high-opening—using their parachutes like hang-gliders, cruising several miles to a point near the El Sol facility, but this time they were using a slightly different method to approach the target zone undetected by both the cartel and Mexican air defenses.

The Gryphon Attack Glider Mark II was, King thought, about as close to flying like a super-hero as a person could get. The Gryphon was similar in design to a wingsuit, but it was made of rigid carbon fiber, which provided even more lift and maneuverability at high altitudes. That was a necessity since they each carried nearly a hundred extra pounds of gear and ammunition. The Gryphon had a fall ratio of about three-to-one, which meant that for every foot of vertical descent, they moved three feet closer to their destination.

The blast of frigid air that permeated King's insulated coveralls was like a double-shot of espresso after hours of sitting in the cargo bay of *Crescent II*. Despite his earlier assurance, Aleman had been unable to pin down a location for the hostages before they reached Mexican airspace, so they had diverted to an aerial refueling tanker over the Caribbean Sea to extend their mission time. However, as the stealth transport headed back toward the mainland, the tech expert made good on his promise. A phone belonging to one of the missing tourists had briefly made contact with a cellular tower, giving Aleman a precise GPS fix. There was no guarantee that they would find the hostages there, but the remote area—about fifty miles northeast of Mexico City and more than a hundred miles from the coast—was reason to hope that the phone had merely been overlooked by the kidnappers. Chess Team had immediately started pre-breathing in anticipation of a high-altitude depressurization, while *Crescent* cruised in circles above the drop zone, taking infra-red pictures of the target location.

The real-time aerial surveillance imagery was now super-imposed on the display of King's glasses, a ghostly outline on the ground, some ten miles away, with a bright red dot at the center. The site was in a field, accessible only by a barely discernible road. That connected to an only slightly better dirt track that ran for several miles, before connecting to a paved, but still evidently remote country road. Unlike Mano's compound in Quintana Roo, there was no evidence of human habitation, or more precisely, no recent occupation. The road ended at what appeared to be the ruins of an ancient city, and the red dot marking the location of the GPS signal was centered on a square structure that looked very much like a step pyramid. The nearest modern structure was a small factory complex a few miles away—also evidently abandoned.

Aleman's research verified that the site was not a registered archaeological ruin, which was not altogether a surprise. The region had hosted numerous civilizations in the thousands of years before contact with European explorers. New sites were being discovered all the time by farmers clearing fields, and not all of those farmers were keen on having government officials and scholars tramping around their land—especially those who were engaged in illicit activities. The unregistered sites were also a trove of antiquities that could be sold on the black market, providing additional revenue for the property owners.

Given the reputation of the El Sol cartel, King was not at all surprised that the hostages were being kept in the ruins, but what did concern him was the complete absence of activity. There were no cars, no lights, no patrols roaming the perimeter of the site. That meant either the cartel had moved on, or there was a lot more to the ruins than met the eye.

He picked a spot a full mile to the north of the pyramid and marked it in the virtual display. "Let's put down there," he murmured, knowing the words would be easily heard by the others and that the same yellow marker had appeared in their glasses as well. "That will be our rally point. We'll hump it in nice and slow. Get a feel for the place."

"You think it's a trap?" Bishop asked, putting into words what King and surely the rest of them were already thinking.

"We'll treat it like it is." King said nothing more, but concentrated on the numbers ticking away in the head's-up display. When he was still a thousand feet up and about two miles from the objective, he deployed his parachute.

The nine-celled ram-air chute snapped up out of its pack and filled with air, dragging him abruptly to what felt like a dead stop. He was still sailing through the skies, the taut canopy overhead giving him the power of flight much like the glider, but compared to the rush of free-flight, drifting under the canopy was about as exciting as lounging on a pool float after a ride in a jet boat. The Gryphon, which had only moments before given him the power to soar like an eagle, now felt like an anchor, dragging him earthward.

Using the toggles, he steered toward the designated landing site and corkscrewed around it until the ground was just below his feet. At the last second, he pulled on the toggles again, braking, and came almost to a complete stop in mid-air, just inches above the loose dirt.

As soon as he was down, he quickly hauled in the chute, stuffing it into a nylon pouch, and then he shrugged out of the Gryphon's multi-point harness. Within seconds of touchdown, he was kneeling, readying his FN SCAR-L rifle—a step up in firepower from the more discreet MP5s they had used the night before. He scanned the area for any sign of activity. "Sound off," he said.

One by one, the team checked in with their callsign and the color code: "Green." All had made it down safely and were fully mission capable.

With Queen and Rook providing security, King and the others began deploying the equipment stored in the Gryphons' wings, after which they stacked the gliders along with their chutes and overalls. Bishop rigged the cache with an incendiary grenade, equipped with a multi-function detonator—time delay, anti-tamper and remote activation.

King turned a slow circle, surveying the landscape in all directions. The field appeared to be open range, with large patches of knee-high grass and shrubs that masked the gentle rise and fall of the terrain. The nearest high ground, aside from the pyramid itself, was more than three miles away, too far to be of any use in establishing an overwatch position. "Knight, it looks like you're gonna get to stay with us for a change. Echelon Black, Rook take the lead."

Echelon Black was their own variation on the infantry tactical marching formation. They lined up in order, corresponding to the starting positions their respective chess pieces would have occupied on the game board, separated by a ten-yard interval. At the order to move, Rook headed out, and when he had gone about fifteen paces, Knight started forward, and then Bishop, King and Queen in turn. The formation was ideal for moving across open terrain toward a target since it gave them maximum forward visibility, and put both Rook's machine gun and Knight's sniper rifle at the forefront, ready to lay down suppressive fire in the event of contact. The trade-off was that they would risk greater exposure to enemy forces, but that danger was significantly reduced with their chameleon suits.

"Got a couple of hot spots," Knight reported.

With his implant, equipped with a thermal scope, Knight could see a lot more than the rest of them.

"Tangos?" King asked, employing the common military jargon that could mean either 'terrorists' or 'targets,' depending on the situation.

Knight scanned the terrain silently for a moment. "I can't tell. There's a heat source at the base of that pyramid, but there are too many walls in the way. Too hot to be human though. Might be the coals of a fire."

"Could mean they've already bugged out," Rook said.

"It could," King agreed. He was more concerned by Knight's grim tone, a definite change from just a few minutes earlier when they had all reported green. "But let's just assume that they haven't. We'll hold up a hundred yards out. Stop, look and listen."

They crossed the open ground silently, checking in all directions for any sign of activity, but the field and the ruined city appeared to be abandoned. King was not sure whether to hope that was the case. If the cartel had indeed moved on, then the mission was a bust and their only lead a dead end. But the alternative—an enemy force that was dug in, and perhaps expecting an intervention—might be a lot worse.

They halted just outside the perimeter of the ruins, looking for some indication of what awaited within. A faint smell of wood smoke and cooking meat hung in the air, but there was something else, too: a familiar musky odor.

"I know that smell," Rook said. "I don't think I'll ever be able to forget it."

"Boars," King confirmed. "Could be a wild herd roaming nearby."

"Not with our luck."

King was inclined to agree. "Knight, you got anything on thermal?"

"Nothing new. If there's anything living here, it's covered up."

King weighed the assessment for a few seconds. "This isn't right."

Deep Blue joined the conversation. "*Crescent* is about ninety minutes to bingo, but that doesn't factor in pick up."

King knew that the process of landing the VTOL used a lot of fuel, which meant that if they couldn't find the hostages and get them to the pick up zone soon—an hour at the outside—*Crescent* would have to leave for another refueling rendezvous.

"We can't leave without at least checking," Queen said. "Even if they're gone, they might have left a clue to where they're headed."

"It's your call, King," Deep Blue said.

"Let's walk the perimeter. Knight, if it flickers, I want to know about it."

They resumed their trek, maintaining a hundred-yard standoff distance from the outermost edge of the ruins. The circuit took another fifteen minutes but yielded no meaningful results. The site was completely dark.

King's gut was telling him to walk away, but he shared Queen's earlier sentiment. They had come too far to just walk away without knowing for sure. "All right, we're going in. Castle and move in, single file."

Just as in chess, 'castle' meant that Rook and King would switch places. In the game it was a tactic designed to protect the king and get the rook into the open, but for the team, this maneuver made

King the point man. Standard military doctrine discouraged a unit commander from taking point for the simple reason that, if the shit hit the fan, he would be the first to die. The rest of the unit would be left leaderless at a time when leadership was needed most. But with their experience and the long-distance guidance from Deep Blue, that possibility was less of a consideration for the Chess Team. Still, it took the team a moment to grasp what King was telling them to do. He didn't wait, but started forward into the ruins.

Despite the complete absence of heat signatures, King scanned each structure he passed. The broken walls showed no sign of any recent activity, but there were enough of them to form a veritable maze, which was almost certainly the intent of the city's original architects. Fortunately, *Crescent*'s aerial surveillance revealed the most direct route to the center, but as King pushed deeper into the labyrinth, the distinctive animal scent grew stronger as did his sense of foreboding.

When he entered an open courtyard near the center of the site, a short distance away he could see twin spots of brightness near the base of the pyramid—the dying embers of the fire Knight had earlier spotted. The pyramid itself was a steeply built succession of tiers, with a staircase running up the middle of the side facing the courtyard. King did not fail to notice the dark smear that stained the steps, and despite the lack of color in the night vision display, he knew exactly what it was.

He had seen enough.

"We're done here. Blue, have *Crescent* waiting for us at the rally point. Queen, take us out." King's tone indicated that the matter was not open to debate.

There was none. Queen set a brisk pace that brought them out of the ruins in less than a minute. King could see the icon marking their goal, the designated pick up zone where they had cached the Gryphon wings, two miles out. It had taken them more than half an hour to make a cautious, stealthy approach. At their current pace, they would cross the distance in half that time.

Too long, King thought. *If this is a trap, we're already in it.* "Double time."

Despite their heavy combat loads, there was not a single protesting groan. Queen broke into a near-sprint and everyone else followed suit, matching her pace.

Perhaps because he was already overloaded on adrenaline, King didn't even flinch when he heard the sound, like the report of a small pistol, echoing across the field. He shouted for everyone to get down, unnecessarily since the others had reacted as quickly as he had. Heeding his own advice, he dove for cover and craned his head around to identify the source of the noise. Something streaked across the night sky, a bright red star, falling from the heavens.

A signal flare.

"I'm detecting movement!" Deep Blue sounded uncharacteristically frantic.

"Where?"

"Everywhere."

As if on cue, a shaft of light appeared in the field off to their left. As the glasses compensated for the sudden brightness, King saw that there were actually two lights, set close together. Headlights.

The beams tilted forward until they were parallel with the ground, partially obscured by the gently undulating terrain, but there was no question that the vehicle was moving. Another pair of lights stabbed into the sky to the right. In the tactical overlay, the vehicles appeared as yellow spots—one on either side and four more rolling up from behind the pyramid.

"The fuck did they come from?" Rook gasped. "Knight, how did you miss those assholes?"

Deep Blue supplied the answer, speaking quickly. "They were dug in, covered with thermal blankets and radar scattering camouflage nets."

King cut in. "Blue, we need *Crescent*. Right here, right now!"

"I do not think they know where we are," Bishop said. She sounded hesitant, as if afraid of stating the obvious.

"Damn it, she's right," Queen said. "We're friggin' invisible."

King stared at the moving dots. While they were definitely converging on the general area where the team was moving, there was no sense of concerted effort. Rather, they seemed to be meandering, sweeping back and forth to flush out their prey. The fact that the vehicles had appeared was proof enough that their presence had been detected, but now with their chameleon camouflage, they were, as Queen had so eloquently observed, invisible.

In the back of his mind, King turned over Deep Blue's hasty assessment of the enemy's tactics. The cartel soldiers had dug concealed fighting positions, hidden themselves under foil blankets and camouflages nets. "They knew we were coming."

"Do you think?" Rook snapped.

"No, I mean they were expecting *us*." Rook had no answer for that. "They knew how to hide from our night vision, thermal... everything."

"We weren't exactly subtle last night," Queen said.

King watched the dots moving in what appeared to be an erratic fashion. One of them was going to pass within fifty yards of their position. He trained his carbine on the approaching headlights. "Time to find out just how well our cloaking devices work. Hold your fire until I give the word."

The glasses easily adjusted for the brilliance of the headlights and the surrounding darkness, revealing two figures in the cab and four more in the bed. The latter were facing out in different directions, sweeping the landscape with their rifles but evidently unable to find a target. As they passed, one of the men seemed to look right at King, but his gaze did not linger. The truck abruptly veered north and headed away, continuing the search.

"All right, here's what we're going to do. Blue, bring *Crescent* in on our position. When our ride shows up, everyone is going to have a pretty good idea where we are, so be ready to lay down suppressive fire. Bishop, stand by to blow the cache. Maybe that will buy us a few seconds."

There was a chorus of affirmative replies, but the only one that mattered to King was Deep Blue's, informing him that the stealth transport would be on the ground and ready to pick them up in two minutes. He had a feeling it would be a very long two minutes.

Crescent came down fast and hard, but its chameleon camouflage made it nearly invisible, even with the glasses. King was only able to judge its location and distance because it, like the team, was tagged in the virtual environment. Unfortunately, even though *Crescent* was outfitted with an experimental acoustic noise-canceling system to muffle the sound of its turbines, there was no concealing the rush of wind created by its downdraft, which even from a few thousand feet up, sounded like a tornado. The last semblance of stealth disappeared when the downward blast stirred up an enormous cloud of dust all around the team's location.

"Bishop, now."

There was a flash of intensely brilliant light almost a mile away, followed a few seconds later by the strident hiss of the thermate core spiking to a temperature of nearly four thousand degrees. It was impossible to tell if the appearance of an artificial sun on the horizon had sufficiently distracted the roving cartel soldiers from the tumult caused by *Crescent*'s impending arrival, but it was a human reflex to turn in the direction of bright light. Up close, the blaze would be bright enough to do permanent damage to the optic nerve of anyone staring at it, and even from a distance, it would effectively destroy a person's night vision for a good twenty minutes.

The downdraft intensified as *Crescent* descended lower still. The dust storm completely obscured King's field of view, but the swarm of trucks remained visible in the virtual landscape, ghostly images generated by the quantum computer at Endgame, using the feed from *Crescent*'s cameras. The vehicles were definitely turning in the direction of the disturbance.

"Open fire!"

Even before he finished giving the command, Rook unleashed the 240B, spraying the nearest truck with a five-second long burst. King concentrated his fire on a different vehicle, aiming at what he hoped was the space right above the left headlight. A moment later, the truck veered sharply and started rolling. He caught a glimpse of bodies flying through the air before his attention switched to another truck. It was about half a mile away, outside the effective range of the SCAR, but only just. He kept the truck in the aiming circle and waited for it to get closer.

There was a flash at the back of the truck, and for a fleeting moment, he thought perhaps Knight had put a round in its gas tank. Then he saw a butterfly-shaped flame race away from the truck and realized that the flash had been a different kind of explosion: a missile launch.

There was a harsh roar as the pilot aboard *Crescent* took immediate evasive action, revving the turbines faster than the compensation rate of the sound-dampening device. The plane started to simultaneously rise and pull away. There was a series of loud pops and a burst of light directly overhead, as the automated defense system on the plane deployed chaff countermeasures designed to confuse heat-seeking and radar-guided missiles. The missile, however, continued on course, moving almost lazily across the distance.

Even though it was little more than a point of light in his display, King knew what the missile was. "It's a TOW!" he shouted, and despite the fact that the truck was still more than five hundred yards out, he opened fire.

The TOW—Tube-launched, Optically-tracked, Wire-guided— anti-tank missile did not rely on a sophisticated internal guidance system. Instead, it was guided by the person who fired it, via a thermal tracking sight connected to the launch tube and a string of wire that could extend more than two miles. The TOW had the reputation of being 'low and slow,' perfect for hitting stationary or slow moving ground targets. It was not designed to engage aerial targets, but *Crescent*'s VTOL capability made it extremely vulnerable to such an attack.

They knew, King thought again, maintaining a steady rate of fire at the truck.

There was no way to jam the communication between the missile and its operator, but to hit a target, especially a *moving* target, the TOW's sights had to remain on the target at all times. That was the system's greatest weakness; once fired, the operator had to remain exposed for the duration of flight. If King could distract the operator, cause him to lose his fix on the target, even for a second...

There was a hissing whoosh as the missile passed overhead. King looked up, an involuntary reflex. *Crescent* was moving away, starting to pick up speed.

But not fast enough.

TWENTY-FOUR
Endgame, New Hampshire

Cold fear slammed through Deep Blue as the feed from *Crescent II* went dark.

No. Not possible.

But it was not only possible, it was the harsh reality. The plane and its two pilots, the team's salvation, was gone, and with it, his ability to see what was happening on the ground.

"King, report." The request sounded impotent in his ears. What could King possibly say, except to confirm the obvious, and what then? What could he do to fix this?

King did not answer him directly, but instead shouted a command to the others. "Fall back to the ruins!"

The ruins? It was the obvious place to regroup, obvious to their enemy as well, but what other choice was there?

He turned to Aleman who sat beside him in the command room, looking as devastated as he felt. "Lew, you're their eyes. Keep them alive until I can get them some help."

He had no idea what shape that 'help' would take. There were no contingencies for something like this. *Crescent* was their only dedicated long-range air asset, and even if he could wrangle another military aircraft or scramble some close-air support, it would take time, perhaps several hours. Since the death of General Michael Keasling, it had been necessary to conduct all dealings with the military through an elaborate system of back-channels, and those wheels turned slowly. He considered involving the Mexican authorities, but even absent the political firestorm that would create, a coordinated response would take time that his people didn't have.

Aleman shook off his paralysis and bent over his keyboard. "I'm patching in Knight's thermal feed. That should increase your visibility until you can get clear of the dust cloud."

Deep Blue saw the immediate change on the wall-mounted plasma screen, but the effect was negligible. The landscape of the virtual environment was filled with blobs of heat, the burning debris of *Crescent* falling from the sky like a meteor shower. Nevertheless, the team was moving, and that was something at least.

A shrill noise startled his already jangled nerves. It was the security hotline phone on the console. *Damn it!* He stabbed a finger at the speaker button. "Whatever it is, deal with it."

"Uh, sir, I think we have an incursion." The male voice, quavering with uncertainty, was another surprise. *Where's Anna?*

He recalled that he had sent Beck to North Carolina to provide security for Sara Fogg. The voice belonged to White One, Scott McCarter, Beck's second-in-command.

McCarter's words finally sank in. "Incursion?"

"A whole bunch of black SUVs just rolled into the campground. They've got federal motor-pool plates. DOJ."

Before Deep Blue could reply, Aleman chimed in. "He's right. And that's not the worst of it. There are four Black Hawks headed this way. Five minutes out."

Deep Blue shook his head, trying unsuccessfully to will away this emerging crisis. The Black Hawks were probably just National Guardsmen on a training exercise. McCarter had misinterpreted the significance of the SUVs.

They were expecting us.'

King's shout still rang in his ears, but now it took on a new urgency. Were these disparate crises connected?

"They're inside the campground," McCarter said, his anxiety rising. "On the road that leads to Post One. Should we engage?"

Post One had been one of the two original entrances to the facility back when it had been Manifold Alpha. In the days that had followed their takeover of the site, Deep Blue had ordered the old entrances sealed, and they had installed new concealed entrances to facilitate movement in and out of Endgame. The significance of this news was not lost on Deep Blue. Someone knew about Manifold Alpha, and they knew how to get into it, or at least they had access to the old plans.

He turned to the other person in the room, Domenick Boucher, who likewise sat stunned at the console. "Dom, what's your gut say?"

Endgame had been hit before, and the possibility that it might be targeted by law enforcement—Homeland Security or some other agency—had always been at the top of Deep Blue's list of concerns. As CIA director, Boucher had helped establish a monitoring protocol so that they would not be taken unaware— listening to inter-agency chatter, eavesdropping on official communiqués, but it was impossible to cover all the bases.

Boucher swallowed and sat up in his chair. "This isn't a coincidence. Someone is making a move against us."

Deep Blue resisted the urge to accuse his friend of stating the obvious, but he needed more. "Who? This didn't come out of nowhere."

Boucher shook his head helplessly.

Long before he was Deep Blue, before he was the President of the United States, Tom Duncan had been a soldier, an Army Ranger. In his earliest days of military training, his instructors had drilled into him the procedure for reacting to contact with the enemy.

Seek cover and return fire. Locate the enemy position, and launch a counter-attack.

The order of the response was important. Immediate action had to be taken, even before the threat was identified, to overcome the paralyzing effect of the ambush.

Ambush.

That was the only way to describe what was happening. A two-stage assault. The trap in Mexico had hit with the devastating force of a roadside IED, stunning them all and leaving them vulnerable to the second phase—the raid on Endgame.

Endgame was by no means defenseless. There were passive and active anti-intruder measures at each of the entrances, including those which had been sealed, and an armory full of weapons, which the ten-man strong White Team—tasked with security and logistics—could use to repel anyone who made it past the doors.

Yet this was not a squad of mercenaries hired by an enemy, not Ridley's gang of dishonorably discharged ex-military psychos. The men in the SUVs were American law enforcement agents.

They were the good guys.

Seek cover and return fire.

King was already doing that in Mexico. The team had taken out at least two of the trucks in the moments before *Crescent*'s destruction. They were outnumbered, but still held a considerable tactical advantage.

Let King do his job, he told himself. *And you do yours.*

Immediate action.

He located the emergency lockdown button on the console. When the site had been Manifold Alpha, conducting hazardous genetic research, the underground complex had been equipped with thick steel bio-safety doors that would instantly seal off sections of the facility. The doors would keep any intruder out, but they would also have the effect of trapping anyone inside, at least temporarily.

Not yet.

Instead, he turned back to the security phone. The indicator light showed that McCarter was still on the line. He took a breath. "White One, initiate Desperado. I say again, *Desperado.*"

TWENTY-FIVE
Manteo, North Carolina

Despite the late hour—or rather the early hour, since it was already after four a.m.—and the fact that she was dead tired, Sara did not sleep. She was afraid that if she slept, she might transform into something like the poor wretches in the isolation ward.

She knew, of course, if she had indeed been infected by the bite, the transformation would happen whether she was conscious or not, but at least she would be able to document the process, providing important data for the next scientist sent to investigate the outbreak. But aside from a perversely contradictory mix of bleary-eyed fatigue and gut-churning anxiety, she felt perfectly healthy.

To stay busy—and awake—she had run a few tests on the blood sample, checking for abnormal acidity, excess protein and microbial agents. The results were irregular, but not conclusive, making it impossible to separate cause from effect. She would need more blood, from all three patients, to run a full battery of tests, and there was no guarantee that even that would yield results. Unlike in movies, there was no machine that could look at a specimen and immediately identify the cause of an illness. It was a process of elimination, looking for specific antibodies and chemical reactions.

After her interview with Ellen Dare, she had ventured back into the isolation ward, this time using the same precautions as the rest of the hospital staff, visually confirming what Dr. Foster had already told her. All three patients were suffering from the same effect; they were all wendigos.

In the absence of any other official diagnosis, she had begun using the term in her notes. It would not have been her first choice, but she had to call it something. Hopefully, further research would give her the actual scientific name for the disorder, but if it was something new, then following medical tradition, the disease would be named for her. Wendigo Disease was preferable to Fogg's Syndrome.

If this had happened next week, it would have been called Sigler's Disease, she thought, with just a hint of regret.

She had no baseline comparison for Haley Stephens or the paramedic, Doug Stovall, but something had definitely changed with Jason Harris. The deformity had become more pronounced, particularly in the skull, where the bony growth had almost completely covered his eyes. His skin also seemed more substantial, no longer paper-thin and translucent, but thicker, like animal hide, and pale white. Although Sara's mind balked at the idea, she could think of only one variable that might account for the change.

Jason Harris had tasted her blood.

Her thoughts kept coming back to Ellen Dare's ominous declaration about the Lost Colony.

There was a well-established link between cannibalism and the spread of certain diseases. The most widely-known example was Kuru, which had plagued the Fore tribe of Papua New Guinea until the 1950s, when scientists connected the disease to the tribe's custom of funerary cannibalism. The practice, as well as the disease itself, had been effectively stopped, but there were other ways for the pathogen—a prion that caused transmissible spongiform encephalopathy—to be spread. A similar prion was responsible for Mad Cow disease, and just as with Kuru, it had been spread, albeit unwittingly, through cannibalism, specifically the addition of ground-up animal protein to the food supply for beef cattle.

Sara would have been inclined to dismiss the cannibalism theory entirely if not for the change in Jason Harris's status. Just a taste of her blood had evidently stimulated the continuation of his metamorphosis. But while the craving for human flesh was evidently a symptom, Sara was hard-pressed to identify it as a cause. There was no reason to believe that any of the three patients had been practicing cannibals.

The one thing that all three did have in common was the archaeological site, and if Ellen was right about the curse on the Lost Colony, then perhaps the same contagion that had wiped them out was still extant in the environment.

But why had it not affected Ellen and the others who had been at the site? Or any of the thousands of other people who had tramped across Roanoke Island in the more than four hundred years since the colonists had vanished?

There was another piece to this puzzle, some other variable that she was missing.

"How goes the search?" a voice from the door inquired. It was Dr. Foster.

"I'm not sure," Sara turned to meet his gaze, and as she did, she saw something that almost made her burst out laughing. Foster's beard was littered with crumbs and the tips of his mustache were dotted with a dark red substance.

"If you're ready for a break, there's some food in the doctor's lounge."

"I see that. I didn't know the cafeteria was open."

"It's not. We ordered out. There's a new barbecue place that's open twenty-four-seven. Mr. Pig. They deliver. We all voted and decided to give it a try. Paid with a credit card and had the delivery guy leave the food outside the front door, because of the quarantine. There's a couple of sandwiches left."

Sara rarely ate out but she was familiar with the new chain. Their stores were popping up everywhere, and they seemed poised to give the industry's giants a run for their money. "Is it any good?"

"Depends on how hungry you are. Wouldn't be my first choice, but I've had worse."

Sara glanced back at her computer and its open Internet browser. She had spent the last ninety minutes combing through a variety of web pages and historical databases, learning everything she could about the Lost Colony and wendigos. It had been a fruitless task, filled with empty speculation, sensationalism, half-baked theories and outright fantasy.

"Maybe some brain-fuel is just what I need. Or at least another cup of coffee."

As she stood and started toward the door, she felt the strange electric sensation at the back of her throat again. *It has to be a smell*, she decided, *something in the air that my nose isn't picking up.*

That happened to her a lot. As a child, she had been diagnosed with Sensory Processing Disorder, an unusual affliction that caused her brain to misinterpret common stimuli, sometimes turning visual inputs into strange smells or turning sounds into physical sensations. It was why she hated traveling by air and generally preferred to avoid exposure to unusual environments whenever possible, two traits that made her job as an infectious disease investigator interesting, to say the least. The biggest challenge was her inability to immediately reconcile a new sensation with its cause. The strange twinge at the back of her throat was probably triggered by something in the air, but it could just as easily be the imperceptible flicker of the fluorescent light bulbs overhead or the ambient hum of the ventilation system.

She followed Foster to the doctor's lounge, where the remains of the meal were spread on the table. Two nurses were seated there, browsing their smartphones and evidently already done eating. One of the Sheriff's deputies was napping on a cot. Sara bypassed the table and headed instead to the coffee urn.

"No guarantees with what's in that pot," Foster declared.

"As long as it's got caffeine," she replied, decanting a stream of the brown liquid into a Styrofoam cup. It didn't look or smell too horrible, but she added a couple of packets of sugar, just in case.

Before she could sit down, the other deputy stepped into the room. "Ah... Dr. Fogg, you've got a visitor."

"A visitor?" Sara raised her eyebrows in surprise. *Who knows I'm here?*

"Asked for you by name," the deputy said with a shrug. "Pretty thing. She's at the ER door. I wouldn't let her in, what with the quarantine and all."

"That's fine, thank you." She turned to Foster. "Guess I'll be right back."

"I'll come with you."

His sudden curiosity about her visitor was faintly annoying, but there was no reason to dissuade him. Instead, she took advantage of the short walk to review the situation. "I don't think we're looking at a contagious illness," she said. "But until we can positively rule it out, let's keep the quarantine in effect. No one in or out of the hospital. That includes me."

"We still have about a dozen patients on the floor, and taking care of them is going to stretch our resources a bit. Can you give me a timetable for how long this lockdown will last?"

"No, I can't." The answer was sharper than she intended, but she had long ago learned the foolishness of making assurances that couldn't be backed up. "It will take as long as it takes. We can't risk letting this get out, so until I'm one hundred percent certain, you're closed for business."

She was spared further discussion on the matter by their arrival at the double glass doors at the Emergency Room entrance. A slim but athletic looking young woman with long brown hair, was pacing anxiously on the sidewalk outside.

It took Sara a moment to recognize the woman, whom she had only ever known in the context of the Endgame headquarters in New Hampshire. Knight's girlfriend. "Anna?"

What is someone from Endgame doing here? She felt her heart skip a beat as she contemplated the possible answers to that question.

The woman whirled at the sound of her name and then peered through the glass. "Dr. Fogg. Is everything all right?"

Anna Beck's voice was muffled by the thick pane, and Sara knew hers probably was as well. She stepped closer. "Why are you here? Is something wrong? Is Jack okay?"

"He's fine, ma'am," Beck replied. "He's the one that asked me to come here. He thought you might need some back-up."

Sara's relief instantly turned to irritation. "Oh, is that what he thought?"

Why, that patronizing son of a—

She stopped herself. While it was true that her fiancé had, of late, become almost suffocating in his desire to protect, not just her but everyone in his life, this was one instance where his interference would actually come in handy. "As a matter of fact, there is a way you can help out."

Beck was not listening. Her gaze was fixed on Sara's hand, on the bandage that now covered the place where Harris had bitten her. "Are you injured, ma'am?"

"It's nothing. And stop calling me 'ma'am.'" She put on her most officious face. "Do you have a phone?"

Beck reached into a pocket and took hers out.

"I'm going to text you a location. I need you to drive out there and have a look around. Look for anything out of the ordinary."

"With all due respect, Dr. Fogg, I was sent here to make sure you stay safe, not run errands."

"Don't call me that either. My name is Sara. We're practically family. And you know as well as I do that Jack is just being overprotective. You know how men are."

"That may be true, but I have my orders. I'd be happy to drive you out there."

"That won't work," she said, trying to sound casual. "The hospital is under quarantine."

"Quarantine? You mean you *can't* leave?" Beck's tone now sounded both concerned and accusatory, and eerily like Jack's. Her eyes dropped to the bandage again. "Have you been exposed to something?"

"Occupational hazard. But don't worry. Exposure doesn't mean infection, and so far I'm not symptomatic.

"You've only been here a few hours," Beck pointed out.

Sara realized that she was going to have to try a different tack with the woman, but before she could figure out exactly what that would mean, a shrill noise pierced the air behind her. She whirled around just in time to see a misshapen figure emerge from the corridor.

There was no question that it was a person who had undergone the wendigo transformation—hairless, transparent skin stretched over unnaturally lengthened bones, eyes sunken into the malformed skull, a jagged row of teeth. Sara had only seen the infected patients laying down, strapped to a hospital bed, so she was unprepared for just how much height the transformation had added. Even hunched over, the thing's back was almost scraping against the ceiling tiles. Then she noticed something else, as well.

Tangled around the stretched torso was a twisted piece of blue fabric. Sara recognized it as part of a set of the scrubs the nursing staff wore, and she immediately understood that this was not one of the three patients that had been brought in earlier, but rather one of the hospital staff.

One of the nurses had changed into a wendigo. The infection was spreading.

She barely had time to process the thought before the creature's head turned in her direction, and with a maniacal howl, it charged.

CR T N

DESPERADO

TWENTY-SIX
Mexico

Parrish felt nothing for the crew of the stealth plane. He felt no sense of success at having accomplished the mission he had been given, no elation at the death of an enemy—no surprise there, since the crew of the plane were not *his* enemy—but neither did he feel any regret. The men were soldiers, just as he had once been, and soldiers sometimes got killed for no good reason, sacrificed like pawns on a chessboard.

But maybe the real reason he felt nothing as he watched the expanding cloud of smoke and fire, and a moment later, heard the boom of the TOW missile—the weapon he had supplied for this very purpose—detonating and tearing the plane in half, was that he was still in shock from Beltran's revelation.

I took care of them.

Parrish knew exactly what that meant. Beltran had killed the hostages. No, not just killed...he had sacrificed them, ripped out their hearts on an altar to a god that had been forgotten more than four hundred years earlier. Forty-six people who had woken up with plans to see the sites of Mexico City, murdered, mutilated. All because of Parrish's plan.

We need to goad them, he had told the cartel leader, just twelve hours earlier. *Take Americans hostage, threaten to kill them in twenty-four hours if your demands aren't met. The President will have to take action, but he can't admit his involvement in what happened last night, so he will have to send the same team back in.*

Beltran was not supposed to kill them, though. Once the president's secret soldiers were dead, then America's champion, the redoubtable Senator Marrs, would take credit for orchestrating the release of the hostages, simultaneously saving the day and destroying his political enemies. Everyone would get what they wanted: Beltran would have his revenge, Marrs would have the glory and Parrish would have a chit from the next President of the United States.

Deal with it, he told himself. *You like a challenge. Well here's the mother of all challenges: Try to get out of this alive.*

Beltran had shown no hostility toward him since he had insulted the cartel leader's heritage. Maybe it was some kind of sick cat-and-mouse game, or maybe Beltran just liked having an audience.

Scratch that. No maybe about it.

Beltran pounded him on the shoulder and pointed at the fireball, as it settled to the ground. He then pumped his fist triumphantly. "See? That's what I do to *pendejos* who mess with me."

There was a veiled threat in his words, but Parrish just nodded. Beltran returned his attention to his binoculars and scanned the flaming debris. "Where are they? I don't see them."

Parrish was not surprised. Although he and Beltran had a good vantage point—concealed under camouflage netting atop the pyramid—it was simply too dark to see anything, especially with ordinary binoculars. What little light there was, from the trucks' headlights and from the burning wreckage of the plane, created a tapestry of impenetrable shadows. Nevertheless, Parrish had a feeling that, even in broad daylight, the American commando unit would be hard to spot. They were using some kind of very sophisticated camouflage that made them almost impossible to target. The plane had been using a similar system, but Parrish had found a way to defeat it.

"Tell your men to look for them with the TOW system."

"You only brought one missile," Beltran complained.

"It's a thermal aiming scope," Parrish explained patiently. "You'll be able to spot their body heat, even if they're concealed."

Beltran gave another whoop of triumph and then relayed the message using a walkie-talkie. Now that the engagement had begun, there was no reason to maintain radio silence. On the field below, the vehicles bearing Beltran's men were lining up in preparation to make a slow sweep through the crash site, pushing the American force into the ruins, where Beltran would be able to spring his trap and exact his bloody revenge.

Parrish felt nothing about that; it was just the job. But there was a sick feeling in the pit of his stomach when he thought about what would come after.

TWENTY-SEVEN

Knight showed them the way out.

Not literally of course. He could barely see anything through the dust and smoke, which not only obscured the camera built into his glasses, but also got into his good eye, stinging and abrading it. Even when he squinted through narrowly slitted eyelids, he couldn't see anything. His implant however was impervious to the environmental conditions, and its thermal capabilities could look right through the cloud. While neither he nor the others could actually see that image, Lewis Aleman, was able to use it to talk them out of the miasma.

They had only just avoided being caught in the firestorm of *Crescent II*'s destruction. Because the aircraft had been attempting evasive maneuvers in the moments before the missile detonation, it had veered off a short distance—less than a hundred yards—before being blown apart. While they had not been smashed under the falling wreckage, they nevertheless felt the pummeling force of the blast wave and had been engulfed in a storm of debris, smoke and burning jet fuel.

As they moved out of the blast zone, Knight tentatively opened his eye. The residue of burning chemicals stung, but it was nothing compared to the all-too-familiar spike of pain that shot through his skull as the projected images began streaming into his retinas.

Getting killed might be preferable to this, he thought, not for the first time. Unfortunately, it wasn't just his life on the line.

"There," Aleman shouted in his ears. "There's something on the pyramid."

Knight had spied the bright spot a moment before Aleman spoke; probably a person concealed under a space blanket to minimize their heat signature. "I see it," he growled, dropping to a knee and aiming his rifle at the indistinct target.

"Hold your fire," King advised. "If we start shooting, they'll be able to figure out where we are. We need to get to a better defensive position."

Knight lowered the weapon and continued forward with the team. As they moved into the open, he glanced back and saw that the four vehicles had lined up on the far side of the crash site. They were no longer moving randomly, but appeared to be advancing in a methodical sweep.

"They're pushing us into the ruins," Queen said. "They already know where we are, and they want us in there."

"Lew," King said, "is our camouflage still working?"

"It checks, but remember, you're not totally invisible."

"We can't let them catch us in the open, but Queen is right. We need a third option."

"Split up," Rook said. "If they follow us, we'll know they can see us."

Knight was inclined to agree with the suggestion, but after a few seconds of consideration, King vetoed it. "Negative. The ruins may be a trap, but they're also our best option for a defensive position. Lew, show us the top-down view."

Ghostly lines appeared in the virtual display, marking not only the position of the advancing picket line but also the maze-like path through of the ancient city. A blue dot appeared above a square shape at the edge of the ruins off to their right. "Go there," King said. "Double time."

As they started to run, the noise of multiple rifle reports and the distinctive zip of bullets creasing the air around them seemed to indicate that the enemy was zeroing in on their position. The trucks were still a hundred yards away but picking up speed as they veered to the right, following the course King had chosen for them.

"I think they can see us," Rook said, matter-of-factly. "So much for technology."

"I will give them something else to think about," Bishop said, slightly out of breath. "Frag out."

Knight glanced over just as Bishop hurled a small spherical object in the direction of the nearest truck. The grenade followed a low arc, traveling nearly forty yards before disappearing into the grass.

Knight looked forward and kept running, confident that they were outside the kill radius, but something in his last glimpse of the pursuers nagged at the back of his mind. There was something about one of the trucks that had begged a second look.

There was a flash, followed a millisecond later by a resonant boom and an overpressure wave that socked him in the gut and did nothing good for the pounding in his skull. Still, his spirits lifted a little as he saw in the top-down view that the truck nearest to the grenade blast had stopped its relentless advance. A quick glance back confirmed that the vehicle was indeed out of the fight. The blast had peeled back its hood and a geyser of steam was pouring from the engine.

A moment later, they reached the spot King had designated as their defensive position. Although the ruin looked like a building on the map, up close it was little more than the outline of the structure it had once been. The broken walls reached no higher than Knight's knees, and there were huge gaps between the sections that still stood. Still, the old stone would stop a bullet and give them something to duck behind as they made their stand.

As he dropped down behind the wall, Rook gave a hoot of triumph. "Bishop for the win. I'll say one thing: You don't throw like a girl."

"You'll pay for that," Queen said.

"Promises, promises."

Knight ignored the banter and scanned the other trucks, which had broken formation following the explosion, but they were continuing their charge. He was not sure exactly what he was looking for, but then he saw it again. A dark spot, like a shadow, seemed to hover over the bed of one truck, partially shrouding the men riding behind the cab. The effect was most pronounced in thermal view; the shadow seemed to be absorbing the body heat of the passengers.

Thermal view, Knight realized with a start. The shadow was absorbing heat because it was freezing cold. "King, they've got a thermal scope. A big one. Cryo-cooled."

"Shit," King said. The curse seemed to be self-directed. "Of course they do. That was a TOW missile that took out *Crescent*."

Although he was not completely read up on the TOW, Knight quickly made the connection. The TOW's optical guidance system incorporated thermal imaging, which had allowed its operator to home in on *Crescent*'s turbine exhaust. While the cartel fighters evidently did not have a second missile, they were using the launcher to detect the team's body heat. Unlike infra-red night vision, a cryogenically cooled scope could detect very minor differences in temperature, but to do so, the device had to be kept very cold at all times, which used an enormous amount of energy and made it extremely cumbersome. When Aleman had designed Knight's implant, he had managed to partially overcome this limitation by using an experimental graphene superconductor, but that technology was still in its infancy. Still, Knight's thermal view was vastly outclassed by the system the enemy was using.

"Well, that explains how they can see us," King went on. "Where is it?"

"Middle truck. In the bed."

"How did a bunch of drug thugs score a piece of hardware like that?" Rook asked, unfolding the bipod legs of his 240B. Before anyone could answer, he strafed the designated vehicle with 7.62mm rounds.

The cold spot fragmented as the bullets slammed into the truck, throwing up little blooms of heat energy. One of the rounds hit the coolant tank, releasing a fog of super-cooled air that quickly boiled away to nothingness.

"You got him," Knight reported, between bursts.

"So they can't see us anymore," Queen remarked, "but now they know exactly where we are."

"A simple thank you will suffice," Rook retorted, shifting to another target.

King's stern voice silenced any further argument. "Queen, Bishop. Watch our six. Knight, do we still have a peeping tom on that pyramid?"

Knight turned his gaze toward the apex of the monument, but there was no longer any indication that the observer was still in place. "Negative."

"One less thing to worry about," Rook muttered, and let lead fly. The remaining trucks had stopped less than a hundred yards from their position, the men inside leaping out and throwing themselves flat to avoid the onslaught. The virtual targeting system marked them each, faster than a human eye could; twelve in all, though there was no way to know if all of the enemy were accounted for.

They had whittled the attacking force down to an almost two-to-one margin. Knight would have felt better about that if not for two things: the fact that the cartel had managed to blow *Crescent II* out of the sky, and Deep Blue's ominous report that Endgame was under siege.

Deal with the immediate problem, he told himself, sweeping the flanks of the pyramid with the muzzle of the CheyTac, and gritting his teeth against the relentless pounding in his skull. There was still no sign of any activity from within the ancient complex. Knight wondered now if perhaps the earlier sighting had been an animal or something equally innocuous.

"Rook, if it's not already too late," King said. "Try to leave one of those vehicles intact. My ankle still hurts, and I'd prefer not to walk out of here."

Rook hummed guiltily. "I think that ship has already sailed. But if it's any consolation, these guys can't shoot for shit."

Knight had noticed that as well. Despite knowing exactly where the team was situated, the sporadic incoming fire was not accompanied by the sound of bullets striking stone. The cartel soldiers evidently had exceptionally poor aim.

Unless they're just trying to keep us pinned down, he realized. *Or they're afraid of hitting their buddies who are sneaking up from behind.*

The latter possibility seemed extremely likely, and Knight was just about to tell King that when he felt the first tremor rise up from the paving stones under foot.

"What the—?"

The floor gave an abrupt heave, and Knight was pitched headlong toward Queen and Bishop, who had likewise been knocked off their feet, but instead of landing on hard stone, he felt the floor give way beneath him, and then he was falling again.

He plummeted into an unseen Stygian darkness for what felt like an absurdly long interval of time, before gravity at last hammered him against the unyielding anvil of stone below. The impact left him dazed for a moment, how long, he couldn't say, but shouted voices—King, Rook and Aleman—brought him back to the surface. He gaped like a fish, trying unsuccessfully to draw breath.

Got my wind knocked out. Is that the worst of it?

He did not dare to hope that he had been that lucky, but if he had broken any bones, he was too numb to feel them. He straightened his glasses and looked around to find Queen and Bishop also picking themselves up off the floor.

The floor of what?

He glanced up and saw an irregular hole, nearly a dozen feet overhead, and peering down into it, the faces of Rook and King. He opened his mouth, intending to tell them that they were all okay—not a lie exactly, just unconfirmed wishful thinking—and to stay focused on the immediate threat topside. But no sound was forthcoming, so he had to settle for a wave off.

He finally caught his breath and was rewarded with a nose full of dust and the smell of high explosives residue. He heard Queen coughing—a good sign, since it meant she was still breathing—and he ventured across the debris-strewn floor to her side.

"I'm okay," she rasped. "Help Bishop."

Bishop was already on her feet, waving him off. "What in hell just happened?"

"There was some kind of pit under the ruins," Knight said. "They must have rigged the support posts and blown them out from under us."

"That's crazy," Queen said. "How did they know we'd choose that particular spot?"

It was a fair question and one for which Knight had no answer, but illogical or not, it had happened. Now they needed to focus on getting out. The muted sound of Rook's machine gun reached his ears, adding urgency to that purpose.

He turned a slow circle and realized that they were not in a pit at all, but rather at a junction, where several subterranean passages intersected. "One of these has to lead back to the surface," he said. He peered down each in turn, testing the dark corridors with thermal view. The mere act of concentrating on the visual input seemed to intensify his migraine, but he ground his teeth through the discomfort. One of the tunnels, which if straight would lead under the pyramid, showed a residual heat trace. "That's the warmest."

"What does that mean?" Bishop asked.

"Probably nothing good," Queen said, bringing her rifle to the ready. "But it's a place to start."

"I'll take the lead," Knight said. It was not merely chivalry that motivated him. His enhanced vision represented their best chance at early detection of booby traps or a force of men waiting in ambush. He slung his sniper rifle across his back—in the close confines of the tunnel, the CheyTac's length and seven-round magazine would be a liability. He switched to the MP5 he carried as his secondary weapon.

The heat signature grew stronger as he advanced into the tunnel, as did his sense of foreboding. The throbbing in his head was growing more intense, and he was having trouble concentrating and making sense of what he was seeing. The temperature changes he was registering seemed to be everywhere, as if the air itself was heating up.

"Disgusting."

Bishop's whispered comment stopped him in his tracks. He had been so focused on trying to see what lay ahead that he had neglected to consult with his other senses. He closed his eyes, and let the warm thick air drift over him. The pungent familiar odor stung his nose, but before he could comment, Queen said aloud what he was thinking.

"Shit. More pigs."

"Back. We need to go back." But before he could take a step, he felt a fetid breeze stir the air, carrying with it the faint noise of animal grunts and the clatter of hooves on stone.

He realized it was already too late.

In Mano's compound, they had faced a few dozen of the creatures Rook had nicknamed 'hell pigs,' and they had narrowly escaped being ripped to shreds. If the seething red blob of heat surging toward them from the depths of the tunnel system was any indication, the herd they now faced numbered in the hundreds.

TWENTY-EIGHT
Endgame, New Hampshire

"Desperado?" **Aleman saw** Boucher's eyes move from Deep Blue to himself, looking for an explanation.

Desperado. Aleman drew in a breath. "It's our walk-away code. Abandon ship."

The protocol was actually a little more involved than that, as was the term itself. In chess, desperado was a strategy for inflicting the most damage from a piece that was already doomed. In this instance, Endgame itself was that piece. While the security team and the various intruder defenses might keep the authorities out or even inflict heavy losses, there was only one possible outcome: Endgame was already lost.

Desperado was a two-stage contingency for dealing with that no-win scenario. The first stage was the evacuation of all non-essential personnel, which in this case meant everyone that wasn't in the control room. When the Black and White support teams heard that code-word, they were to drop everything and head for the nearest safe exit, which for most was the faux outhouse just above the *Labs* section of the complex. The fact that the imminent raid was being staged at the decommissioned Post One entrance suggested that the authorities had access to the original site plans, but the outhouse-elevator was a more recent addition. Once everyone was clear of the complex, their only priority was self-preservation. Get as far from Endgame as possible, start a new life somewhere, and never look back. Once they were clear, the bio-safety doors would drop, buying a little more time for those who remained behind to finish the protocol.

Stage two required complete sterilization of the site. Every piece of physical evidence that might jeopardize the surviving members of Endgame and Chess Team had to be destroyed, including the quantum computer that was now the team's only lifeline.

Deep Blue sank wearily into his chair at the console and stared at the multiple feeds displayed on the wall screens. The team in Mexico, stranded, divided, under fire. Post One, surround-ed by men in tactical gear and blue FBI windbreakers. Radar images of an advancing phalanx of Black Hawk helicopters, probably on their way to reinforce the siege.

"I'll take care of things here," the former president said in a weary, resigned voice. "You guys get clear. Dom, I don't know how much time we'll have. Can you arrange transport out of Mexico City?"

Boucher shook his head in confusion. "Slow down, Tom. What are you saying? Get clear? I'm not leaving."

Aleman jerked in his chair as if he had touched a live wire, but managed a wan smile. "That goes for me, too. You're stuck with us."

"Desperado isn't a suggestion," Deep Blue said, his voice patient but firm. "It's an order. You're going to be able to do a lot more for them on the outside, but you have to go now." He turned back to the screens as if the matter was concluded. "King, you were right about the ruins being a trap. Can you extract the others?"

"Negative." King's voice was startlingly clear in the control room, as was the intermittent noise of gunfire. "But the situation is under control up here. Concentrate on helping them get out of that hole."

"Roger."

"And Blue... Did I hear you correctly? 'Desperado?'"

"Affirmative, King. We've got the law knocking at the door. I'll stay online as long as I can."

"Understood." A pause. "I need you to patch a call through to George Pierce."

Deep Blue did not question the request. "Standby."

With a few keystrokes, he made the connection, and as the ring tone began to sound, Deep Blue muted the feed and turned to face Aleman and Boucher again. "Why are you still here?"

Boucher shook his head. "I'm not going."

Deep Blue's patience evaporated like flash paper. "Damn it, Dom. I need you out there. They need you."

Boucher was adamant. "I can't help them. Don't you see? Whoever did this used me to get to you. I'm damaged goods. All my contacts are compromised. There's nothing I can do and nowhere for me to run, so I might as well stay here and help you."

Aleman could see that Boucher had hit the right pressure point. Unlike the men and women of the support teams, Boucher was a high-profile public figure and the only one of them who was definitely on the authorities' radar.

Deep Blue stared at Boucher, his look of irritation giving way to sadness. Finally, he nodded. "It's the Dom and Tom show, then." He turned to Aleman, his expression hardening in antici-pation of refusal. "You have to go, Lew. Grab a q-phone and get clear. I'll keep the net open as long as I can, but once it goes down, it will be up to you to bring them..." He faltered for second. "To keep them safe."

A wave of cold numbness washed over Aleman. *This can't be happening.*

Deep Blue took something from his pocket and pressed it into Aleman's hands. "Go, Lew. Before it's too late."

Aleman felt his body responding, following the former president's explicit orders to the letter, but his mind was gripped by a fugue of disbelief that did not dissipate until he stepped out through the door to the ramshackle outhouse, which disguised the entrance to the Endgame complex. He wrinkled his nose against the foul odor of raw sewage—a chemical trick to discourage hikers from attempting to utilize the facility for its advertised purpose—and slipped on a pair of sport-frame sunglasses.

The sky was beginning to lighten; it would be dawn soon, but the glasses went automatically into night-vision mode, penetrating the shadows under the canopy of trees. The forest was quiet. The support staff had long since melted into the woods. There was no sign that the FBI agents had grown wise to the alternate entrance. "I'm out."

A somber voice sounded in his head. "Understood. It was a pleasure serving with you, Lew. I have faith in you."

Aleman didn't reply. What could he say?

As he headed into the woods, he squeezed the object in his fist so tightly that his fingers grew stiff. He knew what it was without looking, a uniquely carved piece of ebony that resembled the king chess piece, but instead of the traditional crown and cross, the piece was capped with an eagle's head in flight. When Tom Duncan had handed the carving to him, it was a symbolic message more explicit than anything he could have expressed in words.

Aleman had received it loud and clear.

TWENTY-NINE
Mexico

King felt like a juggler, monitoring three separate events, interacting with each just long enough to maintain control before shifting his attention to the next.

The ongoing battle with the cartel soldiers was happening right before his eyes. Rook was holding them at bay with the machine gun, but how long could that continue?

Queen, Knight and Bishop were running for their lives in the maze of tunnels below. Was there anything he could do to help them?

The sound of a phone, ringing in his ears...a click and a tentative mumbled greeting.

"Hello?"

"George, it's Jack. Take Fi and go. Right now. Keep her safe."

"That bad?"

"That bad." There was no time to articulate a more detailed response, and even if he had been inclined to do so, a deafening burst from the 240B made the point much more succinctly. When the last echoes faded, he continued. "Be careful. Don't trust anyone. You're in charge now."

Pierce was silent for a moment, and King wondered if his old friend understood exactly what he was saying. "Is there anything I...*we*, can do to help?"

"Not this time. Gotta go. Good luck." He ended the call, confident that both his daughter and the secret entrusted to him by his ancestor and friend, Alexander Diotrephes, were in good hands.

One less ball to juggle.

He turned back to the gaping hole in the ruins. The virtual display showed the location of the rest of the team. The parts of the tunnel system they had already navigated appeared as ghost images, but there was little of value there.

"Reloading," Rook called out, pulling King's attention once more to the immediate problem. He dropped down beside Rook and thrust his SCAR in the direction of the enemy, loosing short bursts of covering fire, while Rook fed a fresh belt of ammunition into the machine gun. King could feel the heat radiating from the barrel of the weapon. The battle had already gone on far too long.

Rook slammed the feed-tray cover shut and racked a round into the firing chamber. "I'm up."

"Hold your fire," King advised. The report from a volley of enemy bullets forced him once more behind the stubby walls, but the shots whizzed harmlessly overhead. "Get ready to pick up."

Rook jerked his head in the direction of the recently opened pit. "Going down?"

King glanced over his shoulder, checking the situation below, scanning the ruins for a better position, and more than anything else looking for inspiration. "Bad idea. We'll have a better chance finding an exit for them up here. Let's get to that pyramid."

"Really? 'Cause I got the distinct impression that was the one place we should avoid."

It wasn't like Rook to question his decisions, especially under fire, but then this was an unprecedented situation. Rook was also aware of what was going on, both with their friends and back at Endgame, and King could not ignore the possibility that the other man might be right. "I'm betting one of those tunnels down there leads to the pyramid," he replied, as much to rationalize his course of action for himself as for Rook. "That's our best chance of beating the trap and helping the others."

"Oh." Rook hefted the machine gun into his arms. "Why didn't you just say so?"

King took a fragmentation grenade from his gear pouch and stripped off the safety band. "Ready?"

At a nod from Rook, he pulled the pin and lobbed it in a high arc, out over the field. The explosion that reverberated through the stone floor was like a starter pistol, and both men leaped over the wall of the ruin.

King half-expected the move to be met with a fusillade from the cartel fighters, but instead there was only an eerie silence as they pounded through the rubble-strewn maze. The destruction of the TOW system probably meant that they were nearly invisible again, so maybe the enemy did not yet realize that they were moving.

The silence was broken, not by shots fired at them, but by the sound of multiple reports from underground, as their teammates engaged with an unseen enemy. King took some comfort from the fact that they had anticipated the possibility of another encounter with Beltran's hell pigs, adding shin guards to their protective equipment and upgrading both their weapons and ammunition.

A high-velocity 5.56-millimeter M995 tungsten-core armor-piercing round would have a better chance of penetrating hide and bone than the 9mm pistol rounds they had been packing during their previous encounter with the beasts. But even with those measures, the three trapped in the tunnels below would not be able to hold out forever.

King's injured leg was throbbing from the dynamic leap over the wall. Further complicating matters, the shape of the path through the ruins had changed. Enormous pits had appeared in the avenues and under several of the already broken down buildings, reminding King of the tabletop game, Labyrinth, where the goal was to steer a marble through a maze riddled with holes. The collapse that had sent King's three teammates into the tunnel system had evidently not been an isolated incident.

The implications of this became another item in King's complex mental juggling act. Their enemy had a plan, and so far, they had executed it almost perfectly, first cutting off the team's escape, then driving them into the ruins where pre-rigged pitfalls waited to deliver them into the waiting jaws of the omnivorous boars.

He skidded to a stop a stone's throw from the pyramid steps and raised a hand, cautioning a panting Rook to stay quiet.

"What is it?" Rook whispered, so softly that King would not have been able to hear without the glasses.

"He's got us playing his game," King answered in the same low tone. "We need to turn this around."

"Turn it around?" Rook countered. "Right now, all I care about is making sure that Queen doesn't become pig chow."

King did not fail to notice the singularity of Rook's intent, but he let it slide, focusing instead on the three icons navigating the faintly visible maze below, like the ghosts in a Pac Man game.

Suddenly, the ground beneath him lurched. The noise of another explosion filled his ears, and the stone pavement erupted in a cloud of smoke and shattered stone, right above the place where his trapped teammates had been only a moment before.

THIRTY
Manteo, North Carolina

Anna Beck reacted without hesitation. In a smooth motion, she reached under her light jacket and drew a compact SIG P228 from the holster clipped to her belt at the small of her back. She did not fire, but instead used the muzzle of the semi-automatic pistol to smash through the glass doors separating her from Sara Fogg and the onrushing monstrosity. The shattering noise not only removed the barrier, but also had the effect of making the beleaguered disease investigator duck, which provided Beck with a clear line of fire. She stabbed the pistol toward the creature and squeezed off a pair of shots.

Her first round caught the tall gangly thing almost dead center in the torso, where its heart would have been, if it had been human.

She was pretty sure it wasn't.

The second round hit about eight inches higher, near its left shoulder. The impact caused it to career away from its intended victim and crash into the wall, but a moment later, faster than Beck could shift her aim, it was back up and bounding toward the doctor that accompanied Sara. Beck pushed through the broken remains of the door to get close enough for a clean shot before it reached him.

She almost succeeded.

Her shots had definitely had an effect on the creature. Long streams of brownish blood were flung in all directions, spattering the walls and floor, and when the creature reached out for the man, only one of its spindly arms seemed to be working. The man threw up his hands to ward the thing off and was knocked back, which was exactly the break Beck needed. She fired again, point blank, and took the top of the creature's head off.

The man scrambled backward, narrowly avoiding being pinned beneath the creature, as it toppled forward and skidded a few feet before coming to rest. Beck kept the pistol trained on it for a moment until she was sure that it was not going to get up, and then she hastened to Sara's side.

"Are you okay?"

Sara gaped at her for a moment, but then seemed to gather her wits. She nodded to Beck then moved quickly to the doctor's side. "That was one of your nurses." Sara's voice was taut and breathless. "It's spreading."

The doctor stared up at her in bewilderment. "I don't—"

He broke off suddenly, doubling over with an agonized groan. Sara jerked backward as if she had touched a live wire.

Beck didn't need to see more. She grabbed Sara's arm and drew her toward the exit. "Let's go."

To her astonishment, Sara pulled away. "No. I can't leave."

Before Beck could argue the point, the doctor threw back his head and let out a blood-curdling wail. In that instant, Beck knew that the crisis she had just walked into was far from over.

Her brain struggled to process the transformation that was taking place right before her eyes. Beck was no stranger to such things. Even before she had become a part of Endgame, she had witnessed the monstrous results of Richard Ridley's perversions of science. Her prior experience was probably the only thing that kept her from freezing up or running away in a blind panic, but the spectacle still terrified her.

In the space of just a few seconds, the doctor had become something else, something like the creature that Beck had just killed. She could see his skull shifting and growing beneath skin stretched almost transparent. His hair and beard were falling away in huge tufts. His teeth were growing larger, twisting behind lips that were pulled back in a feral rictus of pain. Beck would not have been surprised to see them burst from his mouth like exploding kernels of popcorn. His arms and legs were lengthening, as if his bones were made of rubber. Even his fingers had nearly doubled in length. Yet as horrible as the process was to behold, what truly chilled Beck was the memory of Sara's earlier comment.

'It's spreading.'

She did not need to be a CDC epidemiologist to figure out what that meant. Sara had come here investigating a disease to which she and everyone in the hospital had been exposed. That contagion, whatever it was, was transforming people into monsters.

And now I've been exposed, too.

Beck, who had in one form or another, been a soldier for nearly all of her adult life, was used to threats that could be answered with force. How was she supposed to deal with this, an invisible enemy that struck without warning?

An enemy that might have already killed her?

As if in response to the doctor's howling, a cacophony of shrieks sounded from further inside the hospital. Then, inexplicably, came the sound of a pistol shot. And then another.

The reports shocked Beck into motion again. "Whatever this is, we have to go."

Sara, still transfixed by the doctor's metamorphosis, offered no argument, but when Beck reached for her arm, she jolted again as if struck by a memory. "Ellen."

"Who's Ellen?"

"Our only chance of figuring this out. We can't leave her."

Beck grimaced in frustration. Too much was happening, too fast. "She's in there?"

A nod.

"Are you sure she's still alive?"

A shrug.

Damn it. "Is there a cure for this?"

"I..." Another shrug.

The stricken doctor continued to convulse violently. Aside from the clothes, which hung loosely on the now oversized frame, the thing was almost identical to the creature that had attacked only moments before. Then, the seizure abruptly ended and the thing looked up at them with eyes that seemed all too human. There was nothing human, however, about the snarl it uttered as it thrust a grotesquely elongated head in Beck's direction. Beck stepped back quickly, and as the hideous teeth snapped shut on the air where her leg had been an instant before, she lowered the pistol and fired a single round.

"That cures everything," she muttered.

Sara stared in disbelief for a moment, but then met Beck's eyes. "Make sure you save a couple for us. Just in case."

"Love your bedside manner, Doc." Beck stared down the corridor. There were still intermittent shrieks issuing from the depths of the hospital, but no more shots. That was a very bad sign, but Beck had a feeling that trying to dissuade Sara would prove fruitless. "You follow my lead and stay behind me, got it?"

Sara nodded again.

"And be sure to let me know if you...you know, start feeling a little monstery."

"Definitely."

With her SIG pointing the way, Beck started down the corridor, checking each intersection and doorway, partly to make sure they would not be ambushed, but also identifying possible fallback positions. About the only thing in their favor was the fact that the creatures did not seem particularly difficult to kill.

As the women pushed deeper into the building, the howls and shrieks intensified, as did Beck's apprehension. Several times, she thought she glimpsed movement out of the corner of her eye, but a second look revealed nothing. She was about to demand a retreat when Sara hastened forward to a closed door.

"This is her room." Sara turned the doorknob, but the door refused to budge.

"Ellen!" She pounded on the door. "It's Sara Fogg!"

"Shhh!" Beck cautioned, though it was too late to make a difference. She stepped past Sara, training her weapon down the corridor in anticipation of a concerted response to the clamor.

"Ellen," Sara said, reducing her volume to a stage whisper. "Are you okay?"

"Go away," a small, high voice replied, and Beck immediately thought of a child hiding in a closet. *Probably not far from the truth.* "You can't come in."

"Ellen, we need to get out of here. I have a friend with me. She has a gun. You'll be safe. Just let us in."

"That's about the worst thing you could have said," Beck muttered, and was surprised when the door opened a crack to reveal a slender face framed with red hair.

"They're everywhere," the woman whispered. "I can hear them."

Sara extended a hand and spoke in a kind but urgent tone. "I know. We have to get out of here. Go somewhere safe."

Something moved at the far end of the hallway, and this time it definitely was not Beck's eyes playing tricks. Three long-limbed figures loped into view, so tall that even bent over nearly double, they were almost scraping the ceiling. One of them was tangled up in what appeared to be a tan police uniform shirt and neck-tie. There was one other noticeable difference from the creatures Beck had already dealt with. The misshapen faces of this trio were streaked with blood, and crimson gore dripped from their mouths.

They had been feeding.

"Too late," Beck shouted, and pushed Sara through the door, into the hospital room. She slammed it closed behind her and threw her back against it. "Can these things open doors?"

Sara and the woman—Ellen—exchanged an uncertain glance.

"That's what I was afraid of," Beck said. "Shove that bed over here. We'll use it to—"

The door lurched behind her, as someone—something—tried to force the door open. Beck lowered herself, bracing her back flat against the door, legs extended at a forty-five degree angle. The door shuddered again.

"Move it!"

Sara leaped into action, quickly finding the foot pedals that disengaged the brakes on the bed. Ellen belatedly joined her, and a few seconds later, they were trundling the bed across the room. Beck felt the creature hit the door again, and this time, it opened a few inches. Spindly fingers slipped through. Beck felt the soles of her shoes losing traction as the creatures pushed harder. "Hurry."

Sara steered the bed next to Beck, and then drove it forward like a battering ram. There was a sickening crunch as the slender fingers were smashed flat between the door and the frame, and from beyond, an anguished wail that sent a shiver down Beck's spine.

Sara locked the brakes in place. "I don't know if that will stop them."

"We only need a few seconds." She nodded toward the windows on the opposite side of the room. "Get those open."

"I tried them," Ellen said. "They only open a few inches. We'll never fit."

Without hesitation, Beck leveled her pistol and fired. The report, deafening in the close confines, made the other two women jump, but instead of shattering the double pane window, the bullet punched a neat hole clean through.

Beck muttered a frustrated curse. Stuff like that never happened in the movies.

The door shook with another impact, but the sturdy hospital bed held it shut. She pushed off and crossed the room, picking up the bedside chair and hurling it toward the damaged window. This time, the thick glass yielded to the impact, exploding out in a spray of jagged shards.

Beck clambered over the sill and dropped down onto the lawn outside. "All clear," she said over her shoulder. "Move."

Sara cajoled a panicky Ellen through and then followed suit.

Beck urged them forward. "Come on."

Out in the open, the horror of what she had just witnessed seemed like just a bad dream. The quiet pre-dawn twilight underscored the sleepy nature of the little island town. It was impossible to believe that monsters could exist in such a place. Beck fought against the inertia of perceived safety, increasing both her pace and her vigilance as she skirted the building toward the small parking lot where she had left her rented Nissan Versa.

"Where are we going?"

Ellen posed the question, but Beck realized that, beyond reaching the safety of the car, she didn't know what the next move would be. Her attention had been consumed with the not inconsiderable task of escaping the flesh-eating mutants. Only now did she have time to stop and think about what had caused that transformation in the first place, and wonder if it was going to happen to them next. She stopped at the corner of the building and peeked slowly around the edge.

Something was moving in the parking lot. Pale bodies, tall and gangly, gleamed a sickly hue in the overhead lights as they roamed between the cars. They moved like wolves or lions, indifferent predators casually on the lookout for a hapless animal to devour. Beck gestured for the other women to remain silent. She mentally measured the distance to her car. Fifty yards, perhaps. If they ran all out, they might get halfway before any of the creatures noticed. The tricky part would come at the end: getting the doors open and climbing inside.

Two more figures emerged from the hospital, but even as they came into view, the others moved out into the empty street. The creatures weren't hunting them per se; they were looking for any prey, and the unsuspecting townspeople would be easy pickings. Or, if what had happened to the doctor was any indication, fertile ground for the infection to spread.

And we were all exposed, she thought.

Sara's safety was her top priority, and all the more so since she was probably the only person who had a grasp on what was really happening. Her job was to find a cure, if there was one, or to initiate the proper containment measures.

As the two creatures moved past the car, Beck gave the signal to move out, but she kept a slow stealthy pace. The creatures remained oblivious to their presence. Beck kept a close watch on them while constantly checking the Emergency Room doors, lest another emerge from within.

One excruciatingly cautious step after another, they crossed the distance unnoticed. It was only when they were within a few feet of the car that Beck switched the pistol to her left hand to take out her key. Instead of using the remote to unlock the doors, she slowly slotted the key in and turned it, manually unlocking the driver's side door with barely a sound. As she eased it open, the overhead light flashed on, and she cringed, but the subtle change went unnoticed by the departing creatures. She motioned for the two women to climb in.

In the near total silence, every noise—the brush of hands on the upholstery of the car seats, the creak of the suspension as weight was added—seemed as loud as a gunshot, but the monstrosities did not look back. By the time Beck was seated behind the wheel, they were barely visible in the distance.

She pulled the door shut, grimacing at the soft but audible click of the latch engaging, and then she let out the breath she had been holding in a long sigh. Beside her, Sara was already in action, dialing a number on her cell phone.

Ellen spoke from the back seat, her voice a rush of panic that had been bottled up too long. "We have to get away from here."

Sara shushed her and then spoke into the phone. "Ira? It's Sara."

Beck could faintly hear a voice at the other end of the line, but was unable to make out what the man was saying. "No, just listen. This place is hot and the fire is spreading fast. I don't know what it is yet, but you have to initiate containment protocols... Red... It's an island for God's sake. Activate the National Guard and have them close off the bridges. Well, all of them. Anywhere there's a connection to the mainland. No one in or out."

"Does that include us?" Ellen asked, her voice rising an octave.

This time it was Beck that silenced her with a withering glance.

"Right," Sara continued, ignoring the disturbance. "And activate the Emergency Notification System. Tell everyone to stay in their homes and lock the doors... No, I'm staying. I'm going to keep working it as long as I can... Too late."

A long silence followed, then the tinny voice sounded again.

"I will. Whatever this is, it's not following a linear vector. As soon as I know more, I'll call. Meanwhile, just shut this place down." She glanced at Beck. "I'd better go."

As soon as she ended the call, Ellen uncorked her bottle of panic. "You just trapped us here!"

Beck ignored the outburst. "Okay, what the hell were those things? What's going on?"

"We're calling them wendigos. It's from an old Native American myth about cannibal monsters." Sara looked back at Ellen. "She's the expert."

Beck frowned. "Those things weren't a myth. And we both saw what happened to that doctor."

Sara shook her head. "Ellen, I need you to calm down and talk me through this again. You were exposed almost a full day ago. What's different about you?"

"It's the curse," Ellen said, desolately. "The curse. I'm Eleanor Dare's ancestor. She was spared, and now I have been, too. But everyone else, all the people here who have perpetuated the myth of the Lost Colony, ignoring their sins... They're all guilty."

"Knock it off," Beck snarled in a voice that shocked Ellen into silence. "This isn't some bullshit curse, okay? It's a disease, and this lady here is the person who can stop it. So give her some straight answers. If you don't like that, you're free to get out right now."

Ellen shrank back in her chair, but nodded.

Sara put a restraining hand on Beck's arm, but the latter could see that her intervention was not unappreciated. "Everybody just take a breath, okay? Ellen, you might be right about the 'curse,' but Anna is right, too. This is a disease, and we can fight it. I need to know how it works, and how it spreads. How did it start? What was the last thing that happened before the appearance of symptoms?"

"Jason found something." Ellen's voice was hollow, beaten. "An old animal bone."

"Are you sure it was an animal bone?" Sara pressed.

"Yes. It was the wrong shape to be..." Ellen trailed off, but then sat up a little straighter. "I thought it was the wrong shape to be human. Too long and thin, but it could have been a wendigo bone."

Sara nodded. "I'll need to see that bone. Can you take me there?"

"It's at the Fort Raleigh historical site."

"Can you walk me to the spot?"

Ellen swallowed. "Okay."

"Fort Raleigh it is," Beck said, slotting the key in the ignition. The engine rumbled to life. She quickly backed out of the parking space, and then shifted into drive.

There was almost no warning. She glimpsed movement in her peripheral vision, and then something slammed into the car, rocking it sideways. Outside the windows, there was a flurry of motion, pale bodies and twisted, misshapen limbs covering the windshield. Beck stomped the accelerator, and the Versa lurched forward, only to encounter resistance, as if the tires had run into a curb.

She touched the brakes, shifted into reverse and hit the gas again, and this time she was rewarded with movement, albeit in the wrong direction. The engine revved louder as the car picked up speed. Outside, the attacking creatures fell back, taken unaware by the move, and in that instant, Beck counted more than a dozen wendigos, at least twice as many as she had seen in the parking lot only a few moments before.

Contagion or curse, whatever the cause, it was spreading fast.

Beck shifted into drive and accelerated forward, this time with enough momentum to break free of the combined strength of the wendigos. One of the creatures crashed noisily onto the hood, but rolled off. Another one rebounded off the front bumper, spilling onto the pavement directly in their path. With a sickening crunch that reverberated through the Versa's interior, they rolled up and over the fallen creature. As the tires hit the pavement again, the car shot forward, slipping the stranglehold.

Beck felt relief at having escaped the attack, but no accompanying sense of satisfaction at having killed another of the creatures. The wendigos were as much victims as the people they hunted. The worst part was the knowledge that the same transformation might at any second add her to their rapidly growing ranks.

THIRTY-ONE
Mexico

Queen pushed forward, leveling her SCAR at the oncoming stampede. "Knight, find us another exit."

Asya felt rooted in place by the sheer scope of the threat they now faced, but the thunderous report of Queen's rifle broke her out of her paralysis. She aimed her own weapon into the seething mass and started firing.

The combined storm of lead slammed into the front of the advancing wave, and several of the pig-faced monsters went down, tumbling forward in a flurry of limbs. Asya kept pulling the trigger, pouring bullets into the boars until, with alarming suddenness, her rifle fell silent. She had fired out the entire thirty-round magazine in mere seconds.

The fallen beasts were piled up in the passage, momentarily blocking the way for the rest, but Asya could see the next wave climbing over the bodies of their dead kindred.

"Bishop," Queen shouted. "Go!"

Asya spun on her heel, orienting on the bobbing blue icon that marked Knight's position, and ran. She buttoned out the magazine, letting it fall, and then she fumbled a fresh one from her gear belt. Her fingers felt fat and clumsy. The simple act of reloading, which ought to have been second-nature after endless hours of rehearsals in training, now felt like a complicated three-dimensional puzzle.

Queen fired again, three-round bursts loosed with almost rhythmic perfection, which only seemed to underscore Asya's inadequacies. With the magazine finally seated, Asya spun around just as Queen's rifle went empty again.

The initial surge had been broken, but the boars were still coming, two and three at a time, the nearest less than ten yards away. Asya dropped it with a single shot that struck right above its porcine snout.

"Leapfrog," Asya shouted. "I cover you."

Queen instantly grasped the strategy and slipped past Asya, reloading as she went. Asya dropped two more boars, and then began backing down the passage.

"I'm up," Queen shouted. "Your turn."

Asya quickly found her stride. Fall back a few steps, turn, fire a few shots to cover Queen's retreat, repeat. Yet the boars kept coming.

They made it back to the rubble strewn pit where the underground journey had begun and followed Knight down another tunnel that seemed to run along the perimeter of the ruin. About twenty yards along that passage, Asya saw another area where the roof had collapsed, littering the floor with huge chunks of rock. Two more tunnels branched off in different directions, but as she started down the tunnel Knight had chosen, she met him coming back out.

"Dead end," he warned.

Queen backed into the open pit, firing down the tunnel. "Keep moving!" she urged.

Knight turned into the remaining passage while Asya covered Queen. The boars were still hunting them.

"I have idea," Asya shouted as soon as Queen was in position again. She let her rifle hang from its sling, and quickly prepped another grenade. "Knight. Come back, quickly."

"Are you crazy?" Queen shouted, not looking away from the advancing beasts. "You'll bring the whole place down on us."

"It will work," Asya countered. There was no time to explain why she was certain they would not be caught in a cave-in. She pulled the pin and then darted back into the open area and hurled the grenade down the passage they had just left. "Frag out."

Knight had just returned to Queen's side when the explosive device detonated. A gout of smoke and debris erupted from the tunnel mouth, showering them with particles, but the deadly storm of shrapnel and the main force of the blast itself had been absorbed by the tunnel walls. The cave-in Queen had feared was indeed happening, but because the place where they stood had already collapsed, there was nothing left to fall on them.

Queen kept her rifle trained on the dust cloud for several seconds but no boars emerged. "Okay," she admitted, sounding just a little bit impressed. "Not bad. Next time though, give us a little more warning."

"Should I not trust instincts?"

Queen inclined her head. "Point taken."

Asya gestured to the rubble that already littered the floor. "I knew we would be safe here."

"Safe, but still trapped."

Before she could reply to that, Asya heard her brother's voice, low and steady. "I take it you guys are still alive down there?"

"Roger," Queen answered. "Bishop dealt with our pig problem. Now we just need to find a way out of this hole. Don't suppose there's a ladder laying around up there."

"No ladder, but Bishop has given me an even better idea."

Asya felt the scrutiny of her teammates. "Way to go, Bishop," Knight murmured.

A blue dot appeared on the virtual map, marking a location that was outside the network of tunnels they had previously explored. "Get as close to this location as you can."

"Is there an exit?" Queen asked.

"There will be."

THIRTY-TWO

The explosion sent a tremor radiating through the surrounding stone, causing Parrish to hug the stone platform on which he lay. The blast had come from somewhere out in the ruins, underground he thought. The top of the pyramid was well outside the blast radius, but the shock had reverberated through the monument, shattering the illusion of safety.

He didn't fully understand Beltran's plan, but it was a safe bet that things were not quite working out as intended. Although the cartel had successfully brought down the stealth plane, the commando team was proving to be elusive, to the point that nobody seemed to have any idea where they were. The underground explosion was a sure sign that the Americans were still fighting, and unless Parrish was very wrong about them, they were probably going on the offensive.

Beltran turned to him and thrust the binoculars into his hands. "Find them."

Parrish had to fight to keep his frustration in check. "You've lost the advantage here. It's time to pull back."

"Not until they are dead."

"We're not going to find them in the dark. Your only chance is to pull your men back and establish a secure perimeter, if it's not already too late."

"They're here," Beltran insisted. "That explosion proves it. The pigs were chasing them."

The pigs. That was the part of this whole scheme that confused Parrish the most. The drug lord had been insistent; drive the Americans into the ruins and either drop them into the tunnels where a huge herd of semi-domesticated wild hogs were waiting to devour them, or force them to seek refuge atop the pyramid, where the bulk of Betran's men lay in wait, poised to capture the intruders and sacrifice them to their bloody Aztec god. Parrish saw this as a needlessly complicated denouement to an otherwise perfect ambush, but Beltran was insistent. "Huitzilopochtli demands blood. Besides, my pigs need to eat," he had said with a laugh, as he had outlined the plan earlier, and then he had added with a wink, "And so do my men."

Parrish had been trying very hard not to think about what that might mean.

"Listen to me. You've already won. Those men out there are nothing. You've taken out a plane worth almost a billion dollars. Right now, Senator Marrs is leading a raid on the people who sent them here, and it's a good bet the trail is going to lead right to the President of the United States. *You have won.*" He enunciated each word for emphasis. "But those soldiers aren't going to just give up. They're going to attack, and believe me, right now, they have the advantage."

He could not tell if his plea was reaching Beltran. The cartel leader was nothing if not unpredictable, a dangerous mix of evil, insanity and intelligence. Parrish could only hope that the man possessed enough of the latter to know when he had reached the point of diminishing returns. The ensuing silence was a hopeful sign. The sky was lightening with the approach of dawn. Perhaps Beltran would at least wait for the arrival of daylight to renew his offensive.

But if the cartel leader had an answer for him, it was drowned out by the boom of yet another explosion. The pyramid heaved beneath Parrish. The binoculars fell from his hands as he threw his arms out once more, but this time the tremor did not abate.

Instead, the sound of stones grinding together intensified, and everything began to move.

THIRTY-THREE

The M67 fragmentation grenade that Bishop had used to collapse the tunnel and block the stampeding boars contained a few ounces of Composition B high-explosives. The charge that she placed near the spot King had designated consisted of five pounds of C-4, and when she activated the remote trigger, most of that energy went straight up into the pyramid.

If he had not already been hunkered down with Rook at the edge of the ruins, anticipating the blast, the explosion would have knocked King flat. Even after the initial shock wave, the ground continued to shake as the pyramid tore itself apart, collapsing like a house of cards.

The comparison was not far off the mark. The explosion had jarred the foundation of the pyramid, like someone kicking a table leg, and fractured the limestone mortar that held everything together. The corner nearest the detonation began to crumble first, and then everything behind it slumped inward to fill the void. King spied movement atop the ancient temple, men with guns frantically trying to escape, but their ultimate fate was hidden from view as the pyramid's collapse was eclipsed by a rising column of dust.

"Queen, what's your status? Are you clear?"

There was silence on the net for a long time, too long, but then he heard coughing sounds. "We're good," Queen managed to say. "Can't tell which way is up, but we're all alive."

King breathed a sigh of relief. "Stay where you are. We're coming to you."

He tapped Rook's arm and together they rose, moving cautiously through the gloom, toward the cluster of blue icons that marked the location of the others. Visibility was nil, and the blast had wreaked havoc on the original map of the ruins, knocking down the few remaining walls and collapsing the sub-surface passages to create treacherous crevasses, forcing them to creep forward one careful step at a time.

"Scratch one more irreplaceable ancient monument off the list," Rook said, as the dust finally started to settle and the scope of the damage became apparent.

Strangely, King felt no regret over the destruction of the pyramid. He had seen the bloodstains on its flanks. Whatever archaeological significance the place might have possessed had been overshadowed by the atrocities committed here in the name of Beltran's perverse religious beliefs. Better to wipe such a place off the face of the Earth. With any luck, they had wiped out the leader of El Sol in the bargain. King was a lot more concerned about the fate of his teammates. Demolishing the pyramid had been a crazy gamble, with the lives of his friends—and his sister—in the balance, but it had paid off.

A few minutes later, they reached the edge of a large hole where Queen, Knight and Bishop had weathered the final demolition of the ruins. Rook peered down into the rubble. "Somebody blink so we'll know where you are."

"Very funny, jackass," Queen said, and even though he was looking right at her, King had trouble distinguishing her from the surrounding rubble.

He looked along the edge of the pit until he found a newly created slope of loose stone, a result of the pyramid's collapse. "There's your exit," he told them. "What are you waiting for?"

THIRTY-FOUR
Endgame, New Hampshire

The sun was just breaking over the mountaintops when the agents made their move. There was a loud *whump* as a shaped charge blew a neat hole in the outer door of Post One. The noise echoed through the empty corridors of the *Labs* section.

Tom Duncan peered at the video feed for the hidden surveillance camera trained on the disused entrance to the facility, watching as FBI SWAT team operators advanced to inspect the results of the attempted breach. The entire latch mechanism had been excised, allowing the door to swing open on its hinges, but beyond it was a wall of solid concrete.

"Will that slow them down?" Boucher asked.

"Maybe for a few minutes," Duncan replied with a shrug. He switched his gaze to the other screen, which showed the ongoing mission in Mexico. He was relieved that King had turned the tables on the cartel, especially as there was very little that he could do to help them.

"So what happens next?" Boucher made a show of looking at the control console. "Is there a self-destruct button around here somewhere?"

"An app, actually. Buttons are so twentieth century."

"So are we."

Duncan smiled ruefully. "A hundred feet below us is a cavern filled with natural gas. We've been using it to generate power for the facility, but when I initiate the self-destruct, the gas will be piped into the ventilation system, filling the entire complex. Ten minutes after that, incendiary charges in critical areas will ignite the gas and completely sanitize the entire facility."

Boucher swallowed. "And everyone in it."

"Desperado was always intended to be a measure of last resort. A literal scorched earth policy. An explosion like that will..." He trailed off, unwilling to articulate the full measure of destruction that would result. He gestured at the screen where the SWAT team was already placing another round of breaching charges. "They might not make it past the barrier in ten minutes, but even if they don't, the resulting explosion will take them out, not to mention setting the forest on fire and probably destroying a good chunk of Pinckney."

"We can't do that, Tom."

Duncan needed no convincing. If the attacking force had been a mercenary army or foreign operatives trying to seize the secrets of Endgame so they could launch a campaign of global domination, he would not have hesitated, but the men on the other side of the barrier were Americans, doing their sworn duty. And that did not begin to account for collateral damage.

"I've always known that I might someday have to make the ultimate sacrifice," Duncan said. "I don't have the right to make that decision for those men out there. But I have to keep my people safe."

"It always comes down to that doesn't it? Sacrifice. Destroy a village to kill one terrorist. Bomb a city to win a war and save millions."

Duncan nodded, still staring at the screen. More vehicles were arriving. Agents in windbreakers were setting up a mobile command center. Another screen showed a second group, National Guardsmen by the look of their uniforms, deploying at the hangar entrance some ten miles away, which while secure, had not been sealed off completely. Those troops would be inside the *Central* portion of the facility in a matter of minutes. "I need a better answer."

"If you take Desperado off the table, you're left with...two options, as I see it." Boucher was thinking out loud, putting his half-formed ideas out in the open in hopes that inspiration would strike. Duncan welcomed the process, but Boucher's next words were anything but inspirational. "Surrender or retreat."

"Surrender is not an option," Duncan said, with unexpected vehemence. Allowing himself to be captured, arrested and put on trial would be a betrayal of the highest magnitude. Not only would he be taking down Chess Team and everyone who had worked and sacrificed to make it a reality, it would also lead to revelations that would throw the entire country into chaos.

Boucher smiled cryptically. "Well then, I guess you've already made your decision. I'll be honest, I didn't much care for the notion of going down with the ship anyway."

Duncan stared at his old friend in dismay. "You think we should run?"

"You do." He stood up. "Making the decision is the easy part. Figuring out how to pull it off, and not second guessing yourself... That's the rub."

"And living with the consequences," Duncan murmured, but he knew Boucher was right. "We can exit through the *Dock*. Either they don't know about it, or they figure it's too inaccessible to be of any use to us."

He did not add that the latter was mostly true. There were only two ways out of the *Dock*: a concealed passage that came up in an old abandoned cabin, which could be reached only via a primitive forest road, and the submarine tunnel that let out under the surface of Lake Winnipesaukee, where another undersea passage—some sixty miles long—connected to the Atlantic Ocean. The latter choice would ensure their escape if not for one small detail. The only vehicle capable of bearing them through the long tunnel was a decommissioned Russian Typhoon submarine, and even if it was possible for two men to operate the 575-foot long vessel, which Duncan very much doubted, the submarine had sustained extensive damage during an incident a few years earlier, and repairing the monstrous undersea craft had been low on the list of priorities.

Fleeing into the woods was only a marginally better choice, but as Boucher had so eloquently demonstrated, when the unacceptable options were subtracted, the only choice was the least undesirable one.

The Manifold Alpha facility had been built to resemble a large letter 'A' with three main areas of operation occupying the points of a triangle. After taking over and rechristening the complex as Endgame headquarters, Duncan had centralized operations in the *Labs* section, at the lower left corner of the triangle, after moving it from *Central*. The *Dock*, situated at the lower right corner, ten miles away, could be reached in a matter of minutes using the dedicated high-speed light-rail train that connected the sections of the sprawling base. Unfortunately, the rail line also joined the *Central* portion at the top of the triangle, where the hangar was located. Once the intruders entered *Central*, their path to the *Dock* would be wide open.

More hard decisions.

He leaned over the console and brought up the systems control subroutine. "I'm cutting all power to the light rail. That will buy us a little time. Unfortunately, it means that we won't be able to use the train to reach the *Dock*."

"Well, there's a reason they call it 'running,'" Boucher replied with a forced laugh.

Duncan executed the command and then closed the system down and locked it out. Given the unique complexity of the quantum computer, it was doubtful that even the most skilled FBI technician would be able to override the lock-out, but Duncan had no intention leaving even that small window of possibility open. The quantum computer would have to be destroyed.

He checked the screen showing the mission feed and saw the team making their way across open ground to the abandoned factory. They were still a long way from safety, but the immediate threat from the cartel appeared to have been neutralized. "King, be advised. The q-net will be going down permanently in a few minutes."

As he delivered the dire news, Duncan felt a pang of guilt for having become so dependent on the innovative technology. The team would be losing not just instantaneous communication with both Endgame and each other, but also the weapons targeting system and their chameleon camouflage. He did not doubt that they were equal to the challenge of finishing the mission without their high-tech gadgets, but that was little comfort. He had let them down.

"Understood," King replied in his characteristically neutral tone. "Good luck."

The words felt like a body blow. *This is it,* he thought. *Everything we've done... Saving the world over and over again... All for nothing.*

No. Not for nothing. We did save the world, after all.

"Well, at least there's that," he muttered to himself. He took a deep breath. "Endgame...out."

"Son of a bitch!"

Boucher's growl shocked Duncan out of the fog of despair. The source of the former CIA director's ire seemed to be on the screen showing the ongoing attempts to break through the barrier at Post One, but at first glance, the situation appeared unchanged. Then he saw what had triggered the outburst.

There were two new faces visible in the crowd of agents and SWAT shooters. The men were immediately conspicuous because they were not wearing the ubiquitous and easily identifiable blue windbreakers favored by FBI special agents. Instead, they wore tailored business suits. Duncan didn't need a second look to identify them. The man closest to the camera, gesticulating wildly as if taking charge of the situation, was US Deputy Attorney General Joe Taits. A political creature with dubious law enforcement credentials, Taits had been a controversial choice for the number two law enforcement position in the nation, but the newly-sworn President Chambers had hoped—futilely as it turned out—that his nomination of Taits, who was popular with the majority opposition party, would be seen as a bipartisan gesture. Duncan had privately advised his successor against the appointment; Taits was, at best, an opportunist, and at worst, an outright fraud.

Duncan however barely noticed the DAG. His attention was transfixed by the other man.

"Marrs. Son of a bitch."

Suddenly, it all made sense. The ambush waiting for the team in Mexico. The raid on Endgame. The senior senator from Utah had two ambitions in life: to become the next president, and to destroy Tom Duncan and everything he stood for.

If Taits was a bad apple, then Marrs was the worm. His first crusade to bring down Duncan's administration had verged on treason, though in a deft move, Duncan had turned the situation to his advantage. Marrs's interference in the more recent Congo crisis, motivated as always by his personal ambition and fueled by generous bribes from special interests, had put the African continent on the brink of total war and nearly triggered an ecological catastrophe that would have killed millions—a calamity that had been averted only by Erik Somers's supreme sacrifice.

Now, with the destruction of *Crescent II* and the kidnapping and probable death of forty-six American tourists, Marrs was directly complicit in both treason and murder.

Duncan shook his head, trying to push down the rising swell of rage. "We have to go, Dom."

Boucher followed him from the control room, his angry eyes watching the screen until they turned the corner. Duncan however did not need to look back. Marrs's appearance had awakened something within him. He had been willing to give his life to preserve the secrets of Endgame and protect the Chess Team from the fallout of his own demise, and still he was not certain that trying to save his own life was the best way to accomplish those goals. Now however, there was a new and far more compelling reason for him to stay alive.

Payback.

THIRTY-FIVE
Mexico

Death, **Colin Parrish** decided, *really sucks.*

He had never believed in an afterlife, which conveniently absolved him of the need to worry about the consequences of questionable moral decisions or the inevitability of karmic payback. He was sure that death was the end, lights out, full stop, but if there was any truth to what untold millions believed, and he was destined for some infernal judgment—slow roasting in the Lake of Fire or sent back to live again as a mosquito—he was okay with that. What he had never anticipated was this: a dark crushing limbo, unable to move, to speak, to even breathe, but completely aware.

His rational mind grasped that this was not the afterlife at all, but the threshold. He was still alive, though the distinction was so trivial as to be meaningless. He knew, with absolute certainty, that he would spend the rest of eternity exactly like this, trapped in the infinite darkness of his own mind.

The first indication that he might be wrong about that, too, was heralded by a faint rustling noise, like someone walking across a graveled path. Then, with startling suddenness, he was yanked out of the darkness and into the twilit aftermath of the apocalypse. He found himself face to face with the Devil himself.

No, he corrected, as the initial sting gave way to a tsunami of pain. *Not the Devil. Someone even worse.*

Hector Beltran was almost unrecognizable. His ritualistically tattooed body, which already gave him the appearance of a demonic creature, was now streaked with dust and blood, making him look utterly inhuman. There was a preternatural fierceness in the man's eyes. His lips were pulled back in what was either a grimace of pain or a grin of bloodlust—probably both. He stood atop a mountain of rubble, the muscles of his arms and chest bulging like something from a comic book as he held Parrish aloft.

Parrish tried to speak, but the only sound to pass his lips was a mewling grunt. Beltran let him fall, and the impact with the rocky ground sent another spike of pain through Parrish's body. Through the haze, he saw Beltran stalking away, bellowing orders to his men in their shared language.

For a few fleeting seconds, Parrish dared to hope that Beltran had forgotten him, but the crunch of footsteps on stone signaled his return. "Get up," he roared in English. "Find them."

Find...who? Parrish longed for the oblivion of unconsciousness, but neither Beltran nor his own body would oblige that retreat. The cartel leader's powerful hands gripped him once more, hauling him erect and drawing him so close that Parrish was nearly suffocated by the other man's sickly sweet breath. "Where are they?"

"I..." At long last, Parrish's inner bulldog began to stir. "Put me down."

Beltran blinked at him in disbelief, and for a moment, Parrish thought the man was going to break him in half. Instead, he set Parrish down on his feet, helping him stand erect, rather than forcing him to do so. "You know how they think," Beltran continued. His tone remained every bit as demanding, but was marginally more civil. "Where will they run to?"

Parrish turned his head to survey the aftermath of the pyramid's collapse. The ruins were barely recognizable. Where the bloodstained temple had once stood, there was only a low misshapen mound of loose stone. A few men with assault rifles were picking through the rubble, searching for other survivors, evidently without success. Beyond that, lay the open field, gently undulating and vanishing into the horizon in every direction. There were mountains to the east, where the sun was just starting to rise, and a blocky shape to the south. Parrish had no idea what the shape was, but it was definitely a man-made structure.

"There," he said, pointing. "What's that place?"

Beltran followed the invisible line of Parrish's finger. "*La matadera*," he muttered. "Of course."

He stepped away and immediately began shouting to his men. The cartel fighters promptly abandoned their search-and-recovery efforts, and with near-military precision, they began marching out of the ruins, with Beltran at the forefront, towering above them like the Lord of Hell incarnate.

Without being consciously aware of doing so, Parrish fell into step behind them. The commands Beltran employed to marshal his troops were incomprehensible to Parrish, but he had no difficulty divining their meaning.

There was one word however, uttered in Spanish rather than Nahuatl, that he did understand: *Matadera*.

Slaughterhouse.

THIRTY-SIX

Knight noticed the change, even before he consciously registered the fact that the virtual display had gone dark. It was as if someone had flicked off the switch on his migraine, leaving only a faint afterimage of pain. His immediate relief was tempered by the gravity of what this development meant.

"I think we just lost Endgame."

There was no answer from the others.

Of course not, he realized. *Comms are down, too.*

He looked up, turning his head to locate the others. Despite the persistent agony of the strobe-light show that had been flashing into his retina for the last few hours, he had come to rely on the constantly updating virtual environment and even on the artificially produced stereoscopic vision of his implant. Yet, even without the chess piece icons to mark them, he had no difficulty finding his teammates, because their adaptive camouflage was also off-line.

In its natural state, the thin over-garment was a pale satin, giving them the appearance of a bulky human-shaped marshmallow. Bishop was about fifty feet away. She had stopped moving and was likewise looking around in apparent confusion at what was happening. Further along, he saw the others. King was ahead of Bishop, and Rook with his machine gun had taken point. Queen, bringing up the rear, was behind him.

King's hand went out in a rapid patting gesture, and then he dropped to the ground. Knight immediately grasped the meaning of the hand signal and repeated it, just as he had learned to do all those years ago in Army basic training. The message was simple enough: *Get down.*

From the prone position, below the low grass cover, his visibility was virtually nonexistent. He could no longer see the rest of the team, nor could he make out their immediate destination, the abandoned factory structure that was still some two hundred yards distant. The ruins were at least a mile behind them, and in the time it had taken them to traverse that distance, there had been no sign of enemy activity. That did not mean, however, that the cartel fighters had been completely defeated.

After a minute of lying motionless, Knight heard a strange clicking sound off to his left. He turned his head toward the noise and mimicked it with his tongue against his teeth. There was a rustling in the grass, and a moment later, King crawled into view.

"Ditch the camo," he said without preamble. King had already done so, stripping off the over-garment to reveal what Rook had dubbed 'work clothes'—in this instance, the latest version of the Army Combat Uniform, which employed the Scorpion W2 multicam pattern. "Where's Queen?"

"My six. About twenty yards," Knight replied.

"Rook is waiting about fifty yards from the factory. That's our rally point. He'll provide fire support if needed. Connect with

Bishop and circle around the building to make sure there are no surprises. We'll meet on the far side."

There was no discussion about the deeper, earthshaking implications of what was happening thousands of miles away at Endgame. All that mattered was the immediate problem. King did not wait for a reply, but resumed his high crawl through the grass. Knight quickly stripped off his chameleon suit, along with the now useless glasses. He stuffed them into his assault pack and began the long slog across the field. It was an arduous task, but he had done this hundreds of times, crawling stealthily from one firing position to the next. He knew that the only way to avoid going crazy was to dissociate the physical ordeal from the more critical mental game of hide and seek. Periodically, he would stop and rise up, just high enough to stay oriented on the objective, looking and listening for any sign of the enemy. After what seemed like an eternity of shuffling along, he caught up to Bishop.

"I am not liking the old ways so much," she said through clenched teeth.

Knight offered a commiserating grin but could not entirely share her outlook, if only because the discomfort he was now experiencing paled in comparison to the relentless headache caused by the implant. Yet, as he continued forward, side-by-side with her, the significance of what was happening finally hit home.

Chess Team was finished.

He had been ready to walk away, to step aside and let someone else take his place, just as Asya had done following Erik's death. Now, the question of his future with the team was moot. Even if they survived this day, managed to regroup and make their way back to American soil, what would happen next?

Would they spend the rest of their lives like this, crawling on their bellies figuratively if not also literally? Would they be forced to hide from the authorities, forced to reinvent themselves and perhaps worst of all, would they be unable to do the very thing that had brought them together in the first place?

Focus, he told himself. *None of that matters now.* But if the last few months had taught him anything, staying focused was a lot harder with just one eye.

They reached the designated rally point, and after a little searching, they located Rook, who was concealed behind a clump of grass with his machine gun trained on the nearby structure. His face was flushed from the exertion, and instead of cracking wise, he simply gave them a nod and resumed his vigil.

As King had instructed, Knight moved off with Bishop in tow, crawling through the grass around the dilapidated two-story structure, which up close, did not appear quite as abandoned as it had from the air. The exterior was streaked with dirt and rust, but the walls were mostly intact, with gaps covered by painted plywood that appeared relatively new. While there was no sign of activity, the dirt around the building, particularly in the area leading up to a large sliding door, was crisscrossed with tire tracks—some of which disappeared into the field on a direct line to the ruins, suggesting that the cartel had used the structure as the staging area for the ambush.

They rendezvoused with the others a few minutes later. Once again, King wasted no time with idle chitchat. This time there was an added urgency to his tone. "We've got movement out in the field. Counted at least fifteen, maybe as many as twenty. I don't think they saw us, but it won't be hard to figure out where to look for us. We need to take that building, now."

Without a moment's hesitation, the team picked up and darted across the open ground, lining up alongside a weathered door. Rook planted a solid kick right below the latch, and the door flew open. The space beyond was dark, lit only by what scant illumination penetrated the exterior walls, but the team moved in quickly, peeling off in different directions to cover every possible enemy position. The building was as unoccupied as it had appeared from outside, but a whiff of the air inside was enough to verify that the building was by no means abandoned.

Knight gagged at the stench of animal excrement, rot and blood. The air was alive with the hum of buzzing flies.

"I know that smell," Rook said, without a trace of his customary wit. "This is a slaughterhouse. They must be butchering those pigs here."

Although the observation seemed irrefutable, it made no sense. Why would a drug cartel be interested in raising wild pigs for slaughter? Like everything else they had discovered about El Sol, the situation defied a logical explanation.

King did not address the subject but immediately began barking orders. "Rook, secure that door. Knight, see if you can find a good position. Bishop, go with him."

It was, Knight thought, either a tacit vote of confidence, or an indication of just how desperate the situation was, that King had sent him to do his old job. *Or maybe he just forgot that I've taken a fifty percent reduction in my ability to see.* Whatever the explanation, Knight had no doubts about his ability to do the job. He ventured deeper into the dark structure, searching for a flight of stairs that would take him to the upper reaches of the building, or ideally to the roof, where he would be able to fire in any direction. There was only open space beyond the entrance—no interior rooms or offices—but he could make out the exposed lattice of rafters and support beams up near the ceiling, and a narrow elevated catwalk that ran lengthwise through the building, supporting some kind of rolling pulley system. With Bishop in tow, he skirted the wall, but after just a few steps, the proof to back up Rook's comment, literally slapped him in the face.

The impact caught him on his blind side, a cold wet collision that almost knocked him down. The object was dense and solid, but had yielded a little—more like running into a person than a wall. He took a step back, bringing both his gaze and his MP5 to bear. Through an almost opaque curtain of flies, he found a carcass hanging from an enormous hook mounted to an overhead rail. The body swayed back and forth. The head and limbs had been removed, and it had been skinned, gutted, and cut in half lengthwise, exposing muscle and bone. As the swarming insects settled back onto the exposed meat, Knight saw that the carcass was only one of several that were lined up in a row in front of them. The floor underfoot was sticky with blood.

He swallowed down his disgust and was about to start forward again when he felt a hand clasp his shoulder.

"Knight," Bishop said, barely able to get the word out. Beneath her dark hair, her face had gone ghostly white, and she looked about ready to vomit. She nodded at the hanging hunk of meat. "That is *not* animal."

THIRTY-SEVEN
Roanoke Island, North Carolina

The shadowy woods near Fort Raleigh reminded Beck of something from a fairy-tale. Not the enchanting happy kind where woodland creatures and magical sprites cavorted to celebrate the beauty of nature, but the dark ominous kind, where monsters and ravenous wolves lurked, ready to devour the unwary.

After the horrors they had witnessed at the hospital, her apprehension was warranted. While they had easily outpaced the wendigos roaming the streets of Manteo, the short drive to the Fort Raleigh National Historical Site had not put enough distance between them and the monsters, or the unseen agent that had created them. Rather, if Sara's suspicions were true, they were now at ground zero for the outbreak.

Ellen brought them to the edge of a shallow hole and began searching the surrounding area. Beck immediately spotted the signs of recent activity, not just the excavation—piles of dirt and a discarded collapsible shovel—but the trampling caused by heavy foot traffic.

"Here." Ellen pointed to something on the ground.

Sara slipped on a pair of sterile gloves before reaching down to retrieve the object. Beck saw that it was a bone. As Ellen had earlier indicated, it was the wrong shape and size to be human, but it did not require a leap of imagination to believe that it was from a wendigo. Sara put the bone in a plastic bio-hazard bag, then turned to Ellen again.

"Jason began showing symptoms after he found this?"

A nod.

Sara looked closely at the contents of the sealed bag. "There are some organic pathogens that can remain dormant for years. Centuries even. I think we have to work from the assumption that it was transmitted on contact. Did Haley touch it, too?"

"I don't recall. He showed it to us, then went back to work. It happened a few minutes later."

"Her exposure could have been secondary. She got it from touching Jason, as did the paramedic. Probably through contact with his sweat or saliva. What I still don't understand is why you weren't affected?"

Beck grimaced a little at Sara's clinical, almost calloused detachment, but she knew that the disease investigator was simply doing her job.

Sara went on. "My first guess would be that you have an immunity to it. Hereditary, if what you say about Eleanor Dare is true." She paused and closed her eyes for a moment. "Back at the hospital, the staff—and me, too... We all received direct exposure, but nothing happened for several hours. What triggered the change?"

"Some people get sick faster than others," Beck ventured, then immediately felt foolish. Sara Fogg was an expert on this subject, while she had little more to go on than unscientific observations.

Sara, however, grasped at the idea. "Okay, let's start with that. Something about Jason and Haley made them more susceptible to rapid onset. A weakened immune system, perhaps. Or something they..."

She trailed off and then stiffened, as if she had received an electrical shock. Without a word of explanation, she tore open the bio-hazard bag and held it close to her face. Beck jolted in alarm at the sudden action and groped for her pistol, half-expecting Sara to begin transforming into a wendigo. Sara was too focused on the contents of the bag to even notice, but after a moment, she lowered it and faced Ellen again.

"Breakfast. What did you eat for breakfast yesterday?"

Nonplussed, Ellen stammered, "Uh, hash browns and coffee."

"And the others? Jason and Haley?"

"I don't... I think Jason got a breakfast burrito." She snapped her fingers. "Yes. I remember now. A chorizo burrito. Haley gave him a hard time about it, but he insisted that she try it."

"But you didn't taste it, did you?"

"No."

"That's the explanation. The common factor." Sara shook the bio-hazard bag emphatically.

"Can you dumb it down for us a little?" Beck asked.

Sara pursed her lips together in thought for a moment. "Think of it like an allergic reaction. Bee stings for instance. A person might get stung once and have only a mild, seemingly ordinary reaction, but if they have a genetic predisposition to becoming allergic to bee venom, that one exposure establishes an immune response in their body, and the next time they get stung...bam."

"Well that clears it up," Beck muttered. "So some people are allergic to wendigos and others aren't?"

Sara shook her head. "No, it's not that simple. You told me to dumb it down, remember?"

"What does that have to do with my breakfast?" Ellen asked.

"Jason and Haley both ate something that contained meat. And just before the outbreak at the hospital, everyone else ate meat, too." She waved the bio-hazard bag again. "There was a strange... I think it was an odor...in the hospital. I noticed it when I first got there. It was really strong in Jason's room, when my suit got ripped. But I also smelled it in the lounge. It was coming from the food. And it's very faint, but I can smell it on this bone. There's a connection between food—specifically meat—and this outbreak.

"And I would guess," she added, "that it's also responsible for what happened to the Lost Colony."

Beck held up her hands. "Let me get this straight. That bone has a disease on it that turns people who eat meat into monsters?"

"There are unique enzymes found in certain types of animal tissue. A good example is something called alpha-gal. It's present in non-primate mammals, like cattle. In a healthy person, alpha-gal poses no problem at all, but there have been cases where people who have been bitten by the Lone Star tick develop an allergic reaction to alpha-gal. They literally become allergic to red meat overnight.

"This is obviously a reaction on a different order of magnitude, but it might explain the causal pathway. Exposure alone isn't enough. You can't become infected unless those enzymes are present in your body."

Ellen's brow furrowed. "This virus—"

"My best guess would be a prion," Sara interjected.

"A prion then, wiped out the Roanoke Colony, except for a few survivors? Then went dormant until we dug it up?"

Sara nodded. "That's my working hypothesis. In a way, you were right about the curse. But it wasn't divine vengeance. Just bad luck."

Ellen shook her head. "We've been trammeling this island for hundreds of years. Archaeologists have excavated everywhere. Are you saying that in all that time, no one ever encountered this...this prion?"

"Well, they may have encountered it, but without the additional catalyst of those specific enzymes, there wouldn't be a reaction."

"The people living in the Roanoke Colony would have eaten wild game and fish," Ellen countered. "The same as the native tribes, and all those who lived here afterward until the twentieth century."

"She's right," Beck said. "There's got to be more to it than that. Those things are alpha predators. They wouldn't just vanish completely." Working for Richard Ridley had given her at least that much of an education in science. "They'd multiply and spread like some kind of zombie outbreak."

Irritation crept into Sara's expression. "It's the best explanation. It may not be perfect, but it's a place..." She stopped midsentence, and then a look of hopeful enthusiasm came over her. "No, you're right. They would have propagated exponentially unless there was some kind of control mechanism in the environment. Ellen, where can I find more information about the native people who lived here? Specifically the tribes that would have interacted with the colony."

"You mean aside from Wikipedia? You can't throw a Frisbee on this island without hitting some kind of museum. Why?"

"Because there's a way to stop this. And we're going to find it."

As if to punctuate the hopeful pronouncement, there was a loud snap—a twig breaking—in the woods nearby. Beck whirled in the direction of the sound, gun drawn, just as a pale figure emerged, loping toward them.

It was not alone.

THIRTY-EIGHT
Mexico

King moved quickly toward the center of the open area, sweeping in every direction with his SCAR. There was still no indication that anyone was laying in wait, but every step forward brought a new revelation about the building and its role in Hector Beltran's grander scheme. He did not question Rook's assessment. The building did indeed house an industrial scale slaughterhouse, replete with butcher's tables, saws, enormous meat-grinders and rolls of paper.

His first thought was that the cartel might be operating a meat-packing business as a way to smuggle product out of the country, but that did not explain why Beltran was herding wild boars when raising domestic livestock, or for that matter simply purchasing animals raised and slaughtered elsewhere, would have been far more efficient. Nor did it mesh with what they had found in Mano's compound to the east, where the boars had, to all appearances, served an entirely different purpose.

The incongruity was worrisome, because King sensed that the underlying purpose was probably darker than anything he could imagine. If they were going to escape and ultimately defeat Beltran, he would need to understand the man's motivations. Plumbing the abyssal depths of Beltran's psyche was not the immediate priority, but King had the nagging sense that he had overlooked something critical.

Too many pieces, and none of them fit.

Queen's voice cut through the fetid air. "King! Over here!"

It was strange to hear his teammates speak in anything but a sub-vocalized whisper. The q-phones and the glasses had so totally revolutionized their techniques that ordinary speech seemed primitive and awkward. *Guess I'd better get used to it*, he thought, but his musings on the dire future they all faced were immediately set aside as he beheld Queen's discovery.

Parked in front of the large sliding door that they had seen from outside, was a medium-sized delivery truck.

"That's more like it!" He half-turned and shouted over his shoulder. "Change of plans. Get down here. We've got wheels!"

Queen raised an eyebrow. "If we can get it started."

"I have faith in you."

"Me?" She shook her head in mock-despair, then climbed up into the cab.

King approached the truck for a better look. Unlike the building, the truck was not only relatively new but it appeared to have been well-maintained. The exterior was streaked with road dust, but the cargo shell, which King now saw was insulated with a refrigeration unit mounted behind the cab, was not only completely intact, but adorned with a detailed likeness of the famous Aztec sun stone. Bold red letters above the disc read 'Azteca.' The legend beneath added 'Proveedor de Carnes.' Loosely translated: meat supplier.

Impelled by morbid curiosity, he circled to the rear of the truck and threw open the roll-up door. Cool air washed over him, but there was nothing visibly sinister in the neat rows of waxed cardboard boxes stacked inside, with stenciled letters that proclaimed carne de cerdo molido. He turned away, leaving the door wide open, and headed forward to check on Queen's progress. As he reached the open door to the cab, the engine roared to life, belching out a black cloud of diesel smoke.

He flashed her a thumb's up and then continued past the truck to the sliding door, where he paused, waiting for the rest of the team to gather. Rook was the first to arrive. He skidded to a halt when he spotted the idling truck, and at King's direction, he clambered into the open cargo area to establish a mobile firing position from which he would be able to cover their escape.

Knight and Bishop were not far behind. As they stepped into view, King was struck by the look of absolute horror on their faces, but neither of them volunteered an explanation. "Knight. Cover me at the door. Bishop, take the shotgun."

Knight hastened forward and aimed his machine pistol at the door, but then he stopped and cocked his head sideways. "Do you hear that?"

The only thing King heard was the chug of the big diesel engine, but he trusted Knight's keen senses. "What is it?"

Knight spun around and began moving toward an area of the building they had not yet explored. Recalling his earlier wariness, King brought his rifle up and started after Knight. The back of the slaughterhouse was cloaked in shadow, but a strange glow was emanating from the floor. The light grew steadily brighter, and he saw that the light was coming from a ramp which descended below the main floor level, as if to a basement or a tunnel.

Suddenly, the connection was clear, or at least a little clearer. He still didn't understand the why of Beltran's ramshackle meat supply operation, but he knew where the cartel fighters were keeping their semi-wild livestock and why Beltran had chosen the old ruins as the place to set his ambush. The slaughterhouse and the ruins were connected by a tunnel system. There were probably dozens of hidden exits and underground warehouses for storing narcotics or guns...but meat?

Why meat?

Wild pigs evidently were not the only creatures that used the tunnels. King could hear the sound clearly now, a loud harsh buzz like an unmuffled chainsaw or a...

"Motorcycle!"

The noise reached a fever pitch, and then *two* motorcycles appeared in the mouth of the tunnel and shot up the ramp. King adjusted his aim and squeezed the trigger twice in rapid succession. At such close range, there was no way he could miss, but the armor piercing tungsten-core rounds seemed to have no effect on the rider. The motorcycle continued forward, forcing King to throw himself to the side to avoid being run down.

Knight fared a little better. What the nine-millimeter rounds from his machine pistol lacked in stopping power, they more than made up for in volume. The rider flinched under the assault, and then both he and his machine were tumbling end over end across the floor.

But in the instant King and Knight engaged the motorcyclists, two more emerged right behind them, and before either of the Chess Team operators could adjust fire, another two appeared.

Knight kept trying to engage targets, with more success than King, but the motorcycles were moving too fast, and the riders, now aware that the enemy was in their midst, were actively trying to reduce the target they presented by ducking low behind their handle bars and zig-zagging randomly as they sought refuge in the dark depths of the slaughterhouse.

"Get to the truck," King shouted.

Knight moved, firing out the last of his magazine one-handed as he ran. King continued searching for a target, but all of the men—save for the one Knight had brought down—had all but vanished from sight.

King ran to the sliding door and threw it back to reveal the newly dawned day. The sudden brightness stung his eyes, forcing him to look away, but the hiss of something whizzing past his head, followed a moment later by the report of a rifle, sent him ducking for cover behind the wall. The shot had come from outside. Beltran's forces were waiting for them.

He turned to meet Queen's gaze and gestured for her to start moving. The truck reluctantly picked up speed. As it rolled past, King broke from cover, launching himself in a high flat dive onto the floor of the cargo bay, where Knight and Rook were already waiting.

Rook opened up with the machine gun, hosing the dark interior of the slaughterhouse with a long sustained burst designed to discourage pursuit, but just a few seconds later, a storm of lead perforated the thin metal walls around them, forcing the three men to seek cover behind the stacked boxes. Although the waxed cardboard was even less effective at stopping a bullet than the sheet metal, the contents of the boxes—paper-wrapped portions of ground meat—kept them safe. The angle of the attack shifted as the truck rolled onward, and a few seconds later the incoming fire ceased altogether.

As it continued to accelerate, the truck bounced violently over the uneven terrain, toppling the stacked boxes and spilling their contents onto the floor. Knight started visibly, as if scalded, when one of the packages brushed his leg, and King saw the same aghast look on his friend's face as he stared at it.

"You okay?"

"No," Knight admitted, shaking his head. He pointed at the jumble of packages and opened his mouth to elaborate, but then faltered, as if unable to find the right words.

"Head's up!" Rook shouted. "Company's coming. Looks like it's Road Warrior time."

Knight's problems would have to wait. Although the slaughterhouse had diminished to a mere blip in the landscape, the objects throwing up horse-tails of dust in the foreground were definitely getting bigger. The motorcycle riders were giving chase.

The violent shaking caused by the truck's passage over the rough ground made accurate fire impossible, but King knew the cartel soldiers would be at an even greater disadvantage on their two-wheeled mounts. "Queen, slow down a little. Let's bring them in a little closer."

Rook regarded him with faint amusement. "I don't think she heard you, boss."

King swore under his breath, only partly out of embarrassment at his goof. His inability to communicate with Queen, just thirty feet away, was only a minor operational inconvenience, but it served as a stark reminder of a catastrophe with which he had not yet begun to truly process. They were on their own. Even if Deep Blue was able to organize a rescue—and something told him that was probably not in the works—there would be no way to coordinate their efforts.

Rook waited until the motorcycle riders were within a hundred yards to trigger a burst. Judging by the arc of the tracer rounds, his shots came nowhere close. Nevertheless, two of the motorcycles skidded to a halt and were immediately left behind by their comrades, who veered away from the truck's dust trail—one going left, the other right, in what appeared to be a flanking maneuver. The reason for the abrupt stop of the first pair became apparent when the flash of muzzle fire signaled an incoming volley of automatic rifle fire. Sure enough, the interior of the cargo bay was suddenly filled with the noise and heat of bullet impacts. King ducked and returned fire, putting the iron sights of the SCAR directly on the tell-tale muzzle flash. He could not tell if he scored a hit, but at least the gunmen stopped firing.

There was another loud report, this time from the front of the truck. It had to be Bishop, fending off a charge from their right side. Even as the echoes of the shot died away, King glimpsed a motorcycle rolling end over end across the field off to the right. The other side however would be vulnerable, since Queen was in no position to drive and shoot simultaneously.

"Knight, see what you can do to protect our left flank."

"On it." Knight immediately crawled forward, passing Rook, and moved to the very edge of the cargo door. Then, in a move that surprised even King, he stuck head and shoulders out into the open and curled his body around the corner. He held himself in place with one hand gripping the doorframe, while his other held his machine pistol. The floor of the cargo area was vibrating so violently that Knight bounced up and down like a dribbled basketball, but after just a few seconds in this precarious position, he started pulling himself back in, and a second downed motorcycle came briefly into view.

King scanned the rising dust cloud behind them, but a minute passed, then two, with no sign of further pursuit. As the adrenaline drained away, he allowed himself to relax, but only a little. The immediate battle had been won, but they were still deep in enemy territory. He did not believe for a second that El Sol's reach was limited to the small group of men that had been deployed at the ruins. It would take only one phone call to organize another ambush, and Beltran had the home court advantage.

I don't even know where we are, he realized, once more feeling the ominous loss of Endgame.

Pull it together, he told himself. *Control the situation before it controls you.*

They were not going to be able to fight their way all the way to the American border, and even if they did, there was no guarantee of refuge there. What did that leave?

"We're going to have to ditch this ride," he said, remembering to speak loud enough to be heard over the roar of the engine and the high-pitched creak of the suspension. "I guess I should go tell Queen."

"Try banging on the walls," Rook suggested, a trace of his customary humor returning. "That's what she does when we run out of toilet paper."

Knight shook his head despairingly. "Tango Mike India."

Rook grinned but then became serious again. "Hey, what was up with you? I thought you were about to jump out of your skin when that package of sausage fell on you. You didn't join some religion that prohibits pork, did you?"

The light moment passed and Knight's face clouded over. "That isn't pork. Bishop and I found...bodies. They're grinding up people."

Rook stared back aghast. "Fuck."

King felt a cold chill at the revelation. "How many? How many bodies?"

"Too many," Knight replied, and King knew exactly what he meant.

"He killed them?" Rook said, incredulous. "The hostages? Killed them and ground them up for taco meat? Why?"

"A sick joke," King said, but the answer felt insufficient. Beltran was unquestionably evil, yet he had not risen to the top of the criminal underworld simply on cruelty alone. There was some darker purpose at work, something that was so far outside the realm of normal human behavior that King felt unable to even make an educated guess.

"He has to die," Rook said, with almost child-like earnestness. "We've got to take that fucker down."

"We will," King promised. He stopped short of adding: *If it's the last thing we do*, because in his heart, he feared that it might be.

THIRTY-NINE

Endgame, New Hampshire

As he exited the light rail tunnel and got his first look at the hangar-sized man-made cavern designated simply as 'Dock,' Boucher let out a low whistle of appreciation. He knew all about the *Dock* but had never actually visited the seldom used corner of the former Manifold Alpha complex, or beheld its contents with his own eyes. The headlights of the Zero SR electric motorcycles that he and Duncan had ridden down the ten-mile long tunnel from the *Labs* were hardly sufficient to reveal the scope of the enclosure, but what they did reveal was beyond all his expectations.

The most prominent feature was the moored Typhoon-class submarine, which stretched across the length of the cavern like a black leviathan from a Jules Verne novel. He could see only a little of it; nearly six hundred feet long—almost the length of two football fields—its full extent was well beyond the reach of the headlights. Even the stubby sail—the tall superstructure that rose just aft of the sub's middle, extending forty feet above the dorsal hull, spiked with various antennae, periscopes and other protuberances that disappeared into the darkness overhead—was almost too much to take in. There had been a time in his long career as an intelligence officer, when he would have killed—literally—for a chance to be this close to one of the largest submarines ever built. Now, it was merely a curiosity to be glanced at and just as quickly forgotten.

Duncan dropped the kickstand on his motorcycle and dismounted. "This way."

Boucher hastened to keep up. Years of sitting behind one desk or another had not slowed the former Army Ranger, but there was an added urgency to his old friend's pace. It was not merely that time was in critically short supply. Duncan was not running away from the forces that were, even now, sweeping through the Endgame facility; he was running toward a different kind of confrontation.

The ongoing conflict between the senior senator from the State of Utah and the former President of the United States, which had run hot and cold over the years, was not merely a bitter political rivalry. Marrs was consumed by a thirst for power, and the man made no secret of how he intended to exercise that power, leveraging populist sentiment into a secretly authoritarian government that would doom the two-century long American experiment in democracy.

Duncan's decision to sacrifice his own presidency to block Marrs's earlier attempts to seize power had not been made lightly, and Boucher knew that his old friend had been plagued by doubt regarding his strategy to preserve both the Chess Team and the world. Those concerns now appeared to have been validated. Duncan's decision to surrender the presidency had been only a temporary victory, not nearly enough to thwart the ambitious Marrs. In a perfect world, Duncan would have been content to allow the democratic process to be the final arbiter. If the American people were willing to be hoodwinked into supporting Marrs, then who was he to stand in the way of the majority? But Marrs had now acted outside the legitimate process, conspiring with international criminals in an act of treason that had cost the life of American servicemen.

Marrs was no longer merely a distasteful political rival. He was the enemy that both Duncan and Boucher had sworn to defend against. Escaping from Endgame was no longer the primary objective. They had to escape so they could strike back.

Duncan ran at what was probably for him, merely a fast jog, to an exposed stairwell that crawled like a fire-escape up the wall of the cavern. Boucher assumed the stairs led up to the concealed cabin entrance and followed along to the extent that his tired old legs and lungs would permit.

There had been precious little time to discuss strategy. They had raced on foot to the computer room, where Duncan had manually initiated the incendiary charges that were part of the self-destruct system. Because the air was not saturated with methane, as the Desperado protocol intended, the damage was limited, but nonetheless far-reaching. The thermate charges had completely slagged the innovative quantum computer, instantly rendering the entire network dead, leaving Chess Team high and dry in the field. Boucher knew that was a preferable alternative to allowing Marrs to gain control of the computer. This was not just a scorched-earth retreat. Marrs would have been able to use the information stored in the computer to expose the entire network of Endgame contacts worldwide, to say nothing of exploiting a technology with the potential to reshape the global power structure.

The acrid smell of burning metal and plastic was still in Boucher's nose, a bitter aftertaste of failure.

From there, it had been a sprint to the light rail tunnel, where the electric motorcycles intended for security patrols and track maintenance, had been waiting to bear them to the *Dock*. Boucher had been relieved to learn that they wouldn't have to make a ten-mile long trek in the dark, but unfortunately, the electric motorbikes could not shorten the ten-story ascent to the exit in the lakeside cabin. He didn't want to think about the long hike that awaited them once they reached the top.

Because his head was filled with the sound of footfalls, tapping out a staccato rhythm on the steps, as well as his labored panting and the rush of blood in his ears, he didn't realize anything was amiss until he heard the crack of rifle fire.

He looked up just in time to see Duncan come about for a hasty descent, hands loose on the rails as he bounded down four or five steps at a time. "Down!" he shouted. Boucher was already pivoting.

Muzzle flashes high above marked the location of several gunmen, FBI, SWAT or possibly National Guard riflemen, who had evidently decided to secure the entrance at the *Dock* after all. If Boucher and Duncan had been just a little faster in their egress, they probably would have run into the waiting arms of the assault team on the surface. That was little consolation now that their only exit was cut off. Boucher stepped aside to let Duncan pass. His friend seemed to be moving with a purpose, and Boucher could only hope that it meant that Duncan had one more ace up his sleeve.

The metal stairs deflected the incoming fire, a fact which did not escape the notice of the shooters, and after the initial volley, the guns fell silent, to be replaced by the ringing of footsteps on the metal treads high above. The reprieve was short-lived however. As soon as Duncan reached the bottom and ventured out into the open, the firing resumed, and this time the bullets did not deflect harmlessly off the stairs, but slammed into the concrete floor all around him. Boucher realized he would have to run the same gauntlet, but without any idea of where exactly he was going.

Duncan made it across the concrete dock to a tall metal structure that reminded Boucher of something he might have made in his childhood, using Tinkertoys or an Erector Set. The scaffold-like contraption sat at the water's edge, and after a moment's scrutiny, Boucher realized that it ended at a catwalk that led out to the Typhoon's sail.

Duncan paused at the base of a ladder leading up the structure. "Dom! Move it!"

Throwing caution to the wind, Boucher launched himself out into the open. He was halfway across before he heard the crack of bullets on the floor and the noise of gunfire high above. He veered off, running headlong into a cloud of concrete dust, then angled in the other direction. His zig-zag course got him safely to the base of the structure, but the evasive maneuvers were not without cost. As he skidded to a halt in front of the ladder, he saw the several men in black tactical gear pouring down the stairs where he had been only moments before.

Duncan's ascent had caused the ladder to vibrate crazily, and Boucher had to fight past his rising trepidation to follow. He felt sure the ladder would come apart in his hands, but that was a less certain outcome than what would await him if he lingered any longer. With an alacrity borne of fear, he scrambled up until he saw Duncan's outstretched hand. He took it, allowing himself to be hauled the rest of the way onto the catwalk, and then Duncan was moving again, crossing the narrow span out to the Typhoon's sail.

Boucher muttered a curse, then rose and chased after his friend. "You can't be serious," he said, the words coming out choppy between labored breaths. "Tom, we don't know how to drive a submarine."

If he heard, Duncan did not acknowledge the implied question. Instead, he vaulted over the rail at the end of the makeshift bridge and spun the flywheel mechanism to open the hatch into the Typhoon's interior. Then, he hauled it open and stepped back, gesturing for Boucher to go first.

Out of the fire and into the frying pan, Boucher thought as he dove through the open hatch. The pitch of incessant rifle fire changed as he transitioned from the vast open space of the *Dock* to the claustrophobic confines of the Typhoon, but the change was less than comforting. There was a scuffling noise as Duncan came through and pulled the hatch shut with a funereal thump, sealing them in the dark belly of the beast.

The oppressive darkness lasted only a moment before a green glow, like the fleeting shine of a lightning bug, appeared before him. The light, which was almost painfully bright, issued from a chemical glow stick that Duncan now held aloft like a torch.

Duncan reached into a small cabinet mounted on the wall next to the hatch and took out a plastic wrapped item about the size and shape off a cigar. He tore it open and shook out another glow stick, which he activated with a quick bending motion, and handed to Boucher. "I've sealed the hatch, but it won't keep them out for long."

"Please tell me you have a plan," Boucher said.

"'Plan' might be overstating it a bit," Duncan admitted "This is more like a Hail Mary pass. If it works we'll be home free. If it doesn't..."

"They'll catch us? Or shoot us?"

"More likely, they'll never find our bodies." Duncan offered no further explanation, and Boucher did not press for one. He had resigned himself to certain death when he had insisted on staying behind. The decision to make a run for it instead of triggering the self-destruct protocol had given him reason to hope that he might be able to postpone his rendezvous with the Grim Reaper, but as far as he was concerned, it was all borrowed time from here on out.

Boucher had no sense of where he was in the submarine, but his gut told him they would not be retracing their steps. Duncan might not have been willing to admit that he had a plan, but the man was clearly moving toward a specific destination as he ventured deeper into the sub's interior. He ducked through the open hatchways connecting one compartment to the next, descending ladders to the lower decks, and Boucher followed. After a few minutes, they entered a cramped space barely larger than a storage closet. One entire wall was comprised entirely of what looked like locker doors.

Duncan tossed his glow stick onto the deck and began rooting in one of the lockers. "Quick. Put this on." He held out something that, in the eerie green glow, looked like a shadow given substance, but as soon as Boucher felt the foam-like texture, he knew what it was.

"A wetsuit?"

Duncan was already stripping out of his own clothes, stuffing each article into a waterproof bag. "Didn't I mention that we're going for a swim?" he said with a half-hearted grin.

"You most certainly did not," Boucher replied, feigning irritation. He quickly doffed his clothes and then began the somewhat more laborious process of pulling on the tight neoprene garment. Duncan had already finished getting his wetsuit on and was now busy procuring the rest of the gear they would need for the 'swim': masks, fins, snorkels and SCUBA gear. When Boucher was finally suited, he followed Duncan through another hatch and into a huge open compartment.

The scant light of the glow stick could only hint at the true dimensions of the space beyond, but it was big by any standards, and positively cavernous situated as it was, inside the submarine. Boucher knew that the Typhoon subs were reportedly large enough to contain swimming pools, and for a moment he thought that was where they were, but the overhead cargo lift suggested that the rectangular opening concealed under large sheets of metal served a different purpose.

"Ridley redecorated," Duncan explained. "He put in a docking bay for a submersible."

"Is that how we're leaving?"

"Yes and no. The submersible is in dry dock, undergoing repairs, but we don't need it. When we open those doors, we can swim right out."

"And go where?"

Duncan moved to one side of the opening and retrieved an object that looked a little like a high-tech vacuum cleaner with the handle removed. At one end, a plastic screen shielded what appeared to be fan blades. Duncan handed the device to Boucher.

"This is one of those underwater propulsion units, right?"

Duncan nodded and selected a similar unit for himself and then set about manually opening the doors to the moon-pool. "Top speed is about three miles per hour, which is a lot faster than it sounds. The battery is good for more than an hour, but our SCUBA bottles won't last that long. Attach your chem-light to the DPV, but try to stay close. If we get separated, we might not find each other again. I already opened the outer door to the lake."

The metal doors slid back to reveal inky black water that seemed preternaturally still until Duncan sat on the pool's edge and broke the surface with his swim fins. "Ready?"

There was a resonant thump from somewhere high above. An explosion—probably from a shaped breaching charge, blowing the main hatch wide open. The SWAT team would be inside the sub within seconds.

"Do I have a choice?" Boucher quickly donned mask and fins and buckled into his SCUBA harness, then joined his friend at the edge of the pool.

"Remember. Stay close. We'll make it out of this alive." With those words of encouragement, Duncan slipped into the water and vanished. Boucher was right behind him.

FORTY

Mexico

As he watched Beltran organizing the pursuit of the American commando force, Parrish had to resist the urge to laugh. The sight of the cartel leader, who not only towered over Parrish but also outweighed him by a good fifty pounds, tattooed to resemble a demonic Aztec deity, streaked with dust and blood like an escapee from Hell, now shouting into a mobile phone, was so absurd it was comical.

There was nothing funny about Beltran's rage, though, and as the reports of failure began to trickle in, the cartel leader's wrath began to grow exponentially. With all of the man's subordinates already engaged in the battle, Parrish found himself alone with the unpredictable crime lord, and there was nothing funny about that either. Beltran struck him as the kind of man who might easily kill the messenger bringing bad news. If the messenger was reporting from a safe distance using mobile phone technology, Beltran might simply lash out in blind rage at the nearest target of opportunity, and right now, that was Parrish.

Parrish was surprised to discover that his initial impression was wrong. When one of his men reported that the Americans had escaped in a stolen truck, killing or wounding everyone who had attempted to stop them, Beltran did not unleash a tornado of impotent rage. Instead, he appeared to focus that potential energy into a flurry of phone calls, sent out to his network of minions, marshaling them in an all-out effort to block his prey's escape. It was this juxtaposition—Beltran, an inked monster coolly working the phones like a predatory CEO or battlefield general—that threatened to crack Parrish up, and giving in to that morbid urge would almost certainly be fatal.

I've got to get out of here, he told himself. *Before this psycho decides he needs more divine help and offers me up to his crazy god.*

Getting away however was not as simple as just slipping away into the background. He had no idea where he was, and he had only his own two feet to bear him away. But then, slinking away with his tail between his legs like a beaten cur was not the Bulldog's style. He stepped in front of Beltran, arms folded over his chest, and stared up into the crime lord's rabid eyes.

"I need a ride out of here," he said. His tone was not confrontational but neither was it pleading. It was a simple statement that allowed no room for further discussion.

Beltran stared at him with undisguised annoyance and then simply turned away, continuing his long distance conversation without pause.

Parrish took this as a good sign and pressed the issue. "Did you hear me?"

Beltran glared at him. "You leave when this is finished."

"As far as I'm concerned, it is finished. Senator Marrs and I handed these guys to you on a silver platter, as promised." He mentioned the senator as a none-too-subtle reminder of the consequences of 'killing the messenger.' Parrish was Marrs's ambassador, and since Marrs was very likely going to be the next President of the United States, treating his agent badly would have far-reaching implications. "Whether or not you can close the deal is not my problem."

Beltran said a few more words into the phone and then thumbed a button to end the call. "A car is on its way for us," he said, with flat indifference. "You can ride with me back to the city. After that, you are on your own."

Parrish carefully avoided letting his relief show, instead creasing his forehead in a look of reluctant acceptance, but he said nothing more. He had won, but it was a tenuous victory, too easily reversed if he kept harping on the issue. Beltran had already moved on, taking another incoming call, and this time, he spoke in English.

"Whatever it is will have to wait. I'm in the middle of something." There was a long pause as Beltran listened, and then his eyes went wide with a mixture of hope and apprehension. When he spoke again, it was in an awed voice. "Are you sure?"

All the anger melted from his expression, replaced by a different kind of fire. "Where did you say?" He nodded, his lips moving as he silently repeated the reply, as if committing it to memory. "This is excellent. You've done well."

Beltran ended the call then immediately dialed another number. When the connection was made, he spoke in rapid Spanish. Parrish caught enough of it to get the gist. Something was happening in America, something that superseded the hunt for the American commandos.

Parrish did not like what he was hearing. Whatever this new development was, it had completely changed the dynamics of the situation, which put him once more on very uncertain ground. "What's going on?" he demanded when Beltran hung up.

The cartel lord was unperturbed by the question. "Something wonderful has happened. A seed that was planted has taken root." He faced Parrish with a broad grin, which looked positively frightening on Beltran's demonic visage. "Good news for you, *Buldog*. I am going to America. You can come with me. And when we get there, you will see something wonderful."

CR AT N

REFUGE

FORTY-ONE

Roanoke Island, North Carolina

Beck fired a headshot that dropped the wendigo at the front of the pack. The next creature, close on its heels, stumbled over the thrashing corpse of its fallen leader and went down in a tangle of misshapen limbs. Beck fired again and again, each shot tearing into the pale creatures, but she saw that she would run out of bullets before she ran out of targets.

"Run! Get to the car!"

She glimpsed movement—Sara and Ellen heeding her advice—and fired out the last of the magazine, buying them a little more time. It worked, though that was of little comfort as the three surviving wendigos closed in.

She resisted the almost overpowering urge to run. With their unnaturally long limbs, they would catch her before she got fifty yards. Instead, she darted toward the excavation, snatching up the shovel that had been left behind.

The digging implement was instantly familiar in her hands. A hinged joint at the spade head, and another where the triangular handle met the foot-long metal shaft, allowed the whole thing to be folded up in a neat little holster that could be clipped to a rucksack. In her Army days, she had known it as an 'E-tool,' short for 'entrenching tool.' While it was usually issued to soldiers to dig fox-holes on the battlefield, it was more frequently used for carving out latrines or as a scythe to hack down weeds, but every soldier knew that it could also be employed as a weapon.

With a loose grip on the handle, Beck swung the E-tool in a lateral swipe that connected with the head of the wendigo leading the charge. It had been a blind swing. A reflex. She had not realized the creature was so close. There was an eruption of foul brown matter as the blade shattered the deformed skull, like a dropped egg.

Beck pirouetted aside as the dead-thing tumbled past, then swung again, lopping off the reaching arm of another. The wendigos, driven by a primal hunger, were oblivious to the lethal potential in her hands. Beck however was no longer mindlessly hacking at the air, but instead timing her strikes, conserving her energy, and whenever possible, checking her six for a flanking attack. The monsters fell, one shattered skull after another, until there were no more. Then she turned in the direction the others had gone, and sprinted after them, the E-tool held out before her like a battle-axe.

As frantic as it had been, the melee had lasted only a few seconds, and she caught up to Sara and Ellen just as they were reaching the car. "Get in," she shouted.

As she threw open the driver's door, she caught a glimpse of movement across the roof of the Nissan. More wendigos were charging across the parking lot. She tossed the E-tool into the footwell, then slid behind the wheel and slammed the door shut. "Is everybody in?" she called without looking, focused on starting the car.

"Yes!" Sara yelled beside her. "Go!"

The engine caught and Beck accelerated forward to the sound of hands and bodies thumping against the fenders. For several seconds, the tumult increased, as arriving wendigos outpaced the little car.

The Nissan revved through first and second gear, finally pulling away from the mass of demonic creatures, but more of them spilled out of the woods all around, trying to intercept them. None succeeded, but their sheer numbers were frightening.

Ellen was on the verge of hysteria. "They're everywhere! You still think this is just a disease?"

"If you don't shut the hell up," Beck growled, "I'll dump you out right now."

"Don't do that," Sara cautioned, as if the threat had been sincere. "We need her to figure out how to cure this thing."

Beck swerved to dodge a wendigo that was running down the road straight at them. "Hate to say it, but could she be right? We're miles from the hospital, and there were only a few of these things when we left. Now there are..." Her gaze flicked to the rear view mirror. "A lot. And something tells me this is just the tip of the iceberg."

"I don't know how it's spreading, but it *is* a contagion. Probably an exotic virus. But that's not the point."

"Then what is?"

"This thing is old. Centuries at least, but something kept it from spreading. It's like you said, this contagion should have gone global, but it didn't, and I think the natives who lived here knew how to keep it in check."

"It's. A. Curse," Ellen said. "The only way to remove a curse is to stop angering the spirits who sent it in the first place."

Beck was about to shout Ellen down again, but Sara forestalled her. "Yes, but how do we appease the spirits? That's what I need to know. Did they make some special offering? Smoke a certain kind of tobacco in their peace pipes?"

"Peace pipes?" Ellen scoffed. "You really don't know anything, do you?"

Sara twisted around to face her. "About tribal practices? No, I don't. That's why I want you to help me understand."

"The native people that lived here were wiped out by the European colonization. They left very little in the way of permaculture, and passed all their traditions down orally. There isn't some special book of native secrets."

"Then where do we start? You tell me."

Ellen shook her head. "Those things are everywhere. Even if I knew where—"

"Just tell us where to go," Beck broke in. "I'll take care of getting us there alive." She sounded more confident than she felt.

Without an ammo re-supply, the E-tool was their only weapon against the wendigos. Unfortunately, while they had passed at least a dozen surf shops and dive outfitters on the short drive from Manteo, she had yet to see a single gun store.

"Well, I don't know if there's anything of real value there, but we can try the Lost Colony Festival Park. It's billed as a replica of the original colony that you can walk through. They have actors playing the colonists...and the natives." There was palpable contempt in Ellen's tone. "There's a museum there, but the place is kind of a tourist trap."

"Let's hope that's the only kind of trap it is," Beck muttered, and put the pedal to the floor.

FORTY-TWO
Mexico City

Asya strolled, with what she hoped would be perceived as nonchalance, down the sidewalk, glancing in store windows as if idly curious about the wares within, but never lingering more than a few seconds. Reflected in the panes, she saw milling passersby and street vendors, none of whom returned more than a cursory glance.

While she was not exactly inconspicuous in the sprawling cosmopolitan megacity, a light-skinned woman with dark hair, wearing camouflage pants and a brown t-shirt was hardly noteworthy. The plastic shopping bag, clutched perhaps a little too protectively in her arms, marked her as a tourist, and there were plenty of those.

She stopped in front of a sidewalk vendor and bought several t-shirts adorned with silk screened images of tropical birds, archaeological ruins and beer labels. One shirt in particular caught her eye, black with the likeness of a world renowned singer; her brother would like that. She handed the vendor several two-hundred-peso notes, waving away the change and stuffing her purchases into the shopping bag before moving on.

Her route meandered back and forth across Mexico City's famed Zocalo, the public square that was a must-see for visitors. She made several more purchases from kiosks chosen at random, snacks mostly, but also five cheap cellular phones, each from a different vendor. Now loaded with two shopping bags, she made another circuit of the square, and then hailed a taxi.

The driver appraised her for a moment, then asked for her destination in nearly perfect English. She feigned incomprehension, just as she had done whenever any of the locals attempted to engage her in conversation, and she mumbled something in Russian before handing him a slip of paper upon which was scrawled the address of a budget hotel on the outskirts of the city. The ride did not take as long as she thought it would, due in no small part to the cab driver's aggressive maneuvering through traffic and his complete disregard for safety.

When she arrived at the hotel, she went through the lobby, and after ensuring that no one was watching, she slipped out the back entrance into a secluded alley. There, she quickly changed into a bright red t-shirt, lightweight cotton shorts and sandals before heading out again.

A short trek brought her to a bridge spanning a canal, and after a quick check for spying eyes, she scrambled down the earthen bank and into the shade beneath the bridge. She waited there for almost a minute before a figure stirred from the midst of what looked like a pile of trash. It was King.

"Any problems?"

Asya shook her head and handed him her purchases. "Easy as cake."

King returned a faint smile, then knelt and began inspecting the contents of the shopping bags. He laid the mobile phones out in a neat row, then delved deeper. When he took out the black t-shirt she had selected for him, he actually laughed. "'El Vez?'"

"Do you like? I know you are a big fan."

"I love." He set it down and kept digging until he found the large envelope, which she had procured at her first stop. Inside were several passports, bundles of American and Mexican currency, and five SIM cards, all retrieved from a safety deposit box in a downtown bank. There was a cache like it in nearly every major city in the world, set aside for just such a possibility. The box had also contained weapons, but Asya had, on King's instructions, left those behind. Guns and knives would not help them make a stealthy exit from the country.

They had ditched the truck after putting a few miles between them and the cartel fighters, and continued on foot until reaching the outskirts of Mexico City. In their combat uniforms, they would almost certainly have drawn the attention of El Sol lookouts, so King had made the decision to send just one person into the city to retrieve the contents of the safety deposit box, and Asya had been the perfect choice. The cartel had not, as far as they knew, gotten a good look at any of them. It was a good bet that Beltran would assume they were all men. With her dark hair and Slavic accent and features, Asya would be the last person a potential El Sol informant would suspect of being part of an elite American combat unit. For her part, Asya felt well-suited to the task. A perennial fish out of water, she had developed a knack for adapting to strange environments. To her, the urban bustle of the Zocalo was no stranger than downtown Pinckney.

King slotted a SIM card into one of the phones and then handed it to her. "I'll pass the rest of this stuff out to the others. You should probably head out now. I'll call you to set up the rendezvous."

Asya did not need to ask for clarification. The contingency plan for the situation in which they now found themselves called for the team to split up. They would go their separate ways to avoid attracting attention, and await further instructions. If any one of them was captured, he or she would not know the whereabouts of the others. Nevertheless, she hesitated. "Should we try to contact Thomas?"

King's stony expression returned. "We're on our own. Blue has his own problems."

She frowned. "That is what I mean. We have to help him."

"Asya, there's a very good chance that Tom is—"

"No!" She shook her head vehemently. "Do not say it."

King took a breath. "We aren't going to be able to do anything until we're clear of this mess."

Asya knew he was right, but that was little comfort. "I want to know," she said, barely louder than a whisper.

King pursed his lips in thought then took back the phone and started scrolling through the pre-loaded contact list. "Even if he got clear of Endgame, there's no guarantee he'll pick up." He hit the 'send' button, then tapped another button, putting the phone in speaker mode. There was a trilling sound as the call went out, then a burst of static, followed by a tinny voice. "Hello?"

King's eyes went wide in surprise. "Lew?"

Asya felt her heart sink. The person on the other end of the line was Lewis Aleman, not Thomas—not Deep Blue.

A strange sound issued from the speaker. It took Asya a moment to realize that it was a sigh of relief. "King. You're alive. What's your status? Is everyone...okay?"

"More or less, but we're in the wind. What's the situation at your end?"

"FUBAR."

Asya had heard the others use the strange term before and knew that it meant nothing good.

"But better now that I know you guys are safe," Aleman finished.

"'Safe' is a relative term."

"Don't I know it. Give me fifteen minutes, and I'll find a way to get you guys out of there."

"What about Thomas?" Asya blurted, unable to contain herself.

"Bishop? Glad you're still with us. The feds raided Endgame. I made it out. Hitched a ride to Manchester. I'm not sure about Blue and Dom." He paused as if trying to figure out how to deliver bad news. "King, there's something else you should know. It's just hitting the news, but there's something happening in North Carolina."

"Sara?" Despite his customary reserve, there was real fear in King's voice.

"I think it might be. The governor has declared a state of emergency. The Outer Banks are shut down. No one is getting in or out. Phones and Internet are down. But some of the reports that got out before the blackout are...well, pretty crazy."

King's expression became even grimmer. "How crazy?"

"People are using the words 'zombie apocalypse.'"

"Lew, I need you to look something up for me."

"Uh, okay. What?"

"El Sol is running a meat supply company. Azteca. Maybe legit, maybe not. I need to know who they're supplying."

There was a long silence, and Asya wondered if Aleman was as confused by the abrupt non sequitur as she was. Although she was still in shock over what they had discovered in the slaughterhouse, she could not believe that King was more interested in taking down Beltran than he was in the fact that his fiancée was caught in the middle of a disease outbreak.

The real reason for Aleman's silence became apparent a moment later. "Azteca is a wholly owned subsidiary of Mid-Atlantic Diversified Holdings LLC. MAD-H looks like a shell company, probably a money laundering outfit for El Sol."

"I don't care who owns them," King snapped. "Where does the meat go?"

"I'm not sure, but MAD-H also owns a fast food chain, Mr. Pig."

King's eyes narrowed. "Never heard of them."

"They're pretty new. Real big in the South, but they have stores in D.C. and New York."

"And North Carolina?"

"Sure."

"But is that possible?" King asked. "How could they get tainted meat, let alone human meat, into the country and onto plates? Wouldn't the FDA catch it?"

"First," Aleman said, "that's nasty. Seriously. Second, we're talking about the FDA, which presents a few problems. They're so understaffed and underfunded that they operate primarily on the honor system, taking action only after the fact, when people get sick. Also, Beltran is probably smuggling the meat across the border and combining it with shipments from legitimate, and inspected, facilities. But probably most important, when the FDA *does* do inspections, they test for things like fecal bacteria, but not whether the pork is actually pork. So it's not only possible, it's probably easy."

King frowned. "You have to get me to North Carolina, Lew."

This time, confusion was the only possible explanation for the long silence.

"Lew?"

"I'm here. This is weird. I'm getting another call."

FORTY-THREE

Rochester, New Hampshire

With a population of almost thirty thousand, Rochester was a sprawling metropolis compared to sleepy little Pinckney, but Duncan nevertheless felt conspicuous as he followed Boucher into the restaurant. It was a 1950s nostalgia-themed diner, surrounded by classic cars, the sort of place that might be frequented by tourists, and where an unfamiliar face might not set the jungle telegraph humming with gossip. Of course, his face was not exactly unfamiliar; he had won New Hampshire handily in both elections, and even though he had been out of the public spotlight for years, he was by no means unrecognizable. He pulled the visor of his borrowed baseball cap down low to cover his face and slid into one of the booths.

His apprehension proved unnecessary. Not a single head turned in their direction. Even the wait-staff seemed oblivious to their arrival. All eyes were fixed on the wall-mounted television in one corner. The set was tuned to a twenty-four hour cable news outlet. The fiery graphics that dominated one side of the screen displayed a map of the eastern seaboard, with the state of North Carolina highlighted in red, and superimposed letters that read: "Hot Zone!"

Duncan squinted to read the captions accompanying footage of National Guard soldiers manning barricades, but it was almost impossible to make sense of the disjointed commentary. As usual, the talking heads were filling up air time with random speculation, but the gist of the story was that the Outer Banks islands of North Carolina had been placed under a strict quarantine due to a possible disease outbreak.

"That's not good," Boucher said. "But at least it's keeping us out of the headlines."

"Sara Fogg is there," Duncan said. "And Anna Beck. They're in the thick of it."

Chastened, Boucher lowered his gaze and lapsed into a silence that ended when a middle-aged waitress appeared a moment later to greet them. "Coffee? You gents look like you could use a whole pot."

"You're not wrong," Boucher replied. "Our car broke down and we had to hoof it in from the turnpike."

It was partly true. The DPVs had born them through the submerged *Dock* exit and as far as the southeastern tip of Lake Winnipesaukee. A shuttered fishing cabin had yielded a few articles of clothing to supplement their wardrobe with warm flannel shirts and the cap that now shaded Duncan's face. They had indeed walked for several miles, until a man driving a pickup had taken pity on them, pulling over and jerking a thumb at the cluttered bed, which had been fine with Duncan.

"You should have called the auto club."

Boucher spread his hands guiltily. "No phone. Actually, do you have a phone we could borrow? I'd be happy to pay."

The woman, who was already digging her cell phone out of her pocket, flashed him a stern 'how dare you even suggest such a thing' look, and handed it over. Boucher returned the same smile he had once used to recruit assets in the early days of his career as an operations officer. As she headed to the kitchen to place their breakfast order, Boucher slid the phone across the table to Duncan.

"Nicely done," Duncan remarked, as he picked the device up and dialed a number from memory. The phone rang several times, and with each iteration, his sense of dread grew, but then to his surprise, a tentative voice said: "Hello?"

"It's me."

Aleman's shock was almost palpable over the line. "Blue? You made it out."

"We did. Have you been able to re-establish contact with the team?"

"Believe it or not, I've got King on the other line. Hang on. I'll conference."

For the first time since their escape from the *Dock*, Duncan allowed himself a relieved sigh. King's voice sounded in his ear a moment later. "Blue?"

He thought he heard another voice, Bishop perhaps, say, "Thomas?" but it was probably his imagination. "I'm here, King. What's your situation?"

"We're alive." King said it quickly, as if the question was irrelevant. "Did Aleman brief you on the situation in North Carolina?"

Duncan glanced at the television screen. "I'm aware of what's happening there. I know you must be sick with worry about Sara, but there's not much we can do to help her right now. We've got bigger problems—"

"Believe me, we don't."

In all the years they had worked together, Duncan had never known King to put anything ahead of the mission. Neither was he prone to exaggeration. "I'm listening."

"Are you familiar with the Lost Colony of Roanoke Island?"

"The first British colony in North America," Duncan answered. "They vanished without a trace. To this day, no one knows what happened to them."

"*I* know."

Duncan had no response to that. He was well aware of King's unique perspective on history. Two years earlier, King had, to all appearances, been killed in an explosion during a mission to North Africa. But just a few hours later he had reappeared, not only alive and well, but making the astonishing claim that he had been transported back in time. Supplied with an immortality serum by the creator of the time travel device, King had been subjected to a journey through the ages, living one lifetime after another in the shadows, awaiting the moment when he could rejoin the team in the present. As preposterous as the story had sounded, Duncan knew that King was not given to flights of fancy. The simplest explanation, particularly in light of some of the other unbelievable things they had all witnessed, was that King had been telling the truth, so when he spoke on matters of history, Duncan took his word for it.

"The winter of 1588 nearly wiped the colonists out. Food was so scarce that some of them resorted to cannibalism. When the others learned what had happened, they hanged the suspected offenders, which oddly enough meant there was enough food for the rest to survive, but that rough justice wasn't good enough for the Secotan tribe, who lived nearby. Cannibalism was their ultimate taboo, and for good reason.

"The Secotan were Algonquins. They believed, as many of their descendants still do today, that when a person consumes the flesh of another human, they open themselves up to possession by a powerful, demonic force, and transform into a creature called a 'wendigo.' A revenant. A living ghost with a ravenous appetite for human flesh.

"The Secotan suspected that some of the surviving colonists had also secretly turned to cannibalism, so they tested the survivors by exposing them to... I guess you could call it wendigo 'essence.' It's a secretion, some kind of pheromone. It might contain a virus... I don't really know for sure, but anyone who had eaten human flesh would almost immediately become a wendigo. Unfortunately for the colonists, there were a few secret cannibals in their midst. They became wendigos and went on a rampage, killing all but a handful of the survivors, who managed to escape and were later assimilated into the tribe."

Duncan broke in. "And you think what's happening now is related to what happened four hundred and thirty years ago?"

Across the table, Boucher raised a questioning eyebrow.

King did not answer directly. "Lew, you said people are calling this a zombie plague?"

Aleman's reply was guarded. "Some of the initial, and I should add unverified, reports coming out the area did indicate that."

"Creatures with distorted limbs and transparent skin," King supplied. "This is happening right now."

Duncan immediately saw a flaw in the argument. "You said that only a cannibal can become one of these things. So how can it be happening now?"

As King explained what they had discovered in Beltran's slaughterhouse, how it connected to the international meat supply, Duncan felt his gorge rise. "He's doing it on purpose? For God's sake, why?"

"I don't think this is a coincidence. The Secotan weren't the only people to believe that cannibalism could unleash powerful supernatural forces. Ceremonial consumption of fallen enemies was part of the rituals for worshipping Huitzilopochtli. Beltran is trying to resurrect the old religion."

"You're saying that Beltran wanted this to happen? He intentionally contaminated the meat supply to make this outbreak happen?" The full weight of what King was telling him hit home. "There are hundreds of those restaurants all across the eastern US."

"He's probably been doing it for years. Feeding his victims to wild pigs, or just grinding them up and turning them into sausage. Anyone who's ever had even a taste of tainted meat is at risk for becoming infected, if even one of those things gets past the quarantine. Even if containment works, it will mean certain death, one way or another, for the thousands of people on those islands."

Including Sara and Anna, Duncan thought.

"There's something else to consider," King continued. "There's a reason why nobody knows the truth about what happened to the Lost Colony. The wendigo contagion is exactly the sort of thing that could be turned into a deadly weapon. Now do you see why I have to be there?"

Duncan was only faintly aware of Boucher's uncomprehending gaze. In the face of what King had just revealed, Marrs's diabolical schemes seemed like a petty high school rivalry.

Four years earlier, he had willingly given up the presidency to save the Chess Team, not to mention the world. Could he do any less now?

"I do," he said at length. "Stand by. I'll call you back when I've made the arrangements."

He ended the call and met Boucher's stare. "Change of plans."

Boucher gestured to the television screen. "Something to do with that?"

Duncan nodded.

"Meanwhile, you'll be doing what exactly?"

"Don't worry about me." He entered another number into the phone. It rang once before the call was picked up. "Please connect me with DAG Taits."

Boucher's eyes went wide as saucers. "Tom, what the hell?"

"I know where he is," Duncan said in response to the receptionist on the other end of the line. "He'll want to take this call. Tell him it's Tom Duncan."

He cupped a hand over the mouthpiece and looked at Boucher again. "You should probably go."

FORTY-FOUR
Mexico

For what was probably the first time in his military career, King felt neither excitement nor relief at the sight of the C-17 Globemaster rolling down the remote airstrip, trailed by a cloud of dust. Instead, he felt only apprehension. If not for Aleman's assurance that Deep Blue himself had arranged for the USAF transport plane to come and retrieve them, to say nothing of the urgent need to reach the Outer Banks as soon as possible, he would probably have stuck with the original plan to disperse the team and lay low. And despite the fact that he trusted Deep Blue implicitly, as the plane rolled to a stop, about a hundred yards from where he stood waiting, King still half expected to see a squad of soldiers swarming down the cargo ramp to take him into custody.

There was, however, only one man in the cargo bay of the plane, and he was, technically speaking, not a soldier, but a sailor.

The man was middle-aged and African-American, with black hair just starting to go gray. He wore USMC desert digital camouflage fatigues without nametapes or rank. When he made eye contact with King, he executed a sharp left turn and strode quickly across the intervening distance.

"You Sigler?" He had to shout to be heard over the noise of the still turning jet engines.

King nodded.

"I was told to expect five. Where's your team?"

King appraised him for several seconds. "Do I know you?"

"Obviously not." The man seemed put out at having to explain himself. "I'm Vice Admiral Ward, commander JSOC. I worked closely with Mike Keasling, God rest his soul, so I know all about you and your little after-school club. You're working for me now."

What the hell? King's brows knit together in a frown. "Forgive me, sir, but I'm going to need to see a copy of those orders."

"Is that supposed to be a joke?" Ward put his hands on his hips. "Look, I'd like nothing better than to stand here and shoot the shit with you, but you're the one ringing the fire bell. So what's it gonna be? Do we stand here dicking around until the Mexicans decide they're curious about an American bird sitting on their turf, or do we finish this conversation in the air?" He snapped his fingers for emphasis.

King felt an immediate and instinctive dislike for the man, but he also sensed that Ward was being forthright. Deep Blue had said to expect military transport. So why did he feel so much anxiety about getting on the plane?

He sighed in resignation. Without turning away, he raised his arms high, as if under arrest and held them that way for several seconds. Ward did not question the odd gesture, a counter-intuitive signal to the team that the situation was safe. King saw the admiral's eyes darting this way and that as the rest of the team emerged from hiding. Ward said nothing, and after a few seconds, he simply turned away and stalked back into the belly of the giant aircraft.

Rook was the first to reach King's side. "Everything cool?"

King shook his head. "I'm not sure, yet." He waited for the others to gather around before continuing. "I really don't know what's going to happen when we get on that plane. We could be headed for Leavenworth—"

"Like that place could hold us," Rook snorted.

"Or worse. I think we might be back under military command."

That was a threat evidently too dire even for Rook to deflect with a witty remark.

"Have you spoken with Blue?" Queen asked. "What's he say?"

"I haven't. He told me he was going dark again, but that he was sending a military plane for us." He nodded at the C-17. "And here it is. I'm going to go ahead and board. If anyone wants to—"

Before he could get the words out, the others were already filing past him, heading to the waiting aircraft.

As soon as they were aboard, the ramp was raised and the engine noise went from a persistent whine to a full-throated roar. Ward sat in a jump seat near the front of the cargo bay, but made no effort to engage with, or even look at them, as the plane climbed into the sky. It was only when they reached cruising altitude that he acknowledged their existence with a single barked word.

"Sigler."

King rose and made his way forward to stand before the admiral. It had been a long time since he had been in a situation like this— required to behave as a subordinate instead of an equal. Even before Chess Team, when he had been part of Delta, rank and rigid military discipline had taken a back seat to camaraderie. Ward's predecessor, General Keasling, had always chafed in their presence, particularly when Rook colored the air with wisecracks and obscenities, but Ward evidently subscribed to a more traditional military philosophy. While it felt strangely familiar to be standing at attention in front of a general officer, it was by no means pleasant.

There was a sound of footsteps behind him, and he turned to find the rest of the team gathering beside him.

A perturbed expression flickered across Ward's face but he did not address the breach of protocol. Instead, he studied each face as if cataloguing them, noting details for future reference: Rook's long goatee, Queen and Bishop—two women in a field where females were still considered a battlefield liability—and Knight's eye patch. Finally, he came back to King. "I'm not going to get in the way of your current mission, whatever that is. Those are *my* orders. You can resupply on ammo—we've got 5.56 and 7.62." He eyed Rook's Desert Eagles. "If you've got anything exotic, I'm afraid I can't help"

"Good thing I loaded for bear before we left," Rook muttered.

Ward ignored him. "You're going to have to decide how you want to enter the AO. If you decide to do a high-altitude jump, you'll need to factor in your pre-breath. Flight time is four hours."

King nodded. "I think we'll just keep it simple. Do things the old fashioned way, low and slow."

"It's your call," Ward said with a shrug, and then added. "This time, anyway. There's commo gear as well. Your mission specialist—Deep Blue?—preloaded your operational freqs. You should be all set."

Blue? That at least was a bit of good news, but Ward did not allow them to savor it.

"I know that you all are used to being off the leash, but that ends right now. This mission is yours, but you are under my authority now, and that means no rogue ops."

"Sir." The word felt strange on King's tongue. "With all due respect, none of us agreed to that."

Ward's eyes narrowed. "You agreed to it when you swore an oath to defend the constitution." He glanced at Bishop. "Except maybe for you, but we'll deal with that later."

"Sir, we cut our ties with the military four years ago."

Ward made a 'look around you' gesture. "I'd say somebody glued the ends back together. But if that's how you feel, I'll put you off right now. You can even have a parachute. My gift to you."

Before King could begin to formulate a reply, Ward went on. "Look, I know what's going on here. I probably know more about it than you do. Tom Duncan's secret strike team; did you think he could pull that off without help? Yes, officially your ties to the military were severed. Hell, technically none of you even exist anymore. But all that's over now. In order to get you guys back, and deal with this crisis in North Carolina, your boss had to make a deal. He agreed to this, and not just so you could catch a ride home. Restoring your active duty service—pretty much undoing everything he did four years ago—is the only way to shield you from prosecution.

"This was Duncan's idea, not mine," he went on. "He did it to protect *you*. I've got a lot of respect for the man. Hell, I voted for him. He was one of us; a shooter. We need leaders like that. But the handwriting is on the wall, and he knows it. He's going down, and he's going to take some very powerful people with him. Do you understand what I'm saying?"

"Yes. Sir."

"Good." Ward settled back in his chair as if contemplating a nap. "You know what to do. Get to it."

The team dispersed, but only for a moment. As soon as they were out of earshot from Ward, they clustered around King.

Queen spoke first. "Is he serious? We're back in the Army?"

King raised a hand to forestall her. "Right now, all that matters is the mission. Ward's wrong. Blue didn't do this to protect us. He did it because he knows how important it is that we stop what's happening in North Carolina."

"And what happens afterward?"

"He's going to break us up," Rook said in a low voice. "I can see it in his eyes."

"That's standard operating procedure," Queen said. "Shuffle the deck. Move experienced troops into leadership positions in new teams."

"I don't think we'll be that lucky," Rook replied. "Old warhorses like us get put out to pasture. Or sent to the glue factory."

"We'll deal with that later," King said. "Right now, we need to prep. This isn't going to be pretty."

"When is it ever?" Rook said.

"We'll be facing an unknown number of hostiles, but that's not the worst of it. Every non-hostile we encounter could turn if exposed. There's no way we'll ever be able to know who was exposed to tainted meat." He gave them all a long hard look. "Actually, we have to consider the very real possibility that we might have been exposed as well."

The statement was met with a collective gasp of disbelief. Queen had the most coherent reply. "I've never even heard of Mr. Pig before this."

"We don't know how long Beltran has been contaminating the meat supply or how widespread this is. There are other considerations as well. We know that people who have..." There was no diplomatic way to say it, "ingested human flesh...are susceptible to infection, but the last time this happened was long before the age of modern medicine."

"What are you saying?" Queen asked.

"We don't know exactly what the pathogen is, but a lot of modern medicines—vaccines and so forth—use proteins derived from human blood and tissue. We're probably safe, but make sure you keep your distance from these things. No direct contact, if you can help it. Just shoot them from a nice safe standoff distance. The good news is, they won't be shooting back."

Queen shook her head. "This is insane. These are innocent people. There's got to be some kind of cure."

King shook his head. "Once a person is infected, they're already dead. We have to eradicate them all. Any uninfected civilians we encounter have to be isolated until we can arrange for them to be evacuated. Blue can coordinate that."

"What about Sara?" Bishop asked.

King winced inwardly but did not allow his face to register any emotion. "Cellular communication to the island was shut off to keep this out of the news, but maybe Blue can find a way past that so we can coordinate with her." He glanced at Knight. "Anna's with her."

Knight stiffened, but said nothing.

King turned away, gesturing to a pallet loaded with ammo cans and green shipping containers. "Let's pack for the trip. Bishop, load up on incendiaries. Blowing stuff up isn't going to help much."

"Well that's a change," Rook said with a chuckle.

King located a container that held half a dozen compact Tadiran PNR 500 tactical comm sets. They were state-of-the-art, but after the q-phones, the walkie-talkie sized radios seemed woefully inadequate. He passed them out to the others and then donned the attached headset before turning it on.

"This is King," he said, speaking in a whisper too soft to be heard even by someone standing next to him. "Radio check, over."

Queen answered first. "Queen, roger out."

It took Bishop a moment to remember that she was the next in the order, and her answer was more hesitant. Knight was next, followed by Rook, who could not pass up a chance to turn even something as mundane as a radio check into an opportunity to crack wise.

Then another voice came over the net.

"Chess Team, this is Deep Blue. It's good to have you back."

In the stunned silence that followed, King felt all eyes looking at him, but he was as shocked as they were. The words were right, but the voice of the man who had identified himself as Deep Blue did not belong to Tom Duncan.

FORTY-FIVE

Rochester, New Hampshire

They arrived from the sky like an army of vengeful angels. Black Hawk helicopters, dark as storm clouds, swept in from every direction, converging on the airspace directly above the diner. The response of local citizens fell into two categories: some gawked at the aircraft, holding their mobile phones up to record the exciting drama as it unfolded and some fled in a panic.

Only one man remained immune to the polarized hysteria. He sat calmly at a table inside the diner, sipping his coffee beneath the shadow of the brim of his borrowed ball cap, which was emblazoned with, ironically, the state's official motto: Live Free or Die.

Ironic, because Tom Duncan had discovered that the real world was not bound by those absolutes. There were other ways to live. Other ways to win.

The door of the diner burst open and men in black tactical garb flooded into the restaurant, brandishing M4 carbines and shouting conflicting orders.

"Don't move."

"Hands up."

"Get down."

Duncan drained the last few drops from his cup as they closed in around him. None of them fired, and while they continued to barrage him with testosterone-fueled commands, not one of them came within arm's reach. They were waiting for something. Additional orders perhaps. Duncan was content to wait as well. He had done what he could—for the team, and for the country that he loved. Now it was time to face the consequences.

He raised one hand. "Check, please."

Sardonic laughter erupted from behind the assembled SWAT operators. Two men, one wearing an FBI windbreaker, the other a Brooks Brothers suit, stepped forward. The latter was still chuckling. "I've got the check right here, Duncan. And believe me, you're going to pay."

Duncan raised his eyes, locked stares with Senator Lance Marrs until the oily politician stopped laughing and looked away in discomfort, and then switched his gaze to the other man. "You really didn't need to go to all this bother, Mr. Taits. I surrendered already, remember? That was our deal."

The deputy attorney general did not answer, and that, more than anything else that had happened, fanned a coal of anxiety in Duncan's gut.

"You're a dangerous criminal," Marrs said, almost crooning in satisfaction. "The American people need to see how we deal with criminals."

"I'm sure the American people will be very interested in your role in all of this, Senator."

"Get up," Taits growled. "You're coming with us."

Duncan inclined his head and then slid out of the booth, hands extended as if offering a benediction. Taits stepped back and nodded to one of his men, who promptly seized Duncan's wrists and secured them with flexi-cuffs.

They hustled him from the diner, clustering around him, and then bundled him into a helicopter that waited, rotor still turning, on the road just beyond the parking lot. Marrs and Taits climbed in as well.

"Taits!" Duncan had to shout to be heard over the engine noise. "We have a deal, right?"

"Screw your deal," Marrs retorted. "You're finished. You're going to testify before a Senate committee. Tell them and the American people how you and President Chambers created an illegal paramilitary unit."

"If you want my cooperation, I need to know you kept your end of the bargain."

"I don't need your cooperation. I've got enough evidence to roast you and Chambers. All I have to do is ask the questions. You don't even have to answer. When you plead the Fifth, that will be answer enough," Marrs kept gloating.

Duncan ignored him and kept his focus on Taits. "I need to know."

Taits's contemptuous mask cracked just a little, and he gave a terse nod.

Duncan breathed a relieved sigh, then turned to Marrs. "Don't worry, Lance. I won't say a word."

FORTY-SIX

Manteo, North Carolina

There were no cars in the parking lot of the Lost Colony Festival Park. It was still early, but Beck had a feeling that this day's visitor turnout was not going to break any records. The good news was that the wendigos appeared to have little interest in the theme park. Driven by their primal hunger, they went where the people were. During the drive from Fort Raleigh, they had glimpsed packs of the creatures roaming the neighborhoods, crawling all over houses like enormous pale white spiders, looking for some way inside. A few had looked at the passing vehicle but none had given chase. Perhaps at some level, they retained enough intelligence to know that they had zero chance of catching up to the little Nissan.

The park occupied a small island, one of several that jutted out into the Roanoke Sound. The only approach was a narrow two-lane bridge. The road from the bridge passed a complex of rustic-looking shingled buildings, surrounded by neatly manicured lawns, trees and flowering shrubs. Just past the buildings, separated by a short path, was the empty parking area. Beck shut off the engine and surveyed their surroundings for several minutes to see if anyone—human or wendigo—would come to investigate their presence.

"Looks clear, but let's move with a purpose."

She waited for acknowledging nods, then threw open the door, grabbed hold of her recently acquired E-tool, and sprinted to the covered porch that fronted the largest building. Double doors with large glass panes blocked their entrance. Locked. No surprise there. Beck peered through the panes into the lobby beyond, then made a decision.

Bracing herself for the shrill alarm that she expected would surely ring out, she swung the E-tool at the door-panes. The glass shattered inward, but the only sound was of the shards tinkling on the stone tiles inside. Not one to question a stroke of luck, she used the spade head to knock down several jagged protrusions and then stepped through the narrow opening.

The museum lay just beyond the ticket lobby, with several small galleries arranged in a walking tour that began with the geological history of the Outer Banks, and worked forward through the native occupation of the area, and eventually to the Lost Colony. Although she was no expert in history or archaeology, Beck did not fail to notice that the exhibits were all style and little substance. There were reproductions of simple tools and artifacts, as well as dioramas of native men—bodies painted, wearing beads, feathers and not much else—hunting and fishing. Women were shown laying the catch out on drying racks to preserve the meat. There were even miniature depictions of entire villages. Missing was anything with provenance.

"I told you," Ellen said in a glum voice. "There's nothing here. The native people who lived here left very little behind. What few artifacts have been discovered went to more reputable museums. And most of what we know of early Native American culture is from the observations of the earliest European visitors. Half this stuff is completely inaccurate. The rest is guesswork."

Sara was clearly making an effort to be patient with her. "Think. Does looking at this trigger any memories? What about the wendigo stories? Is there anything in them about how to defeat a wendigo?"

"Starve it," Ellen replied, bleakly.

"But how? How do you keep the monster from eating you?"

"You don't understand. The wendigo legend was meant as a deterrent. The mere threat of turning into such a demon was enough to discourage breaking the taboo."

Sara frowned, clearly unwilling to give up but evidently unsure of what button to press next. "Let's keep looking," Beck suggested, "If this place is a dead end, the sooner we're out of here, the better."

That seemed to satisfy Ellen. She headed forward into the next gallery. Beck and Sara followed and found the historian gazing at the largest display yet, an exhibit built around a section of upright wooden planks, fitted together to form a palisade. Carved conspicuously onto one of the boards was a word: 'Croatoan.' Behind the replica of the wall that had once encircled the Roanoke Colony, was an interpretive sign that bore the headline: 'Where did they go?'

Beyond the palisade, a series of smaller displays explored some of the more popular theories relating to the disappearance of the colonists. Beck gave them only a cursory glance. She did not know enough about the story to separate fact from elaborate speculation, and there seemed to be plenty of the latter. She found Ellen standing in front of another display, gazing at a shelf containing several flat rocks, each one inscribed with carved cryptic letters.

"This is it," she said, pointing at the first one in the line. "The last message of my ancestor, Eleanor Dare. This isn't the real one of course. That's still in the collection at Brenau University in Georgia. This is just a replica."

"What about the others?" Sara asked, a hopeful note in her voice.

"Fakes. The first one—the real one—was found in 1937, the same year that the Lost Colony play started running here in town. After that, everyone and his uncle started showing up with new 'Dare Stones,' each one purporting to be the continuation of Eleanor Dare's story."

"How do you know they're fake?"

"Inconsistencies in the carving style, the language, contradictions in the narrative. Unfortunately, when the hoax was revealed, it was assumed that the original stone was also a fake. But I know it's true."

Beck was curious about how Ellen knew this, but she sensed that the answer to that question might not be entirely satisfactory. Sara asked a more obvious question. "What does it say?"

"'Father, soon after you went to England, we came here.'" Ellen seemed to be reciting the message from memory instead of reading it, and her voice took on a haunting quality. It was like listening to a ghost.

"'Only misery and a war torn year. About half are dead for two years or more from sickness, we are four and twenty. Savage with a message of a ship was brought to us. In a small space of time they became afraid of revenge and all ran away. We believe it was not you. Soon after, the savages, fearing angry spirits, suddenly murdered all, save seven. My child, Ananias, too, were slain with much misery. Buried all four miles east of this river on a small hill. Names are written there on a rock. Put this there also. Savage show this unto you and hither we promise you will give great and plenty presents.'"

Beck stared at the carved rock. Evidently, she would also have to accept Ellen's translation as well. Other than the fact that some of the carved symbols looked like letters, the stone was completely illegible.

"Again," Sara said, a gleam in her eyes. "Slower this time."

Ellen obliged, but as soon as the first line was out, Sara stopped her. "Where is 'here'? Where was this stone found?"

"The stone was found by the Chowan River, near Edenton on the other side of the Abelmarle Sound, almost sixty miles from here. But I believe the stone may have been moved there. I haven't published this research yet, but I have reason to believe that the stone was originally found near Buffalo City, on the banks of Mill Tail Creek. That's the river Eleanor mentioned in the message. The whole area is a marsh, but there is a slight elevation change about four miles from that area. That's the small hill where the others are buried."

Sara's eyes darted up, looking at nothing as she processed this information. "How long do you think it would have taken to carve that message? Hours? Days?"

Ellen's brows knitted together as if the question had never occurred to her. "I suppose."

"Your ancestor sat down and carved out a message to...her father, right? Why? Put yourself in her shoes. She wrote this two years after the colony was abandoned. What changed?"

"My hypothesis is that the tribe she was with was relocating, probably to a hidden refuge to avoid reprisals. The Secotan knew that more Europeans would arrive. The message says as much."

Sara nodded. "And no one has ever investigated the actual location where the stone was found?"

"No. Remember, most academics believe the stone is a fake, so there's no reason for them to take it seriously. If I had been able to find proof that the first part of the message is true—the remains of those colonists who died in the first year—I could have gone forward with the search for the graves of Ananias and Virginia Dare."

Sara gripped her arm. "You did find proof."

Ellen looked up in surprise.

"You were right," Sara continued. "About everything. And that means you're right about this, too. The native refuge where your ancestor lived is out there. And somehow, they knew how to beat this...this curse. How to make the wendigos leave them alone."

The look of hope in Ellen's eyes faded as quickly as it had dawned, replaced by an almost feral glint. "No. There's nothing left of it. Even if we knew exactly where to look, the refuge is gone. They would have taken everything of value when they abandoned it. And whatever was left behind would have decomposed. It's hopeless."

Beck could see that Ellen was on the verge of slipping into hysteria again, and came to Sara's rescue. "It's the only chance we've got," she said. "Snap out of it. Like Sara said, you were right about what happened to the colony. If anyone can figure this out, it's you."

For a few moments, Beck wondered if she had overplayed her hand. But then the hopeful look came back and Ellen nodded. "The Secotan, and really all the native tribes in the region before contact, were very simple. Primitive. So if they had some way of resisting the wendigo curse, it would be something equally simple. A certain kind of plant maybe. Something they would eat, or burn in a fire to make toxic smoke."

"Something that can only be found in that one place," Sara said. "That's more like it. Now, where's this Buffalo City?"

"On the mainland, about ten miles from here. Only there's no city there anymore. It went into decline after Prohibition, and died out completely in the fifties. The site has been reclaimed by the wilderness. Now the whole area is a wildlife preserve."

"The mainland?" The dark cloud of defeat abruptly shifted to Sara. "Outside the quarantined area?"

"Works for me," Beck muttered.

"You don't understand. They've shut the island down. No one in or out. That's what a quarantine means."

"Yeah, but they'll let you out. You're the expert. If anyone can clear us, it's you."

Sara shook her head. "It doesn't work that way. And the soldiers manning the barricades aren't going to let us get close enough to explain it. If we come too close, they'll shoot first, no questions later."

"Just call your office. Explain it to them."

"There's no service."

"Of course there is. We all got the Emergency Alert, right after you called it in." Beck took out her own cell phone, but where there should have been signal bars, there was instead a 'No Network' message.

"In a situation like this, access to the cellular network is restricted to official traffic," Sara explained. "We won't be able to—" She stopped abruptly and dug into her pocket for her own cell phone, which was buzzing furiously. She stared at the caller ID in consternation, then hit the button to receive the call. "Hello?"

Her face lit up. "Jack!"

FORTY-SEVEN

Before getting on his private jet, Hector Beltran had found the time to shower and change his clothes. Gone was the feathered cape, along with the blood and dust that had covered him following the destruction of the pyramid. Instead, he wore slacks and a tailored shirt, which revealed only a hint of the tattoos underneath. Parrish was no judge, but the clothes looked expensive. The cartel leader would have been unrecognizable but for his eyes. There was no mistaking the look of madness in those bloody orbs.

Beltran's men had also cleaned up, but there were considerably fewer of them now. Just four other men, aside from Beltran and himself, doubtless the surviving members of the cartel's leadership. Like Beltran, they wore designer clothes that almost, but not quite, covered their ritual tattoos. Not one of them carried a weapon. Parrish sat in their midst like a party crashing refugee.

He kept to himself, which seemed to suit Beltran just fine. Sunlight streaming in through the windows on the right side of the aircraft told him they were heading northeast, which meant they were indeed going somewhere in the United States. Beltran had been telling the truth about that much, at least. But the knowledge that he was once more in the skies above America failed to buoy Parrish's spirits. Whatever it was that Beltran was up to, whatever had shaken him loose from his monomaniacal quest for revenge against the American commandos who had taken his brother, had to be worse than anything Parrish could conceive.

As the flight wore on, the other men idly conversing in a hash of Spanish and Nahuatl, Parrish caught Beltran watching him. He sensed that the cartel leader was eager to share information, to satiate his guest's curiosity, if only Parrish would ask. Parrish did not take the bait. He did not actually want to know. Curiosity was for cats. He was a bulldog, focused on one task and one alone: survival.

He slept fitfully, alternately lulled to sleep by the droning hum of the engines, and startled awake by murmured voices and episodes of turbulence. Later, much later, he was roused by a change in the plane's attitude. They were descending.

He could no longer see the sun, which either meant they were traveling due east or that it was midday. As he blinked away the last vestiges of bleariness, he saw Beltran moving through the cabin toward the cockpit door. Though he could only hear Beltran's voice, shouting in Spanish, it was enough for him to get the gist of what was being discussed. There were evidently some issues at the destination airport, which Beltran seemed to believe could be resolved by simply ignoring air traffic control and doing as he pleased.

Parrish rose and moved down the aisle to learn more about the situation. Maybe Beltran's ultimate goal didn't matter to him, but getting the plane down in one piece certainly did.

"What's going on?" he asked in English.

"Nothing that concerns you, *Buldog*. Relax. You're almost home."

"I am concerned. It sounds like there's a problem. Maybe I can help."

To his surprise, the pilot spoke up, likewise in English. "They say the airport is closed."

"So land somewhere else. Where are we anyway?"

"We need to land at this airport." Beltran said with a frown, pointedly ignoring the question.

Parrish leaned his head into the cramped cockpit. Through the windscreen, he could see land—a patchwork of green and brown—and beyond that, an endless expanse of gray ocean. "Why is it closed? Tell them it's an emergency."

"I tried that."

Parrish shuffled through a variety of responses, but without knowing more about their destination, it was impossible to know which was the right one. What might work at some backwater airstrip in the middle of nowhere would get them shot out of the sky if they approached a more heavily populated area.

He looked out the window again. East coast. Barrier islands. Florida? The Carolinas? "Where are you going?"

"Dare County Regional Airport," Beltran supplied.

Parrish was unfamiliar with the name, which meant rural. "Tell them you'll divert. Then drop below radar and double back."

"That's not the only problem," the pilot said. "It's like I told Señor Beltran. The runway is only four thousand feet long."

"So?"

"This aircraft needs at least five thousand feet to take-off."

Parrish almost laughed aloud. He turned to Beltran. "There you go. Pick another airport."

"That is where we must land," Beltran insisted.

"If we land there," the pilot said, "we won't be able to take off again."

Beltran gripped the man's shirtfront. "I don't care. Do it."

Parrish wondered if he should be concerned by Beltran's lack of concern over that not-inconsiderable logistical detail, but whether or not the aircraft made it back into the sky made no difference to him. Once his feet hit the ground, there was no way in hell he would ever get back into Beltran's plane.

The pilot capitulated, raising his hands and nodding. Beltran released him and then turned to Parrish. "*Gracias, Buldog*. It is good I brought you along."

"I'm just deadheading."

Beltran puzzled over the word a moment, then shook his head, his face becoming unexpectedly earnest. "When we land, something very special is going to happen. You can be a part of it, if you wish."

"Thanks, but no thanks. I already have a job."

Beltran chuckled softly. "With Senator Marrs? I don't think you have much of a future with him. The world is about to become a very different place."

Parrish kept a diplomatic smile fixed to his lips as he shook his head again. Beneath him, the plane tilted and began to slow. "We should probably buckle up."

"There's still time, if you change your mind. Think about it."

Yeah, that'll happen.

Parrish found his seat and buckled up. Perhaps because he was so eager to be back on terra firma, the descent seemed to take forever. The plane descended for several minutes, then leveled out and banked through a long turn before continuing down.

The landing gear dropped with a thump. He could see the ground coming up fast, verdant forests, threaded with ribbons of asphalt, dotted with houses and other buildings. There was no sign of the runway, and when the plane dropped below the level of the tallest trees, Parrish started looking for the escape exit. Then, with a screech, the plane was down.

The pilot reversed the engine thrust with what seemed like frantic urgency. Parrish recalled the man saying that the strip was just four thousand feet long. One thousand three hundred yards, give or take. Thirteen football fields. How many football fields did the plane need to stop? How many did they have left?

Enough, evidently.

The g-forces of deceleration finally relented, allowing him to settle back, and then the plane stopped altogether, with the wheels still on hard tarmac. As soon as all motion ceased, Beltran rose and faced the seated men, raising his hands.

"Four years ago, I called out to you." He spoke in English, almost certainly for Parrish's benefit. "I said, 'Join me as fellow sons of Huitzilopochtli,' and you did. Together, we brought back the old ways. We killed our enemies. We gave their hearts to Huitzilopochtli. We feasted on their flesh."

The offhand declaration went through Parrish like an electric shock. *He's serious. He's been eating people.*

The tourists on that bus… That's what they were eating last night at the pyramid.

He tried to get me to eat them.

It was all he could do to keep from throwing up, but Beltran was plowing forward, unaware of Parrish's revulsion. "We sowed our enemies as seed, cast them upon the wind. Now, the seed we planted has borne fruit."

The atmosphere in the cabin was charged with religious fervor. Murmured words, a prayer perhaps, grew together into a hum that sounded like a wire about to snap.

"Many ages ago, long before the Spaniards took our land, the people of the north told of a fearsome demon they called *windigo*; a creature who devours the flesh of men. When I heard these stories, I knew that what they feared, *we* worshipped." He thumped his chest for emphasis. "Huitzilopochtli and the *windigo* are one and the same. We have awakened Huitzilopochtli with our offering of flesh. Now, let us go forth to meet our god!"

With that, he threw open the door located just aft of the cockpit. The men exited their seats and descended to the tarmac, leaving Parrish alone with Beltran. The cartel leader stared at him and nodded, as if sharing some silent joke, and then he too turned and headed down the steps. Parrish just sat there a moment, trying to wrap his head around Beltran's confession. Yet, beyond the horror of the man's admission of cannibalism lay something even more troubling.

The seed we planted has borne fruit. What did that mean? And why had Beltran come here? Why had he insisted on this place?

He rose and moved to the open hatch. Beltran's men were gathered in a loose cluster on the grass at the edge of the tarmac, waiting it seemed for something to happen. Parrish looked past them, searching for a building or a road, anything that he could use as a signpost to guide him out of this nightmare.

His eye was drawn to movement at the edge of the field, but it was only an animal, probably a deer, moving faster than his eye could follow.

That was no deer.

An enthusiastic murmur rippled through the assembled men, but to Parrish, the sound was like warning bells. Another shape moved into view.

Definitely not a deer, but what the hell is it?

The thing was vaguely human in form, but hairless, with pale skin and extraordinarily long limbs. Parrish's first instinct was to deny the reality of what he was seeing. It had to be a trick of the light. A hallucination. A dream...

On the ground below, Beltran and the others opened their arms as if to offer a welcoming embrace. There were at least a dozen of the creatures, and more were emerging from the woods with each passing second.

Beltran moved to the forefront, arms spread wide, shouting in Nahuatl, and then suddenly the leading edge of the swarm was on him. The powerfully built crime lord was dwarfed by the towering creature. A spray of blood erupted from the midst of the flurry of white limbs, and then the struggle was repeated over and over again as the monstrous forms fell upon the defiant crowd of believers.

The violence shocked Parrish out of his paralysis. He jumped back inside the cabin and fumbled with the lever that would pull the door back up. The steps lifted with agonizing slowness, folding flat against the door before rising like a drawbridge to seal him inside the plane.

He sagged against the hatch as if the weight of his body would be enough to keep the creatures from getting in. After a moment, he realized that the pilot and co-pilot were staring at him from the cockpit, their wide eyes and shocked expressions confirming that the nightmare was real.

Suddenly the fuselage shook with an impact. Parrish spread-eagled, but there was nothing to hold onto. The deck tilted crazily, and he was thrown against the opposite bulkhead and then rolled back against the door. The plane rocked back and forth a few times but there were no more jolts. Then, for several seconds, there was only silence. Parrish crawled to the nearest porthole window and cautiously peeked around its edge.

He saw ghostly white shapes, eyeless faces streaked with blood. Elongated torsos hunched over, standing on long spindly legs, milling about as if looking for their next meal. Windigo or Huitzilopochtli, Beltran had met his god at last, and paid dearly for the privilege.

Parrish eased forward a little more, expecting to find a scene of carnage, with the creatures hunched over the remains of Beltran and his men, gnawing on their bones and slurping down their entrails.

What he saw instead was much, much worse.

FORTY-EIGHT

At a signal from the loadmaster, the Chess Team trundled down the ramp and leapt out into space. There was nothing fancy about the jump. No wing suits or ram-air canopies. No oxygen bottles, full face masks or thermal jumpsuits. No pre-breathing for high altitude, and no long free-fall or drift to the surface. They jumped from a rather unimpressive 1,200 feet, static lines opening their chutes right away, and they dropped unceremoniously groundward.

The brief conversation with Sara had left King cautiously optimistic. That she had responded at all was nothing short of a miracle. She was alive and Anna Beck was with her, which was more than he had allowed himself to hope for. The possibility of a treatment or cure was even better. Sara believed that the means to stop the spread of the wendigo infection would be found at the site of an old native refuge on the mainland, only a few miles from Roanoke Island. But reaching her location—about a mile northeast of their designated drop zone—was not going to be a walk in the park. Sara had also revealed that the island was crawling with wendigos.

As they drifted down beneath the mushroom-dome canopies of their T-11 round chutes—standard issue for the Army's airborne divisions—King surveyed the landscape below. Roanoke Island looked serene, perhaps a little too much so. It took him a moment to realize what was missing: there were no cars moving on the highways and streets.

"King, this is Deep Blue, over."

King was still trying to get used to hearing Lewis Aleman identify himself as Deep Blue. This was not the first time that Aleman had taken on the role of remote handler, but the fact that he was using Duncan's callsign was still disconcerting.

Their callsigns, even that of Deep Blue, were not just nicknames. The designations were like positions on a sports team: quarterback, center, coach. You couldn't play without someone in each critical position, and if a player had to leave the field, someone else took his place. But there was a difference between substitution and replacement. Although Aleman had not gone into great detail about what had happened at Endgame—King got the impression that there were things he was not at liberty to disclose—the fact that Aleman identified himself as Deep Blue was ominous. It meant that Tom Duncan was not coming back.

'Duncan did this to protect you,' Admiral Ward had said. Evidently, that umbrella of protection did not extend to Duncan himself.

They had adjusted to Asya in the role of Bishop—well, *were adjusting* anyway—and they would get used to having someone else as Deep Blue, but it wasn't going to happen overnight. Of course, if Rook was correct—and King thought he probably was—this would be their last mission as Chess Team, so the issue was moot.

"King, here. Send it."

"Be advised. A civilian aircraft just violated the no-fly zone. They made an unauthorized landing at Dare County airfield."

"Where's that?"

"A few miles northwest of your drop zone."

King turned his head in that general direction but he was already too low to make out anything in the distance. There was probably an innocent explanation for the violation, but King had long ago stopped believing in coincidences.

"Find out what you can about that plane," King said. He glanced down. The vast green expanse of the soccer field they had chosen as a drop zone stretched out beneath his feet. Just a few seconds to touchdown. "I'll get back to you when we're secure. King out."

The ground came up fast. The T-11 chutes were strictly minimalist, designed to put large numbers of troops on the ground in a hurry. The chute slowed the descent, but landing still felt a little like jumping off the roof of a one story house. As soon as his feet hit, he threw himself sideways into a roll designed to spread out the impact and avoid injuries. There was a stab of pain in the ankle he had injured the day before, but that was both expected and unavoidable. He recovered quickly, pulling in his chute from a semi-prone position before the wind could catch it and drag him across the field. Then he jumped up, rifle at the ready, scanning for a target. For a moment, all he could see were collapsing bubbles of pale green silk.

"Report in."

Queen was close enough that he heard her reply without the aid of the radio. A second later, her message came over the net. *Satellite lag*, King thought. *One more thing we'll have to get used to.*

The rest of the team called in, reporting no injuries and a fully ready status, then Rook's voice sounded again. "I've got movement. Something coming out of the trees to the west."

"Damn," King muttered. He had hoped for a little more time on the ground before contact.

"One hundred yards, but closing fast. Oh, you are one ugly son-of-a... Correction, make that *a lot of somethings*. Here they come."

"Rally on Rook," King called, sprinting forward. "Maintain sectors of fire. Do not let them get within fifty yards."

He could see them clearly now, long sinewy limbs, flesh the color of squirming maggots, heads and bodies that looked like the distorted reflection of a funhouse mirror. They were not exactly as he remembered them. Despite their height and speed, the creatures appeared sickly and weak.

"Light them up," he shouted.

Rook unleashed the 240. He was practically sniping with the machine gun, triggering short bursts with deadly accuracy. Tracers arced across the open field. Pale bodies burst apart in eruptions of red. One wendigo after another went down, as the 7.62mm rounds shredded the leading wave.

Knight's rifle sounded a loud report, and as King turned to see what he was shooting at, Queen and Bishop opened up with their SCARs. Each team member was facing a different direction, which meant there were targets coming in from every side. King stood in the center of the formation, turning like the second hand of a clock, backing up each of the others in turn, providing covering fire while they reloaded. Queen and Bishop had already discovered that single shots weren't effective at stopping the creatures, so they were firing in burst mode, three rapid shots with each trigger pull. Sometimes it took several bursts to finally put a wendigo down. Soon, they were surrounded by an ever-shrinking ring of bodies, far too many to count, some as close as twenty yards, and the number of creatures emerging from the tree line was growing.

"There's too many," Queen shouted. "The noise is bringing them in."

King knew she was right. They were going to have to find a more defensible position to deal with the mass attack, or risk being overrun. He spotted a small concrete structure—a maintenance shed or possibly a restroom—about a hundred yards away. "Pick up. We're moving to that building."

Without turning away from their respective sectors of fire, the team made their way across the field, avoiding wendigo carcasses as they might landmines. When they got within ten yards of the building, Knight scrambled up onto the roof and ran to the opposite edge to ensure that no wendigos were lurking on the blind side. When he signaled that the coast was clear, they all clambered up to join him.

There were now wendigos moving in from all directions, bounding across the open field to converge on the building. The tumult of gunfire was almost constant, yet they kept coming, drawn magnetically to the noise of battle and the prospect of fresh meat.

The team had already killed dozens of them. How many more would they have to kill? Hundreds more? Thousands?

Was there anyone left on the island to save?

"I think we may have packed too light," Rook shouted, as he slapped a fresh belt of linked ammunition into the machine gun.

King looked at the scattering of brass cartridges that was beginning to accumulate around their feet, and he knew that Rook was probably understating the situation. He keyed his mic. "Blue, we're going to need resupply, and soon. Some air support might be nice, too."

"I'll see what I can do. Hang in there."

Out of the corner of his eye, he saw Bishop step to the edge of the roof and aim almost straight down. There was a flash from her muzzle, then another, and another. "A little help here."

King raced to her side and started firing, point blank, into a veritable sea of grasping arms. He fired out his magazine, reloaded and kept firing. And still they kept coming.

Then something changed. He was so focused on repelling the attack that he almost missed the abrupt shift. For no apparent reason, the wendigos stopped their attack and began retreating. As they scuttled away, several more dropping from well-aimed shots, King realized that the creatures were all moving in the same direction: northwest.

"Hold your fire!" he shouted. The ringing in his ears was so loud, he could barely hear his own voice, but he augmented the command by waving his hand in front of his face, the universal gesture for immediate ceasefire. It took a moment for the message to break through the fog of war, but by the time all their guns fell silent, there was no mistaking what was happening: the wendigos were in full retreat.

"Okay," Rook said. "What just happened? Did we scare them off?"

"They're all going the same direction," Queen observed. "I don't think they're running away from us, but toward something else."

King shook his head uncertainly. The museum where Sara and Beck were holed up lay to the east. While there was no way of knowing what had drawn the attackers off, they could not let this window of opportunity close. "Let's get moving."

They cautiously descended, threading their way through the tangle of unmoving wendigo bodies. King noticed that Knight was particularly hesitant about making the traverse, probably because of his impaired depth perception. The disability had not been a limitation during the battle; Knight's performance had been the very essence of the unofficial sniper motto: One shot, one kill. Yet, even with both feet solidly on the ground, Knight moved with almost excessive caution until he was clear of the fallen wendigos.

Before he could inquire about Knight's odd behavior, Aleman's voice came over the net. "Thought you might want to know. I ran the tail numbers on that mystery plane that violated the no fly zone. Give you one guess who owns it."

"Beltran."

"His holding company anyway. It looks like you were right about him being involved. His restaurants have been shut down, and all his assets have been seized."

King was less than sanguine about the news. "Too little, too late. What Beltran wants is here. It's always been here."

"What exactly is it that he wants?"

King looked in the direction the wendigos had gone. Northwest. The same direction as the airport where Beltran's plane had landed. "I have a feeling we're going to find out sooner than we want."

FORTY-NINE

It was not his reduced eyesight that prompted Knight to exercise what seemed like an excessive degree of caution as he made his way across the field strewn with wendigo carcasses, but a limitation of an entirely different sort.

He wondered, not for the first time since King's explanation of the threat they faced, if he should reveal his concerns. He had kept silent on the plane because King would have almost certainly sidelined him, and he was not about to stay behind now—not with Anna in danger.

Besides, he wasn't even sure that there was a problem. The immunosuppressant drugs that he was taking to prevent his body from rejecting the now defunct ocular implant made him vulnerable to ordinary infections, and King had indicated that this disease was something else altogether.

But what if he was wrong?

It was a chance he had been willing to take when contemplated from a distance, but now that the battle had been joined, now that the full scope of what they would have to do had been revealed, he realized that he had let his confidence override good judgment.

Would there be any warning? Would he have enough time to put a bullet through his brain before he lost all control of his body and transformed into one of those demonic creatures?

He pushed the idea out of his head. There were a lot of ways to die on the battlefield, and being overly fixated on one threat was the surest way to get blindsided.

They reached the highway and moved at a fast walk along the pavement. There was no need for stealth, but they maintained situational awareness. Everywhere they looked, they saw the footprint of wendigo activity. Houses with doors left wide open, front porches streaked with blood, driveways littered with scraps of torn clothing. Half a mile from the soccer field, they found a car abandoned in the middle of the road, doors open, engine still running. Black streaks on the pavement showed how the vehicle had skidded to a stop. There were dents in the fenders and smears of blood on windows, but no sign of the driver.

Rook nodded at the car. "Finders keepers, right?"

Knight fixed his gaze on the empty space behind the steering wheel. "What do you think happened to the driver?"

Rook rolled his eyes. "Jeez, I was kidding. We'll give it back."

"Taken or turned?" Knight said, ignoring him.

King got within a few yards of the car. "The blood is on the outside. It looks like the wendigos stopped this car. The driver probably tried to make a run for it on foot."

"If that's wendigo blood," Knight said, "then the car is contaminated."

Rook laughed. "You worried about cooties now?"

"Knight's right," King said. "We don't need to take any chances. Leave it."

Rook accepted this without further comment, and they resumed their trek.

They found survivors, too, people who had been awakened by the emergency alert and followed the instructions to lock themselves in their houses and wait. A few came out to meet them, wondering aloud if the crisis was over, or in some cases, volunteering to join the fight. King urged one and all to return to the safety of their homes and continue waiting for further guidance from the authorities.

Managing the survivors slowed them down considerably, and it was nearly half an hour before they crossed the narrow bridge that led to the island where the Lost Colony Festival Park was located. As soon as they were within sight of the main building, Sara Fogg burst from the entrance as if shot from a cannon. She made a beeline for King.

The two embraced as if they hadn't seen each other for years. Knight turned his head slightly, giving them the privacy of his blind side, and in the process he glimpsed another figure approaching with considerably more restraint.

"Anna!"

Beck smiled and quickened her pace, but refused to run. She was too much a soldier to let her guard down, even for a moment of joyful reunion, and that gave Knight time to notice the dark stains on her clothes, the streaks of blood on her face, and most conspicuous of all, the entrenching tool she hefted in her right hand.

He threw up his hands, palms out. "Stop!"

Confusion immediately registered on her face, giving way to concern. "Dae? What's wrong?"

"Don't come any closer." He could see by the look in her eyes that the warning stung her as much as it did him. King and Sara were still locked in an embrace like something from a romantic movie, while he was telling Beck to keep her distance.

"It's the meds, Anna." He kept his voice low, a futile effort to preserve his secret a little while longer. "The immuno-suppressants. They might make me more susceptible to this."

She gave a cautious laugh, amused but nevertheless fraught with worry. "I'm not contagious, Dae. Tell him Sara."

"You might not be, but there's blood all over you."

At the sound of her name, Sara pulled away from King, and Knight realized that everyone was looking at him. "Actually, Dae-jung is right. I'm afraid in all the chaos we kind of threw bio-safety protocols out the window, but it is possible for a person to be a carrier without becoming symptomatic."

The explanation did not put Beck at ease. "So I'm a carrier now? I can't ever touch my boyfriend again?"

"Of course not," Sara was quick to say. "A disinfectant shower should take care of it." She turned to Knight. "My gut says that you're not at any particular risk... You haven't eaten at Mr. Pig, I hope."

Knight shook his head.

"Well then you probably aren't at risk."

Beck gave a weak shrug and looked away. "Better safe than sorry, I guess."

The words felt like a gut punch, but King came to the rescue. "Okay, break's over. We've got to get to the refuge site." He keyed his radio. "Blue, we need pickup from this location."

Aleman's voice came back immediately. "Easier said than done, I'm afraid. The island is still locked down, and I don't have direct access to the CDC or the National Guard. It may take more than just your say so to convince them it's safe to—"

The rest of the sentence was rendered inaudible by a loud crashing noise in the distance. Knight immediately turned toward the source, as did everyone else, but there was no visible sign of the disturbance.

"What the hell was that?" Rook asked. "It sounded like an avalanche."

A moment later, a dark cloud rose above the treetops, and a few seconds later, the noise repeated. "Whatever that is," Knight said, "it's about a mile away."

Worry creased King's forehead. "Sara, this site you want to investigate... You really think there's a cure there?"

Sara gave a helpless shrug. "I don't know if we'll find anything there at all. But if Ellen is right, then that's where the Lost Colony survivors lived, at least for a time. There might be something about that place that keeps the wendigos away. It's not a great lead, but it's all I've got."

"Blue, keep working it. We need to get Sara out of here, ASAP."

"Will do."

The noise came again, and then with barely a pause, it repeated.

"Getting closer," Bishop said.

"It's the wendigos," King said, with grave certainty. "Tearing their way into houses."

Rook raised a dubious eyebrow. "I don't think kicking in a door makes that much noise."

"They aren't kicking in doors." King turned to Sara again. "We need to get moving. You have a car?"

Beck answered first, pointing to a small hatchback in the nearby parking lot. "It's over there, but I'm not sure we'll all fit."

Rook laughed. "Ever see one of those clown cars?"

King shook his head. "Queen, Bishop. Take Sara and the others out in the car. We'll follow on foot."

Queen shook her head. "Screw the 'women and children first' macho bullshit, King. You're the one who can barely walk. You take the car. We'll catch up."

"This isn't a democracy." King's tone was flat but there was no mistaking the underlying aura of command. "Do it."

A noise as loud as a gunshot silenced any further discussion. A hundred yards away to the west, what appeared to be most of a large tree, the trunk splintered at the base, limbs still attached and flinging out a flurry of leaves, arced up into the air, spinning end over end like a juggler's club, before crashing down in a cloud of dust.

"They're coming," King shouted. "Go."

It was already too late. Five pale figures emerged from the direction of the bridge, long limbs and ungainly gait belying their incredible speed. Rook braced the massive 240B against one hip and fired from a standing position like some kind of action-movie superstar. The burst ripped into the charging wendigos, felling two of them and wounding the others, but more were already racing forward to take their place.

Knight brought his rifle up, but the wendigos were too close and moving too fast for him to acquire a target. Around him, the others were firing their SCARs, dropping one wendigo after another, but the creatures weren't just mindlessly running toward anything on two legs. They were spreading out, as if trying to dodge the team's shots or flank their position.

That's exactly what they're trying to do, Knight realized. He whirled around and saw Beck racing for the parked car with Sara and Ellen in tow. A wendigo appeared in the periphery of his vision. The creature had slipped past the team, though the trails of blood streaming across its torso indicated it had not made it through unnoticed. It was homing in on the retreating women like a heat-seeking missile. With two good eyes, he would have noticed it sooner. He brought his rifle up, putting the crosshairs on the back of its skull, but as its head bobbed up and down with each step, he saw that Beck and the others were in his line of fire.

If I miss...

He squeezed the trigger. Felt the stiff recoil rock against his shoulder. The crosshairs jerked up, ever so slightly, and then the wendigo's head burst apart.

He glanced around, acutely aware of the fact that by focusing on the threat to the others, he had left himself completely vulnerable. The vigilance and combined firepower of his teammates had kept him safe, but if one of the wendigos could get through, then it was only a matter of time before others did. There was something different about this attack. These wendigos seemed smarter than those they had first encountered, behaving more like pack hunters than rabid dogs.

He felt like he was missing something else vitally important, but the job of picking off individual wendigos consumed his attention. He peered through the scope, sweeping back and forth until he acquired a target, fired and then resumed sweeping.

Tunnel vision. His intense focus, so essential to scoring one lethal hit after another, made it impossible for him to see what was happening practically right in front of him.

"Oh, hell no!"

Rook's shout broke the spell. Knight looked up and immediately recognized the nagging detail he had earlier overlooked.

The attacking wendigos might have been more intelligent, but they did not appear to be physically different from those they had fought at the drop zone. They certainly weren't large or strong enough to demolish entire houses or rip trees in half and toss them into the sky like horseshoes.

The same could not be said of the dump-truck sized monstrosity lumbering across the bridge.

FIFTY

Beck shoved Sara ahead, then wheeled around, caught Ellen's hand and whipped her past, propelling her toward the car. She switched the E-tool from her left hand to her right, and faced the advancing horde. The team was holding the line, but a few of the creatures had made it through; one lay twitching just a few yards away.

She glanced over her shoulder. Sara was circling around to get in the passenger seat. "No." Beck fished out the key and tossed it to Sara over the top of the Nissan. "You drive. I'll help them clear a path."

Sara caught the keys and stared at them. "Anna, I can't—"

Her protest fell abruptly silent, her eyes suddenly wide as saucers and focused on something just past Beck's shoulder. Beck turned back and felt the blood in her veins go ice cold.

It was a wendigo in the same way that her rented Nissan and an Abrams tank were both vehicles. It had the same ghastly translucent skin stretched taut over corded muscles, but the similarities ended there. This creature's chest and arms were mottled with a strange colored pattern that coiled around the torso and down the arms. Unlike the other wendigos, which were misshapen and distorted, the limbs of the creature stalking across the bridge were solid, skeleton and musculature in perfect proportion. The same could not be said for its head, which now appeared to be just an enormous set of jaws—like the mouth of a killer whale—protruding from the creature's shoulders. Aside from twin rows of jagged teeth, the head was almost completely featureless, without eyes or nose, only a pair of dark gaping nostrils above the bear-trap jagged rows of teeth. The prodigious weight of the bestial head had caused the wendigo to walk in a hunched over fashion, on all fours like a gorilla, but even bent nearly double, it was still almost twenty feet high.

The sheer size of the monstrosity commanded her attention like the gravity of a black hole, and appeared to be having the same effect on the rest of the team. She heard the buzzsaw report of Rook's machine gun, and saw blossoms of red appear on the enormous torpedo-shaped head, but the 7.62-millimeter rounds had about as much effect as mosquito bites. The others were firing at it as well, with no more impressive results, but while their firepower was concentrated on the massive creature, nearly a dozen smaller wendigos slipped out from its shadow and broke for the relative cover of the trees.

Beck tore her eyes away from the battle, turning back to Sara. "Get out of here!"

Sara needed no further convincing. She had circled the car and was sliding behind the driver's seat. Ellen was already inside.

"Whatever you do," Beck shouted, "don't let those things stop you. Keep driving."

She did not wait for an answer but pivoted back toward the battle. To her amazement, the behemoth appeared to be struggling. The cumulative damage was accomplishing what no single weapon could.

That was the good news. Unfortunately, while they drilled away at the massive monster, more than a dozen wendigos made it past and were closing in on Beck's location.

The Nissan started with a barely audible purr and backed out of the parking spot.

At least Sara will make it, Beck thought as she hefted the E-tool and started toward the nearest creature. *She'll find a way to stop this disease in its tracks. Maybe even find a cure.*

The thought brought some comfort as death closed in around her.

A swipe of the E-tool caved in a wendigo's head, but the impact rang down the length of the handle. It was all she could do to hold on as she drew back for another swing. The spade-head sliced deeply into another. She drew back, then thrust it forward like a spear, impaling the wounded creature.

She thought she heard someone calling her name. Her given name. Was it Dae-jung? He was one of only a few people who called her 'Anna.' She tried to catch one last glimpse of him, but the ever-tightening ring of wendigos blocked her view. All she could see was the car with Sara and Ellen driving away, slipping past evidently unnoticed. Then even that sight was taken from her as the creatures moved in for the kill.

FIFTY-ONE

"**Anna!**"

Knight's howl rose above the din, and Queen risked a quick backward glance to see what was happening. He stood poised to fire, his rifle aimed at something behind them. Then she saw what he was aiming at. A cluster of wendigos had gotten past them, possibly by hiding in the trees or even taking a circuitous route through the nearby complex of buildings. They had made it to the parking lot less than fifty yards away.

Knight had the shot but did not pull the trigger. Instead, he just howled in impotent rage. In front of Queen, Rook's machine gun was still pouring a hailstorm of lead into the enormous wendigo, and King and Bishop were backing him up. The beast's flesh was a ragged map of wounds streaming dark blood, but it was still moving faster than she would have thought possible.

The monster on one side, a pack of wendigos on the other. What was the more immediate threat?

The little Nissan tore out of the parking area and headed along the road to the place where the team had chosen to make its stand. One of the creatures took notice and started to pursue, but Queen felled it with a three-round burst that obliterated its ghoulish face. As she brought her sights to bear on the grouped wendigos, she glimpsed Sara behind the wheel of the car, and Ellen Dare in the back seat.

Where's Beck?

Queen knew the answer as soon as the question formed, and her heart sank. Beck had stayed to fight the wendigos off, so Sara could get away. Queen took aim at the pack.

"No!" Knight cried. "You'll hit Anna."

She's already dead.

Queen didn't say it aloud. Before she could pull the trigger, another shout split the air. From out of nowhere, Bishop dashed right across Queen's line of fire, and ran headlong at the wendigos, uttering a long fierce battle cry that might have been a curse in her native tongue or simply a berserker scream.

"Shit!" Queen jerked her rifle away without loosing a shot. Bishop's desperate charge wasn't likely to accomplish anything more than getting her killed, too. Worse, it had left Rook and King to deal with the monster that was still relentlessly advancing.

Queen swung around just in time to see Rook push away from his machine gun. The weapon's removable barrel was glowing a dangerous hue of orange. Continuing to fire the overheated weapon might cause a malfunction or worse—deform the barrel, which could have explosive consequences. Also, the creature would be on them before he could swap out the barrel. Instead he drew one of his Desert Eagle pistols. As if inspired by Bishop's recklessness, he ran toward the monster.

He held the pistol in a two-handed grip, shooting on the move, but instead of aiming for a vital spot—head or heart—he concentrated his fire on the beast's legs. The half-inch thick bullets didn't have the speed or penetration of the sleeker, high-powered rifle rounds from the 240B, but they slammed into the monster's knee with jackhammer force. The bone shattered under the assault, and no amount of primal fury could keep the monster upright. The wounded leg folded under its weight, and the giant pitched forward like a felled tree.

King and Rook both dodged out of the way of its wildly flailing arms and snapping jaws, but as the monster crashed down with an impact that sent a tremor rippling underfoot, they kept firing until the thing finally stopped moving.

It seemed to take an eternity for it to die, but when Queen heard Sara shouting and turned to see the little car still rolling toward them, she knew that only a few seconds had passed.

"Get in!" Sara yelled from the open window. "Hurry!"

Queen felt rooted in place, caught in a gyre of too many conflicting priorities. In the parking lot, a stone's throw away, Bishop was locked in a hopeless hand-to-hand battle with half-a-dozen wendigos, in a surely futile attempt to save Anna Beck. Knight was halfway there as well, but staggering, as if the weight of loss was already bearing him down.

"Queen!" King's snapped her out of her despair. She jerked her head around to meet his steady gaze. "Go with her. Keep her safe. She has to find the cure. That's the only thing that matters."

Queen stared at him in disbelief. She heard Rook's voice, fierce and urgent. "Go with her, boss. Like you said, it's the only thing that matters."

Before either she or King could reply, Rook took off at a run after Knight, his right fist still gripping the Desert Eagle. "Don't worry," he shouted without looking back. "I got this."

Now it was King that seemed paralyzed by indecision. Queen could easily guess what was going through his mind. Half the team in peril. Beck, probably dead. Bishop, too—his own flesh and blood. Leaving might mean abandoning Knight and Rook to the same fate. And for what? To escape with Sara? Was he supposed to sacrifice the team to save his fiancée?

Queen knew it was not as simple as that. There was an island crawling with wendigos between them and the refuge, and no guarantees that any of them would make it out alive.

Her own choice was just as stark. Stay and fight with Rook, or help Sara reach the refuge and hopefully stop the wendigo outbreak?

"King, he's right. We have to go!"

A flicker of movement near the bridge caught her attention, a lone wendigo, late to the party. Queen sighted and fired. The creature went down, but two more appeared even as it fell, and then another. Not stragglers, but the vanguard of another horde.

The report jolted King into action. Without another word, he crossed to the Nissan and got in the back seat.

Fighting the urge to take one last look in the direction Rook had gone, Queen followed suit. Sara started to get out, but Queen shook her head. "You drive. I'll shoot."

FIFTY-TWO

Parrish had just worked up the courage to open the plane's exit door and venture out onto the tarmac, when the noise of what sounded like an avalanche reached his ears. He backed away from the door and returned to the window. Nothing moved on the runway, but just over the treetops, he saw an enormous plume of dust and smoke lofting into the heavens.

"What was that?" the frightened co-pilot asked.

"Those things are tearing up the city." Parrish watched a few seconds more, then reached for the lever again.

The pilot forestalled him. "Are you sure that's a good idea?"

"If they decide to come back, do you think we'll be safe in here?" He did not wait for an answer. The door fell smoothly away from the fuselage, the steps unfolding to kiss the pavement. Parrish descended quickly and looked up and down the length of the runway. There were small planes parked at the far end of the strip and some kind of structure. It was a place to start.

Behind him, the plane's crew had closed the door again. The two pilots were either trusting in the thin shell of aluminum to protect them, or in the best tradition of naval officers, they had simply elected to go down with the ship. Further away, the noise of relentless destruction continued without let up, but the dust cloud seemed smaller, more distant. Maybe the pilots had made the right choice.

Parrish was still trying to wrap his head around what he had just seen. If not for the sheer horror of it, he might have laughed. The cartel leader had been such a fool, trusting in his primitive god to protect him, to reward him.

Or maybe this was exactly what Beltran had been expecting.

Parrish had heard stories about Aztec warriors who competed for the dubious honor of being sacrificed to their bloodthirsty gods, probably the very same god Beltran claimed to worship. Maybe that was how Beltran and his men saw themselves: blessed ones, chosen sacrifices to Huitzilopochtli.

"Careful what you wish for," he murmured. Good advice, but too late to be of any use to Hector Beltran.

Parrish reached the building and tried the door. It was unlocked, but there was no sign of anyone inside. The phone was dead, but he noticed a pickup, the Dare County seal on the door, parked outside. He found the keys hanging from a hook on the wall, but after unlocking it and getting inside, he hesitated. He had only a vague idea about where he was, and those creatures were between him and freedom. On the other hand, he was finally out from under Beltran's thumb.

The more he thought about it, the better he felt. The entire ordeal, which hadn't even lasted a whole day, was finally over. Beltran wasn't going to be a problem for anyone, anymore, which was good news for Marrs, on top of everything else Parrish had done for him.

And the monsters? Wild dogs and the power of suggestion... something like that. There was a rational explanation for all of this. There had to be.

Yet, as he threaded his way through streets littered with debris, past overturned cars and one house after another that appeared to have been knocked flat with an army of bulldozers, he knew better.

This was the end of the world.

FIFTY-THREE

Rook aimed his Desert Eagle at the writhing mass of wendigos, but just as Knight had done, he withheld firing the weapon, not because of the very real possibility that a round from the .50 caliber pistol might punch right through one of the creatures and hit Bishop, but rather because he couldn't believe what he was seeing.

Bishop was kicking serious ass.

Rook would not have guessed a person could move so fast—and he had even seen her fight Queen once. Bishop was a blur of motion, launching kicks and punches that deflected snapping jaws and knocked the attacking creatures back before they could grasp hold with their freakishly long fingers.

Rook started at the noise of a rifle shot and whirled around, just as Knight fired a second time. The sniper was not targeting the creatures around Bishop, but rather picking off a fresh wave of the monsters coming across the bridge. The CheyTac thundered again and again, and with each report, a wendigo head split apart. Rook took aim with his Desert Eagle, but each time he was about to pull the trigger, his target was felled by one of Knight's bullets.

He turned back to find Bishop, almost unrecognizable beneath a layer of gore. It was impossible to tell how much of it was hers. Probably not much, judging by the fact that she was still on her feet. She was surrounded by wendigos, but most of them were sprawled out around her, limbs bent at unnatural angles or torn off completely. Only two were still standing, still trying to succeed where their brethren had failed.

Quicker than his eye could follow, Bishop wrapped her arms around the neck of one creature and flipped herself up and over its shoulders, twisting savagely as she flew through the air. An instant later, the wendigo toppled forward, minus its head, which was still gripped in Bishop's arms. The remaining creature struck at her like a biting viper, but Bishop thrust the severed head forward, jamming it into the wendigo's gaping mouth with such force that the creature's lower jaw broke away. She side-stepped, allowing its momentum to carry it past, and then she delivered a two-handed hammer blow to the base of the monster's skull. Even from several yards away, Rook could hear the sound of bones breaking.

He whirled back around to help Knight, but there were no more wendigos left to kill.

"Well, shit," he muttered. "What did I stay behind for?"

His quip failed to elicit even a glimmer of amusement from Knight, who was now staring desolately toward the parking lot. Bishop just stood there, breathing heavily, eyes darting to and fro, as if expecting another wave of creatures to appear at any moment, but otherwise unmoving. At her feet, partly covered by wendigo bodies, curled in a fetal ball, was the almost indistinguishable form of Anna Beck.

Knight took an uncertain step forward, then broke into a run. Rook holstered his pistol and sprinted to interpose himself. He put his hands on Knight's shoulders. "Don't."

Knight tried to wrestle out of his grasp, but even in his rage and grief, he was no match for Rook's strength. "Let go of me. I have to..."

"No, you don't," Rook said, firm but gentle. "You don't need to see that, brother."

Rook did not completely understand why Knight had been so reluctant to approach Beck earlier, but even absent the risk of infection, there was no way he was going to let Knight get close to Beck. Knight had been through too much, lost too much. His eye. His best friend, Erik Somers. His grandmother. Now his girlfriend.

Knight did not need to see what was left of her body.

"*Bohze moi!*"

Bishop's sudden exclamation turned Rook's head, distracting him just enough to allow Knight to slip free. As Rook spun around, making a futile grab for his friend's arm, he saw the reason for her outburst.

Anna Beck was moving.

The apparent resurrection left Rook completely stunned. As Beck slowly uncurled, a low moan escaped her lips.

"Shit!" Rook gasped. He tried to recall what King had said about how people transformed into wendigos. Was it like the zombie virus in movies, dead people reanimating after they were bitten? He fumbled for his pistol, but before he could get it out, Bishop knelt and hugged Beck, and Beck, despite her injuries, returned the embrace.

Just as the adrenaline of the false alarm was starting to drain out of Rook's extremities, Knight reached Beck's side and threw his arms around her as well.

"Dae. Don't." Beck's protest was weak, barely audible, and too late to matter. Knight hugged her close, as if afraid that she might evaporate if he let go.

Bishop pulled away abruptly and shot a nervous glance at Rook.

"Knight. Why don't you move away from her for a minute?" Rook spoke in the low tone and calm manner usually reserved for negotiating with suicidal maniacs. "Let Bish and I have a look at her injuries?"

If Knight's earlier fears proved true, if the medication he was taking to prevent his body from rejecting the ocular implant also left him vulnerable to the wendigo infection, how long before the first symptoms started to manifest? Would there be any warning at all? Rook gripped the Desert Eagle, ready to draw it at the first sign of a transformation.

Knight did not let go of Beck, did not even acknowledge Rook's presence. Thirty seconds passed, a minute, and then Beck spoke through clenched teeth. "It's okay."

For a moment, Rook thought she was speaking to Knight, trying to convince him to let go, but then he realized that Beck was looking at him. Her face was taut, agonized, but she was lucid. "I think...we're safe," she continued, laboring over every word. "He isn't...going to turn."

"Are you sure?"

"It would have...happened...already."

Rook let out his breath in a long sigh then closed the remaining distance and laid a firm hand on Knight's shoulder. Knight met his gaze, tears streaming from his good eye, and Rook looked away, not so much embarrassed by the display of emotion as afraid that it might prove contagious. "Seriously, pal. Save it for later. We need to get your lady patched up."

"And we need to go before more of those things show up," Bishop said.

"After what you just did," Rook said, with an approving nod, "that's the last thing I'm worried about."

Bishop shook her head. "I am not wanting to do that again."

"Amen to that."

Knight relaxed his fierce embrace, but only enough to allow Rook to begin treating Beck's wounds. Her fetal curl had protected her vital organs and saved her life, but the wendigos had torn her exposed back to shreds. Rook winced when he saw the damage. "Great. Now that I really need her, Queen's off running around with Mr. and Mrs. King."

He dug into his assault pack and brought out a combat life-saver pack, which contained a variety of field dressings and three one-liter bags of saline solution. Although Queen was the designated medic, every member of the team was cross-trained in battlefield medical care, and carried a similar kit on every mission.

"This may sting," he warned, as he used one of the bags to rinse away the blood, revealing several huge bite marks and large divots torn from her flesh. The damage was superficial but extensive. She flinched at the first touch of the solution, but then steeled herself and endured his ministrations without further reaction.

Rook was impressed. He had no idea how she was even conscious, much less able to talk. He covered the worst of her wounds with large field dressings. When he was done, she grasped his shoulder and used it to haul herself erect.

"I'm good," she rasped. "Let's go."

Despite her strong resolve, Beck nearly collapsed when she tried to walk on her own. Rook swept her up in his arms, carrying her as he might a small child. "It's okay. I got you."

"You can't..."

"There's a car about half a mile from here. I can carry you that far." When Beck offered no further protest, he started forward.

Bishop raced ahead, evidently making the unilateral decision to take point. After sluicing away the blood that coated her body, she looked almost human again. The wendigos had left their mark, with bite wounds on her arms and a nasty looking welt on one cheek, but she had fared considerably better than Beck.

Rook was surprised to see Bishop kneel down to retrieve his machine gun, draping its sling around her neck. The gun looked huge in her grasp, almost as long as she was tall. The muscles of her arms bulged under the heavy load, but her face betrayed none of the effort. "We need this, I think."

Rook just stared in disbelief. Bishop, who had just ripped apart a half dozen wendigos with her bare hands, was now hefting the enormous 240B and ready for battle again. Beside him, Knight, as lethal with only one eye as he had been with two.

It was like having the old team together again.

As they passed the carcass of the enormous wendigo, Rook wondered aloud if there were others.

"First one like that I've seen," Beck said. "But I think...they grow...after they eat."

Rook wracked his brain for a witty reply, but the thought of what it was the wendigo had eaten to get that big robbed him of every last vestige of humor. Once past the bridge, they got their first look at the chaos the wendigo pack had left in its wake.

Smoke billowed from a score of fires scattered across the landscape. Houses had been cracked open like eggs, the broken pieces discarded with indifference. The giant had done that, Rook knew, ripping down the walls to get at the frightened people hiding within. Some had no doubt turned, adding to the growing army. The rest had been devoured.

"I think there must be more than one of the big guys," Rook ventured.

"Given the amount of destruction," Knight said. "I think you're right."

"Frickin' wonderful. Well, they're gone now. I say we get some wheels and head in any direction that is away from them." He paused, trying to decide if what he had said made any sense, then shook his head and continued walking.

They had done okay so far, but he had no illusions about what would happen if they were attacked again. If there really were several of the jumbo-sized wendigos, and hundreds or possibly thousands of the regular ones, then beating them was a job for an entire army.

"Rook," Bishop called out. "Someone is coming."

Rook followed Bishop's gaze and spotted a lone pickup rolling down the abandoned highway. "A concerned citizen. Perfect."

"How do you know he's concerned?"

"I'll make sure of it." He gently lowered Beck to the ground, then strode to the center line, and held up both hands in a slight variation of the universal symbol for stop—the difference being that each hand held one of his enormous Desert Eagle pistols.

The truck stopped a good fifty yards away, as if the driver was afraid to come any closer. Rook made a rolling gesture with the barrel of one pistol, and the truck grudgingly advanced until it was right in front of them. The driver rolled his window down and poked his head out.

There was undisguised wariness in the man's expression. No surprise there. Rook's own upbringing had taught him that rural folks, while hospitable, were naturally suspicious of outsiders, especially those who didn't quite fit in. The four of them looked like refugees from some post-apocalyptic future, which actually wasn't far from the truth.

The man studied them for a moment, noting the camouflage and heavy weaponry. "Army?"

"Something like that. We're trying to get back to our unit. Think you could give us a ride?"

The man shrugged. "Why not? Hop in. You'll have to roshambo for the front seat, though."

Rook holstered the pistols and gave his friendliest smile. "Much appreciated."

Knight and Bishop assisted Beck into the open bed, then climbed in with her. Since Knight was not about to leave Beck's side, and Bishop's Russian accent was a liability when it came to conversing with the locals, Rook got the dubious honor of sharing the cab with the driver.

"Which way?" the man asked.

There were two bridges across the Croatan Sound, one at the north end of the island, and another southwest of their present location. Both bridges would deliver them to the mainland near the town of Manns Harbor, but Rook was pretty sure that King and the others would have taken the southern route, away from the rolling wave of destruction that had begun in the north.

"Stick to the highway," Rook told him. "Head south, and then across the bridge."

The man nodded, and then put the truck in gear and started forward without comment, which struck Rook as a little off.

"Hope you don't mind me asking, but how did you manage to survive..." Rook jerked a thumb over his shoulder. "All that?"

"Just lucky, I guess. Actually, I was inside and pretty much missed the whole thing. Heard lots of noise and figured it must be a tornado or something. When I finally came out, I saw...those things."

Something about the explanation only made Rook more suspicious. After a disaster, the first thing people in rural communities did was check on their neighbors. They didn't jump in the truck and run.

"Where are my manners?" Rook thrust out his hand. "I'm Stan."

The abruptness of the gesture surprised the man, but he recovered quickly, clasping the proffered hand. "Folks call me Bulldog," he said.

"And what folks would those be?" Rook said with a knowing smile. "Because you sure as hell aren't from around here."

FIFTY-FOUR

King rested his SCAR on the door frame, scanning the roadside for any sign of current wendigo activity. There was plenty of evidence that they had been there. The highway they had walked down earlier was now strewn with wreckage from houses and shops that had been demolished. Trees and power lines had been knocked down like blades of grass trampled underfoot. Dodging the rubble had slowed them to a crawl. The scale of the destruction was far too great to be the work of just one monster wendigo, which meant that the thing with the snake tattoo was not the only example of its kind. The giants were something new, something outside his experience.

"Sara, that big one we fought. Have you seen others like it?"

Sara glanced in the rearview mirror, meeting his eyes. "In the hospital, one of them bit me."

King drew in a sharp breath but withheld comment.

"Afterward, he—it—got bigger. I think feeding makes them grow."

"You're right. Feeding on human flesh does make them grow larger. Most of the ones we've encountered so far were victims of the tainted meat supply. They never would have willingly engaged in cannibalism, so the infection has driven them mad. It's different for those who make the conscious decision to eat the flesh of another person."

He realized that the others were staring at him in astonishment, and he looked away, returning his gaze to the landscape of destruction.

"Like the colonists," Ellen said in a small voice. "The ones who were cursed."

King nodded without looking at her.

"Well," Sara said, "I suppose that repeated ingestion of...uh, could build up extreme levels of certain proteins in the body, which might result in a more dramatic presentation of the symptoms. Perhaps those... What should we call them? Alpha wendigos? Maybe they were living on Mr. Pig before this started."

King suspected there might be a different explanation, but did not share. They had enough to worry about.

"Stop!" Queen shouted.

Sara hit the brakes. King turned and peered through the windshield. There were no wendigos but the road directly ahead of them was completely impassable, blocked by an unending string of cars that had been overturned and tossed around like toys. Some of the vehicles had been ripped apart, and were streaked with blood. A hundred yards further along, the line of cars followed the turn onto the bypass road that ran west toward the Virginia Dare Memorial Bridge. In the distance, King could see clouds of smoke rising, and huge pieces of debris, even entire cars, hurled up into the air.

"I think we've caught up to them," Queen said.

"Oh, my God," Sara whispered. "This is my fault."

The comment shocked King into silence.

Queen shook her head. "Unless you fed thousands of people tainted meat and then set the wendigo virus loose, I don't think so."

"Not that." Sara pointed at the wreckage. "These people were trying to flee. I stopped them by ordering the quarantine. Now they're trapped here, with nowhere to go. Those things are going to wipe them all out."

King found his voice. "You're wrong. You gave the order for everyone to stay inside, shelter in place."

Judging by the level of destruction wrought upon the houses, it seemed unlikely that anyone who had followed Sara's instructions would have fared much better, but she could not have known about the alpha wendigos. Sara was right about the fate facing those caught on the road, though. The trapped motorists were an all-you-can-eat buffet stretching out all the way across the bridge to the barricades erected on the far side.

He keyed his mic. "Blue, this is King."

"Go."

"You need to coordinate with the National Guard. Tell them to let people off the islands."

"King, I don't have that authority."

"Then find someone who does. Tell them it's Sara's recommendation. The people who are caught at the roadblocks are not infected. They can't spread this. We have to get them off the island."

Queen cut in, speaking directly to King. "You do that, and you'll be uncorking the bottle. Those things will have a straight shot to the mainland, and once they get there—"

"I know what will happen." King left the mic open so Aleman could hear his answer. "How many of those people have eaten tainted meat? Ten percent? More? The longer we leave them out there, the bigger the wendigo army will get. Everyone on the road will be killed or turned. We can't afford to let either one happen."

"And what happens when the wendigos hit the barricade? You think those weekend warriors have a prayer of stopping them?"

"No," King admitted. "That's going to be our job. But we need to find a way off this island."

"It *is* an island." Ellen's voice was timid, as if she expected her idea to be dismissed out of hand. "We could take a boat."

King could have kicked himself. "Ellen, your ancestor would be proud. Where can we find one?"

The compliment had the desired effect. Ellen sat up a little straighter. "There are several marinas on Shallowbag Bay. We just passed it."

King consulted his mental map of the island. Shallowbag Bay was on the eastern shore of the island. To get to the mainland, they would have to take a circuitous route, but that would still be faster, and presumably safer, than trying to run the gauntlet on the highway.

Sara turned the Nissan around and headed back up the road half a mile, until she saw a parking lot with a low wooden sign pointing the way to the docks. King understood now why he had not noticed it earlier. Like everything else alongside the highway, the marina building, along with several boats that had been parked out in front of trailers, was now almost unrecognizable. But as Sara steered down the narrow lane that fronted the pier, the damage was less pronounced, and the boats in the water appeared to be unscathed.

They got out and ran down to the deserted dock. King picked out a twenty-three foot long Super Air Nautique G-23 ski boat, which according to the sandwich board sign located nearby, was available for rental use on an hourly or daily basis. The boat's operator, however, was nowhere to be found. King climbed aboard and was helping Sara and Ellen do the same when Queen called out. "King! We've got company."

King followed her gaze and spotted a small pack of wendigos, coming from the direction of the highway. Queen took aim but King forestalled her. "Get the boat started. I've got this."

He readied his rifle but did not fire. If there were more wendigos in the neighborhood, the shots would bring them running. Instead, as soon as Queen was aboard, he freed the mooring rope from the cleat and shoved off from the pier. The boat seemed rooted in place by inertia, drifting sluggishly away from the dock. One foot. Two. The wendigos were moving a lot faster than the boat.

The engine turned over with a cough and Queen gave a shout of triumph. "That's what I'm talking about."

King felt the shift in his center of gravity as the screws started turning under the hull. A froth of white rose up behind the craft, but as it started to pull away, the lead wendigo reached the dock and leaped into the air.

King fired, a point blank burst that struck the wendigo in the torso. The impact was just enough to alter the trajectory of the creature's jump, so instead of landing squarely on the stern seats, it dropped with a splash a few feet behind the churning wake.

The other creatures were undeterred by the demise of the frontrunner. They ran to the edge at full tilt and hurled themselves out into space. King fired again, hitting one and missing the others, but ultimately it did not matter. The boat had finally picked up some speed. All the wendigos fell short, splashing into the water and disappearing. Several more followed, throwing themselves lemming-like from the pier.

King watched the spot where the wendigos had gone in, waiting to see if they would break the surface, swimming after the fleeing boat, but there was no sign of the creatures. No desperate thrashing, no bobbing to the surface for desperate gasps of breath. The wendigos, creatures of lean muscle and dense bone, had sunk to the bottom of the bay like stones.

King keyed his mic again. "Blue. How are we doing on clearing those roads?"

"Admiral Ward is making it happen. He said 'please' with extreme prejudice. I think it's going to happen, but it sounds like it's already complete pandemonium on those bridges."

King's estimation of Ward went up a notch. "Tell the National Guard that as soon as they get the civilians safely evacuated, they need to blow up all the bridges leading out of the infected area."

"Blow up the bridges," Aleman repeated, a hint of skepticism in his tone. "I'm sure that will go over well."

"Trust me on this. Wendigos can't swim. They'll be trapped on the islands, unable to spread the infection."

"I'll pass it along. No promises. Can I tell them that you've got a plan?"

King glanced over at Sara, who was watching him intently. "Tell them I'm working on it."

FIFTY-FIVE

Parrish felt a wave of numbness shoot through his extremities at the accusation. Was it even an accusation at all? His passenger's smile seemed sincere enough, but Parrish could sense that there was a lot more going on behind it.

The people were military. He could tell that from the Scorpion W2 multicam Army Combat Uniforms they wore—soon to be general issue for all US Army troops, and already fielded to certain elite units. The blond man's rowdy hair and goatee also marked him as a member of an elite service—Special Forces, maybe even a Delta team—and that meant he was smarter than the average bear. Despite the Hollywood stereotype of Green Berets and Navy SEALs as muscle-bound testosterone addicts, the selection process for special operations relied far more on mental acuity than physical ability.

There was something else about the man, a nagging suspicion that he had seen him before. Maybe they had crossed paths when Parrish had been a CID investigator. Regardless, he was certain the man in the passenger's seat—Stan—was testing him, and if he lied and was caught, he would be in for a world of hurt.

"Is it that obvious?" Parrish said with a laugh. "You're right. In fact, I'm not even sure where I am. I was on a plane that made an unscheduled landing at the airport just north of here. I know that this is Dare County, North Carolina, but beyond that I'm completely lost."

Had he said too much? Given the circumstances, there was no upside to making up a bullshit story, and filling the expectant silence would alleviate suspicion and give him time to come up with something more substantial that did not incriminate him.

Stan nodded. "The airspace over the island is restricted. You took quite a chance landing here."

"You're telling me. It wasn't my idea. I was just along for the ride."

"Whose idea was it?"

I think you already know the answer to that question, Parrish thought. *This will blow your mind.* He met Stan's stare and held it. "A man named Hector Beltran. He's a Mexican crime lord. I'm DEA. Been working undercover to infiltrate the El Sol cartel. Ever heard of them?"

Stan gave a noncommittal shrug.

Parrish took a breath. He was committed to the narrative now but he had to be careful about not trying to sell it too hard. "Those guys are into some really weird shit. Human sacrifices, cannibalism." He shook his head in disgust. Stan remained silent. Time to change the subject. "Hey, do you know what's going on here? I mean...those things? What the hell are they?"

"There's been a disease outbreak," Stan revealed. "Some kind of rage virus, like in the movies."

Parrish did not have to fabricate his response to that. "Bullshit. I saw those things. That's not some rage virus. Those things weren't..." He trailed off. They *were* human. As much as he wanted to deny it, he had seen it with his own eyes. He stopped the truck in the middle of the road and looked the soldier in the eyes. "Beltran and his men. They changed. I saw it happen."

There was a glimmer of curiosity in Stan's blue eyes. "Tell me."

"Beltran insisted on landing the plane here. He knew it was closed, but he made the pilot land anyway. I think he knew about...about your 'rage virus.' After we landed, he went outside and a bunch of those creatures showed up. He called them *windigos*. It's an old Indian word. American Indian, not India Indian. Anyway, I thought the windigos were going to rip them to shreds, but Beltran and his men fought them off. Killed a few even."

Parrish found himself breathing faster as he relived the horror of what he had seen. Concealing his true identity and purpose was now the last thing on his mind. "And then it happened. They started changing." He shook his head. It sounded so crazy. Maybe his imagination had gotten carried away.

"Go on," Stan prompted.

"It was like something in a movie. Like when people change into werewolves. They got big. I mean huge. Big enough to do all this." He gestured at the landscape of destruction. "So I'm not buying that this is just some rage virus."

Stan nodded thoughtfully. "Sounds like this Beltran guy wanted to get infected."

"I think that's exactly what he wanted. He's crazy. I mean absolutely psycho. He thinks he's some kind of Aztec god." Another piece of the puzzle clicked, and Parrish snapped his fingers. "I think he might be responsible for all of this. He kept talking about 'planting a seed.' I didn't know what he meant, but maybe he put this disease out there, and was just waiting for something like this to happen so he could have his chance to become one of those things."

"You said Beltran and his men. How many? How many of these mega wendigos are there?"

"Five. Beltran and four others."

"We waxed one, so that means four left."

"You killed one?" Parrish was impressed.

Stan nodded. "Yep. And now we're going after the others."

FIFTY-SIX

As she guided the ski-boat across the placid surface of the Roanoke Sound, Queen listened intently to the conversation taking place just a short distance away. She was bursting with questions. What had happened after she had left with the others? Was Bishop okay? Knight?

She had been relieved to hear Rook's voice come over the radio net, but instead of checking in and reporting their status, he was broadcasting a conversation with someone who called himself 'Bulldog.'

The transmission had started just a few seconds after King had ended his call to Lewis Aleman, picking up in mid-sentence, as if Rook had suddenly realized that the rest of the team needed to hear Bulldog's story. King had prompted Rook to ask a few specific questions toward the end. The PNR 500 radios allowed for two-way conversations, just like a telephone, so Rook did not have to release his transmit button to receive. Mostly, King and Queen just listened.

It had been Rook's idea to go after the remaining alphas.

"I would strongly advise you to find a boat and get off the island," King interjected.

"We killed one, we can kill the rest." Rook seemed to be speaking to Bulldog, but he was clearly replying to King's suggestion. "If we can draw them away from the populated areas, it will give more people a chance to escape."

"He's right," Queen said, despite her misgivings. Rook was not the kind of man to run from a fight, especially when there were innocent lives at stake. "The regular wendigos aren't strong enough to break into houses or tear open cars. If Rook can draw the alphas away, those people on the bridge will have a fighting chance."

King's eyes reflected her own apprehension, but he nodded. "Rook, hit and run. Get them to follow you to the east side of the island, then get a boat and move offshore. The wendigos can't swim. You might be able to lure some of them into the water and drown them."

"We'll lure them into the water and drown them," Rook echoed. "Just like the Pied Piper."

"The Pied Piper wasn't dealing with rats the size of school buses," Queen said into her microphone. "Be careful."

"After all," Rook continued. "There's five of us, counting you, Bulldog, and only four more of them."

Five? Had they all made it out? Even Anna Beck?

"Do what you can," King said. "But don't take any unnecessary chances. You're no good to anyone dead."

"No guts, no glory," Rook said, as if trying to give Bulldog a pep talk, and then with a rasp of static, the transmission ended.

Queen glanced back at King, who shook his head in response to her unasked question. "We've got to reach the refuge. Rook knows what he's doing."

"What if there's nothing at the refuge?" she countered. "It's been centuries since anyone lived there. We don't know what to look for, and probably won't know if we find it."

"We'll find it," Sara said in a calm voice.

Queen stared at her. The CDC investigator had not overheard the conversation, so she could only guess at the subtext of the exchange between King and Queen. Sara Fogg had earned their trust, though. Her expertise had been invaluable in saving the world from the Brugada outbreak six years earlier. If Sara promised a cure, Queen had no doubt that she would deliver.

But how long would that take? Hours? Years?

She turned her eyes forward, keeping the boat parallel to the island shore. The boat skimmed across the water, leaving a broad V-shaped wake that would have been perfect for wakeboarding. The pitometer on the dash panel put their speed at just over forty miles per hour, and in no time at all they were rounding the north end of the island. To the south, a low bridge extended out from the island and across the water, all the way to the faintly visible irregularity that was the mainland a few miles to the west. This was the old original bridge to Manns Harbor on the mainland, a two-lane, two-and-a-half-mile-long affair that looked like it should have been demolished decades ago. Although the bridge was still a mile away, Queen could see the cars, hundreds of them, lined up bumper-to-bumper, not moving an inch. She craned her head around, gazing back at the island, where columns of smoke were rising to mark the destructive rampage of the alpha wendigos along the approach to the newer bridge.

"Looks like the roads are still blocked."

"Not much more we can do about that," King said as he settled into the seat next to her and activated the onboard GPS. "Sara, where exactly is this refuge?"

Sara turned to Ellen. "You know better than I do."

Grateful for a chance to contribute, Ellen leaned forward and pointed to a spot about a mile south of where the highway crossed the peninsula and then continued across the Alligator River. "Buffalo City was right there. This is Mill Tail Creek." She traced the course of a narrow stream that ran from the Alligator River, east into the middle of the refuge, broadening out just below the old Buffalo City site.

"We can take the boat up the creek," King declared. He plotted the distance, roughly twenty-five miles from their current position, around the top of the peninsula and then down the Alligator River. "We should be able to make it in about forty minutes."

Queen regarded him with a solemn look. "Forty minutes is a lifetime," she said. "Especially for those people trapped on the island."

King had no answer for that.

FIFTY-SEVEN

Asya tied off the length of wire and then raced back to the waiting pickup. "Done," she told Rook.

"All right. Get on the gun. We're probably going to have to do some shooting even if this works."

She nodded and climbed into the bed of the truck and braced the 240B on the tailgate. Knight was also watching the road through the scope of his CheyTac. Beck was huddled in a corner, trying not to aggravate her injuries with unnecessary movement, but she still had Bishop's SCAR at the low ready, just in case.

They had not seen a wendigo since leaving the park, but the evidence of the creatures' unrelenting push toward the mainland was writ large across the sky in black clouds of smoke.

"Let's do this," Rook shouted, and then he fired his pistol twice into the air.

The noise rolled across the flat landscape and died away, returning them to the eerie quiet, where the only sound for miles around was the distant symphony of tearing metal and crunching fiberglass.

"Bishop?"

Asya heard Knight's voice, but did not look away from the machine gun's iron sights. "What?"

"Thank you."

His gratitude brought an unexpected lump of emotion in her throat. "Is just what we do, no?"

"No," Knight said. His tone was soft but solemn. "That was something else."

Asya didn't know what to say, so she just shrugged.

Knight was not finished. "Do you remember yesterday, when I told you no one expects you to be what Erik was?"

She remembered the conversation well, but...had it only been one day? It felt like a lifetime. "I remember."

"I didn't give you nearly enough credit. You *are* Bishop."

A smile crept across her face. *Yes, I* am *Bishop.*

"Here they come!"

Knight's shout snapped her out of the self-congratulatory moment. She peered down the road, but it was several seconds before she spotted the first wendigo, a moving figure that looked no bigger than her pinkie finger. Knight's rifle cracked loudly beside her. A moment later, the lone figure fell back, but several more moved up behind it, undeterred by the other's fate.

"Bishop," Rook shouted. "Give them a taste."

She pulled the trigger and felt the 240 buck against her shoulder. The report was so loud, she couldn't hear the noise of spent brass and separated links rattling onto the bed liner. Three red tracer rounds arced out across the open road, marking the trajectory of the rest of the burst, and at least some of the bullets found their targets.

The pickup lurched into motion and rolled away from the battle, heading back toward the devastated town center. As it pulled away, she saw that the small group of wendigos was now a rolling wave of pale gangly bodies, sprinting forward almost as fast as the truck was moving. There was no sign of an alpha wendigo. Evidently it would take more than a few pot shots to lure them away from their single-minded push to the mainland, but this was a war where victory required absolute annihilation of the enemy. She triggered several more bursts, just to keep them interested, and then she looked away as the first of the creatures reached the spot where they had parked only a few moments before.

"Cover up!" she shouted.

The warning was almost too late. Knight had barely averted his eyes when several small artificial suns exploded on the road behind them. Bishop had placed six incendiary grenades, daisy-chained with a monofilament trip wire, near the wrecked cars along a quarter-mile stretch of road. To increase the destructive potential of the booby trap, she had punctured the gas tanks of several more cars, saturating the ground with flammable liquid. When the lead wendigo hit the trip wire, detonating the grenades, the resulting firestorm engulfed the dozens that were caught in the midst of the sudden eruption of light and heat.

A few flaming bodies emerged from the firestorm, only to collapse dead after a couple of steps. After that, there was nothing to see for a long time. The pickup stopped, two hundred yards from the edge of the inferno, and Rook got out to assess the damage. It was impossible to say how many had been caught in the flames, or if any more, in their blind hunger, had run heedless into the furnace, but it took less than a minute for some of the creatures to figure out how to go around it.

Suddenly there was another explosion from the midst of the conflagration. Flaming debris erupted in every direction. An entire car rose into the sky in a fireball. At first, Bishop thought it was a fuel tank going up, but then something emerged from the heart of the inferno.

It was an alpha.

The beast moved quickly, running through the flames like a firewalker crossing a bed of coals. There were carbon black streaks on its flanks, but it did not appear to have suffered any injuries from the heat.

"Someone woke up on the wrong side of the bed," Rook said. His triumphant grin slipped a notch when a second alpha burst from the flames. He took a step back toward the truck. "I think maybe we should go now."

A third alpha wendigo came through, close on the heels of the other two.

Rook vaulted into the bed and rapped his fist on the cab roof. "Go!"

Bulldog got the message. The pickup took off with a squeal of rubber on pavement, but the truck was no sports car. The alphas, with their ten foot stride, covered the intervening distance with astonishing speed.

Bishop aimed the machine gun at the feet of the leading alpha and opened up. The creature waved its monstrous arms as if swatting flies.

Knight fired the CheyTac. His bullet punching into the thing's skull with the force of a sledge hammer blow, throwing up a geyser of blood. The wendigo stumbled, but then shook its weirdly-shaped head, as if shrugging off a run-in with an open cupboard door, and resumed its pursuit, pounding forward with heavy steps that shook the earth. In a matter of just a few seconds, it was close enough that Bishop could see its jagged teeth and the great pink maw of its jaws. She aimed into it and pulled the trigger again.

The top of the long, featureless skull blew apart. The alpha reared back abruptly then collapsed like its bones had turned to jelly.

"Lucky shot," Rook grumbled, as he continued pumping rounds from both Desert Eagles into the legs of the next monstrous alpha. Bishop hoped he was wrong. She swiveled her gun to the creature Rook was engaging and raked it with a burst while Knight sent one bullet after another into the head of the third.

The gun fell silent, the ammo belt completely fired out.

She looked around for another canvas drum magazine but quickly realized that the battle would be over, one way or another, before she could reload. Beck was on her knees next to Rook, firing the SCAR into the jaws of the nearest alpha, but with less effectiveness than Bishop's fire.

The creature stumbled, the bones of one leg smashed by Rook's bullets and no longer able to bear weight. It sprawled forward on its belly, sliding with enough momentum to almost kiss the pickup's bumper. The third alpha appeared to be on a collision course with the thrashing form, but just as it was about to be tripped up, the creature flexed its massive legs and leaped over the crippled alpha. The jump supplied just enough momentum to launch the creature into a low arc, and as it sailed through the air, Bishop saw that its trajectory would inevitably bring it down right on top of the pickup.

FIFTY-EIGHT

Huitzilopochtli feasted.

There was food aplenty on the road that lay before him. Men and women, families, trapped in a line of unmoving cars that stretched to the horizon. He tore the vehicles open and plucked out the occupants inside as easily as one might crack a walnut. Some of them began to change immediately, and these he permitted to live; after all, were they not also Huitzilopochtli? The rest, he tore apart and devoured.

As he consumed more human flesh, his earthly form grew larger, and so also did his ravenous, insatiable hunger.

There was a part of him that remembered being Hector Beltran, but his transformation into Huitzilopochtli, had begun long before the metamorphosis of his flesh. It had started merely as an act of adolescent defiance, repudiating the tired old traditions of his Catholic forbears by willfully engaging in the savagely violent practices of earlier ancestors, or rather, what he imagined those rituals to be.

Killing was easy. In the world of Los Zetas, it was a routine occurrence, hardly more noteworthy than swatting a fly. But to eat the flesh of a conquered adversary? That was something that, once done, could never be undone, and so was the perfect symbol of the new life he would make for himself. Yet, until that first taste, he had not truly understood what it would mean. It had been like stepping through a door into another life. The power of the ancient god had awakened within him, and set him on a path to a destiny greater than anything the cartel could offer. The wealth his fellow *narcotraficantes* craved was ephemeral, a goal unworthy of the god he aspired to be.

Like the Aztec emperor Tlacaelel, who had elevated Huitzilopochtli from the status of minor tribal deity to the highest position in the Nahua pantheon, and in so doing, had elevated the Aztecs to a position of divine favor, Beltran had reimagined the worship of Huitzilopochtli. Instead of offering sacrifices to keep the sun burning in the heavens, Beltran and his followers would consume the flesh of their enemies in a ritual communion, which would allow their god to reside within them.

Although he continued to control one of the most powerful criminal enterprises in the Americas, he saw these illicit endeavors merely as a means to an end, and that end was the complete transformation into Huitzilopochtli. He began to crave human flesh the way some men crave sex, and when he learned of the Algonquin legend of the windigo, he began to believe that a literal transformation was indeed possible. If the legends were true, it had happened before. He would make it happen again with an offering of flesh.

He *had* made it happen.

That the windigo might be the result of a contagion—a virus or some similar microbial organism—did not occur to him, nor would it have mattered. He was no scientist, but a true believer. He did experiment, first with the wild boars, which grew fat on what remained of those he sacrificed, along with a cocktail of hormones and steroids. He used the money from his illicit activities to establish the restaurant chain where he mixed in the meat of wild pigs, fattened on human flesh, with that of domestic livestock. While the experiment did not yield the desired results, it was extremely profitable and had the patina of legitimacy, which had laid the foundation for what would follow. And that had worked exactly as planned. Now, all that remained was to leave this island behind and reach one of the nearby cities. The roads would take him where he needed to go, and there would be no shortage of people who had, unknowingly, already shared in the great communion with Huitzilopochtli.

The part of him that was still Beltran knew this. The feast now set before him was nothing compared to what awaited him on the other side of the water. His offerings had spread across the southern United States. Thousands of people, millions, had unknowingly eaten portions of tainted meat. It would take only a touch to make them like him. He would lead an army of windigos to devour the world.

But first, he would have to cross the water.

He was faintly aware of gunfire behind him. Several of the smaller windigos, those who had only recently changed and were driven purely by the primal need to eat, broke off and headed in the direction of the disturbance. He let them go. While they had answered his call, like wolves joining a pack and submitting to the will of the alpha male, he did not control them, nor did he care to. They served his purpose regardless of whether they stayed in his shadow. At first, just a few raised their heads and turned toward the shooting. Then the rest joined in the stampede, choosing to risk the guns of victims in the open, over the less certain prospect of waiting for scraps to fall from their great leader's mouth.

He was Huitzilopochtli; he did not fear humans or their guns, but their presence did concern him. They were a threat that would have to be dealt with. When he felt the fire on his back, he realized that the threat behind them might be more significant than he had first believed. The others, his trusted lieutenants who had come with him from Mexico, turned back to deal with the attackers, but the only thing that mattered to him was what lay ahead.

Something was happening. On the five-mile-long span across the water, the cars were moving. Nearly half the bridge was cleared, and in the moment that it took him to realize this, several more cars began moving, accelerating to top speed in their haste to escape the island.

He struggled to understand the significance of this development, but could grasp nothing beyond the fact that his prey was slipping away. He reached down, snatched up a car and ripped its roof off in his hands. He no longer perceived the world visually, but his other senses, hearing and smell especially, painted the world more vividly than anything he had ever seen with his eyes.

Although they were screaming in terror, the people in the car were ready for the change. He opened his jaws and made a hissing sound, not to threaten but rather to spray some of his saliva on them. That was all it took. A bit of spittle, a drop of sweat, even the touch of a misshapen hand.

In seconds, they were windigos, slavering in anticipation of their first meal as manifestations of Huitzilopochtli. But he did not set them loose right away. Instead, he turned his attention to the bridge, where still more vehicles were slipping away. Only a few still remained, their engines revving in anticipation of the long run to freedom.

Curious, he started forward, picking up speed until his enormous feet were thundering against the bridge deck. One foot caught a fleeing car and sent it tumbling down the road like a toy kicked by a mischievous child, but the others accelerated away. Soon he had matched the pace of the escaping cars, but they were no longer of interest to him. All that mattered was crossing the water and reaching the far side.

Suddenly, the bridge deck lurched beneath him with such force that he was thrown back. His powerful hands closed involuntarily, crushing the already damaged vehicle in his right fist, pulverizing the recently changed windigos within. He barely took note of their fate. An instant later, a blast of intense heat radiated across him, followed by a storm of dust and debris.

He remembered enough of his former life to recognize an explosion.

Some of the fragments tore into his skin, but he shrugged the inconsequential injury off as easily as his former self might ignore the bite of a mosquito. He was back on his feet before the last echoes of the detonation died away. A portion of the bridge had been destroyed. He could hear the tumult of its collapse, smell the residue of explosives and the acrid tang of burning metal and petrochemicals.

He started forward again, moving cautiously now lest more of the damaged span collapse underfoot. A gap of at least fifty yards now separated him from his goal. Several idling military vehicles waited there, along with at least a score of soldiers.

Something stung his skin, and he heard the crack of a rifle report. The soldiers were shooting at him. The bullets were merely an irritation, but he knew that there might be other, more dangerous weapons in their arsenal.

He drew back and hurled the crushed remains of the vehicle across the gap. The car flew like a guided missile, smashing into one of the military trucks, even as the soldiers scattered before it. There was a pause in the volley of gunfire as the men tried to regroup, but disrupting the attack had not been his primary goal.

The firing resumed, but he ducked his head, weathering the assault as he waited for his counter-attack to bear fruit.

He did not have to wait long.

It had taken only a few drops of blood, spattered from the collision of the car he had thrown at the soldiers, falling on the exposed skin of just one man who had unknowingly partaken of the offering to Huitzilopochtli. Even from a distance, he could tell that nearly all of the soldiers had eaten and would change if exposed. He heard more shots fired but none of the bullets were aimed at him, and after a few seconds, the guns fell silent.

A score of windigos now stood on the far shore, feasting on what remained of the soldiers who had been killed before they too could be changed.

He felt a mild thrill of satisfaction, but simply having some of the lesser ones on the other side was not enough. He paced at the edge of the gap, testing its stability, gauging the distance as precisely as he could, and then, he jumped.

FIFTY-NINE

Queen throttled back the boat as they slipped through the narrow mouth of Mill Tail Creek and into the dark woods of the Alligator River Wildlife Refuge. Black tupelo and cypress trees growing out of the marsh to either side obscured the point at which solid ground gave way to wetland.

King peered into the shadowy woods, trying to imagine how the area would have appeared three hundred years earlier.

Despite the fact that the eastern seaboard had been occupied for millennia, there were still a lot of places that were much the same as they had been before the arrival of European colonists: inhospitable wilderness. The low-lying peninsula between the Alligator River and the Outer Banks was just such a place, which in some ways made it the perfect place for a short-term refuge from an invading force of white settlers with guns, but what about bloodthirsty wendigos that were more animal than human?

"Do you...?" Sara didn't finish the question, but cocked her head sideways as if sniffing the air or listening, or some strange combination of both.

"What is it?"

"Something." She shook her head. "I can't quite put my finger on it, but there's something very different about this place."

"It's outdoors," Queen remarked.

King caught the hint of what might have been either annoyance or amusement in Queen's tone. Sara evidently did not, but continued to gaze out across the water. "Maybe."

King knew that Sara, with her sensory processing disorder, was probably feeling overwhelmed by the plethora of sensations, sounds and smells that existed nowhere in the climate controlled environs favored by modern humans. Yet, he also knew that Sara's unique perspective afforded her insights about the various stimuli she experienced that were not immediately apparent to others.

The GPS signaled their arrival at the target coordinates, but there was little else to distinguish the section of the creek. Queen steered into a narrow channel that was barely wide enough to accommodate the boat. A dirt road ran parallel to the channel, and there was a small dock about a hundred yards up the course. When Queen pulled alongside it, King hopped out and tied the boat off.

"I thought there was supposed to be a city here," Queen said.

Ellen shook her head. "The city was abandoned in the 1950s. It was originally just a logging camp, built after the Civil War, but during Prohibition it became a boom town because of moonshine production. There were over three thousand people living here, and nearly every one of them was a moonshiner. There was even a boat, the *Hattie Creef*, that ran 'shine across the Abelmarle Sound. I'm pretty sure that's how the Dare Stone ended up all the way north on the Chowan River."

Whether it was the opportunity to share her expertise, or simply being away from the constant threat posed by the wendigos, Ellen's mood was greatly improved. "Anyway, the town was always sort of a ramshackle affair. The houses were built with scrap wood, salvaged from the logging operation. The ground is soft and waterlogged, so nothing is very permanent. When Prohibition ended, the town's main source of revenue disappeared, and gradually, so did the population. Nothing lasts long here. That's why I don't think we're going to find anything to help us. The swamp erased any trace of the Secotan and their refuge hundreds of years ago."

Sara, who had been staring out into the woods as if entranced, turned to Ellen. "Obviously not every trace. The Dare Stone turned up."

Ellen conceded the point with a shrug.

King studied the surrounding landscape, trying to visualize—trying to remember—what it had looked like during the time of the Secotan, when the last surviving members of the Lost Colony would have occupied the spot. Why had they chosen this place? It was not the ideal habitat, yet something had drawn them here... Something about this place protected them from the wendigo.

No, that isn't quite right, he realized. The natives weren't afraid of the wendigo curse. They had used it like a bio-weapon, exposing the colonists to the contagion. They had probably served it to them in food, knowing full well that if any of the colonists did transform, they would be unable to harm the Secotan men, women and children. The natives had inoculated themselves with some kind of wendigo repellant. Something that the colonists would have known nothing about. Something they kept in their secret refuge.

But what?

Queen shook her head, muttering, "This is…"

She didn't finish the complaint, but King could fill in the blank. Hopeless? A waste of time?

He was starting to feel the same way.

Sara however appeared to have become energized. She stepped onto the dock and then headed straight out into the woods, as if drawn by an invisible homing beacon, but as soon as she left the dirt road, the tangled understory stopped her cold.

King caught up to her. "What is it?"

"This place. It's…" She turned to him. "When I got to the hospital, there was something, a smell I think, that was like biting on tin foil. It set my teeth on edge. I noticed it in the patient rooms and whenever there were wendigos around."

King was immediately wary. "Are you sensing it now?"

"No. Just the opposite. Whatever is here is like… I guess I'd compare it to putting cortisone cream on a mosquito bite. Instant relief. It's soothing. And it's stronger in there. In the woods."

King sniffed the air, which was redolent with organic smells—the sweet aroma of flowers and the sulfite smell of decay—but he found nothing to correspond to what Sara was describing.

"All right, let's do a little trailblazing." He drew his KA-BAR knife and started hacking through the tangle. The seven-inch long blade, once standard issue for the US Marine Corp, lacked the chopping heft of a machete but it was adequate to the job of sawing through vines and small branches. Queen came forward and joined the effort, but the four-inch blade of her SOG Ops combat knife was even less effective for the task.

"Careful what you touch," he cautioned. "There are a lot of poisonous plants out here. Sumac, poison ivy, stinging nettles."

"Creepy crawlies, too," Queen said. She showed the others the back of her hand, which was almost completely covered by something brown, fuzzy and eight-legged.

Ellen let out a yelp of surprise and drew back. "How can you do that?"

"It's easy. Here, give it a try?" She extended her hand toward Ellen, but the movement startled the spider, causing it to dart up Queen's arm to disappear over her shoulder.

Ellen shuddered. "What if it had bitten you?"

"I think it did," Queen said, inspecting the back of her hand where a faint red bump was starting to rise. "But it's no big deal. That was a wolf spider. Their venom isn't dangerous to humans."

"Even so, I could never let a spider crawl on me like that."

Queen shrugged and resumed hacking. "It's all in your head. I used to be terrified of spiders. Actually, I was pretty terrified of everything. I got over it."

"How?"

"Immersion therapy. When you tackle the source of your fear head on, you just kind of burn out the part of your brain that was afraid."

Sara suddenly grabbed Queen's hand. Queen stiffened defensively, and King started toward them, ready to interpose himself and save Sara from a reflexive and possibly violent reaction. Queen, however, did not move. She merely regarded Sara with an irritated frown. King was amazed at her restraint, but Sara noticed none of it. She was staring intently at the red spot on Queen's hand.

"That bite. It's—"

Whatever she was about to say was cut off by a loud, deep boom— not thunder but an explosion. "That was the bridge," King said.

"Does that mean everyone got away?" Ellen asked. "Those things are trapped?"

As if in answer to her question, Aleman's voice sounded in King's ear. "King, the soldiers at the bridge are going nuts. It sounds like some of those things made it across. Do you copy? They've reached the mainland."

King turned to Sara and spoke in an urgent tone. "Take Ellen back to the boat. Take it back out into open water, and stay away from shore."

"What are you going to do?"

"Whatever I can."

SIXTY

Rook had less than a second to make the decision and no time at all to second-guess or worry about the consequences. The choice was between getting killed when the alpha crashed down on top of them, or risking a similar fate by trying to get out of the way. Because there was marginally more uncertainty in the latter course of action, he threw his arms wide, sweeping the others into his embrace, and leaped from the bed.

They hit the pavement at almost the exact same instant that the alpha wendigo landed on the truck.

As soon as he made his jump, Rook let go of Bishop, Knight and Beck, propelling them away from him so he would not crush them on impact. He tried to tuck and roll, just as he had when making the parachute landing in the soccer field. But the leftover momentum from the truck's acceleration shredded his clothes and the skin underneath, as he rolled over and over on the ground. Being pummeled relentlessly over every square inch of his body, drove him to the edge of consciousness.

He was only peripherally aware of the alpha landing in the bed, its weight driving the undercarriage of the pickup down into the pavement with a shriek of friction and a flurry of sparks. The sudden deceleration pitched the creature headlong, but it caught hold of the cab, and then both the creature and the vehicle were turning in crazy circles.

Get up! Move!

The world spun around him, but through the fog of pain and vertigo, he realized that he was no longer moving. He struggled to rise, managed to push himself up to hands and knees and saw at least a dozen wendigos racing up the road, heading toward him. Closer still, the alpha he had crippled was advancing, crawling as fast as a person could walk.

Bishop lay nearby, fighting the after-effects of the desperate leap from the truck. Further away, Knight and Beck lay unmoving, sprawled out like offerings to the devouring monsters.

"Move!" The word came out in a gasp, and suddenly he could breathe again. He lurched upright and spied one of his Desert Eagles close by. He staggered toward it and bent to retrieve it. Only then did he realize that its twin was still clenched in his right hand.

The solid hunk of metal in his hand filled him with a sense of purpose. Muscle memory took over. He took a steady firing position, and with both arms extended, took aim and began shooting.

The Desert Eagles thundered in his hands, first the right, then the left, like a well-oiled engine of destruction. The .50 caliber rounds tore into the charging wendigos, knocking them down like targets in a penny arcade shooting gallery, scattering shattered torsos and headless carcasses. He got off six shots in total before the pistol in his right hand went silent. Two more and then the left was out as well. Eight shots, eight dead wendigos.

But they were still coming. A trio who had survived Rook's counterattack overtook the injured alpha and moved relentlessly toward Knight and Beck. Frantic, Rook buttoned out the spent magazines and was reaching for replacements, when he saw a blur of motion out of the corner of his eye.

Before he could react, the blur resolved into the compact form of Bishop, back on her feet and running to intercept the wendigos. She threw herself at them like a wrecking ball, bowling them over with a full body slam. Even as she hit them, she succeeded in hooking one creature's neck in the crook of her elbow, and pulled herself in tight around its deformed head. Her weight bore it to the ground, the impact crushing its spindly bones.

Rook got one of the pistols loaded and immediately resumed firing, taking out several more wendigos that were rushing up to reinforce the attack, while Bishop, moving with an unrestrained fury to match the primal hunger of her foes, tore the remaining monsters apart before they could reach Knight and Beck.

For a moment, Rook almost believed they would survive the onslaught. Then he felt a tremor rippling the ground underfoot and heard a savage roar from behind. He whirled around just as the alpha—the one that had demolished the truck—reached out and caught him.

SIXTY-ONE

Queen pulled her hand from Sara's grasp and started after King. She had no clue how the two of them were supposed to stop the wendigo invasion, but who else was there? The rest of the team had gone silent. The barricade was down, the National Guard soldiers manning it evidently overrun. If there was a cure to be found in the refuge, it would come too late to make a difference.

She stopped.

The cure, or wendigo repellent, or whatever it was Sara was trying to find, might be humanity's only hope if she and King failed. She ripped off her headset and took the radio unit from her belt, then backtracked to where Sara and Ellen stood, paralyzed by inertia. Queen pressed the radio into Sara's hands. "Take this. You can use it to talk to Lewis. Organize whatever has to happen next."

Sara nodded dumbly. Queen led the two women back along the trail they had just blazed, and then pointed to the boat. "Get going."

She didn't dare wait for an acknowledgement. King was already gone, a good half-minute ahead of her, pounding down the dirt road that led, Queen presumed, to the highway and an army of wendigos.

As she sprinted to catch him, the spider bite on her hand began itching furiously. She wasn't worried about the venom. Unlike black widows and other dangerous arachnids, the poison of the wolf spider was neither systemic nor neurotoxic, and caused only mild local skin irritation. Of course, the prescribed treatment for a bite did not include running a thousand yard dash in full combat gear, and the harder she ran, the more intense the sensation became.

She ignored it, locking the discomfort away in the same part of her brain where she had once buried her fear of all crawling creatures. She had overcome her phobias the same way she had overcome all her weaknesses, by turning them upside down, transforming fear into conviction, pain into resolve.

Over the pounding of her own feet and the rush of blood in her ears, she could just make out the pop of distant gunfire. The reports were not as loud as the earlier explosion, the shooting probably several miles away, but there was no question that the battle was being fought on the mainland. It was their worst-case scenario. The wendigos had not been contained. They would have to be hunted down and eradicated, and if even a single one survived...

She spied King, a hundred feet away, and she managed to pour on a little more speed, quickly catching up to him. The dense forest to either side was cut through with drainage channels and a few side roads, but there was little sign of immediate human activity until they rounded a gentle bend in the road and caught sight of the highway.

The pavement was a clogged artery of cars, all fleeing the destruction of Roanoke Island. Although it was a two-lane road, the drivers had managed to create two additional lanes of traffic, so that the cars were running four abreast, although the cars in the outer lanes were rolling with their wheels on the grassy shoulder. The congestion arose from the fact that the road eventually led to a narrow bridge across the Alligator River.

King took one look at the gridlock and then angled to the east, running along the roadside, against the flow of the exodus. In just a few minutes, they came to the tail end of the traffic jam, but King kept going.

"They'll have to...come through here," he said. It took a couple breaths to get it out, but he did not break stride. "There's no other way out of here."

"What about through the forest?"

He glanced at her. "Would you go that way?"

She glanced at the densely packed woods and the tangled understory. She shook her head.

"We better hope they don't," King continued. "If they go in there, we'll never be able to run them down."

"You're optimistic," she muttered. "I'll give you that."

"What?"

"I hope you have some kind of plan."

"These things can die," he said, shouldering his SCAR. "So, we kill them before they kill us."

His confidence did not allay her concerns. It was not fear for her own safety. The possibility of getting killed was an occupational hazard with which she had long ago come to terms. She was worried about what would happen *after*. After they failed, after they ran out of bullets, after the wendigos tore them apart and there was no one left to stop the infection from spreading. Nevertheless, she brought her own weapon to the high ready and charged ahead, prepared to meet the advance head on.

Smoke and the sulfur smell of burnt gunpowder stung her nose. Directly ahead, the road was lined with dark green military vehicles—Humvees and five-ton trucks—but there was no sign of the soldiers who had driven them.

King motioned for her to get down, and together they low-crawled forward until they could make out movement near some of the trucks: wendigos feasting on the bodies of the fallen. Queen saw tattered remnants of clothing still clinging to some of the creatures, and recognized the familiar green and white universal camouflage pattern of the Army Combat Uniform—standard issue for the National Guard.

These wendigos were fellow soldiers...or had been just a few minutes ago.

Something big was moving behind the trucks. It was bigger than the largest vehicle but it was made of flesh and blood, and as it slouched down the road, she saw that beneath a coating of blood and grime, its skin was mottled with an elaborate faded pattern that looked like green and red scales.

"That's Beltran," King whispered.

Queen studied the approaching alpha. There was not a trace of recognizable humanity in the creature's deformed body.

"That tattoo," King went on. "He thinks he's Huitzilopochtli."

Queen aimed her rifle at the creature's head but did not fire. She had seen how ineffective bullets were at stopping the alphas. It had taken their combined firepower to kill the one at the Festival Park, and this one looked even bigger.

Beside her, King also took aim. "Wait for it," he advised. "Let him get close, then concentrate your fire center mass."

The advice was sound. The alphas' skulls were like armor plate, but the hunched over posture made a clean shot to the torso impossible. To kill it, they would have to practically be standing within reach of its grasping arms.

Despite the fact that the Beltran-thing was moving at, what for *it* was probably just a walking pace, it closed the distance in seconds. Queen took a breath and held it, waiting for the moment when its oblong head would turn toward them, but if it noticed them, it paid no heed. Instead, it continued ambling down the road.

"Damn it," Queen whispered when it was past. She kept her weapon trained on its tattooed back, but she knew the chances of a killing shot were slim. Even if she did score a lucky hit, the noise would bring the rest of the wendigos running. *We're fucked no matter what we do.* The realization brought clarity. "Desperado."

King glanced at her sidelong. "Maximum damage before we go down?"

"You have a better idea?"

"Not really." He keyed his transmitter. "Blue, this is King. We're going to try to take out this alpha. It's Beltran."

Queen couldn't hear the other side of the conversation, but it wasn't difficult to fill in the gaps. "He's the biggest threat, but even if we succeed, there's no way we'll be able to kill them all. You'll need to send in the cavalry. Air power. Troops in MOPP gear. But you have to contain this." A pause. "Thanks. King, out."

In the brief time it took for him to send the message, Beltran had nearly vanished in the distance. Even at a full sprint, they would be hard pressed to catch him, but King evidently had no intention of giving chase on foot. "We need to get one of those trucks. There's a fifty on that five-ton."

Queen picked out the truck he was referring to—a large six-wheeled transport with an M2 machine gun mounted on the roof turret. If anything could take down the alpha in short order, it was that combination of heavy machinery and firepower, but the vicinity was crawling with wendigos. "There's no way we'll make it through that. I'll draw them off. You get the truck and go after Beltran."

"Absolutely not. It will take both of us. One to drive, one to shoot."

"You'll have to figure it out," Queen replied. "A diversion is the best chance you've got of making it to the truck alive. Get ready."

She started to rise but he grabbed her shoulder. "Then I'll do it. You go after Beltran. That's an order."

She returned a grim smile. "Rules of chess. The king has to survive."

Before he could say another word, she wrenched out of his grasp and bolted to her feet, running out into the center of the highway. She took aim at a group of wendigos and fired off a pair of shots. One of the creatures went down. The rest looked up in hungry unison. Pale faces began to appear from the gaps between the parked vehicles, dozens of them.

Damn, there's a lot of them, Queen thought. The soldiers of the North Carolina National Guard had, it seemed, developed a fatal fondness for Mr. Pig.

"That's right, bitches," she shouted. "Fresh meat, right here."

She fired into their midst again, then spun on her heel and took off running. That they would eventually catch her was a foregone conclusion. The only thing that mattered was drawing them away long enough for King to reach the trucks. She was a fast runner, but with their abnormally long legs, the wendigos were faster. She counted to ten, then twisted around and triggered a burst in hopes of buying a few more seconds.

She fired before her brain received any feedback from her eyes, but the rounds found a target. It was impossible to miss. A wendigo, maybe ten yards behind her, went down, tripping up those behind him, but it hardly mattered. The entire road was a wall of spindly limbs and misshapen bodies, poised to sweep over her.

She veered off the road and headed for the trees, wondering if she had bought King enough time to reach the truck. Instead of trying to blaze a path through the underbrush, she whirled around and started firing. The trees at her back kept the creatures from surrounding her, and the lead spewing from the muzzle of her SCAR kept the front-runners at bay.

She felled several with point blank shots, twisting back and forth, practically jamming the muzzle into the gaping mouths of wendigos as they tried to strike at her like vipers. When the last round was fired, she swung the smoking weapon back and forth like a scythe, batting away reaching hands and jabbing at the demonic faces that seemed to be everywhere. Then the rifle was ripped from her grasp.

She whipped her knife from its sheath, driving it into another of the creatures, but as it fell, it took the blade with it. Surrounded, Queen raised her fists, the only weapon she had left.

As the wendigos closed in, she heard the distant throaty roar of a diesel engine coming to life, and she knew that she had accomplished at least that much.

SIXTY-TWO

Knight came to with a start, looking around frantically. Since losing his eye, he often woke up this way, disoriented at the abrupt transition from dreams, where he had unrestricted vision, to a reality where half the world was hidden from view. This time, he had not been dreaming, but what he found upon waking was a nightmare.

Beck lay nearby, bruised and bloody, groaning but not quite conscious. One hand was still gripping the stock of her borrowed SCAR, but the other seemed to have developed an extra joint. Her left arm was bent at an unnatural angle between the wrist and elbow, and a jagged splinter of bone protruded from her forearm.

A little further away, Bishop was fighting a trio of wendigos with the same berserker fury that had saved Beck's life earlier, but a crippled alpha was crawling to join the fight.

He realized, belatedly, that the booming report of Rook's Desert Eagles had awakened him, but where was Rook now?

He twisted around just in time to see a second alpha reach down and grab hold of Rook with both arms. With astonishing speed, the creature thrust its captured prey into its gaping maw, but just as it was about to chomp Rook in half, there were several more loud booms, and the back of the alpha's head exploded in red mist. The monster went down with a crash that reverberated through the ground, and Knight lost sight of Rook.

The crash jolted Knight into action. He grabbed the SCAR out of Beck's hands, eliciting an anguished cry from her as he jostled her broken arm. He took aim at the alpha closing on Bishop. The rifle bucked against his shoulder, and a red flower bloomed on the alpha's featureless head, but the shot accomplished little else. Knight scrambled to his feet...and nearly collapsed again as a wave of pain shot through his left ankle.

Broken? He had no idea, but it hurt like hell. He fought back the wave of blackness that threatened to overtake him, and fired again, putting a shot directly into the nostril slit above the alpha's gaping jaws.

The creature twitched, and a stream of dark blood began gushing down into the serrated grimace of its teeth, but it kept coming.

Bishop, spinning like an Olympic gymnast, locked her legs around the neck of a wendigo and then whipped her body, along with its head, around one hundred and eighty degrees. As it dropped lifeless to the ground, joining several others that had already been dispatched, she managed to land on her feet, and scrambled away just as the alpha heaved into the space she had occupied an instant earlier. It lurched forward again, now just ten yards from Knight and Beck.

The enormous creature filled Knight's lone eye. He pulled the trigger again, but nothing happened, and only now did he see that the magazine was bent nearly as badly as Beck's arm. It was a wonder the weapon had fired at all.

The enormous maw opened wide, blasting Knight with a vaporous exhalation that stank of rotten meat. Beside him, Bishop was struggling to pull Beck out of the way, but there simply was not enough time. The jaws came forward.

Knight thrust the useless gun forward, jamming it between the jaws as they started to close. The hardened steel crunched against the jagged teeth but did not give. In frustration, the monster began whipping its head back and forth. Knight caught a glancing blow and went sprawling. Another wave of pain shot through his ankle, but he shook it off and started crawling toward Beck and Bishop, desperate to reach them before the alpha.

A noise as loud as a cannon boomed from somewhere on his blindside. The noise repeated, again and again, and with each report, there was an eruption of gore from the monster's head.

Knight turned to see Rook, covered in the blood of the other alpha head he had killed, striding forward with the relentless determination of a Hollywood killer-cyborg, pumping rounds from his Desert Eagles into the creature's head. The thing shuddered and collapsed, but Rook did not stop firing until both guns were empty.

Knight sagged in relief, but saw that the respite would be short-lived. More wendigos were appearing from every direction.

"Gotta go," Rook said, hastening to Knight's side. "You okay?"

"Do I have a choice?" He clasped Rook's hand and stood again, purposefully putting his weight on his injured foot. The pain was like a baptism in fire, but pain was something he could deal with. "A sprain," he said through clenched teeth. "Not broken. I can walk."

Rook nodded. "Good. Can you run?"

"Do I have a choice?" he said again.

Bishop helped Beck to her feet. Together the four of them hobbled in the direction of the pickup, which had come to a stop across the lanes in the middle of the highway, as if trying to block the road. The cab had been partially peeled back and a front fender was missing, but as they reached it, Knight saw that Bulldog was still behind the wheel, or more precisely, slumped over it, with blood streaming from a gash in his forehead.

Rook ripped the door open and shoved the unconscious man aside. He settled into the driver's seat and tried the key. The engine made a mechanical chugging sound, but refused to turn over. Rook swore and tried again to no better effect.

Knight turned, looking for another vehicle, but the rampaging alphas had left nothing intact. All he saw were more wendigos, rushing down the road, emerging from the woods, streaming toward them from every direction.

Rook stomped the gas pedal to the floor, held it down, and tried the key again. The engine caught with a roar and belched a cloud of noxious exhaust. "Back seat!"

Bishop and Knight hoisted Beck into the bed and then threw themselves in as well, even as the first of the wendigos caught up to the truck. Rook hit the accelerator. The truck fish-tailed, leaving rubber on the pavement, then shot away. Knight spied grasping fingers hooked over the edge of the tailgate. Two creatures had made a desperate grab for the truck as it pulled away. They were now being dragged along behind it. He kicked his heel against the fingers, and the wendigos fell away, but more of them were trying to seize hold of the truck as it passed. There were repeated thumps from the front, as wendigos tried to stop the truck with their bodies. A few of them rolled up and over the windshield, dropping lifeless into the bed. Even though the impact shattered their spindly bones, the dying wendigos put up a fight as Bishop and Knight heaved them into the path of the swelling horde chasing behind the pickup. There were too many to count—at least a hundred, and more joined the hunt with each passing second.

Knight exchanged a glance with Bishop, and knew she was thinking the same thing. They were trapped on the island, with nowhere to go and no way to win against such overwhelming odds. He shook his head. "Sorry. I got nothing."

Bishop shrugged in resignation. "Was good fight."

He laughed. "Yes, it was."

He sank down next to Beck and put his arm around her, holding her close. Bishop settled down beside them, her expression stoic.

There were better ways to die, but at least he wouldn't be alone at the end.

"Where do you think he's going?" Bishop said after a moment.

"What?"

"Rook. He seems to have a plan."

Knight tore his gaze away from the chasing wendigos and looked around at the familiar landscape passing by. Rook was driving just fast enough to stay ahead of the horde, making no effort to outrun them. He abruptly turned off the highway and onto the road back to the site of their first battle with an alpha: the Lost Colony Festival Park. The truck slowed a little as Rook steered around wendigo corpses on the bridge, and then they were rolling past the corpse of the slain alpha, past the shingled buildings of the visitor center.

Knight leaned close to the half-demolished cab. "Rook, Bish thinks you have a plan."

"Fucking-A right, I do," Rook chortled. "Hang on, back there. The Pied Piper is about to take care of the rat problem."

The parking lot flashed by, then a large empty amphitheater, and then suddenly it was as if they were transported back in time. Crude log buildings, a blacksmith's forge, a well, empty pillories—they were driving down the middle of a primitive colonial village, a recreation of the Roanoke colony. Behind them, wendigos were crowding into the open streets, filling the village square.

With a lurch, the truck smashed through a wooden palisade, crossed a narrow beach, and then splashed into the placid waters of Shallowbag Bay. The combined impacts stole most of the truck's momentum, throwing the passengers forward. The engine revved as Rook tried to eke out a few more feet of progress, but the wheels just spun impotently in the soft mud, and then the engine died with an ominous clank.

"Everybody out! Swim for it!"

Knight was already taking steps to heed the advice. He scooped Beck up in his arms and heaved her over the side of the pickup, into the four-foot deep water. He dove in after her, and gripping her hand, began to swim for open water.

Behind them, a seething mass of wendigos poured through the breach in the palisade and ran headlong into the bay in pursuit of their fleeing prey. At first the water barely reached their elongated knees, but as they pushed further out, the silty mud slowed them down, even as the bottom dropped away.

Knight saw Bishop in the water. Rook as well, pulling the still dazed Bulldog along behind him. He swam furiously, ignoring the throb of pain in his foot as he kicked away from shore, tugging Beck along with him, but instead of the desperation that had motivated him during the struggle to reach the truck, he was now borne along by hope.

The wendigos did not even attempt to swim. Their lean bodies weren't buoyant enough to stay afloat, but their primal hunger was so great that they were incapable of recognizing the need to turn back. Instead, they kept going, striding forward as fast as the water would allow, until the water closed over their heads.

And they drowned.

All of them.

SIXTY-THREE

King caught just a glimpse of Queen before the wendigos closed in around her. He did not look again. The only way to give her sacrifice meaning was to stop Beltran. That was what he had to stay focused on. He turned his eyes back to the road and kept the five-ton rolling down the center line.

A mile and a half down the highway, he caught sight of the lumbering alpha, and Beltran evidently heard him coming. The monster turned around, facing him, and then started to run toward the truck.

King had about two seconds to weigh his options. The .50 caliber gun, a weapon designed to engage armored vehicles, would make quick work of the monster, but was there time to stop the truck and climb up into the gun turret? Probably not.

The machine gun wasn't his only weapon, though.

"If it's a game of chicken you want," King muttered, "I'll play."

He pushed the accelerator pedal to the floor and aimed the front of the truck squarely at the advancing alpha. Beltran did not relent. Neither did King.

The distance between them shrank so quickly that King did not have time to second guess his decision. The alpha grew large, and then suddenly King was thrown forward into the steering wheel when the truck slammed into the enormous creature.

The truck slewed sideways as the wheels turned sharply. Then it spun around, out of control, and veered off the road. King was thrown out of his seat to slam against the passenger side door, and then he bounced around the interior like a sock in a tumble dryer.

It took a moment for him to recognize that the truck had come to a stop, and another to realize that it might take more than getting hit by a truck to stop Beltran. He scrambled to right himself, ignoring the sharp pain in his ribs, but when he sat up, everything was crooked and disorienting. The truck had nosed slightly down at an angle, just enough to throw off his equilibrium. Keeping one steadying hand on the dash, he rose up to grasp the lip of the gun turret, and then gingerly hauled himself erect.

The machine gun was pointing ahead and slightly down into the trees. A glance back showed the highway, empty in both directions. Where was Beltran?

Something jostled the truck, alerting King to danger. He braced himself against the turret, gripping the gun so that he could swivel in the direction of a target. He spun around, searching for the alpha. There was a flicker of movement in his peripheral vision, and then Beltran sprang up in front of the truck like an overwound jack-in-the-box. There was no time to fire the gun. King dropped out of the turret a millisecond before one of the alpha's powerful arms raked across it, ripping the gun from its mount, sending it crashing noisily into the trees at the roadside.

The monster's bulk blocked out everything else, darkening the interior of the cab, but King could see, amidst the intaglio of tattooed red and green feathers, the damage that had been wrought by the head-on collision. King surmised that, instead of being knocked clear by the impact, the alpha had been dragged underneath the truck. Beltran's torso was a mass of mangled flesh and protruding bones. Blood poured out of his body, splattering the truck's hood and windshield. The internal injuries had to be mortal, even for a creature as massive as Beltran had become, but death wouldn't come fast enough to save King.

With another swipe of its arm, the creature removed the top of the cab, peeling back the roof like the lid of a sardine can. As its enormous head came down, jaws open wide, King rolled off the seat, curling into the footwell. Blood and saliva showered down on him. He felt the thing's hot breath on his face. The entire truck shuddered as the massive jaws clamped shut right above him, again and again.

Beltran reared up and then reached in with his monstrously huge fingers. King felt them brush against him, and he wormed deeper under the steering wheel, just out of reach. He did not fool himself into thinking he was safe, however. Hiding from the monster was not the same as fighting it. Queen hadn't given her life so that he could huddle in a corner and hope everything would turn out okay.

Beltran curled the fingers of both hands under the dash, and then with a mighty heave, split the cab apart like the halves of an oyster shell. It was the moment King had been waiting for. He launched himself out of the ruined interior and straight at Beltran's exposed torso, plunging one hand into exposed viscera, the other grasping a protruding rib, as big as a rafter.

Beltran threw back his head and let out a deafening howl. King felt hands closing around him, and he gripped even tighter. When Beltran tried to rip him loose, he gave the broken rib a savage twist that elicited another howl of agony. Then he jammed his other hand deeper into the open wound in the alpha's abdomen. He could feel Beltran's heart throbbing against muscles and membranes, the pulsing beat like the rumble of some industrial machine on an assembly line.

He let go of the rib, yanked his hand out and drew his KA-BAR. For a fleeting instant, he envisioned himself cutting out the monster's heart. What better way to balance the cosmic scales? But the practicality of it defeated him. If the alpha's organs were proportionate to its body, Beltran's heart was probably now the size of an engine block, the veins and arteries that connected it to the rest of his body, as thick as tree branches.

No, he decided. *No symbolic actions today. Just get the job done.*

He thrust the seven-inch-long blade point first into the wound, and drove it home.

SIXTY-FOUR

The wendigos towered above Queen, closing in on her like a wall of putrefying flesh. She lashed out with her fists, beating at them. At first she tried to direct her blows, but they shied away, and she was only able to score glancing, ineffectual hits. As her fists met only air, her punches became more desperate. She was not fighting because she thought she might win, but only because she refused to simply give up and accept the inevitable. She would die on her feet, not on her knees.

But the wendigos did not attack. The pack continued to writhe and churn. Those at the rear fought to move forward, clawing and jostling, driven by insatiable hunger, while those at the front shrank back in what seemed almost like a state of panic.

It was as if an invisible force field had been erected around Queen.

She stopped flailing and stood still, wondering at the cause of this strange phenomenon. As a group, the wendigos weren't fleeing, but individuals within the horde were shying away from her, only to try again when their nerve returned.

She reached out for one of them but it drew back, as if scalded.

Emboldened, she took a step forward, and the whole mass of them shifted back.

"What the hell?"

Wendigo repellent. That was what they had been looking for out here, and somehow she had found it. *But what is it? What's keeping them back?*

Even as she asked herself the question, she knew.

"The spider bite."

Sara would probably be able to explain it better, but something about the proteins in the venom the wolf spider had injected into her hand was driving the wendigos back like mosquitoes fleeing citronella smoke.

She took another step. The wendigos shifted, filling in behind her as she moved away from the woods, but none got closer than eighteen inches.

"That's how they did it," she said aloud. "Fat lot of good knowing it does me now. Except..."

She feinted forward as if charging the wendigos and watched them pull away in a panic.

"I wonder what would happen if a spider bit you?"

She turned and headed back in the direction of the woods. The creatures squirmed at her approach and gave way. When the way was clear, she pushed into the tangled understory, wrestling through the foliage with her bare hands.

The wendigos followed, perhaps hoping that the strange effect would dissipate, freeing them to rip her apart and devour her flesh.

The possibility imparted a sense of urgency to her task.

It wasn't long at all before she spotted an inch-long brown spider sitting motionless on a tree branch. Wolf spiders were hunters, sometimes jumping on or chasing down their prey, rather than waiting for an unlucky insect to blunder into a web. Like most animals, they preferred to avoid humans, rather than waste their precious venom on prey that was too large to consume. They would bite if aggravated, though, so Queen was exceedingly careful as she goaded the spider onto her open palm.

Then, she flung it at the nearest wendigo.

The creature seemed oblivious to the little arachnid scrambling for a purchase on its papery skin. Then, without any sort of precursory symptoms, the wendigo went rigid and pitched forward like a felled tree.

Queen scanned the area for the spider, but it scurried away and disappeared into the underbrush before she could grab it.

"This is going to take a while," she muttered. She knew better than to think that she could collect enough spiders to take out the pack that dogged her every step. What she really needed to do was find Sara and tell her about this.

Unless she already knows. She recalled how Sara had grabbed her hand, just before she and King had been called away. Somehow, maybe because of her weird sensory disorder, she had figured it out. With any luck, Sara was already whistling up a bunch of synthetic spider venom—surely there was such a thing—to inoculate everyone, or even better, to spray the whole area with it and permanently wipe out the wendigos.

She took a moment to orient herself, and then headed south, toward the creek, where she hoped Sara was still waiting.

SIXTY-FIVE

Death was never pretty, but Hector Beltran's death was exceptional in its ugliness.

When King's blade pierced the membrane around the alpha wendigo's heart, a gush of hot blood and fluid nearly drowned him. The smell, a mixture of hot copper and putrefying flesh made him gag, but King did not relent. He pushed the knife a few inches further, and rammed it into the throbbing muscle.

Beltran's heart swelled suddenly, not in reaction to the attack, but merely the normal diastolic phase of the organ, filling up with blood. When the systolic phase began a moment later, it was as if a dam had burst. The muscle contracted, and Beltran's heart, overstressed by the battle and damaged by King's blade, ripped itself apart.

The eruption blasted King away, knocking him back onto the hood of the truck. He scrambled for purchase, preparing himself for the next attack, but it never came. The monstrous alpha crumpled to the ground, and aside from a few twitches, it did not move.

King felt no sense of victory. Too much had been lost, and while this battle was won, the war was not over. After a minute to catch his breath and wipe some of the gore away, he keyed his radio. "Blue, it's King. Beltran is dead."

An ear-splitting whoop made him wince. As he fumbled for the volume control, he heard a voice, not Aleman, but Rook. "Big fucking deal. We took out three alphas and then played Pied Piper with all the rest of 'em."

King's elation at hearing Rook's voice was quickly buried under an avalanche of grief. How was he going to break the news about Queen?

Another voice came over the net. "Jack? It's me."

Sara! At least she was safe.

"Great news here. Queen helped me figure it out. We know how to stop the wendigos. It's spider venom. That's how the natives were able to stay safe while using the wendigo contagion like a bio-weapon. And it's why they came here after they turned it loose."

A new voice jumped in, fainter, the person obviously not talking directly into the microphone. "Sara, let me tell him."

King was stunned. The voice belonged to Queen. There was a shuffling noise and then she spoke again, louder this time. "Remember that spider bite I got? It's like industrial-strength wendigo repellant. They wouldn't even touch me. And one drop of the stuff is enough to kill them."

"It's got to be some kind of allergic reaction," Sara chimed in from the background. "I need to get back to the lab so I can watch it happen under the microscope. Maybe we can come up with a vaccine to keep people from getting infected in the first place."

Sara kept talking, but King barely heard her. "Queen?" He croaked. "You're alive."

"Of course I am. You didn't think I had any intention of letting those ugly bastards eat me, did you?"

She said it with such confidence that King almost believed her.

It took him fifteen minutes to hobble back down the road to where the speedboat was docked and Queen and Sara were waiting, along with a very relieved Ellen Dare. With the crisis finally past, all his hurts, starting with the gash in his ankle, decided to pay him back with interest. Before boarding, he immersed himself in the creek, washing away most of the blood, and with it, all of the despair he had felt earlier.

As impossible as it seemed, they had survived.

Aleman's next call, as the boat sped back across the bay to rendezvous with the rest of the team, reminded him that other battles had been fought and other sacrifices made. "King, when you get a chance, remind me to tell you about a call I got from an old friend of ours. You might remember him. His company helped us out a few times."

King did not miss the conspicuous coded-language, nor its subtext. The 'company' obviously referred to the CIA, and the old friend had to be Domenick Boucher. Boucher and Duncan had escaped Endgame together, but King knew nothing more about what had happened beyond the fact that Duncan had personally anointed Lew Aleman to take over the role of Deep Blue. The fact that Aleman was trying to hide that information suggested that someone—probably Admiral Ward—might be monitoring their secure communications. King doubted very much that they had any secrets from Ward, but he knew that Aleman surely had his reasons.

What was Aleman trying to tell him?

A call...

"Sara, do you have your phone?"

She looked at him in surprise, but then dug in her pockets until she found her mobile. She thumbed it on and glanced at the screen. "Network is back up. Battery's almost dead though."

He took it from her and quickly composed a brief text message—two words: 'What's up?'—and sent it to the same number he had used to make contact in Mexico.

A few seconds later, the reply came back. "Call me." Followed by a ten-digit string—not a phone number but a math problem. He reversed each digit in his head, four become six, three was seven, and vice versa, a simple expedient code. Then he dialed the new number.

Domenick Boucher answered. "I've some bad news, King. Tom was arrested by the FBI. He surrendered to them, as part of a plea bargain, which included protecting you guys."

"I know."

Boucher's tone suggested that King did not know as much as he thought he did. "They flew him to Washington, and my contacts tell me that Marrs plans to drag him in front of the Senate Judiciary Committee. Tonight. He's called for an emergency meeting."

The revelation made no sense, and King told Boucher as much. "The Senate doesn't have jurisdiction over a former president."

"I don't think Marrs cares about what is or is not within his jurisdiction. He'll do whatever it takes to get ahead. But I think he's really after something else."

"The President."

"If he can make the case that President Chambers is ultimately responsible for what we've been doing, the senate will have no choice but to call for impeachment proceedings."

King recalled what Ward had said during the flight. *'He's going down, and he's going to take some very powerful people with him.'*

Anger gripped King's throat. "Marrs is a traitor. He's the one that should be on trial."

"You don't need to tell me that." A pause. "We have to get Tom out of there."

King's answer came without hesitation. "Absolutely."

"If you can make it to D.C., I'll take care of the rest. I should warn you, though. If we do this, there's no going back. We'll have to disappear completely."

King raised his eyes, meeting Queen's gaze. A short distance away, he saw five figures standing on the shore. Beck was there, along with a shorter man that he didn't recognize, but King's stare lingered on his teammates: Knight, Bishop and Rook. He would offer them the choice, of course, but he had no doubt about what their answer would be.

"Set it up. I'll call when we get there."

As the speedboat neared the shore, King felt a thump against the hull. He looked over the side, expecting to see a piece of driftwood, but instead saw a veritable field of pale round objects just below the surface. Some of them were looking up, faces frozen in death.

Drowned wendigos.

He waited until they were a little closer to shore to jump out. Rook greeted him with a fierce bear hug that made him wince. Bishop squeezed even harder, while Knight settled for a handshake and Beck, a smile and a nod.

There was just one introduction to make, and Rook took care of it. "King, this is Bulldog. Bulldog, King."

There was a sudden glimmer of fear in the small man's eyes, recognition, of the name or perhaps his face, but he hid it quickly behind a smile and offered his hand.

"Bulldog helped us out big time," Rook went on in a friendly tone. "Hell, it's almost enough to make up for the fact that he's the piece of shit who sold us out to Beltran and blew up *Crescent.*"

Bulldog's smile evaporated, and he tried to bolt away, but Rook's hands had clamped down on his shoulders, pinning him to the spot.

"You didn't really think I bought that bullshit story about you being DEA?" Rook said.

Bulldog's eyes danced, and King expected to hear him offer protestations of ignorance, but after a moment, he sagged in resignation and shook his head. "I thought you looked familiar," he said to Rook. "I saw you at that party in New Hampshire. Can't believe I forgot that. I usually don't screw up on the little details. I guess running from flesh-eating monsters can mess with your head."

"You get used to it after a while."

King took a step closer to the small man. He had harbored similar suspicions about Bulldog from the moment Rook reported the encounter. "Are you working with Marrs?"

Bulldog blinked at him, but said nothing.

King took another step forward, bending his head down until their faces were almost touching. He raised his wrist, displaying his stainless steel watch, but did not break eye contact. "In exactly sixty seconds, my friend Rook here is going to put a bullet in the back of your head. After having spent some time with the El Sol cartel, I'm sure you'll recognize just how merciful that method of execution is. It's better than you deserve. I know that you supplied Beltran with the TOW missile that destroyed our plane in Mexico, and that by itself is reason enough for me to end your life. I wouldn't be at all surprised to learn that you played a part in the kidnapping, murder and ritual *consumption* of a bus full of American tourists, but maybe that was all Beltran's doing." King gave a little shrug then let his eyes flicker to his watch. "Oh, look. Only thirty seconds left."

"What do you want?"

"Ah, yes. The deal. Well, it's simple really. You're the little fish. Marrs is the big fish." He checked his watch again. "Ten seconds. Rook."

Rook made a very dramatic show of drawing one of his Desert Eagles, placing it against the back of the man's head.

"Save it," Bulldog said, with a snort. "I used to work CID. Even if I believed that you meant to—"

There was a loud metallic click as Rook pulled the trigger. "Shit," Rook's voice was filled with what sounded like sincere embarrassment. "I forgot to reload."

Bulldog was speechless for a moment, but as Rook ejected an empty magazine and slotted a fresh one into the enormous pistol, he swallowed and resumed speaking. "Fine. I'm tempted to say 'do it.' But the truth is, I'm not willing to die for that piece of filth."

Rook made a clucking sound. "Said Mr. Pot, of Mr. Kettle."

"It was a job. I had no idea Marrs was working with..." Bulldog shuddered. "Someone capable of doing..."

"Is that supposed to mean something?" King asked.

Bulldog met his stare. "You want the big fish? You want Marrs? All you had to do was ask."

SIXTY-SIX
Washington, D.C.

It was just after six p.m. when a line of black SUVs pulled up in front of the Dirksen Senate Office building, a stone's throw from the Capitol. A scattering of journalists, who were perpetually camped out on the steps of the building hoping for a scoop, shifted toward the convoy, sensing that something newsworthy was about to happen. The vehicles disgorged a veritable army of men in blue windbreakers who swarmed around the central SUV, hiding its passengers from the cameras and the eyes of the journalists. The cluster then moved quickly to the doors and inside, leaving the reporters to speculate about the nature of this after-hours activity. Some murmured that it must surely have something to do with the strange news coming out of North Carolina.

The man at the center of the moving cluster knew almost nothing about what had transpired in the Outer Banks. Duncan had been kept isolated and incommunicado since his arrival in the nation's capital. Aside from some empty gloating on the part of Senator Marrs, who had departed the group shortly after the helicopter touched down, no one had spoken to him at all. Whether the news out of North Carolina was good or bad, there was nothing more he could do about it. The die had been cast.

The agents ushered him to the second floor, and into a familiar wood-paneled gallery. There was no audience present, but twelve of the seventeen chairs on the elevated semi-circular podium at the back of the room were occupied. Duncan recognized all of the men and women seated there. Once, he had been on a first-name basis with several of them. He had played golf with them. Spent long hours in late-night strategy sessions at their side. Stumped for them on the campaign trail. Now, they all regarded him with frank suspicion, contempt even, as if he were a leper in their hallowed presence. Lance Marrs sat in the outermost seat on the left hand side, barely able to contain himself.

The agents brought him forward to a table positioned in front of the bench. Deputy Attorney General Taits moved to his side and motioned for him to sit. Duncan sat. Nothing more was expected of him. The chairman called the meeting to order, but Duncan paid little attention to the formalities. His role here was simple. Marrs and the other members of the Senate Judiciary Committee would harangue him with questions, and he would invoke his Fifth Amendment rights against self-incrimination, freeing Marrs to build his case against the president on innuendo and circumstantial evidence.

He doubted that Marrs would ever find a smoking gun, but in politics, such absolutes were rarely needed. Regardless of the outcome, the nation would suffer greatly, becoming further polarized and ultimately weakened. He hoped that the other men and women in the chamber would recognize that, and see Marrs for what he was, but whether or not that happened was out of his control. He had given everything to protect the nation that he loved; now it was up to the rest of them to save it.

Marrs's voice cut through his musings. "Mr. Chairman, I want to thank you for convening this special session. It is my intention to reveal a conspiracy to undermine the constitutional authority of this body and establish a military dictatorship in the White House. It is a conspiracy that has its roots with this man." He gestured to Duncan. "Disgraced ex-president Thomas Duncan. And like a poisonous tree, the branches of this conspiracy have spread far and wide, infiltrating the military, our intelligence and law enforcement agencies, all the way to the office of President Chambers."

A murmur rippled through the committee, but Marrs pressed on. "Mr. Chairman, with your permission, I would like to question the witness."

"I believe we all have questions for President Duncan," the chairman said. "But as you are the most familiar with this alleged conspiracy, by all means, proceed."

Duncan did not fail to note the way the chairman had subtly corrected Marrs—calling him 'President Duncan' as was customary—and the use of the qualifier 'alleged.' It was almost enough to make Duncan hopeful.

Marrs was clearly more interested in talking than in asking questions. He launched into a narrative of the closing days of Duncan's administration, emphasizing perceived failures and using loaded language to imply a widespread cover-up. Several of the senators on the committee shifted uncomfortably as the accusations came close to sweeping them into the so-called conspiracy. Duncan sensed that many of them knew that Marrs was fabricating his accusations, but that would matter little when Marrs went public. To save their own skins, they would have to throw Duncan under the bus.

Just as Marrs's monologue seemed to be building toward some kind of climax, another murmur went through the room. Duncan heard a few gasps from the committee but these were quickly drowned out as the FBI agents began moving quickly in response to a disturbance at the back of the room. Duncan craned his head around and saw a compact man in street clothes standing near the door.

There were cuts and bruises on the man's face. He looked like he had gone ten rounds with Mike Tyson.

And won, Duncan thought. There was an air of unyielding confidence about the man. Even as the agents swarmed around him, forcing him to the floor, he remained unflappable.

The chairman shouted for order, but Duncan was more interested in Marrs's reaction. The senator from Utah was staring at the newcomer through narrowly slitted eyes. There was uncertainty in the gaze but also recognition.

Marrs's voice rose above the tumult. "Mr. Chairman, if I may?"

"Senator, do you know this man?"

Marrs weighed the question with evident apprehension, staring at the stranger as if trying to read his mind. "I do, Mr. Chairman. This is my special investigator, Mr. Colin Parrish. He's been leading the probe that unmasked this conspiracy."

"Senator Marrs, this is highly irregular. These are closed proceedings. I won't have you turn them into a circus."

"My sincerest apologies, Mr. Chairman. I can only guess that Mr. Parrish here has some new critical information, which has just come to light. Isn't that right, Mr. Parrish?"

Parrish pulled free of the agents, stood, and said simply. "It is."

Marrs's face split in a triumphant grin. "If it's answers you want, Mr. Chairman, then look no further."

The chairman frowned but gestured for Parrish to come forward. The newcomer strode to the table and took a seat beside Duncan.

Marrs quickly took charge, ignoring the standard introductions and protocols. "Mr. Parrish, we're all eager to hear what you've discovered."

Parrish leaned forward and spoke into the microphone. "Thank you, Senator. Mr. Chairman.

"I'll begin with my personal involvement in this affair. Yesterday, Senator Marrs approached me and asked me to look into rumors of a secret paramilitary group operating on foreign soil—specifically, an operation against the El Sol drug cartel in Mexico, undertaken without official sanction, but with the support of the military. I quickly discovered evidence to support these allegations and identified President Thomas Duncan as one of the key players."

Parrish glanced sidelong at Duncan and nodded. It was a curious gesture that was lost on neither Duncan nor Marrs.

"I'd like to see this evidence," the chairman said.

"I'm sure Senator Marrs can provide you with that," Parrish answered. "But that's not why I'm here."

Marrs's face creased in apprehension. He leaned into his microphone. "Mr. Chairman, perhaps we should recess—"

Parrish spoke over Marrs. "Senator Marrs instructed me to coordinate with Hector Beltran, the leader of the El Sol cartel, to arrange a trap for the paramilitary force."

Duncan thought he had misheard, but the sudden buzz of low conversation in the room told him otherwise.

"That's enough," Marrs said sharply, but Parrish kept talking.

"With the Senator's blessing, Beltran abducted a bus full of American tourists to lure the paramilitaries back onto Mexican soil. Our plan was to isolate them by destroying their transport—a military stealth aircraft—using a TOW missile, which Senator Marrs provided, and then kill or capture the team on the ground. We were partly successful. The plane was destroyed and the crew aboard was killed."

Because he was sitting next to the man, Duncan heard every word Parrish said, but it was impossible to know if the rest of the committee had heard. Marrs kept shouting for Parrish to shut up, and when that accomplished nothing, the senator turned to Taits. "Arrest him. Shut him up."

Duncan grabbed the table in front of him, wondering if he was losing his grip on reality. Was this really happening?

"I later learned that the hostages Beltran had taken were also executed," Parrish went on. "Ritually murdered and eaten by—"

Screaming a string of curses, Marrs leapt from the dais and rushed toward the table. Time seemed to stand still. None of the FBI agents had been prepared for it, and their disbelief left them stunned into paralysis. No one realized what Marrs intended until it was too late.

There was a flurry of movement, and then suddenly Marrs had an agent's gun in his hands, aimed at the table.

Duncan made a desperate attempt to pull Parrish down, out of the line of fire, but as he reached out, someone grabbed him from behind and dragged him back.

Parrish was still talking when the noise of the shot filled the room. Duncan felt something warm and wet on his face. More shots were fired, but as the room descended into total pandemonium, Duncan was hauled back through the exit door. The chaos had not yet extended to the corridor outside Room 226, but Duncan's savior kept going, as if he intended to drag Duncan all the way to the street. It wasn't until they rounded a corner that the agent stopped and helped Duncan stand on his own.

"Well, that didn't quite go according to plan," the man said.

After everything that had happened, it took Duncan a moment to process the voice. He turned to look his savior in the face, but could not reconcile the unrecognizable visage with the very familiar voice. "King?"

The man standing in front of him looked nothing like King, but as Duncan scrutinized the face, he realized that he wasn't actually looking at a face at all. It was a projection, a reproduction of a face on a flexible liquid crystal display worn as a mask to hide King's true appearance.

"Here." King thrust a piece of the same material into Duncan's hands. "Put this on. We don't have much time."

"A chameleon suit? How is that possible? The quantum computer was destroyed."

"Aleman figured out a way to program them with static images. Virtual faces are the best we can manage right now. They're great as long as nobody looks too closely."

"That's how Parrish got in? He was working with you?"

"It didn't take as much persuasion as you might think. He loathes Marrs. Maybe I should say 'loathed.' I guess the feeling was mutual."

Duncan stared into the unfamiliar eyes. "Is everyone...?"

"Dinged up, but alive." He gestured at the mask in Duncan's hands. "These things burn through batteries fast, so the rest of the explanation will have to wait until we're out of here."

Duncan breathed a sigh of relief. He took the mask in his hands and prepared to roll it down over his head like a stocking cap. "What's the plan?"

"Still working on that. Getting you back was priority one. Taking down Marrs was just gravy."

Duncan froze and then lowered his hands without donning the mask. "I can't go with you."

"What? Don't be stupid, Tom."

"It's not stupid, Jack. If I run, they'll never stop looking for me, and you and the others will never be safe. I can't let you destroy your lives."

"That's our decision, and it's already been made. Unanimously."

"And this is mine." Duncan thrust the mask into King's hands. "Walk away. Live your life. Chess Team is finished."

He walked away, and did not look back.

SIXTY-SEVEN

King stared in disbelief at Duncan's retreating form. Of all the possible outcomes to his crazy scheme for springing his old friend from custody, this was one he had never contemplated. He considered running after Duncan, subduing him with a chokehold or using some other means to compel him to go along with the plan, but the opportunity to do so had already slipped away. FBI agents were swarming around him, uncertain whether to arrest or protect, but they were certainly intent on making sure that the former president did not also become a casualty.

An electronic ping warned King that the battery powering his chameleon mask was down to a twenty percent charge. It was time to go. When the team had a chance to regroup, they could come up with a better plan. Hopefully, Duncan would be more responsive the next time around.

King headed down the stairs, wincing as every step brought a twinge of pain to his injured ankle. He headed for the exit doors just as a parade of police cars and fire trucks arrived outside. The FBI jacket he had earlier appropriated was probably more effective than the mask at getting him past the security checkpoint. The guard at the station was too busy keeping track of who went in to give him more than a passing glance. Once outside, he removed both the jacket and the mask, and headed for the National Mall, where he would be able to disappear into the crowd.

"Sigler!"

The shout caught him off guard. He hesitated, ever so slightly, but kept walking.

"Damn it, I know it's you, Sigler. Stop."

The pounding of feet warned that someone was giving chase. King tensed his body, ready to fight, but when the man caught up, he simply fell into step beside King. Out of the corner of his eye, King visually confirmed what his ears had already told him. "Admiral Ward. What a surprise."

"I was pretty sure you'd put in an appearance here. When I heard the sirens, I knew I was right."

"I can honestly say that I had nothing to do with that. Senator Marrs had a breakdown and started shooting. That's all I know." He quickened his pace, wondering exactly how he was going to ditch the admiral.

"What about Duncan?"

"What about him?"

"That's why you came here, right? 'Leave no man behind.' We all live and breathe those words. So, where is he? Why didn't he come with you?"

King had no answer, so he kept walking.

Ward walked in silence beside him for almost a full minute. "You went off line so fast, I didn't get a chance to tell you. You and your team did... Well, 'outstanding' hardly seems to cover it. I understand why Duncan picked you."

"You're welcome."

Ward uttered a short humorless laugh, then stepped in front of King, blocking his path. "I'm only going to say this once, so pay attention."

King folded his arms across his chest. "You have my undivided attention. Sir."

"There are things that I can do to protect you. But there are also limits to what I can do. That's the way things work in the military. Do you understand what I'm saying?"

"Not exactly," King answered.

"Then let me put it another way." Ward made a point of locking stares with him before continuing. "In thirty-six hours, you and your people need to report to my office at Fort Bragg to discuss the future of Chess Team. Consider that an order. If you don't show up, I'll have no choice but to declare you AWOL. Do you get me? Thirty-six hours."

Ward executed a precise right-face and strode away without another word, leaving King dumbfounded. He shook his head and started walking again. Because of the unexpected encounter, as well as the ominous threat that accompanied it, he did not go immediately to the safe house Aleman had set up for them. Instead, he roamed the Mall, stopping frequently to give his wounded ankle a break and to check his six, to make sure Ward did not already have men shadowing him.

If he was being followed, though, he would probably never know. As the commander of joint special ops forces, Ward had at his disposal the very best the military had to offer.

The walk gave King plenty of time to think about what had happened. Duncan believed that by sacrificing himself, the rest of them could maintain the status quo, or at the very least, return to the life they had had before joining the team. King understood that kind of thinking, because every single one of them would have been willing to do the same... In fact, they were all willing to do that for Duncan.

Ward had been right about that much. 'Leave no man behind' was not an empty slogan. King would not rest until Duncan was free, and he had no doubt the rest of the team would feel the same way. The more he thought about it, the more he understood what Ward had actually been trying to tell him.

As darkness began to settle over the city, he boarded a random metro train, transferred half a dozen times, and then finally arrived at the safe house, where the rest of the team was waiting, along with Aleman and Boucher.

They had taken the boat north to Virginia Beach, and there parted company with Ellen and Sara. The latter was eager to get to work on researching a counter-agent to the wendigo pathogen. Beck's injuries, while not life-threatening, had required hospitalization, so they had made the difficult decision to leave her behind as well.

Upon arriving in D.C., they had met with Boucher and Aleman, and learned of Marrs's plan to crucify Duncan and launch a witch-hunt that would eventually take down President Chambers. The senate hearing had been the perfect place to make the rescue attempt, and Parrish had volunteered to create a diversion by exposing Marrs's involvement with Beltran and his culpability in the destruction of *Crescent II*.

"You know you'll be incriminating yourself," King had warned.

Parrish had been unconcerned. "It shouldn't be too hard to swing an immunity deal with what I know."

Parrish obviously hadn't considered how far Marrs would be willing to go to silence him.

Bishop met King at the door, a look of alarm on her face. "Where is Thomas?"

He motioned her back inside. "I only want to tell the story once," he said.

They gathered around the table. Knight hobbled in on a sprained ankle. Bishop was covered in abrasions and bites. Everyone was moving gingerly, with too many scrapes and bruises...except for

Queen. Somehow, she had come through the ordeal almost unscathed, aside from a red welt on the back of her hand, which evidently itched furiously.

"Stop scratching," Rook warned her. "You'll just make it worse."

Her eyes shot daggers at him.

King recounted what had happened at the senate meeting. What ought to have been the climax of his story—Marrs's violent breakdown—was overshadowed by King's revelation that Duncan had refused the offer of escape, and by Admiral Ward's ultimatum.

Rook spoke up. "You told him to go to hell, right?"

"Does everyone feel that way?"

"The decision is made," Queen said, and everyone else nodded.

King studied their faces to make sure the sentiment was shared by all. It was. "Admiral Ward doesn't actually expect any of us to show up. It was a warning. He's giving us a head start."

When King had finally realized exactly what Ward was telling him, his estimation of the man had increased ten-fold. Ward, like Keasling before him, was the kind of officer that inspired soldiers to greatness. It was a pity that fate had cast them in the role of antagonists.

"In thirty-six hours...make that thirty-three...we will all be declared AWOL, and Ward will release the hounds. That's how long we have to say whatever good-byes we have to say and then disappear."

"Then what?" Bishop asked.

"Then? We get our friend back."

SIXTY-EIGHT

The President of the United States closed his eyes, shutting out the hyper-active news pundits and the seizure-inducing graphics of the cable news channel, as he pressed his fingertips to his temples.

"...confirming reports of a shooting in the capital that left one man dead. Police say the shooter is in custody, but are not yet releasing any names."

He was tempted to cover his ears as well, to block out the audio, to fully retreat from what was, without question, the worst day of his presidency, but that kind of escape simply wasn't possible. His job was to weather the storm, keep it together in the darkest hour, and inspire the nation to believe that things might get better.

It was hard to imagine them getting worse.

More than a thousand people were dead or missing in the Outer Banks. The entire island chain would probably be uninhabitable for years to come. Worse, there was no way to suppress the stories of people transforming into flesh-eating monsters or the rumors that the food supply had been tainted with human remains. And now? Someone had been killed in a meeting of the Senate Judiciary Committee, and rumor had it that the meeting had been called for the purpose of initiating impeachment proceedings.

His enemies were circling like sharks. His friends and allies were distancing themselves with ambiguous support. The best thing for him to do would be to resign, dump the mess in Nicholas May's lap. He'd never wanted May for VP anyway; the party had pressured him into the selection. He seriously considered it for a moment, but he was not convinced that would be the best thing for the country.

The audio abruptly cut off, plunging the room into silence. He opened his eyes and was surprised to see that he was not alone in his private office.

"Well," he said, after overcoming his initial surprise. "I guess I should have expected a visit from you."

"Yes," the visitor replied. She was a tall woman, dressed in a tailored skirt and jacket, which accentuated her slender physique.

With raven-black hair framing high cheekbones, full lips and dark smoldering eyes, she might easily have been mistaken for a fashion model. She turned those eyes on him now. "Actually, *you* should have called *me.*"

He endured her reproof without comment, straightening in his chair to face her.

"Fortunately," she continued. "We just might be able to salvage this, thanks to Senator Marrs."

"Marrs? He's been a thorn in my side since the day I took office."

"No one told you? The senator from Utah won't be a problem anymore."

President Chambers quickly connected the dots. "The shooting? He was the victim?"

"Even better. He was the shooter, and the man he shot was in the process of exposing Marrs's dealings with the Mexican drug cartel that killed those American tourists, shipped tainted meat to fast food restaurants and probably engineered the bio-terror attack in North Carolina."

"Marrs is responsible for...all of this?"

"Only peripherally, but his involvement, not to mention the fact that he murdered a man in front of a roomful of FBI agents and his fellow senators, will take the heat off you." She paused a beat, making sure that she had his attention. "There is a wrinkle however."

"A wrinkle?"

"Marrs was planning to make the case that you conspired with former-President Duncan in the creation of an illegal paramilitary force that carried out foreign policy initiatives, and that you diverted tax-payer funds and military equipment to pay for it." She avoided asking him if any of it was true. In fact, a denial was on Chambers's tongue—there was no conspiracy. He had asked Domenick Boucher for a couple of favors, nothing more—but she did not give him the opportunity to speak. "Duncan has been arrested, and it was Marrs's intention to question him before the committee. Marrs may be out of the picture, but the allegations are still in the open. Whether or not Duncan implicates you is irrelevant. He cannot be allowed to testify before that committee."

"I'm not sure what I can do to stop that from happening."

She leaned forward, placing her palms flat against his desk. Her pose would have been provocative if not for the fact that he was truly afraid of this woman. "The Consortium believes in you, Mr. President. We are invested in your success, and I am prepared to send a very clear message to that effect. But first, there's something you have to do."

"What?"

"Tom Duncan must disappear."

CR AT AN

EPILOGUE: FAREWELL

EPILOGUE
Florida

It was a small service, attended only by a handful of staff from the assisted living home—a doctor, a nurse, some orderlies and cooks. The staff was encouraged to attend the memorial services for patients who had passed, as a way of preserving their dignity at the end. So many of the people for whom they cared were already dead—gone and forgotten, as far as their families were concerned.

No one believed that would be true of the woman being laid to rest today. She had only one living family member, a grandson— a man of means, who had spared no expense to ensure his grandmother's comfort during her final days. It was unthinkable that he would not be present on this day. He had made all the arrangements by telephone a few days earlier, and had given every indication that he would be present to say his final farewell.

But there was no sign of him.

The staff members were disappointed, but it was not the first time a survivor had chickened out at the last minute. The service went ahead, more or less on schedule. The attendees paid their final respects, and then they dispersed to go on about the business of their lives.

They would have been surprised, and perhaps a little dismayed, to learn that their every move was being observed through a high-powered sniper scope.

A treetop perch two hundred yards away was as close as Knight dared get to his grandmother's funeral. Admiral Ward's thirty-six hour deadline had come and gone, and now he and the rest of the team were officially fugitives from justice.

The irony of the situation was not lost on him. Just a few days ago, he had been ready to walk away. To leave the team because he no longer felt capable of doing what was required of him. Now, in spite of what it would mean, possibly for the rest of his life, he couldn't imagine being anything else. He did not regret that his decision to stay with King and the others had cost him a chance to say good-bye to his grandmother, but that did not mean he felt nothing. He felt grief, he felt sorrow. Most of all, he felt anger.

Anger at the fact that he and the others, after having given so much, so often, were now forced to skulk in the shadows, cut off from the rest of the world, treated like criminals when they should have been treated like heroes. He had never been in it for the glory, but damn it...was it too much to ask for a simple *thank you?*

He felt anger at being left alone. For more years than he could remember, his grandmother had been his only living relative, and even though her mind had been slipping away, she had always been in his life. She was his connection to his past, to his heritage and culture. And now she was gone forever, and he couldn't even say good-bye.

He trained the scope on the grave and watched as two workmen lowered the casket into the ground. It had been his intention to arrange for a traditional Buddhist funeral, but subsequent events had required him to sacrifice tradition in favor of expediency, and that too contributed to his anger. Instead of a ceremonial cremation, her mortal remains would be buried in the ground.

"When all of this is done, *halmeoni*," he whispered, "I will return and honor you in the right way."

After the workmen left, a lone figure approached the plot—a young woman with long dark hair. She was dressed in a simple black dress, with a long coat draped over her shoulders. With her back to Knight, she knelt, grabbed a handful of dirt, and tossed it into the open grave. She contemplated the open hole in the ground for a moment, then turned away slowly, gazing into the woods as if searching for someone.

Now Knight could see that one of her arms was in a sling. He kept watching her. The scope was powerful enough that he could see the tears that streaked her pretty face.

After a moment, she turned back to the grave, knelt again and placed something on the ground in front of the low gravestone. When she stood up again, Knight could see wisps of smoke rising from a pair of incense sticks that protruded from the soil.

Knight sighed and moved the scope away from the grave site. He scanned the cemetery and the surrounding woods, and when he was certain that no one else was lurking nearby, he put the scope away and climbed down, wincing as his sprained ankle met the ground. He gritted his teeth through the discomfort and moved through the woods with a stealth that belied his injury. He caught up to her just as she reached the edge of the lawn.

"Anna!"

She turned, the smile already on her face, and embraced him. He returned the hug gently, fearful of aggravating her injuries. "I'm glad you could make it," he breathed into her ear.

"Where else would I be?"

He held her in silence for a few moments, drawing strength from the feel of her body next to his. "How's the arm?"

"Still broken," she said with what might have been a chuckle. "It will be at least a year before I can arm wrestle again. But it beats the alternative."

That brought a smile to his face, and he hugged her again. "I have to go."

"I'm coming with you."

He thought about how to respond to that. Part of him felt guilty. He wanted to protect her, to keep her safe, not drag her down into his new fugitive existence. Rootless, rudderless, always looking over their shoulders. And if they screwed up, if the hunters eventually caught up to them, she would share his fate: imprisonment or worse. What right did he have to subject her to that?

Part of him was desperately happy that she wanted to be with him.

"Well, you can always change your mind."

"Why would I do that?"

He could have listed a dozen reasons, but instead said simply, "Where's your car?"

"I took a cab."

"That simplifies things." He took a step back and gestured to the woods. "My car is that way. It's a bit of a hike."

She shrugged. "Don't worry about me. You're the one that can barely walk. Maybe you should just give me the keys. I'll go get the car and bring it around."

"You? You've only got one good arm."

"You've only got one good eye. And one working foot."

"I guess together, we make up one functional person."

"I would have put it more romantically," she said, "but isn't that pretty much the definition of love?"

Georgia

Although she had been working for over fourteen hours without interruption, Sara felt a mixture of guilt and anxiety as she left the Bio-Safety Level Four laboratory. Guilt because the work was far from complete, and even though the outbreak had been stopped, the threat would remain until she could find a way to eradicate it forever. Anxiety because work was her only refuge from the pain of what had been lost.

Always driven, and a classic loner, Sara had lived most of her life content with the idea that she would never marry, never have a family. She told herself those things didn't matter to her. She rationalized that the world was much too dangerous a place to bring children into, and for the most part, she had succeeded in convincing herself. Even when Jack had entered her life, she had persisted in her belief, and why not? Their respective careers kept them far too busy for the sort of traditional family life that everyone else seemed to think was the very pinnacle of human existence.

Yet, as the day of their wedding drew closer, she had allowed herself to contemplate what that might be like, and had realized that all her protestations had simply been a way of protecting herself from the possibility of disappointment.

Disappointment like what she felt right now.

She had been able to put that disappointment out of her mind while working, especially given the urgency of the task at hand, but all the tests that could be run were either in progress or already complete, and as her colleagues had pointed out repeatedly, she was due for a break.

As she made her way out of the facility, she contemplated different scenarios for the next round of testing. She had successfully isolated the proteins secreted in the wendigo bodily fluids that caused a reaction in susceptible test subjects. The tests were limited to samples of human blood taken from people who admitted to having eaten at Mr. Pig. Not everyone in that group produced a positive result, suggesting that contamination of the meat supply had been random, but there were a few samples where a violent and instantaneous reaction was observed. Specific protein sequences in the cells—proteins that could only be created when the body digested human tissue—reacted to the presence of the wendigo like switching on a light, triggering a cascade effect. Her working theory was that a unique confluence of proteins activated a latent sequence of non-coded, or as it was often called, 'junk DNA' that made up the majority of the human genome. Proving that would require months, perhaps years, of research. Right now, all that mattered was stopping the disease cold.

The next step had been to observe the reaction when wolf spider venom was introduced to the cells. Once again, the reaction was immediate. A specific protein in the spider venom killed the wendigo protein by triggering an anaphylactic response. Wendigos, it seemed, were allergic to spider bites.

Her highest priority now was to find a way to inoculate those at risk for infection. All the thousands of Americans who had unwittingly ingested human protein in their barbecued pork sandwiches. Would the venom make them immune? Or would it kill them when exposed?

The results so far were very promising, but she would have to collect a lot more data before she would even contemplate a human trial. Unfortunately, the infection was unique to humans; there would be no way to test it on laboratory animals.

The ethical ramifications, as well as trying to forecast scenarios based on different sets of results, helped keep her mind off her personal woes as she crossed the parking lot and got into her car. She was mentally drafting a set of protocols for initiating human testing, when a voice spoke to her.

"New course set." It was the onboard GPS. "In three hundred feet, turn left."

Her eyebrows drew together in a frown. She had not put in a new destination, and she rarely ever used the GPS, since most of her driving was limited to commuting to work or to the airport. She tapped the screen of the device, tracing the blue line on the map that showed a route leading out of the Atlanta metro area, north and east some fifty miles to the north end of a big lake that infiltrated dozens of little valleys, giving it the appearance of a crazy Rorschach blot.

"Lake Sidney Lanier," she murmured. "Never been there."

She traced the line with her fingers to a spot near the lake shore. Her heart skipped a beat when she reached the end of the line. Instead of the customary pin, the destination was marked with a tiny chess piece.

A King.

For the next seventy minutes, she was barely aware of anything but the voice of the GPS, guiding her through Atlanta traffic, onto the freeway and then off again near the city of Gainesville. From there, she hung on every synthesized word, navigating a maze of roads to the lakeshore, and ultimately to a large A-frame cabin built of stone and cedar.

Jack Sigler stood in the driveway, as if he'd been waiting all day for her to arrive. "You made it," he said, grinning.

"How did you manage to hack my GPS?"

"Deep Blue—Lew did that. Said it was child's play. I'll have to take his word for it."

She was in his arms before she knew it, hugging him and kissing him, and yet her joy at seeing him could not quite remove the anxiety that had been plaguing her for days now. When he had left her with Ellen and Beck, he had warned her that it might be a while before they saw each other again. There had not been time for specifics, let alone to talk about their future together, but seeing him again now, so soon after parting, filled her with dread rather than hope.

She pulled away. "What's wrong, Jack? Something is wrong. Don't try to tell me it's not."

His eyebrows drew together in a frown. "Remember how I told you that we would be going off the grid for a while? Well, we're officially there. The military is going to come after us, so we'll be dodging them for a while."

"How long is a while?"

"That's what I wanted to talk to you about." He put his arm around her shoulders, gently guiding her toward the steps that led up the deck that wrapped around the house. "If we turned ourselves in right now, we'd get a slap on the wrist. Administrative punishment. The worst they'd do is a court martial and maybe a dishonorable discharge, but that would be a lot more trouble than we're worth."

"So do it. Get out. You were happy leaving the military behind."

"That's not the problem." He took a deep breath. "Deep Blue— President Duncan—has been arrested. We're going to try to spring him. Doing that is probably going to put us on the FBI's most wanted list. We'll have to create new lives, sever all ties with the past. Zero contact."

Despite the humid lake air, Sara felt a chill. Her worst fears were being realized. "You mean me."

"I'm...sorry."

Part of her wanted to tell him not to do it. To choose her and their life together, over Duncan, but she knew how unfair that would be. The man she had fallen in love with was not someone who would leave a friend to rot in prison.

Part of her wanted to go with him. If he was going to have to invent a new life, why not one with her? But that too was something she couldn't do. Her work at the CDC was more than just a career, it was a calling. He saved the world by fighting terrorists and monsters. She saved it by stopping pandemics. The woman Jack Sigler had fallen in love with was not someone who would turn her back on something like that.

"I always knew that being married to you might mean that one day you wouldn't come back," she said, a little surprised that she was able to get the words out. "I just didn't think it would be quite like this."

"I guess it's good that we never officially tied the knot."

She pulled away and faced him. "Why would you say that, Jack? I love you, and I'm going to keep on loving you no matter what happens. I want to be your wife. Do you get that?"

He stared back at her for a long time. "Come with me. I have something to show you."

He led her inside the cabin. She was not at all surprised to find the others there: Queen and Rook, Knight and Anna Beck, Bishop,

Lewis Aleman and a man who was introduced as Domenick Boucher. Strangely, they were all wearing formal attire—the men wore tuxedoes and the women were in elegant evening gowns. There was one other person in the room, a middle-aged man wearing black clerical attire.

"This is Father Santini," Jack told her. "I've asked him to perform the ceremony."

Sara gaped first at the priest then at Jack. She leaned close to his ear and whispered. "Uh, I'm not Catholic. Come to think of it, neither are you."

Santini must have overheard. "I won't hold that again you, Miss Fogg," he said with a grin.

"Father Santini is a friend of a friend. I'm afraid this won't exactly be a conventional wedding," Jack explained. "We can't very well apply for a marriage license, so legally we won't really be married."

She mulled this over for about half a second and then smiled. "Screw legality. If we say 'I do,' that's all that matters."

He gave a relieved sigh. "I'm glad you feel that way."

Jack Sigler and Sara Fogg said "I do," and vowed to love, honor, comfort and keep each other, forsaking all others, until the end of their days. They exchanged rings and a kiss, and then became Mr. and Mrs. Jack Sigler in every way that mattered to them.

King did not allow his anxieties about what lay ahead to darken this moment, the culmination of one journey and the beginning of another.

He was acutely aware of those who were not present—Fiona, George Pierce, his parents, Tom Duncan—but one lesson life had taught him was that circumstances were almost never perfect, and to wait for ideal conditions was to waste precious time that could never be recovered. Life was too short and tragedy could close a window of opportunity all too suddenly. Maybe one day they would have a real wedding, but for now, this was enough.

Sara was resplendent in her dress—Queen and Bishop had somehow managed to penetrate the FBI presence at the Bible Conference Grounds in Pinckney to retrieve both the gown and the rings from the Honeymoon Nook cabin, where King and Sara were to have spent their first night together as man and wife.

"How did you pick this place anyway?" Sara asked.

"The owner is an old friend. He's out of the country right now, but he said we could crash here for a while. I figured since it was pretty close to Atlanta..."

"Must be a pretty good friend."

"The best. We had a few adventures together back in the day." One of the benefits of living a few extra lifetimes was that you made friends that no one else knew about. King had a feeling that would come in handy in the days to come. "He's pissed that he wasn't here for the wedding, but he'll keep our secret. He's the one who recommended Father Santini."

"Well, it's not what I imagined, but it's still perfect." She gave him another long passionate kiss. "I have to ask, though, are we all staying here? Because I was kind of hoping to get you alone."

Before he could answer, Boucher called for everyone's attention. King thought the former CIA director was going to offer another toast, but instead he directed everyone to the large plasma screen television in the house's living room. "One of my contacts just called. The President is about to speak."

Despite the timing, King was curious to hear what President Chambers would say. As far as anyone knew, Marrs's plot to unseat the president had ended with his arrest, but there were plenty of other reasons for this special address.

The screen filled with a shot of the White House Press Briefing Room, where a procession of people were stepping onto the podium, lining up in front of the blue backdrop. There was a buzz of conversation in the room, and then the announcement, "Ladies and gentleman, the President of the United States."

King watched as Chambers stepped onto the dais and took his place at the lectern adorned with the Presidential Seal, but as the president began talking, he noticed something else. At first, he tried to dismiss it. Just one of those things. But as the president offered his assurances that the crisis in North Carolina was over, and he was rewarded with a round of applause led by the other people on the stage, King felt compelled to take a closer look. He let go of Sara's hand and moved forward until he was just a few feet away from the screen.

"Jack?" Sara asked. "What is it?"

King shook his head, still unwilling to believe what his eyes were telling him, and he continued to stare at the screen. "Can we pause this? Or run it back?"

"Sure," Aleman said. "Just say when."

"Now." He said it without any urgency. Although the camera view was centered on the president, the person just behind his right shoulder had been in the shot the whole time. Now that the frame was frozen, King focused his attention on the figure standing there, hoping desperately to find something that would allow him to dismiss the matter altogether.

Sara came alongside him and took his hand. "Jack, what is it? What do you see?"

He touched a finger to the face frozen on the screen. "It can't be her. It's not possible."

His long life had taught him one other lesson: nothing was impossible.

"That's Julie. That's my sister."

CROATAN

CODA
Virginia Colony, 1588

After the surviving colonists, just two dozen of them, made their peace with the natives and returned to the mainland to permanently join the tribe—the only conditions under which the native chief would agree to shelter them—the privateer known to the colonists as John King made his way back to the abandoned village.

He had what he wanted now. He had the answer to one of the most enduring mysteries of all time. But that answer was something he could never share.

It was not merely the horror of what the colonists had done to each other, so they could live a few days longer. In extremis, such moral lapses were forgivable, if not quite universally acceptable. No, it was not the fact that some had fallen to cannibalism that frightened the man who called himself John King, but rather the possibility, however slight, that the truth—the final truth—about the fate of the colonists might one day be used for a terrible purpose.

Over the next few weeks, he set about disassembling the settlement. He ripped down the houses, carrying the wood to the shore where he used it to build a small boat—just enough to bear him south, where he would be able to find passage aboard a Spanish galleon or perhaps sign on with an English privateer. He scattered the stones of cook fires and forges. He kept some of their goods—a few tools and some clothes to replenish his own. The rest he pitched into the sea.

When others arrived, as they surely would a few years hence, they would find no trace at all of the colony. They would assume, correctly, that the colonists had been assimilated by one of the local native tribes. They might, in time, learn about the wendigo curse, and how the natives had unleashed a horror upon the colonists who had broken the tribe's most sacred taboo. And someday, someone would wonder if the power of the wendigo might be used as a terrible weapon. He could not allow that to happen, and the only way to ensure that no one ever stumbled across the truth was to give the world something else to think about.

Borrowing a page from sleight-of-hand conjurers, he would use misdirection to hide the truth.

With his boat ready to sail, he returned to the site one last time. All that remained to mark the place was the wooden palisade, part of the old fort built by the expedition that preceded the colonists. In time, that too would disappear, its exact location lost to memory. There was one thing however that would never be forgotten.

Using a chisel, he carved a message onto the palisade. A single word, not at all cryptic. If taken literally, it would prompt future searchers to look for the missing colony to the south, on Hatteras Island, instead of inland. But King knew that as the years passed, the message would take on a mythical, haunting quality. One word that, despite meaning very little, would forever evoke a sense of both mystery and terror:

CROATOAN

ABOUT THE AUTHORS

JEREMY ROBINSON is the international bestselling author of fifty novels and novellas including *Uprising*, *Island 731*, *SecondWorld*, the Jack Sigler thriller series, and *Project Nemesis*, the highest selling original (non-licensed) kaiju novel of all time. He's known for mixing elements of science, history and mythology, which has earned him the #1 spot in Science Fiction and Action-Adventure, and secured him as the top creature feature author.

Robinson is also known as the bestselling horror writer, Jeremy Bishop, author of *The Sentinel* and the controversial novel, *Torment*. His novels have been translated into twelve languages. He lives in New Hampshire with his wife and three children.

Visit him online at www.jeremyrobinsononline.com.

SEAN ELLIS is the international bestselling author *Magic Mirror* and several thriller and adventure novels. He is a veteran of Operation Enduring Freedom, and he has a Bachelor of Science degree in Natural Resources Policy from Oregon State University. Sean is also a member of the International Thriller Writers organization. He currently resides in Arizona, where he divides his time between writing, adventure sports and trying to figure out how to save the world.

Visit him on the web at: seanellisthrillers.webs.com

"JEREMY ROBINSON IS THE NEXT JAMES ROLLINS."
— CHRIS KUZNESKI, NY TIMES BESTSELLING AUTHOR

HERCULEAN

A CERBERUS GROUP NOVEL

JEREMY ROBINSON
AND SEAN ELLIS
INTERNATIONAL BESTSELLING DUO OF SAVAGE AND CANNIBAL

Coming in 2015

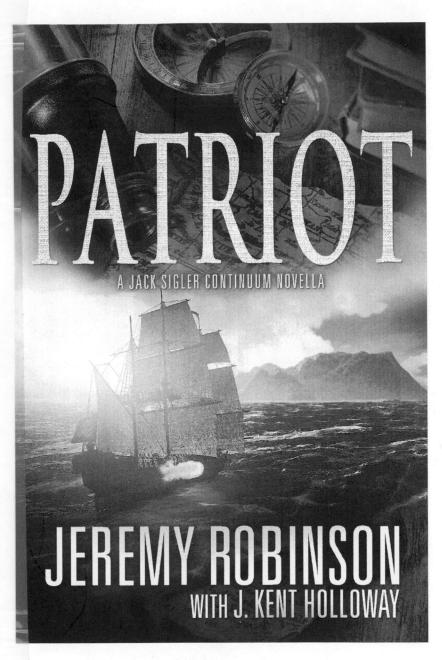

PATRIOT

A JACK SIGLER CONTINUUM NOVELLA

JEREMY ROBINSON
WITH J. KENT HOLLOWAY

Coming in 2015

Made in the USA
Middletown, DE
14 February 2015